MEDICAL

Life and love in the world of modern medicine.

The Midwife's Secret Fling
JC Harroway

Las Vegas Night With Her Best Friend
Tina Beckett

MILLS & BOON

THE MIDWIFE'S SECTRET FLING
© 2024 by JC Harroway
Philippine Copyright 2024
Australian Copyright 2024
New Zealand Copyright 2024

First Published 2024
First Australian Paperback Edition 2024
ISBN 978 1 038 93894 7

LAS VEGAS NIGHT WITH HER BEST FRIEND
© 2024 by Tina Beckett
Philippine Copyright 2024
Australian Copyright 2024
New Zealand Copyright 2024

First Published 2024
First Australian Paperback Edition 2024
ISBN 978 1 038 93894 7

MIX
Paper | Supporting
responsible forestry
FSC® C001695

Published by
Harlequin Mills & Boon
An imprint of Harlequin Enterprises (Australia) Pty Limited
(ABN 47 001 180 918), a subsidiary of HarperCollins
Publishers Australia Pty Limited
(ABN 36 009 913 517)
Level 19, 201 Elizabeth Street
SYDNEY NSW 2000 AUSTRALIA

Cover art used by arrangement with Harlequin Books S.A.. All rights reserved.

Printed and bound in Australia by McPherson's Printing Group

The Midwife's Secret Fling

JC Harroway

MILLS & BOON

Lifelong romance addict **JC Harroway** took a break from her career as a junior doctor to raise a family and found her calling as a Mills & Boon author instead. She now lives in New Zealand and finds that writing feeds her very real obsession with happy endings and the endorphin rush they create. You can follow her at jcharroway.com, and on Facebook, X and Instagram.

To my mum.

CHAPTER ONE

EARLY BOXING DAY MORNING, Zara Wood parked her car and left the cosy interior for the sub-zero temperatures outside. Craving a hot shower and a decadent five hours of uninterrupted sleep after her night shift at the hospital delivering babies, she pushed open the front gate to her Derbyshire cottage.

This early, the village of Morholme was quiet as people slept off the excesses of Christmas Day. Zara sighed; no matter which way she looked at it, working on Christmas night had sounded desperately lonely. But unless she counted watching her five-year-old son, Zach, sleep, something she still enjoyed, she'd had nothing better to do. Besides, most of the other midwives had families and partners, and Zach had been so excited for a sleepover at her mum's, where he'd no doubt eaten too many treats and stayed up late.

As she headed for the front door of the end-of-terrace cottage she'd inherited from her late father, a noise—the metallic scrape of the squeaky side gate—grabbed her attention.

Zara peered around the side of the house to see a strange woman disappear down the lane that ran between Zara's cottage and that of her neighbour. Zara raced into the garden, confusion turning to panic. Had she been burgled while she'd been at work? She'd spent six months renovating the basement rental flat while also working full-time to support her son single-handedly. Had the stranger broken in using the key Zara had hidden under a flowerpot for her new lodger—a man visiting from Australia—who was due later today?

With adrenaline ramping up her pulse, Zara yanked open the gate, outraged that someone had taken advantage of all her hard work. But by the time she'd made it into the lane, the woman had vanished.

Indignant, she entered the rental with her master key, fearful she'd find the lovely cosy accommodation she'd slaved over on her days off while Zach was at school completely ransacked, but everything appeared undisturbed. Even the television and portable speaker, the only items of real value, were still present. Perhaps the woman wasn't a thief at all, but a squatter.

Zara sighed, her five hours of sleep dissolving. She'd need to wait up for a locksmith to change the locks. Her mood worsened as she moved to the bedroom, finding evidence that the squatter had indeed spent the night. The bed Zara had left immaculately made for her lodger with clean luxury sheets and a cosy duvet was all rumpled and had obviously been slept in.

Just then, she caught the sound of the shower door closing in the en-suite bathroom. Her pulse soared. There were two squatters. And one of them was using *her* hot water and *her* luxury body wash. The cheek of people!

Melodic humming came from behind the closed bathroom door. *Male* humming. With a sudden chill of fear spreading through her veins, Zara grabbed the nearest heavy object—a ceramic candlestick from the mantel. She should probably call the police, but first, this guy was going to get a piece of her mind.

The bathroom door flew open. A stark-naked man appeared. On seeing Zara, he came to an abrupt halt in the doorway, his expression registering shock, which quickly morphed into a hesitant smile.

'I come in peace,' he said, holding up his hands in surrender as he nervously eyed the candlestick she'd menacingly raised. 'But if you're going to use that, do you mind if I cover myself first?' His eyes darted to the nearby towel rack.

'You can't be here,' Zara said, too strung out to place his accent, but it was clear he wasn't local. She yanked an expensive Egyptian-cotton towel from the rail and tossed it at his naked chest.

He caught it with one hand and quickly wrapped it around his hips. 'Why don't you put down the candlestick before someone gets hurt?' he said, one side of his mouth kicking up, a playful edge to the nervousness now.

'There's nothing funny about breaking and entering,' Zara said, inflamed that he seemed to find this situation amusing. 'You're trespassing. If you don't leave immediately, I'll call the police.'

How dared these people take advantage of all her hard work? Renting out the newly finished flat would help subsidise her wages so she could give Zach everything he deserved in life, given that she'd never received a single penny of support from his father, a man Zara considered the biggest mistake of her life.

He held up his hands again now that the towel was securely tucked. 'Hey, there's no need for the police,' he said, as if she were overreacting. 'Let's just chill out for a second.'

'No, you chill out,' she volleyed back. 'And while you're at it, get out.' Thanks to this freeloader and his lady friend, she'd have to spend valuable time that she could have been sleeping fixing up the flat for the arrival of her lodger.

'I'm not trespassing,' the stranger said with amused patience, his inquisitive stare taking in Zara's creased midwife's uniform. 'Are you Mrs Wood? I'm Conrad Reed.'

At the mention of his name, Zara sagged with relief, her adrenaline draining away.

'It's *Ms* Wood, actually. I'm not married,' she snapped, feeling stupid. 'So you're Conrad Reed...from Australia?' There'd be no need to use the candlestick, call the police or change the locks, because *this* was her lodger, the man who'd signed a month-long lease and was supposed to be arriving that afternoon.

'Yep,' he said, his smile widening as he stuck out his hand. 'Good to meet you. If I'd known you were going to let yourself in, I'd have put on some clothes.' Humour flashed in his eyes.

Reluctantly, she shook his hand, her face flaming at the misunderstanding. But was everything a joke to this guy? Perhaps Aussies were just naturally easy-going thanks to all that sunshine and surfing. His accent was so obvious to her now, she cringed at her eagerness to jump to the wrong conclusion.

'Sorry,' she muttered. 'I thought you were a thief, or a squatter.' She lowered the candlestick to her side.

'Nope. But you weren't really going to use that, were you?' He eyed her makeshift weapon doubtfully.

'I don't know...' She narrowed her eyes and stood a little taller. 'Maybe.'

He laughed then, but she couldn't join in or see the funny side. She was too tired.

'I hadn't thought it all the way through,' she continued. 'I just know that I worked hard to single-handedly renovate this place, and I've just got home from work after a night shift, and I have to pick up my son in five and a half hours so I was looking forward to some sleep and—'

She took a breath; she was waffling. This man didn't need her sad life story. And now that there was no need to evict him, she couldn't help but notice his attractiveness. Dirty-blond hair still damp from the shower. Piercing grey eyes, sparking with amusement. Tall and tanned with a muscular physique, his broad chest dotted with water droplets. Helpfully, her brain chose that moment to remind her that she'd seen him naked, even if she'd been too scared and outraged to enjoy it at the time.

But Conrad Reed's smokin' body and roguish good looks were irrelevant. Since a holiday fling six years ago had resulted in her precious baby, and after Zach's biological father had declared he wanted nothing to do with Zara or his son, her sole focus was taking care of Zach so he never once felt the loss of a positive male role model in his life. What with her shift work and her five-year-old, there was no energy left for members of the opposite sex, not even an exotic one with a drool-worthy body and a charming smile that came far too easily and made her think of all the things she'd denied herself since that pregnancy test had turned positive—partying, dates, *sex*.

'Hold on a second… You were meant to be arriving later this afternoon?' she reminded him, her voice pinched with fresh annoyance. She hoped her very first lodger, as hot as he was, wasn't going to be problematic.

'Change of plan. I took an earlier flight.' He gave a casual shrug, one hand pushing his wet hair back from his handsome face so his biceps bulged.

Zara grew hot, all too aware that it had been almost six years since she'd been intimate with a man, and that, but for her Egyptian-cotton towel and a cheeky grin, he was stark naked and impressively endowed.

'I did message late last night to let you know I'd arrived,' he said. 'Thanks for leaving out the key, by the way.'

'I don't check my phone when I'm working,' she said tightly, desperate to get away from his male confidence and amused curiosity. He was making her feel like an ancient, uptight freak.

'So is it too soon to joke about this yet?' he asked, flashing her the kind of smile that had probably rescued him from many a tricky situation. 'It's one hell of an introduction story.'

Zara raised her chin, feeling foolish for her part in the misunderstanding. 'Yes, I'm afraid it is.' He, on the other hand, seemed to find everything amusing. 'I'll…let you get dressed,' she said, wishing he were wearing more than a towel, his tall, lean body tauntingly on display.

She flushed hard. She was clearly exhausted; she wouldn't normally be susceptible to a guy's sexy confidence and charming smile. She turned for the bedroom door and then froze. The rumpled bed, the steamy bathroom, his freshly showered appearance finally registered, the pieces falling into place. Obviously her new laid-back lodger had entertained female company last night, and the mystery woman sneaking out of the side gate had not long left his bed. Or, more correctly, *Zara's* bed. Ignoring the sudden flare of irrational loneliness—her own nocturnal activities were non-existent by choice, despite her friend Sharon's constant urging she *have a little fun*—she fisted her hands on her hips and spun to confront him once more.

Having clocked the name badge on her uniform, Conrad had been about to mention that he'd taken a locum position at the same hospital, when she spun around, her lush mouth pursed with suspicion.

'Wait...' She frowned, her big hazel eyes taking another sweep of his naked torso before she met his stare. 'I just saw a woman leave here, but the lease was for you alone. Single occupancy.'

She looked embarrassed to mention it, but clearly wasn't scared of a little confrontation. And she clearly hadn't finished confronting him. At least she hadn't decked him with that heavy-looking candlestick...

'It *is* just me. Don't worry, she won't be back.' Conrad shrugged. What was a single doctor a long way from home supposed to do?

She flicked a glance at the unmade bed, her lip curling with disapproval as she slowly nodded. 'Oh, I see... So that woman isn't your girlfriend?'

Her stare returned to his, and then shifted over his chest. Ever since she'd decided he posed no threat, she couldn't seem to stop checking him out. And the curiosity, the attraction, was mutual. Zara Wood was a complete bombshell— petite, brunette, her body boasting the kind of curves that made him think of bikinis.

'Nah.' He shook his head, not in the slightest bit embarrassed to have been caught in the act of the morning after. 'I met her on the train. She gave me a lift from the station. It was just a one-time thing. No big deal.'

But from the way his feisty landlady was looking at him, he could tell she wasn't impressed.

'A one-night stand on your first night in town,' she said with a disbelieving slight shake of her head. 'Impressively fast work.'

Conrad smiled wider, wondering exactly what her problem was. She was only in her twenties, too young to be a prude. She had a son. Surely she must have had a one-night stand before.

'Is that not allowed?' he asked, fascinated by her prickly attitude. 'I don't recall anything in the lease agreement I signed that prohibits your tenants from having casual sex.'

'No problem at all,' she said, flushing but raising her chin defiantly. 'You can have as much casual sex as you like as far as I'm concerned. Who am I to judge?'

Conrad folded his arms over his chest, chuckling to himself when her stare dipped there once more. 'And yet you sound as if you're judging.'

His curiosity sharpened. Who was this intriguing woman and why was she so...uptight? He could understand the whole intruder misunderstanding, but she was acting as if she'd never once let her hair down.

'I'm not,' she bluffed haughtily. 'Your sex life is none of my business.' She blushed furiously, looking away.

'Well, I'm glad we've got that cleared up.' Conrad nodded, smiling to himself.

'However...' Zara thrust the candlestick at him, so he took it with an incredulous snort of amusement. 'I do have a small son, so, as your landlady, I'd appreciate it if your, um...*guests* could limit themselves to your half of the garden.' She backed away towards the bedroom door as she spoke, as if she couldn't wait to get away from him now that she had him pegged as some sort of player.

'Of course, no worries,' he said with a shrug and a non-threatening smile. 'With this weather—' he glanced pointedly at the window and the grey skies beyond '—I don't think it will be an issue. It's hardly barbecue season. But I'll be sure to let you know of anyone else sleeping over. I don't want my *guests* bludgeoned in their sleep.' He held up the candlestick, his lips twitching with amusement. She was fascinating, formidable and so sexy.

'There's no need for that,' she said, appalled, the pitch of her voice rising. 'I don't need to know every time you have casual sex.'

'Are you sure?' he teased, unable to resist coaxing out the fiery sparks of challenge from her eyes. 'It's no problem to flick you a message.'

He should stop antagonising her and let her get some sleep, but, for some reason, he really wanted to see her smile.

'I'm positive, thanks.' The smile she offered him was frustratingly tight and insincere. Then she glanced down and muttered, 'I don't want to be inundated with messages.'

'What's that supposed to mean?' he asked, his stare narrowing. For someone with a son and no husband, she was acting fairly high and mighty. She'd obviously made some snap judgements about him, when all he'd actually done was arrive at a property he'd legally rented half a day early. Perhaps he and his landlady weren't going to get along after all. Shame, given they were most likely going to be work colleagues. But he wouldn't drop that bombshell now, not when his every move seemed to infuriate her.

'It means you clearly enjoy being single.' She smiled brightly. 'I know the type.'

Conrad sighed. They'd clearly got off to a terrible start and, by the sounds of it, she didn't think much of men.

'Anyway,' she went on, 'I need some sleep. I'll leave you to it.' She backed towards the door, practically vibrating with nervous energy, so all he could do was watch her, bewildered. 'It was...good to meet you.'

'You too.' He replaced the candlestick on the mantelpiece and followed her from the bedroom into the kitchen, where she made for the front door as if the building were on fire.

'And merry Christmas, for yesterday,' he said as she yanked open the door, letting in a blast of frigid air that made him shiver.

'Merry Christmas,' she said, on a nervous squawk before she kept her stare lowered and fled up the path to her part of the house, leaving Conrad to scratch his head and wonder if he and his wildly sexy English landlady could be any more different.

CHAPTER TWO

A WEEK LATER, on his third shift as a locum obstetrics registrar, Conrad strode onto the labour ward at Derby's Abbey Hill Hospital, his footsteps slowing to a halt. Up ahead at the nurses' station stood his incredibly sexy but uptight landlady, Zara Wood. Internally, he groaned, his heart sinking. To say they'd got off to a bad start last week was an understatement. He'd never met anyone as wary as her, and she clearly thought him some sort of philandering creep. Sadly, that hadn't stopped him wondering about her incessantly, knowing this day, when their paths would cross again, would come. But if they *had* to work together, it made sense to clear the air.

Expecting their reunion to be as frosty as the English winter weather outside, Conrad hesitantly approached, watching Zara, who wore a harassed expression as she stabbed at the computer keyboard in frustration.

'Do we actually have a registrar working today?' she asked her midwife colleagues, Sharon and Bella, whom Conrad had already met. 'They don't seem to be answering their pager.'

'We certainly do,' Sharon said with a knowing smile as she wiped patient names off the whiteboard behind the desk. 'Haven't you met our locum?' She winked suggestively at Bella, who chuckled and rolled her eyes.

'Oh...are you in for a treat,' Sharon continued, with her back to Zara. 'In fact, I think he's single. I know I sound like a broken record here, and I know that you "don't need a man"...'

Clearly Zara often threw around this argument.

'But for him,' Sharon said, 'it might be worth finally breaking your long dry spell.'

Conrad hid a smile, his ego posturing as Bella fanned her face dramatically. 'Right...that accent,' she said to Sharon, 'the body, those eyes. I certainly wouldn't kick him out of bed for not emptying the bins. Makes you wanna move to Australia.'

Conrad crept closer on softened footfalls so he could eavesdrop for a little longer. He worked hard at keeping in shape. It was good to know that his efforts at the gym hadn't gone unnoticed. He was only in town for another three weeks, and, after past events in his personal life he was trying not to think about, it had been a long time since he'd felt in a relationship kind of place. That didn't stop him wondering what Zara Wood really thought about him though.

'Wait,' Zara said, rounding on her colleagues, her back to Conrad and her hands on her hips so he had an uninterrupted view of the gorgeous outline of her figure. 'Did you say Australian?'

Bella nodded and Conrad froze, wondering if Zara would make the connection.

'He's not tall with grey eyes, is he?' she went on. 'A smile that could melt off your clothes?'

His lips twitched as he forced his stare from the curve of Zara's hips, although she'd certainly checked out his nakedness a week ago, before she'd torn a few strips off him and almost kicked him out of the flat he'd legally rented. But it was good to hear confirmation that their attraction, their chemistry, was mutual.

'Yes, that's the one,' Sharon said as she wrote new names on the board. 'Dr Reed.'

'Oh, no…' Zara muttered, her shoulders sagging.

'So you *have* met?' Sharon turned to fully face Zara, a delighted smile on her face. Then the older woman caught sight of Conrad in the background, her eyes widening with surprise and a flicker of guilt.

'Good afternoon, ladies,' he said, announcing himself with a straight face. 'Did I hear my name mentioned?' He came to a halt behind Zara, who seemed to freeze, her shoulders tensing.

Zara spun on her heel, her expression impressively innocent considering how they'd just been gossiping about him. 'Of course you're a doctor here…' she muttered stonily. 'I suspected as much when I saw your stethoscope hanging by the door last week.' Her voice was clipped with annoyance and accusation, telling him he was in trouble again. But at least she wasn't wielding a weapon this time.

'That's right. A locum.' Conrad smiled and dropped his voice, unable to resist teasing her again. 'But at least this week I've got my clothes on.'

Despite trying very hard to look busy, the other two midwives were obviously shamelessly eavesdropping, because they gaped excitedly and then hid stunned smiles.

'You couldn't have mentioned that you worked at *my* hospital when we met?' Zara said, ignoring the delighted, slightly impressed mirth of her colleagues. She grabbed one of the ward tablets from the charging station and glared his way, clearly still furious with him.

'I had planned on bringing it up when I saw your name badge,' he said, his lips twitching as he glanced down from her green-brown eyes to where she clutched the device the way she'd gripped that candlestick—with malicious intent. 'But my fight-or-flight response got in the way. You looked menacing wielding that candlestick.'

Zara sighed and glanced at her colleagues, who were pretending not to listen. 'It's not what it seems.'

Sharon and Bella looked up, innocently.

'She's right,' he added. 'It was just a simple misunderstanding.'

'Okay, okay, don't protest too much. We believe you,' Sharon said, eyeing Zara with an impressed and questioning look. Clearly Sharon *didn't* believe them and wanted all the juicy details. In trying to smooth over their misunderstanding, he'd only made it worse.

'I thought he was a squatter,' Zara exclaimed to the other women, 'so I accidentally confronted him getting out of the shower. He's renting my basement flat, although he's one infringement shy of being evicted.'

Zara returned her glare to Conrad and the other two midwives chuckled and trailed away, back to work.

'As we're housemates as well as colleagues…' Conrad said with his most charming smile. How had she described it? Capable of melting off clothes? He could work with that. 'I take it you won't mind me calling you Zara?'

Her eyes narrowed with suspicion. 'As you're *finally* here,' she said, pointedly, 'I have a thirty-three-year-old primip who's been in second-stage labour for forty-five minutes that I'd like you to examine.' Without further preamble, she marched down the ward, heading for one of the delivery rooms as if he were an obedient dog who would come to heel.

Conrad followed, setting aside the invigorating friction with his prickly landlady for now, although it was certainly helping him to forget why he'd as good as run away from Australia to hide for a while in deepest, darkest midwinter England.

He paused outside the delivery room to wash his hands. 'I take it the foetal heart rate is stable? No sign of distress?' he asked, his mind now on work.

'It is, but mum-to-be is pretty exhausted. She's been labouring for eighteen hours.' She pressed her lips together as if Conrad were to blame for her patient's predicament.

'Have the membranes ruptured?' he asked, tossing the paper towels in the bin.

'Yes, and the neonatal registrar is on their way,' Zara replied, pushing open the door and nodding to the other midwife in the room before addressing the patient.

'Angela, this is Dr Reed, the obstetrician. I've asked him to examine you because you've been pushing for a while now and this baby doesn't seem to want to be born.'

As another contraction took hold of their patient, Conrad observed the foetal heart monitor for signs of distress and pulled on some sterile gloves.

'Angela,' he said, 'on the next contraction, I just need to examine you, okay?'

The woman nodded, bracing herself as another wave of pain struck. Conrad quickly examined the birth canal, felt the baby's head and the fully dilated cervix before meeting Zara's stare. 'The baby is right occiput-transverse,' Conrad told her.

Zara nodded, a flash of relief in her big expressive eyes.

'The baby is absolutely fine,' Conrad explained to Angela and her partner, a concerned-looking guy with round glasses and dark curly hair. 'But its head is a little rotated. He or she needs a little bit of help coming out, so, if you agree, I'm going to use the ventouse suction to help things along.'

Angela nodded weakly, her grip tightening on her partner's hand as another contraction took hold. Zara set up the instrument tray for the delivery while the second midwife assisted Angela through her contractions and her breathing. The neonatal registrar arrived, the small delivery room filling up with bodies. While the baby seemed fine at the moment, instrumental delivery could be a traumatic experience and the newborn would need checking immediately after birth.

'Okay,' Conrad said to all concerned. 'Let's get this little one delivered.' He slipped on fresh gloves and set up the instrument, while Zara positioned herself at his side, the second midwife and the partner holding the patient's hands.

'On the next contraction, Angela,' Zara instructed, 'Dr Reed is going to straighten the baby's head and apply suction, okay? You keep pushing until we tell you to stop and soon you'll have your baby.'

With that familiar surge of adrenaline in his veins, Conrad attached the suction cup to the top of the baby's head and applied gentle traction while rotating slightly to reposition the baby's head. He never tired of the thrill of helping to welcome a human being into the world. He loved his job, and it was immediately obvious that so too did Zara. At least that was one thing they had in common.

With the baby's head in the usual position of occiput-anterior, the next contraction delivered the baby's head.

'Okay, Angela, pant now,' Zara instructed, watching his every move.

Conrad quickly removed the cord from around the baby's neck, becoming aware that Zara was tightly gripping his shoulder, as if fully invested in the safe delivery of her patient's baby.

In the pause between contractions, Conrad glanced up and met her stare, a flicker of respect blooming in his chest. Given they'd be living together and working together for a few weeks, it made sense that they try and get along. Life was too short for disagreements and misunderstandings.

'Just one more push now,' Zara told the mother, releasing Conrad's shoulder with a slightly embarrassed shrug, 'and you'll meet your baby.'

Now that the hardest part of the delivery was over, Conrad shifted sideways to make room for the feisty but fascinating midwife. As an obstetric trainee, he'd soon learned how midwives could be very possessive of the babies they delivered. Where midwifery specialised in normal pregnancy and birth, Conrad was only really required when things weren't going to plan. That said, the specialities depended on one another. Everyone involved in obstetrics was there for the same reason: to ensure the safety of both the mother and the baby.

The baby's shoulders were delivered with the next contraction, followed by the rest of the newborn, a baby boy with a lusty cry and a full head of dark hair just like his father. Conrad detached the suction cup from the baby's head and wheeled his stool aside to allow Zara close enough to lift the newborn onto his mother's stomach.

'You have a son,' Zara said. 'Congratulations.' Her eyes

shone with emotion as she supervised Dad to cut the umbilical cord.

Conrad smiled to himself, glad that the situation was so easily resolved. While the tearful couple met their baby, Conrad assessed the woman's birth canal for damage. 'Just the placenta to deliver now, Angela, then I just need to give you a couple of stitches and we're all done.'

The woman nodded her consent, too in awe of the new life in her arms to worry about the business end of things, so Conrad got to work. The room emptied of the now redundant extra bodies—the neonatal registrar and the second midwife—leaving Conrad and Zara alone with the new family.

'I'll bring you some toast and tea,' Zara said to Angela as Conrad finished up the sutures and pulled a blanket over Angela's legs.

'Congratulations,' he said, taking a second to glance at the contented newborn, who, after all the excitement, had dozed off to sleep, before leaving the new family to get to know each other.

He found Zara in the ward kitchen, making toast.

'I feel like we got off to a bad start last week,' he said, slouching against the door frame and watching her brusque movements with fascination. 'We should probably try to get along, seeing that we're not only working together but also living in the same house, don't you think?'

She shot him a sideways glance. He raised his eyebrows expectantly, his pulse bounding with excitement, because he'd been right earlier: their attraction was clearly mutual.

'Did you have to mention the lack of clothes in front of my colleagues earlier?' she said, eyes narrowed with suspicion. 'It sounded bad.'

'I'm sorry. I didn't mean for them to hear. And I was just teasing you. I hoped to coax out a smile after the misunderstanding of our first meeting.'

'It seems everything's a joke to you,' she huffed. 'But you should know that it's hard to keep a secret around here.'

'That's a bit harsh,' he said, wondering exactly how he'd managed to get so far under her skin. 'I take my work very seriously. And I did overhear you all talking about me behind my back earlier. Why don't we call it even and call a truce?'

His apology, the reminder that he'd been the topic of some pretty unprofessional conversation, seemed to appease some of her indignation, but not all of it, because she went on. 'I know you seemed to have charmed everyone else here with your... This...' She waved her finger in his general direction.

'With my *clothes-melting smile*?' he offered, enjoying the sparks in her stare. But he rarely clicked with someone this strongly and instantly.

Her scowl deepened. 'But, just for the record, you're wasting your time trying to charm me. I work and take care of my son. That's all I have time for.'

'Noted,' he said, his expression serious. 'It can't be easy being a single parent. I take my hat off to you.'

Ignoring his comment, she looked up sharply. 'So you understand that I'm not interested in being your next casual conquest?' She shot him a pitying smirk, even though *she* was the one rumoured to be stuck in a prolonged dry spell. But his first impressions had clearly been spot on. Zara Wood obviously had no time for men. And despite finding his landlady incredibly attractive, Conrad hadn't dated seriously for over six years.

'Of course I do. But from what I've seen of Morholme,' he added about the village just outside Derby where they both lived, 'we seem to be the only two residents under the age of sixty. I'm only in the UK for another three weeks, but it makes sense for you and I to at least be friendly, don't you think? After all, life is too short for drama.'

Sadly, he knew that first hand. His brother's violent death six months earlier had been sudden and shocking. A man he'd loved and looked up to, there one minute and inexplicably gone the next when all he'd been doing was his job. It had made Conrad all too aware of the fleeting nature of life. You could lose what you loved in a split second.

Conrad dragged his thoughts from his still fresh grief and watched Zara set her features in an unreadable expression. 'I don't have much time for friends, so don't get your hopes up.' She smirked. 'You might want to consider other forms of…entertainment.'

Of course, by entertainment she meant sex. Because she'd obviously picked up on his casual attitude to dating, something he'd perfected over the past six years, since he'd moved too fast and been dumped.

'I understand,' he said with a smile, desperately trying to work his charm. 'But I was really just talking about a friendly coffee between two colleagues.' It was her mind that had turned immediately to sex. 'I don't want any awkwardness between us; that's not my style. Do you have a break coming up?' he asked, gratified to see her flush.

If they didn't have to work together *and* live together, he'd have given up trying to win her over by now. But there was something about her he couldn't seem to ignore. Despite their misunderstanding and their other differences, she, like him, was a straight talker. After the betrayals of his past from the one person he'd trusted more than anyone else, his late brother, he instantly respected that about Zara.

'I'm due a break in ten minutes,' she said, placing the buttered toast on a tray with two mugs of strong tea. 'I'll finish up with Angela and meet you in the staff canteen.'

'Great,' he said, his heart banging as if he'd won an epic victory. 'Coffee is on me.'

She raised her chin. 'I can buy my own coffee, thanks.'

Feisty and fiercely independent... 'Got it.' He sighed. What was it about Zara Wood that intrigued him?

'I'll see you later.' With an inscrutable glance, she picked up the tray and passed him, the sway of her hips as she walked down the ward his only reward for bravely extending the Anglo-Australian olive branch.

CHAPTER THREE

TEN MINUTES LATER, in the cafeteria, a flustered Zara took the seat opposite Conrad. What were the chances that her Australian lodger was also the new obstetric locum? If only she'd asked him what he did for a living that first day instead of shamelessly ogling him and judging him for being young, free and single, she might have avoided further embarrassment.

'Thanks for coming,' he said, all easy charm, those grey eyes of his smiling.

Zara shrugged, still mortified that he'd overheard her comments on his attractiveness earlier. But at least he hadn't gloated too much. She unwrapped her sandwich, although her stomach clenched with nerves. She blamed her colleagues on the delivery ward. The minute Sharon and Bella had discovered she was meeting the new locum doctor, who also happened to be her tenant, for a coffee, they'd shrieked like a couple of silly excited schoolgirls. Matchmaker Sharon, who was always encouraging Zara to *live a little* and *have fun*, had even fussed with Zara's hair and tried to persuade her to put on some lip gloss. As if…

'So, what brings you all the way to the middle of England from Australia?' she asked, trying her best to be friendly. 'As you pointed out, it's not for our barbecue weather,' she scoffed.

Outside, it was another dreary, grey and bitterly cold winter's day. But no matter what the state of the weather, she couldn't seem to forget she'd seen him stark naked. That was what six years without sex did to you.

'I finished my registrar training back in Australia, but I didn't want to apply for a consultant post yet.' Conrad smiled that killer smile, shrugging casually as if his easy-going personality was natural and in no way contrived. 'So I applied for a locum position and here I am.'

He took a sip of his coffee and she forced herself to take a bite of the sandwich, knowing from past experience she should take the opportunity to eat while she could. But despite all her tough talk, despite blaming Sharon for her nerves, there was something about Dr Reed that made her edgy.

Maybe because they were opposites, chalk and cheese. Maybe because he was the first Australian she'd ever met. Maybe because he was the only man in six years she'd found attractive enough to make her wonder if Sharon was right when it came to dating and sex and relationships: Zara *was* selling herself short. And she had to reluctantly admit that, whatever his other faults, he seemed to be good at his job.

But she didn't suffer fools. She'd meant what she'd said. His charisma, the good looks, the hot body—all irrelevant. She'd fallen for that kind of charm offensive once before. Zach's father had been one of *those* guys—avoiding commitment or being tied down, simply out for a good time. Her mistake had come with consequences for the most precious person in her life: her son.

'I actually like the contrast,' he said, still referring to

the weather. 'Where I'm from, winter temperatures rarely drop below twelve degrees Celsius.'

Zara sneered, wondering again why he'd come all the way to the middle of England in the winter. She couldn't imagine that Derby, or even Morholme, would be anyone's choice of travel destination. Looking at his light tan, the sun-kissed ends of his hair, the laughter lines around his eyes and mouth, Zara imagined the exotic heat and golden sand beaches of Australia, a place of surfing and picnics and laid-back vibes. A place she'd never been.

'Where in Australia are you from?' she asked, thawing to him a little, not that she wanted him to know she'd spent the past week daydreaming about her sexy new tenant or furtively hoping for another glimpse of him leaving the flat. When Bella had mentioned the new doctor was Australian, she'd even secretly hoped him and her lodger, the only Australian she knew, were one and the same.

'Brisbane,' he said, watching her intently as if, to him, she was equally exotic. 'Well, the Sunshine Coast to be precise.'

Zara rolled her eyes disbelievingly. *The Sunshine Coast...?* That sounds like a dreadful place to live. No wonder you prefer sleepy, freezing-cold Morholme.' What on earth was he doing there?

He laughed, his smile lighting those gorgeous grey eyes that seemed to bore into hers. Zara couldn't help but smile back. It had been a long time since she'd clicked with a man or found a shared sense of humour, not that this mild flirtation could go anywhere, of course.

'Have you ever been to Australia?' he asked, something in his laid-back attitude surprisingly intriguing now that she knew he took his work seriously, something she could respect.

Zara shook her head. 'No. I've always wanted to visit. It's on my list.' She didn't want to tell him the last time she'd been abroad she'd been a twenty-year-old student midwife. She'd saved up for a friends' holiday to Spain, where she'd fallen for a handsome Spanish waiter, had a dreamy holiday romance and come home pregnant. She already felt pretty unworldly compared to Conrad Reed.

And the last thing she wanted to think about in front of him was her youthful naivety and how, even after all these years, there was a part of her that blamed herself for Zach's situation. Holiday romances never lasted, and she didn't regret having her wonderful boy. But she wished she'd chosen a better father for him, one interested in knowing him, even if he and Zara weren't together.

'Holidays for me are usually a rainy week in South Wales.' She shrugged, her face heating. 'Or a road trip to Chester Zoo, but I wouldn't change a thing, obviously.'

She pressed her lips together, experiencing the familiar sharp ache of rejection on Zach's behalf. Spain wasn't that far away from England, and if Lorenzo had asked, she'd have brought baby Zach to meet his father. Instead she'd learned just how little she'd meant to the Spanish waiter, who probably had a different fling with a fresh holiday-maker every two weeks. A man like that, just selfishly out for a good time, had no use for a kid cramping his style.

'So, how old is your son?' Conrad asked, seeming genuinely interested.

'Zach. He's five.'

Conrad raised his eyebrows, his smile filled with satisfaction. 'Same age as my nephew, James.' Something shifted over his expression—pride, longing, a flicker of sadness, gone before she could be sure of it. 'Is he at school?'

Zara nodded, instinctively sensing that Conrad and James were close. She recognised the adoring look on his face. 'He goes to Morholme Primary School.'

'So how do you juggle shift work and childcare?'

'I'm lucky to have my mum living close by. She often picks Zach up from school while I'm at work. And, depending on my pattern of shifts, has him for sleepovers, which he loves.' In many ways, she had a great life: a good job she adored, a secure home thanks to her father, a son who made her smile, every day. No wonder she couldn't find the energy to bother with something as dissatisfying as dating, not when, in her experience, men were so unreliable.

'So is your nephew in Australia?' she asked, curious that they seemed to have the love of a five-year-old in common. Would she need to revise her first impressions of this man?

'Yeah, in Brisbane. I miss the little guy.' He glanced down at his coffee, telling her he didn't want to say more on the subject.

'It must be quite a culture shock for you coming here,' she said. 'Derby isn't exactly a cosmopolitan city and there's literally nothing to do in Morholme unless you're into pensioners' bingo at the village hall.'

He laughed again, meeting her stare. 'Morholme is very quaint, I guess. But you've done a beautiful job with the flat. It's very comfortable.' His expression was full of warmth and curiosity that left Zara aware of his observation to the tips of her fingers and toes.

'Thank you,' she said, his compliment bringing an unexpected ache to her throat. 'My father left me the house, so Zach and I are lucky.'

'Your father has passed?' he asked, with a frown.

'Yes, five years ago, just after Zach was born. He had pancreatic cancer.' Why was she telling him this? She barely knew him. But he was right; life *was* short. Her father's untimely death was proof of that. Not a day went by where she didn't miss her dad. She owed her parents so much. She could never have finished her midwifery training and established herself at the hospital without the support from Pam and, thanks to her father, she and Zach would always have a roof over their heads.

'I'm sorry,' he said, simply. 'I understand what that's like. I've lost someone, too.'

Zara blinked away the sting in her eyes. 'Then I'm sorry, too,' she said, feeling awkward and wondering if the real reason he'd left Australia was to mourn.

'So what *do* you do for fun, *Ms* Wood,' he asked, pasting on a bright smile and changing the subject, 'if it's not pensioners' bingo at the village hall?'

Zara smiled, grateful that they could shift back to lighter topics. 'Well, nothing as exciting as I'm imagining you do on the Sunshine Coast, perhaps barbecues and beach walks.' If only he knew how mundane her life was—not that she needed his pity. She and Zach were fine.

She smiled a genuine smile, thinking about her son. 'After a week of juggling childcare and shift work, the highlight of my week is usually feeding the ducks at the village pond on a Sunday, followed by a trip to the playground.' There was nothing better than spending time with her little boy, the centre of her world. If her own personal life lacked a certain…sizzle, it was a small price to pay for Zach's happiness and security.

'So no New Year's Eve party lined up for tonight?' he asked. 'Perhaps a hot date?' His stare glittered with that curiosity that told her their attraction was obviously mutual, even if they had no intention of acting on it. 'I heard mention of a dry spell earlier, so I just wondered…'

Zara blushed furiously. She couldn't even recall what a *hot date* felt like. In fact, she'd barely had a couple before having Zach. But she was going to throttle Sharon. 'No, no date tonight.' And she'd already declined an invite to drinks at Sharon's house.

'Really?' he asked with flattering astonishment. 'But New Year's Eve only comes around once a year. You're too young and too interesting *not* to have a date tonight.'

Zara shrugged, abandoning the rest of her sandwich, because her appetite had vanished. While his comments were flattering, she felt the need to defend herself. 'I'll probably have an early night, actually, given I have the early shift tomorrow and Zach spends every Friday sleeping over at his grandma's. She has a little dog he adores, and she spoils him. But I don't mind.'

He nodded, and she continued her justifications. 'Besides, I've kind of had my fingers burned in the past. I've raised Zach single-handed. My spare time is precious. I'd rather give it all to my son.' And having made one mistake with her holiday romance, having exposed her innocent baby boy to his father's rejection, she just couldn't face the effort of meeting some stranger who'd most likely do a runner as soon as she mentioned she was a single mum.

'Of course,' he said with a guilty wince. 'It must be a lot to juggle.'

'What about you?' she asked, desperate to change the subject back to Conrad. 'Any kids of your own? A wife or girlfriend back in Australia? Or maybe both?'

She needed some nugget of information she could give to Sharon and Bella when she returned to the ward. Her colleagues would be hungry to know what she and the hunky Australian had talked about, and Sharon would go ballistic if all Zara had done was talk about why she was so sworn off relationships.

He shrugged, looking mildly uncomfortable for the first time. 'I've dated in the past, but, you know, nothing serious in recent years.'

She sensed there might be more to the story, but, like her, he obviously didn't want to talk about his past relationships. 'You're just having a good time, right?'

Why was she poking at him this way? She wasn't normally rude. But there was something about him that was forcing her to revise her first impressions and messing with her head. She blamed Sharon, who'd acted as if Zara were going on a real date, when in reality *she* wouldn't know a good time if it came up and kissed her senseless.

'You don't think much of me, do you, Zara?' He smiled, holding her eye contact for a long while, making her squirm.

'I don't know you,' she said, all bluster now that he'd called her out. 'But I think you're a good doctor. You paid your rent on time. The rest is none of my business.'

He laughed and Zara couldn't help but smile too, glad to pretend she'd been joking, because, otherwise, she'd sounded like a bitter old shrew who judged every man she met against her disappointment with Zach's father.

But now that she'd met this sexy Australian with such a different outlook from hers, the huge hole in her personal life gaped open. If she didn't know better, she'd think he'd been sent there to shake up the life she'd assumed she had under control and make her restless for something more. She'd just cast that ridiculous thought out of her head when Conrad's pager sounded an urgent tone.

'It's Labour Ward,' he said, looking down, abandoning what was left of his coffee and jerking to his feet.

'I'll come with you.' Even though she had fifteen minutes of her break left, Zara grabbed her bag and they both started running.

The alarm led them to one of the delivery rooms. Sharon glanced up as they entered, her expression sagging with relief, but Zara's blood froze. She and Sharon had been looking after this woman together, before Zara had gone on her break.

'This is Jane Phillips,' Zara told Conrad. 'A twenty-eight-year-old multiparous mum on her third pregnancy.'

More help arrived: the obstetrics SHO, Max, and a crash team anaesthetist.

'Normal vaginal delivery four minutes ago,' Sharon added in a panicked voice, her stare flicking to the newborn in the arms of the father, who was looking on anxiously. 'Sudden post-partum haemorrhage following third stage,' Sharon continued, reaching to the wall behind the new mother to adjust the flow of oxygen to a mask she fitted over Jane's face.

Conrad grabbed a wide bore cannula and a tourniquet, quickly introducing himself to the patient as he sited the cannula in her arm.

'We need cross match. Four units,' he said, extracting a blood sample and passing it to Max.

While Sharon set up an infusion of intravenous fluids,

and Zara drew up syntocinon, a drug that would contract the uterus and hopefully slow down the bleeding, Conrad placed a hand on Jane's abdomen, manually massaging the uterus.

'Start the syntocinon transfusion,' Conrad told Zara, his alarm obvious in the clipped tone of his voice. 'Was the placenta intact?' he asked Sharon.

'I thought so.' Sharon nodded as the woman's blood pressure dropped, the alarms sounding once more.

With panic and fear in charge of her heart rate, Zara took over the compression of the uterus while Conrad examined the patient.

'There's no obvious tear,' he said, meeting Zara's stare. 'The bleeding is coming from high up. Keep massaging.' He reached for a second intravenous cannula and sited it in the woman's other arm, the sense of urgency in the room building. Catastrophic post-partum haemorrhage was fortunately rare but life-threatening, and every midwife and obstetrician's worst nightmare.

'If we can't get the bleeding to stop,' Zara explained to the alarmed couple, who hadn't had a chance to enjoy their newborn baby, 'you might need to go to Theatre.'

'Get a second bag of fluids up, please,' Conrad told Sharon, who rushed to do his bidding. 'Zara, can you draw up some prostaglandin?' asked Conrad as they nervously watched the blood pressure monitor, willing the drugs to work and the bleeding to slow.

Zara reached for the second line drug as Conrad took over with the uterine massage, their efforts coordinated, their differences and misunderstandings forgotten as they worked as a team.

Zara injected the prostaglandin into the muscle of Jane's thigh and looked to Conrad for guidance.

'Blood loss isn't slowing as quickly as I would like,' he said, addressing the patient and her partner. 'Do you consent to surgery?'

The couple nodded, wide-eyed now with the same fear Zara was desperately trying to control.

'Call Theatre,' Conrad told Sharon, clearly reaching the limit of his composure. 'Tell them we're on our way.' He unlocked the wheels of the bed and nodded to Zara. 'Take over here with uterine compression and, Max, get the blood sent round to Theatre.'

Leaving Dad and the baby in Sharon's care, she, Conrad and the anaesthetist steered the patient out of the delivery room and rushed towards the lifts that would take them straight to the operating suites.

Inside the department, Zara handed the patient over to the waiting theatre staff, her job for now done. 'Keep me posted,' she told Conrad as the doors swung closed.

He gave her a determined nod. Of respect, of thanks, of promise. Then he disappeared out of sight, racing to surgery with their patient. Zara headed back to the delivery ward, her adrenaline draining away to be replaced by concern. She hoped for their patient's sake, for Jane's newborn and her husband, that her instincts were right: that Conrad *was* a good surgeon. For now, all she could do was wait.

CHAPTER FOUR

LATER THAT NIGHT, back in Morholme, Conrad knocked on Zara's front door, nervous excitement making his heart skip a beat. He understood how Zara's alternating shifts created issues with childcare, but he hated the idea of her being alone on New Year's Eve. He waited in the freezing pitch black. Days were dark when he arrived at work in the morning and dark again by the time he left the hospital in the evening. It made him wonder if he'd ever again see the sun.

The door opened and Zara appeared, her expression one of surprise. Warmth flooded onto the doorstep from the house. She looked relaxed and sexy in her jeans and sweater. She'd been on his mind all day since their talk in the cafeteria and the emergency they'd dealt with together.

'Hi,' he said, trying to keep his voice serious. 'I wondered if you could point me in the direction of pensioners' bingo? I hear it's the most exciting thing that happens around here.'

Her laughter lit her eyes and raised his sun-starved spirits, so his smile widened. There was something about her laugh, her sense of humour, that mocking challenge in her stare, that took his mind off his own troubles. She'd admitted she'd had her fingers burned when it came to dating, and he wondered how far her trust issues went. That would be another thing they had in common, although Conrad's own sense of betrayal was complex and snared up with his grief over losing his brother, Marcus. It was hard to be angry with a dead man, especially one Conrad had always looked up to, the one person he'd thought he could trust.

'Actually,' he went on, keen to change the direction of his thoughts away from his late brother, and his reasons for leaving Australia so he'd had space to think and grieve, 'I'm going to try out the local pub, and wondered if you'd like to join me, seeing as you're alone tonight and we're probably the only two non-retired people in the whole of Morholme.'

A moment's hesitation flicked over her expression. 'Um… I have to be up at five.'

'I know, but it's New Year's Eve. We don't have to stay long, but I hear there's live music,' he cajoled playfully, switching on the smile she found charming, 'a buffet, and, if you need further convincing, even a meat raffle donated by the local butcher! How could you possibly resist?'

She laughed again, her refusal clearly waning.

'We might have a good time,' he urged. 'I don't know about you, but after today, I could use a few laughs.'

At mention of their emergency, she seemed to change her mind, to his relief. 'Sure, why not? Although I can't promise I'll make it to midnight. And I hope you like your beer warm and your sandwiches curly, not a barbecued prawn in sight.'

'They're my favourite, as it happens,' he joked, elated that he'd managed to persuade her and draw her a little more out of her shell. Today, he'd revised his opinion that she was prickly and uptight. She was smart and funny. She was clearly a dedicated midwife and was understandably devoted to her young son. When she let down her guard, her attractiveness shot through the roof. When she laughed with him, he didn't miss Australia quite as much.

'I'll just grab my coat.' She disappeared for a second, reappearing wearing boots, a puffer jacket and woollen hat with a furry pompom. They set off on the short walk to the Miner's Arms, side by side.

'So how did the surgery go?' she asked. 'Thanks for texting me to say she was out of Theatre, by the way.'

'You're welcome. I'm not going to lie, it was stressful,' he said, watching a small frown of worry tug at her mouth. 'I found some retained placental tissue that was causing the bleeding, so she lost a lot of blood.' Post-partum haemorrhage was one of the worst emergencies he ever had to treat.

Zara glanced up at him with obvious concern. 'You were still in Theatre when my shift ended, so I've been worrying about the outcome. Will she be okay?'

Conrad nodded. 'I hope so. I had to transfuse three litres of blood and her renal function went off a bit. So she's recovering on the high-dependency unit for now, but I hope to transfer her to the postnatal ward in the morning, as long as she's remained stable overnight. How was the baby?' he asked, recalling how emotional and exhausted the husband had been when Conrad had spoken to him on HDU.

Zara's frown eased slightly. 'He's well. Perfectly healthy. So that's one good thing.'

'Yeah.' He dragged in a deep breath. 'Sometimes it's hard to leave the job behind, isn't it?' There was something very attractive about Zara's dedication to her patients. It spoke of loyalty and compassion, two very attractive qualities in Conrad's book.

'It is,' she agreed. 'It can be emotionally draining.'

'That's why I'm so glad I could persuade you to come for a drink tonight.'

She smiled and some of the tension around her eyes eased. 'Why did you choose obstetrics?' she asked, eyeing him with curiosity as they crossed the deserted road towards the quintessential English pub, which had brass carriage lamps beside the door and climbing ivy growing along the stonework.

'Well, my mother is a midwife,' he said, pulling open the door to the pub for Zara to enter first, 'and, believe it or not, I like the happy endings. If we do our jobs right, we not only help the patient, but we also send her home a mother to a healthy baby. That's pretty cool in my book.'

'I agree, it is,' Zara said, her observation intensifying as if she'd warmed to him since their earlier chat in the hospital canteen. And the feeling was mutual. Faced with an evening alone with only his ruminations on why he was there in England, Conrad had remembered Zara say her son was spending the night at her mum's place. The idea of getting to know her a bit better, a woman who'd pretty much been on his mind since the day they met, had galvanised him off the sofa.

Inside the Miner's Arms, the antiquated theme continued with low ceilings criss-crossed with wooden beams, old guys in flat caps propping up the bar and a roaring log fire in a massive blackened grate.

'What can I get you,' he asked over the sound of the band, who were playing popular classics no one was dancing to.

Zara removed her hat and unzipped her coat, her cheeks rosy from the cold. 'I'll have a pint of Chatsworth Gold ale, please.'

Conrad nodded, impressed by her drink of choice. While Zara smiled at a few locals and wandered off to find them a table near the fire, he ordered two pints of Chatsworth Gold, his attraction to his landlady building. He wasn't looking for a relationship. He was only in the UK for another three weeks. But Zara Wood was exactly his type: stunning, smart, funny and clearly dedicated to her work and her son.

Wondering again about her dry spell and what it meant for a harmless bit of flirtation, he joined her at the table and took a seat.

'Cheers,' he said, raising his glass. 'To the end of a busy week and the end of another year.'

'Cheers!' She smiled and clinked her glass to his, taking a sip.

'Oh, that's good,' he said, the hops and honey blending on his tongue.

'As good as your Australian beer?' she asked, her hazel eyes twinkling in the glow from the fire.

'Better,' he said. 'And perfectly chilled too. You promised me warm beer...'

'Well, warm beer is the house special,' she teased. 'You have to ask for it with a secret handshake.' She winked. 'I'll teach it to you.'

Conrad laughed, delighted that she seemed to be enjoying herself. 'Obviously beer drinking is how you Brits manage your seasonal mood disorders,' he countered. 'Is winter always this dark? I literally haven't seen the sun for days.'

'Don't be such a baby,' she said, laughing at him.

Conrad basked in the sound, his curiosity for this woman building to an unreachable itch. 'What made you change your mind about joining me tonight?'

'It's a woman's prerogative,' she said. Then she shrugged, mischief in her eyes. 'Actually, I think it was your willingness to eat curly sandwiches, or maybe what you said earlier about life being short and New Year's Eve only coming around once a year. As you might have overheard this morning, Sharon is always trying to fix me up with single men, although dating is the last thing on my mind. Don't tell her about this, by the way. She's a dreadful matchmaker. If she finds out we had an innocent drink, she'll have us married by next Tuesday.'

'Your secret is safe with me.' He smiled, something she'd said earlier niggling at him. 'So, is Zach's father in the picture at all?'

At his mention of her son's name, she looked surprised, as if she hadn't expected him to listen or to remember.

'Nope,' she said, with a shake of her head. 'It was a holiday fling. He's Spanish. When he found out he was going to be a father, he declined the offer to stay in touch.' She shrugged, her eyes darting away as if she was embarrassed. 'And can you really be called a father if by choice you've never met your son or contributed to his life in any way?'

'I guess not.' He winced, appalled on Zara and Zach's behalf. 'So he doesn't even support Zach financially?'

She shook her head again, looking uncomfortable. 'But I see to it that Zach has everything he needs.'

Conrad nodded, the steely glint in her eyes highlighting the fierce independence he both admired and wondered if it masked more vulnerable feelings. 'I'm sorry,' he said. 'That's his loss.'

She glanced at him sharply, as if he'd caught her off guard in return. 'It's fine. My son doesn't need a male role model like that.'

'So is he the reason you don't date, even if you had time?' he asked, cautiously, wary of crossing the line and upsetting her again. He hated that someone with so much going for her had closed off that part of her life. She was in her mid-twenties, way too young to have sworn off relationships, although these days, he too took things slow.

Zara flushed, shifting in her seat. 'Don't get me wrong, I like men, well, the dependable, responsible ones, that is.' She shrugged. 'I guess I've had to learn to rely on myself and it's become a bit of a habit. And I go out of my way to ensure my mistake doesn't define my son or allow him to suffer in any way.'

'Fair enough.' He nodded because he'd made his own mistakes, rushed into a relationship with the last serious girlfriend he'd had, like the proverbial fool, and lost her. Of course, the heartache he'd experienced when she'd broken up with him was nothing compared to the sense of betrayal he'd known later when she'd moved on to his brother. It seemed he hadn't in fact lost her because he'd moved too fast. Tessa just hadn't wanted Conrad.

'So what would New Year's Eve in Brisbane look like?' Zara asked, drawing him away from thoughts he always seemed to get snagged on: how the brother he'd loved and looked up to could have deceived and betrayed him like that.

'Definite beer consumption,' he said, smiling through the flicker of homesickness pinching his ribs. 'Parties in every bar and restaurant along the river. Fireworks at midnight.'

She looked wistful for a second, before she blinked the expression away. 'You must miss home?'

'I miss some things.' Conrad paused, taking another swallow of the delicious ale. 'Family, obviously—my parents, my nephew. The weather…' His smile stretched, and he realised he was already pretty addicted to drawing out Zara Wood's brand of throaty laughter. First impressions aside, they actually shared quite a bit in common.

'Tell me about James,' she said. 'You two are obviously very close.'

'We are.' Conrad swallowed, his chest hollowing out with a sudden rush of sadness. 'Although I haven't seen him for a while, but he loves dinosaurs and anything with wheels, particularly trains.'

'Don't you live close by in Australia?' she pushed, her stare shifting over his face as she tried to figure him out.

'I do,' he admitted, reluctant to spill the complexities of his past, despite feeling relaxed from the beer and the warmth of the fire and already pretty confident that Zara was a loyal person. 'But… Well, the person I lost recently was my brother, James's dad. Six months ago.'

She gasped, her hand coming to rest on his arm and her stare full of that compassion she shared with her patients. 'I'm so sorry; that's terrible.'

He shrugged, still getting used to saying the words aloud. 'Obviously my sister-in-law, Tessa, is still in a pretty bad place. She's grieving, and you know how hard it is to raise a child alone.'

Of course, his relationship with both Marcus and Tessa had already been strained, before Marcus's death. How could it not have been, given that Conrad and Tessa had once dated, way before she'd slept with Marcus and fallen immediately pregnant with James. Not that it was *her* betrayal that stuck in Conrad's throat. His romantic feelings for Tessa had been long gone by the time she'd hooked up with Marcus. But his brother had owed him some consideration and loyalty and an explanation. Instead they'd sneaked around behind Conrad's back.

'But she's not alone,' Zara pointed out. 'She had you and your parents, right?'

'Yeah.' He nodded, glancing away. 'But since the funeral, Tessa has kind of withdrawn from our family out of grief, taking James with her, obviously.'

'I'm so sorry,' she whispered.

Conrad shrugged. 'When James was born, I promised my brother I'd always look out for him. But after he died, I obviously overdid the concern. Tessa told me to back off. So I figured I'd get away for a few weeks so we all had some space to grieve for Marcus.' And, of course, his and Tessa's history had also clouded the issue.

'So you chose a locum position in the UK?'

He nodded. 'I understand that Tessa is dealing with a lot,' he went on, 'but I miss James. I just hope that when I return to Brisbane, she's ready to let us back into his life.'

'I hope so too, for your sake and for your parents.' Her frown deepened and he could have kicked himself for killing the mood. But he was still trying to get used to talking about Marcus's senseless death without his voice breaking, still trying to make sense of it all.

'It's...complicated,' he said. In more ways than one. 'But the last thing we want to do is push Tessa further away.'

'Do you mind me asking what happened, with your brother?' she whispered when he looked up. 'It's fine if you don't want to talk about it.'

'I don't mind talking about Marcus.' Conrad took a gulp of beer, preparing himself, focussed on the uncomplicated time when Marcus had simply been the older brother he'd looked up to. 'He was amazing. There was only a year be-tween us, so, growing up, we were best friends.'

And that had made the breach of trust harder to bare. He didn't blame Tessa and Marcus for falling in love. But he hated that his brother hadn't come to him straight away, that he'd kept it a secret until discovering Tessa was preg-nant, until he'd been forced to come clean. Marcus had tried to heal the rift, and Conrad had been forced to swal-low down his sense of betrayal and confusion for the sake of family harmony. But his absolute trust in his brother had been broken, the issue for Conrad going unresolved as life moved on.

'Marcus worked as a paramedic,' he continued, block-ing out how he'd felt backed into a corner back then, before James was born, as if his feelings didn't matter because there was a baby coming, a wedding to plan, a sister-in-law to welcome into the Reed family. Then Marcus had died. Conrad's grief was compounded by those lingering feel-ings of betrayal he'd never quite dealt with. He knew he should let the past go, but he was stuck somehow with no hope of a resolution now that Marcus was gone.

'One day, he attended a call—a case of domestic vio-lence.' Conrad gripped his pint glass, his knuckles white. 'The perpetrator had pushed his wife down the stairs and then called the ambulance. Marcus arrived before the po-lice. He could see from the front door that the woman had a head injury, was lying unconscious and needed urgent help, but he probably should have waited for support. The guy was armed with a knife. He was smart enough to know he was going to jail, so he became belligerent, tried to jus-tify what he'd done. Things escalated when Marcus tried to treat the casualty. He stabbed my brother in the neck before the police arrived. Marcus died later in hospital.'

'That's so terrible.' Zara swallowed hard, her eyes shining with tears. 'So senseless. I'm so sorry.'

Conrad nodded, shocked by how much of the story had come pouring out. But Zara really cared about people. She was easy to talk to.

'Sorry,' he said, drawing a line under the conversation. 'I didn't mean to bring down the mood. It's meant to be a party. It's New Year's Eve.'

'It's okay,' Zara said, her eyes full of empathy. 'I shouldn't have been so curious.'

Conrad eyed their near-empty glasses, eager to pack away his complex feelings for which there seemed to be no end, just an infinite loop. 'I'll um…get us another drink.' He pushed back his chair and stood. 'Unless…' He glanced at the band, who were doing a valiant job considering nearly everyone in the pub was ignoring them. 'Are you up for a dance?' He held out his hand, determined to get the party mood back on track.

Zara frowned at his abrupt change of pace. She looked around the pub, self-consciously. 'Dance…? Really?' She hesitated, eyeing his hand with uncertainty.

Admittedly the place was pretty dead, by New Year's Eve standards, but the band were reasonably good, the tunes catchy and recognisable.

'Definitely,' Conrad said, desperate for her laughter over her pity. If only she knew the other half of the story… 'I've let things get too heavy. And who cares what the old farmers think of us?'

'Okay.' Her eyes glowed with excitement as she put her hand in his, the decision made. Conrad pulled her to her feet and led her to the small carpeted area in front of the make-shift stage, glad to move his body after the serious turn the conversation had taken. With his heart pounding, he scooped his arm around her waist, holding her close, spinning her, making her laugh. The sound shifted the heaviness in his chest to a muted throb he could easily ignore.

Within minutes, another couple had joined them dancing and then another. Zara lost that self-consciousness, throwing herself into enjoying the music as if she hadn't danced in a very long time.

'Now it's a New Year's Eve party,' he said, dipping his head close so he caught the scent of her shampoo, felt the heat of her body, heard the exhilarating catch of her breath.

'It's been a while since I've been to one,' she said, blinking up at him with the same excitement he felt at her closeness. Could she feel this chemistry too? Was she, like him, torn between acting on it or pretending it didn't exist? Whatever happened between them, friendship or more, could only be temporary given he was headed back to Australia in three weeks. But they didn't need to trust each other to have a good time.

'Then I'm glad I persuaded you to come,' he said, simply focussing on enjoying the moment, her company, the building atmosphere, the fact that they were young and alive and on the cusp of a brand-new year.

'Me too.' She smiled and he believed her.

CHAPTER FIVE

'THREE...TWO...ONE. Happy new year!' Zara yelled at the top of her voice as Sid, the normally gruff owner of the Miner's Arms, fired a confetti cannon into the air and gold glittered down on the biggest crowd Zara had ever seen in the village pub.

Conrad scooped her into a big bear hug, his smile infectious. 'Happy new year, Zara,' he said, his warm breath tickling her neck, and the yummy scent of him making her head spin faster than the effects of the alcohol and the party vibe combined. 'I hope it's a great one for you and Zach.'

With her throat choked that he'd included her son in his well wishes and before she could overthink the foreign impulse, she hugged him back and pressed a brief kiss to his cheek. 'You too,' she said, laughing up at him as all around them people hugged and kissed and raised their glasses in toasts.

Conrad grinned. The sexy Aussie was surprisingly great company, effortlessly bringing her out of herself with his sense of humour and his laid-back personality. She'd danced as if no one was watching, laughed at Conrad's improbable tales and drank more beer than she should have drunk given she had to be at work in seven hours. She'd even thrashed Conrad in a highly contested game of England versus Australia darts.

'Wanna head home?' he asked, his hands sliding from her shoulders. 'We both have work tomorrow, and you said you have to be up at five.'

Zara nodded, knocked sideways by his thoughtfulness and by their chemistry that had been simmering away all night. Despite her first impressions of him as a Jack the Lad, he hadn't once crossed the line. There'd been plenty of touching while they'd danced, some flirtatious looks, lots of laughter. But now she wondered if she'd imagined his interest. She was so out of practice when it came to members of the opposite sex. She almost wished Sharon were there for advice. Perhaps he didn't fancy her the way she fancied him. Perhaps he just needed a friend.

Zara blinked, sobered by the memory of his grief earlier when he'd told her about his brother. Now his locum job there, so far from home, made sense. There must be a part of him running away from the pain, the memories, the grief. But those realisations brought more questions, like why he didn't date and why his relationship with his sister-in-law was so tense.

At their table, they collected their hats and coats before spilling out of the pub into the sub-zero temperatures. 'That was so much fun,' she said. 'Thanks for dragging me along. I can't remember ever having such a good time at the local pub.' Despite her earlier reluctance, part of her didn't want such a great night to end.

'You're welcome,' he said. 'All we need now is the fireworks.' He looked up at the clear night sky dotted with stars, before flashing her a cheeky grin that set her pulse aflutter and left her wondering if her life did indeed lack a certain spark. 'Although I guess that's expecting a bit too much.'

'I think so,' she agreed with a chuckle.

They walked in silence for a few minutes, their breath misting the cold, damp air, close, but not too close. After all the touching on the dance floor, the 'happy new year' hug, the way he'd helped her into her coat, Zara missed the contact. Through her own actions, she'd been starved of intimate touch for over five years. As Sharon often pointed out, she'd shut herself off from relationships. Because they were a low priority? Yes. Because she'd had her trust damaged? Probably. Because she was desperately trying to make up for her mistake by being everything Zach needed, mother and father? So what if that was the case? It harmed no one.

'You okay?' he asked as they arrived at her cottage.

She nodded feeling as if his casual flirtations, his thoughtfulness and sense of humour had brought her back to life. He was ridiculously hot, a nice guy too, once you looked beneath the surface. Behind those dreamy bedroom eyes of his, the laid-back, good-time attitude hid more complex emotions, but even that called to her. Glancing over at his handsome profile, she'd never been more aware of what she'd denied herself since Zach was born—good times with someone her own age, connection, sex. But she should probably think of him as off limits. Kiss him goodnight and leave it there... So why did that idea send her stomach to her boots?

Conrad pushed open the garden gate and stepped aside. 'After you.' He even pulled out his phone and switched on the torch so she could see the path that bisected the lawn and led to her front door.

This was it. Decision time. Give him a peck on the cheek and say goodnight or go for it? She was so confused. And a bit tipsy. And turned on.

They'd barely made it two or three steps inside the garden when he reached for her arm. 'Wait—I think I saw something move.'

Zara froze, peering into the shadowy blackness of the back garden, her fear muted by the heat from his touch and the protective way he stepped forward, putting his body between hers and danger. It had been so long since someone other than her mum had cared and looked out for her, and this was different somehow. Sexier. Gallant.

'It's probably just a fox,' she whispered, trying to pull herself together. 'We get lots of those here.' She needed to calm down. He was just being considerate. Just because he was sexy, funny and charming and a dedicated doctor, didn't mean she seriously wanted to take flirting to the next level, did she? Could she even remember what the next level was? Perhaps that was exactly why she needed to live a little. Sharon was right...

'No, it was smaller than that,' he said, keeping a protective hold on her elbow as they crept further into the garden.

Zara released a tipsy giggle, enjoying that this urbane Australian who most likely didn't even own a pair of wellies was willing throw himself into the path of whatever beast was lurking in the dark. Then her blood ran cold as realisation struck.

'Billy Boy,' she whispered, her panic instantly fullblown.

'Is that an ex of yours?' Conrad said, standing taller as if fully prepared to face up to some thug in her honour.

Zara shook her head and pressed her lips together as another giggle threatened. But an escaped, much-loved pet was no laughing matter. 'No, it's Zach's pet rabbit. He's always escaping. He has a death wish.' She gripped Conrad's arm. 'We have to catch him before a fox does. Zach will be devastated if anything happens to Billy Boy.'

Stepping cautiously onto the frosty grass, Zara walked underneath the house's security-light sensor, triggering a blinding halogen beam that flooded the garden in light. From the corner of her eye, she spied a flash of movement, a blur of grey against the greenery.

'There.' She hurried towards the rabbit, cornering it behind a bush. Conrad stood at the opposite end of the hedge, his stare alive with excitement and amusement, as if he was enjoying himself as much as when they'd danced and played a very competitive game of darts.

'Don't laugh,' she chided, her own lips twitching. 'We need to catch him before he escapes into the fields, or my life won't be worth living.'

'Right.' Conrad nodded, his expression falling serious, which somehow made Zara want to laugh even more.

'Ready?' Zara shook the branches of the hedge to flush Billy Boy out.

The rabbit hopped sedately from his hiding place, utterly unaware of the dangers out in the dark. Zara crouched low, her hands out in front, ready to intercept the fluffy bundle. But before she could get within grasping distance, Conrad dived onto his stomach, his arms outstretched like a rugby player landing a try. His hands closed around thin air. Billy Boy hopped away, evading them both.

Zara burst out laughing, her mirth momentarily outweighing her concern for the pet. She fell back onto her backside with laughter, the dampness from the grass soaking through her jeans.

'What was that?' she asked, tears running down her

cheeks as Conrad climbed to his feet and brushed the wet grass from his front.

'I've never caught a rabbit before,' he said, seemingly delighted that he'd made her laugh so hard. 'They're a pest in Australia. Farmers shoot them.'

'Shh,' she hissed, scrambling to her feet. 'He'll hear you.' With her hand on Conrad's arm, they followed the rabbit deeper into the recesses of the garden.

'This time, stay low but nimble,' she instructed Conrad, impervious to the cold because she was enjoying herself so much. 'I normally have to catch him all by myself with Zach too busy giggling to help out.'

Conrad nodded, mock serious. 'So what's the plan this time? Do I catch him while *you* giggle?'

Zara held in another bubble of laughter. She liked that he could laugh at himself, and she'd pay good money to see this tall, sun-kissed Australian catch a pet rabbit in the dark, muddy garden alone. Suddenly his attractiveness tripled.

'I'll flush him out,' she said, trying to be serious, 'and one of us just grabs him. He's not actually that fast because he's a bit over-loved and overfed.'

Conrad limbered up by bouncing on the balls of his feet and shadow-boxing like a like a prize-fighter. Zara rolled her eyes and hid another smile, picking her way silently to the far side of the rabbit hutch. She crouched down to find Billy Boy happily munching on a patch of dandelion leaves that had somehow survived the cold. She tried to reach for him but he was already spooked by Conrad's unorthodox belly-dive. He darted away, Zara's fingertips grazing his fur, but he hopped straight into the waiting hands of a very smug Conrad.

'Just like catching a baby,' he said as he stood, a triumphant smile stretching his sexy mouth.

Zara breathed a sigh of both relief and longing. He was far too gorgeous and confident for his own good. And now that Billy Boy was safe, all she could think was how much she wanted to kiss him. Properly.

'Well done,' she said. 'We'll make a rabbit wrangler out of you yet.' She looked away from his victorious expression, his eyes dancing with merriment and something else she wasn't sure she was ready to see: desire.

Did she really want anything to happen between them? Would sleeping with him be reckless? Or just a safe, fun way to explore something she'd denied herself for far too long?

Ignoring the excited flutter in her stomach, Zara opened the hutch and grabbed a handful of fresh straw, shoving it inside Billy Boy's bedroom. While Conrad placed the bunny back inside and closed the door, Zara inspected the cage, finding a corner where the chicken wire had come loose. She stretched the wire over the makeshift nail she'd hammered in the last time the bunny had escaped, reclosing the gap. Tomorrow, after work, she'd dig out a hammer and repair the hutch properly.

'So it's not just pensioners' bingo that gets pulses racing around here,' Conrad said playfully as they headed towards the door to his flat.

Zara smiled up at him, her own pulse still leaping at the power of his sexy smile and the awoken urges pounding through her body. 'We only bring out the escaped bunnies for people who are rubbish at darts,' she said dryly.

He laughed, tossing back his head. Smiling at each other, they paused under the security light beside his door.

'Thanks for tonight,' she said, her voice a little croaky with lust. 'It will be a long time before I'll forget that hilarious rugby dive.'

'You're welcome.' He grinned wider. 'It's nice to see you laugh; you should do it more often.'

Zara stilled, embarrassed by how right he was and by how much she'd neglected her own needs to focus on Zach. No, that wasn't fair. It wasn't Zach's fault. It was fear that had held her back. Fear to be vulnerable with another man after Lorenzo. Of course her son would always be the most important person in her life, but maybe the universe was trying to tell her that it was okay to act her age and have a good time. And she didn't have to be vulnerable with Conrad, not when it could be for just one night.

'Well…goodnight, Zara,' he said when she stayed silent and unmoving for too long. 'Any time you need help catching Billy Boy, just give me a shout.' He leaned close, gripped her shoulder and pressed a cold kiss to her cheek.

Zara's breath trapped in her chest, her heart bounding as his lips lingered on her skin. It was now or never. If she didn't do something right that second, she would always regret it. Before he pulled back, she turned her face and grazed his lips with hers in the merest brush of a kiss.

Conrad peered down at her intensely, his hand on her shoulder still holding her in place. They stared, one second stretching into another, a loaded moment of possibility.

'Sorry,' Zara whispered, uncertain after being so rusty at flirtation for so long. But something had shifted between them, a crackle of awareness. Surely he'd felt it too, this chemistry between them, there all night, just waiting for one of them to acknowledge it? If she was going to put herself out there again, Conrad was as safe a bet as any.

He knew her situation, her priorities. Like her, he wasn't looking for a relationship, and he'd be going back to Australia in a few weeks.

'Are you?' he asked, simply, his voice husky and his stare unwavering. 'You shouldn't be.'

She shook her head. 'I'm not really. I'm just aware that I'm seriously back-pedalling. This afternoon at work, I said I wasn't interested in being your next casual conquest. I kind of regret that now.'

She tried to smile and he cupped her cold cheek, his thumb grazing her cheekbone. 'I don't recall that conversation. And life is too short for regrets.'

She flushed, nodding because he was right. 'You can probably tell I don't do this very often...' She couldn't make her feet move away, but was this, kissing him properly, perhaps sleeping with him, a stupid idea? With them practically living together and definitely working together, there'd be no escaping him for the few weeks he was in town. But it was only one night. Just casual sex. What had he called it that first day they met? *No big deal?* If only she was brave enough, it could be the perfect end to a New Year's Eve party unlike any other.

'You haven't done anything yet,' he pointed out, his stare dipping to her lips, as if he wanted more. 'No one is keeping score, Zara. I fancy you. If you fancy me, we could have a good time, nothing serious. Just for tonight if you like.'

He made it sound so easy. She *did* fancy him, and right then 'a good time, nothing serious' was *all* she wanted, *all* she could think about. 'I do want that,' she whispered, her body dragged down with relief and lust.

With an intense stare, he cupped her face in both his hands. 'And I've wanted to kiss you all evening.'

With a jolt of action on both sides, their lips collided in a rush. Conrad wrapped his arms around her and dragged her body flush to his. His lips parted, coaxing her mouth open, and their tongues touched. So turned on she thought she might pass out right there in the frozen garden, Zara kissed him harder, deeper, her hands finding and gripping his hips as she surged onto her tiptoes to keep their lips in contact.

He crushed her mouth under his, a sexy little grunt sounding in his throat as their tongues slid together, back and forth. Zara shut down her thoughts, closed her eyes and surrendered to the hormonal rush. The uninhibited excitement of feeling attractive again, kissing a sexy man who treated her with respect and made her laugh. She spent her every waking moment caring for other people—Zach, her patients, the babies she delivered. She deserved something that was just for her, didn't she? To start the new year off differently from the previous five—with a promise to take better care of herself and her own needs going forward.

Conrad pulled back, his hands still cupping her frozen face, his fingers restlessly sliding into her hair. 'Come inside. It's freezing.'

Zara nodded. He put the key in the lock, ushering her into the cosy, warm flat she'd worked hard to renovate. Before he could speak again, perhaps to offer her a drink or take her coat, Zara turned and kissed him once more, now drunk on the idea that tonight was about sex. He was used to that. Probably good at it, too. And she'd been without it for far too long, as if punishing herself for that one mistake in recklessly choosing Zach's father.

But she wasn't a naive twenty-year-old any more. She

was a woman. She knew what she wanted and what she didn't want. And she wanted Conrad.

With his lips on hers, Conrad removed her hat and pushed her coat from her shoulders. His kisses drove her wild and made her forget her responsibilities and the habitual way she kept men at arm's length. Zara caressed his tongue with hers, unbuttoning his coat and reaching for his belt, frantic now that this was really going to happen.

'Are you sure?' he asked when he'd yanked his mouth from hers, his breathing ragged as he pulled her close.

Zara nodded, abandoning his belt buckle as another moment of doubt crept in. 'Although I haven't done this in a very long time, but you've heard about my famous dry spell.' She shrugged, smiled, trying to keep the light playful vibe between them going, because it was a major part of her attraction to him.

'Should I ask how long?' he said, his eyes searching hers while his hands slid restlessly up and down her arms as if he couldn't *not* touch her.

'Since before Zach was born,' she admitted, her high from their kisses dimming slightly.

'Really?' he asked, incredulous, cupping her cheek. 'You're so sexy. It's hard to imagine you're not beating off Englishmen with a stick.'

Zara chuckled, grateful that even now, when part of her was besieged by nerves, he could make her laugh. Then she sobered. 'We should probably keep this between us, though. No one at work needs to know, right?'

Zara didn't want her night with the sexy Australian doctor to be gossip fodder on the maternity ward, not when she was so famously single. Sharon, in particular, would read far too much into it, and it was just one night…

'I hate secrets,' he said, his eyes hardening slightly, 'but this is our business, Zara.' As if sealing the promise with a kiss, he tilted her face up and lowered his lips to hers.

She had no time to wonder why he hated secrets, because this kiss was different, slower, deeper, more determined and thorough, as if it was leading somewhere she definitely wanted to go. Thank goodness she'd shaved her legs in the shower earlier, although her underwear was decidedly practical and no frills, but hopefully it wouldn't be on long enough that he'd notice.

When he slid his lips down the side of her neck and scooped his arm around her waist, pressing her restless body to his hardness, she couldn't hold in her moan. Then they were on the move, her hand clasped in his as he strode to the bedroom. Zara took a split second to notice that he'd changed the sheets since last week, these ones dove grey, not the original snowy white ones, before she gave herself fully over to the thrill and heat of their chemistry.

'You are *so* sexy,' he said, dragging her close once more, his hands in her hair. One hand slid under her jumper to the small of her back and she shuddered under his deep, drugging kisses. 'I promise I'll make this good for you, given you've waited so long,' he whispered against her lips, not that Zara was in any doubt. This was already the best sexual experience of her life and he'd barely touched her yet. But where Lorenzo had been a boy, barely out of his teens, Conrad was a man.

'Okay,' she said, pulling at the hem of his sweater until he yanked it off and threw it aside. His bronzed and defined naked torso called to her hands, so she indulged herself, sliding her palms over his abs, across the mounds of his pecs and the rounded muscles of his shudders. He was indeed all man. Strong and lean. Making her feel small.

Her fingers slid into his hair, and she craned herself up on her tiptoes to kiss him again, her desire flaring to an inferno of need she had no hope of fighting. They kissed, stripping, laughing at a stubborn jeans button and a welded-closed bra clasp. Even the serious business of getting naked was somehow fun with Conrad.

When they stood before each other in just their underwear, he scooped his arms around her waist and tumbled them both onto the bed with a chuckle that turned into a groan.

'I'm so glad you wanted this as much as me.' His hands skimmed her body, his lips, the heat of his breath, trailing over her skin. 'After our first meeting when I thought you seriously meant me harm, it could have so easily gone the other way.'

Zara smiled despite the way his touch inflamed her entire body. 'Never mess with a mama bear defending her den.'

'I wouldn't dream of it.' He slid her body under his, limbs tangled, his body heat scalding, his hands in her hair as his tongue surged against hers. 'And you are one seriously hot mama bear.'

Zara sighed, completely surrounded by and immersed in him, his sexy scent on her skin, the rasp of his facial hair against her chin, encircled in the flexing strength of his toned body. Finally she could relax and surrender, safe in the knowledge that they only wanted this from each other. No relationship, no feelings, no consequences.

He cupped her breast, his thumb rubbing the nipple erect, and she gasped, holding him closer, hooking one leg over his hip, her pelvis bucking against the hard length of his erection.

'Conrad,' she moaned as he dipped his head and captured the same nipple with his mouth. She was insane with want, scorched with heat, already so close to climaxing. Frantic to have more of him, Zara shoved at his boxers and slid her hand between their bodies, wrapping her fingers around him so he groaned into their kiss. He pulled back, kneeled beside her and removed her underwear, reaching for a condom from his jeans and tossing it onto the bed.

He gazed down at her naked body and Zara had a moment of self-consciousness. She wasn't a tanned, toned pin-up like him. She was an English rose, pale, and had stretch marks, her boobs less perky thanks to breastfeeding Zach. But Conrad didn't seem to care. His stare moved over her nakedness as an art fan admired a Constable. He cupped her breast, slid his hand over her waist and hip and then stroked between her legs.

Zara gasped at his slow, thorough touch. Her heavy stare latched to his as he watched her reactions, learning what made her moan and gasp and reach for him. When he lay beside her, Zara turned to kiss him, her hand finding him once more so they pleasured each other, face to face, hot breath mingling in between heated kisses.

But Zara had waited too long for this degree of intimacy to hold out. His touch infected her entire body in a wave of heat and longing and paralysing bliss that she welcomed, craved, needed.

'You're close,' he said, brushing his lips over hers, his fingers moving between her legs as he peered down at her with that confidence she should find arrogant but only found wildly attractive.

She nodded, impressed that he knew, moaned louder as he captured one nipple with his mouth and sucked. Lights flashed behind Zara's eyes, but then he shifted on top of her and handed her the condom. She tore it open, desperate to have him inside her. She rolled it onto him, fumbling in her haste because he continued to kiss her and stroke her, driving her closer to the edge.

Finally, he scooped his arm around her waist and hauled her under him. Zara panted, parted her legs and then he was kissing her and pushing inside her, so all she could do was cling to him and hold on tight as wonderful pleasure consumed her.

'You okay?' He paused, staring down at her as he pushed her wild hair back from her flushed face and brushed her lips with his.

'Don't stop,' she said, begging, gripping his broad shoulders, her fingertips digging into his steely muscles. Zara crossed her ankles in the small of his back and he sank lower, started to move, watching her reactions in between deep, drugging kisses as if ensuring she was there with him on this journey to oblivion.

'Yes,' Zara said as he gripped her hip and thrust harder, faster. She tunnelled her fingers into his hair and met the surges of his tongue in her mouth with her own, her body pure sensation, her every nerve ending alive, poised on the brink of ecstasy.

Then she was falling, shattered, her body awash with heat and wave after wave of pleasure as her orgasm struck, and she cried out his name in confirmation of the best sex of her life.

Conrad groaned as he picked up the pace, his hips jerking erratically now as he chased his own release. Zara kissed him once more, desperate that this be as good for him as it was for her. With a final jerk, he tore his lips from hers and crushed her tighter, his body taut and his groan muffled against the side of her neck.

She lay under him, panting, coming to her senses. Finally, he rolled sideways, each of them staring up at the ceiling and laughing, while they caught their breath.

'I can't believe I put that off for so long,' she said, her voice full of wonder and euphoria. Had she denied herself sex all these years because she'd been determined to make good on her mistake and be the best mother she could possibly be? Because she was scared to be vulnerable with another man in case she was, once again, rejected? But sex with Conrad was different. Freeing. Truly strings-free.

'That was something else,' Conrad said, tugging her close to press his lips to her temple. '*You* are something else, Zara Wood.'

Zara propped herself up on one elbow, beyond pleased with herself. 'So is this part where you kick me out and I do the walk of shame?' She grinned, enjoying that there was no overthinking to do, no bone-deep trepidation that he might not want to see her again, that he might not want a relationship with her, because *she* didn't want one with *him*.

'You can leave if you want.' He smiled, pressed a kiss to lips and then climbed from the bed and stalked naked to bathroom to take care of the condom. 'But if you give me a few minutes,' he said, casting her a cheeky wink over his shoulder, 'I'd like to do that again.'

'Okay,' she said, watching his toned backside disappear into the en suite before falling back against the pillow with a delighted chuckle.

'Happy new year,' she whispered to herself, hugging

her secret close. One day, when Conrad had gone back to Australia, she'd confess to Sharon that she'd finally broken her dry spell. And it had been totally worth the wait.

CHAPTER SIX

ON MONDAY, Conrad arrived at the hospital's outpatient department for an antenatal clinic, his stare scanning the name board for which midwives were present that morning. Seeing Zara's name, he felt his pulse bound violently with anticipation.

When he'd woken up New Year's Day morning, Zara had gone, leaving behind only the scent of her perfume on his pillow. Thanks to their differing shifts, and a series of emergency surgeries that had kept Conrad away from the wards and in Theatre, he hadn't seen her since. But a little distance was a good thing. A chance to process what had been, at least for Conrad, an unexpected and seriously hot night.

Entering his designated clinic room, he logged on to the computer and brought up his list of patients to take his mind off Zara. He'd just started to read the notes of the first patient on his list when there was a knock at the door.

'Come in,' he called, looking up from the computer.

The door opened and Zara appeared. Before his instantaneous smile had formed, before he could open his mouth to speak again, the urge to kiss her slammed into him and stole his breath.

'Hi,' he said, his heart rate going nuts. 'Good to see you.' If he'd thought she was sexy before, now that he knew how hot they were together, he really wanted to see her again. They had a great time together. They shared a career and understood the demands of each other's jobs and neither of them wanted a relationship. For him, it didn't get any better than that. But now wasn't the time to raise the possibility.

'You too,' she said, sounding detached. 'Do you have a second to discuss a patient?' She made eye contact but he could tell her guard was back up as if New Year's Eve hadn't happened.

'Of course.' He stood and beckoned her inside.

She entered and left the door ajar, telling him this conversation would definitely be patient-related and in no way personal. 'I've just seen a thirty-four-year-old primip following her twenty-week scan,' she said. 'The placenta is low lying, and she has type one von Willebrand's disease.'

Conrad nodded. 'Thanks for bringing this to my attention. It sounds as if I should see her myself today. She'll need repeated scans,' he went on, outlining an action plan. 'The placenta previa might correct itself as the baby grows, but the bleeding disorder certainly complicates the risks for the mother.'

Placenta previa, when the placenta blocked the opening of the uterus, was enough of a risk of haemorrhage without adding in an inherited blood-clotting disorder in the mother.

'Yes, that's what I thought,' she said, her concern obvious. 'I'll warn you now, before you see her—she's keen to have a home birth.'

'That complicates things.' Conrad winced. This pregnancy definitely qualified as high risk. 'Okay, let's go examine her.'

In Zara's clinic room, he introduced himself to her patient, Helen, and quickly examined the woman's abdomen to confirm the foetal growth matched the scans and corroborated the baby's due date, but everything seemed in order.

'Okay,' he said as the patient adjusted her clothing. 'As I'm sure Zara has explained, your scan shows that the baby is healthy and developing normally. But the scan also shows that the placenta has attached in a low position, near the internal opening of the womb.'

Helen frowned, worry tightening her mouth as she looked between him and Zara. 'What does that mean for my birth plan?'

Conrad drew in a deep breath, preparing to offer the patient news that might be poorly received. 'Well, the first thing we need to do is monitor your pregnancy a little more closely than we normally would. Sometimes, as the baby grows and the uterus grows too, the position of the placenta can elevate. I'd like you to have another scan in ten weeks' time.'

'Okay,' Helen said, looking relieved.

Zara shot him another meaningful look, full of encouragement, and Conrad nodded, their silent communication telling him they had the same concerns. Part of their job was to try and facilitate the patient's choice when it came to the birth of their child, but their job also involved explaining all of the potential difficulties.

'That being said,' he continued, 'the main risks of a low-lying placenta, which, by the way, affects one in every two hundred pregnancies, is premature labour and haemorrhage, which would obviously be complicated by your inherited bleeding disorder. If the placenta stays where it is, blocking the birth canal, the baby's exit route, I'm afraid I'll be recommending a planned caesarean section around thirty-seven weeks for your safety and that of the baby.'

Tears built in Helen's eyes. Zara passed her a box of tissues, nodding at Conrad in emotional support.

'I understand it's a lot to process, right now,' Conrad said, hating that he'd made the patient cry, 'but no decisions need to be made today. As I said, the situation could change. Do you have someone you want to call, to meet you here? A support person?'

Helen shook her head, sniffing into the tissue. 'My husband is working in Scotland at the moment.'

Zara rested a comforting hand on the woman's shoulder. 'What about a friend or other relative?'

'My sister actually works in this hospital as a medical secretary,' Helen said, looking up at them.

Conrad nodded encouragingly. 'Why don't you give her a ring? Maybe she could meet you in the café upstairs. They do a wicked scone, and the tea is strong.' He smiled, and Helen laughed through her tears.

'Thank you, Doctor. Thank you, both. I will call my sister. A cup of tea and a scone sounds wonderful.'

Zara shot him a grateful smile he enjoyed way too much.

'Remember,' Conrad said to Helen in parting, 'the most important thing is that the baby is healthy and growing well. Our job—' he glanced at Zara, including her in his statement '—is to present you with all the information so you're aware of all the options and to help you deliver your baby as safely as possible.'

Before he left, his own list of patients calling, Zara looked up from comforting Helen. *Thanks*, she mouthed, her stare glimmering with respect.

He smiled, grateful that that night hadn't altered their

working relationship. They were so attuned, so professionally supportive. He'd never worked with anyone quite like Zara. Surely she couldn't ignore their chemistry? Surely she still wanted him the way he wanted her? If not, he would, of course, respect her decision. But with a busy clinic to get through, he'd have to bide his time to ask the question.

Mid-morning, Zara had just added hot water to her instant coffee in the outpatient's break room, when she grew aware of someone at her side. She looked up to see Conrad smiling down at her.

Their eyes locked, and her stomach knotted with giddy anticipation, the same feeling she'd carried since waking up in his bed in the early hours of New Year's Day. Since then, she'd lived on tenterhooks, craving the gorgeous sight of him like a drug but scared to run into him on the ward in case anyone, mainly Sharon, noticed something was different between them.

'Hi, again,' she said, stepping aside to allow him access to the kettle.

'I thought you might like to know that I transferred Jane Phillips to the postnatal ward from HDU last night,' he said, reaching for a spare mug. 'I'm pleased to say that she's doing much better.'

'That's great news,' Zara said in a breathy-sounding voice, nervously glancing over her shoulder, only to discover they had the break room to themselves. 'Thanks for keeping me updated.'

He was such a good doctor, dedicated and compassionate. That he knew she'd be worried about their post-partum haemorrhage patient and wanted to reassure her also spoke to the kind of man he was—caring, intelligent and funny.

Now that she knew him better, she saw so much more than a hot guy out for a good time. She saw the doctor who struggled to break bad news to patients because he obviously cared. She saw the man grieving for his brother and missing his young nephew. She saw someone perhaps hiding from something and wondered how she could help him the way he supported her.

'So, how are you?' he asked, his voice low. 'We've managed to somehow accidentally avoid each other since New Year's. But I've been thinking about you.'

'I'm good. Just busy,' she said, stirring her drink with a trembling hand. 'Never a dull moment around here...'

'True,' he said, that intense interest in his eyes, as if she might be the only woman in the world. 'But I wasn't talking about work. I wondered if you're free for lunch, after clinic? I think we should talk about what happened between us.'

'Talk?' she said, her pulse flying. What was there to say? That she couldn't stop thinking about him either? That she couldn't forget their night together.

'Yes, talk.' He smiled, and she lost her train of thought. 'I'd like to know if you had a good time. Make sure you have no regrets. I don't want us to tiptoe around each other for the next few weeks.'

'I don't have any regrets,' she said, her stare drawn to his mouth. He was awesome at kissing. 'What about you?' Her question emerged as an embarrassing choked whisper.

'None whatsoever, Zara. In fact, I'd like to see you again, perhaps when Zach next sleeps over at your mother's place. I thought we could explore Derby, maybe go dancing. Plus I've been dying to know if Billy Boy is okay after his escape.'

At his mention of the rabbit, Zara laughed, her nerves

settling. 'Zach's with my mum Friday, but… I don't know, Conrad. It was supposed to be one night. Zach is still my priority.'

She glanced at the door, worried they'd be interrupted. Worried that someone would be able to tell they were no longer just colleagues. But she was sorely tempted to say yes. They could extend their *nothing serious* into a temporary fling until he left for Australia. What better way to get her confidence back? After all, she wasn't looking for a relationship right now, but she didn't want to be alone for ever.

'Of course he is,' Conrad said with a casual shrug. 'I wouldn't expect anything else. As you know, I'm heading back to Australia in a few weeks. I'm not suggesting we date. I don't really do that any more.'

'Why don't you date any more?' Had someone broken his heart? She'd assumed he was running away from his grief, but maybe it was heartbreak that had chased him from Australia.

He glanced away, looking uncomfortable, and Zara shook her head. 'Sorry, forget I asked. It's none of my business.'

Just because they'd developed a close, supportive working relationship, just because they'd had sex, didn't mean he owed her anything. And the hospital was the last place they could talk.

Conrad inhaled deeply. 'Maybe I'll tell you some time, away from work. Look, I had a good time New Year's Eve, that's all. I got the impression you did too.'

'I did.' She nodded, her body turning instantly molten with that thrilling need he'd brought back to life on New Year's Eve.

'So, if you wanted to have some more good times, nothing serious, same as New Year's, I'd be interested.' He smiled and she got lost in his eyes for a second. 'I enjoy your company. You have a great sense of humour. It's been a long time since I could laugh with a woman.' He shot her a hopeful smile.

'I enjoy your company, too,' she said, still hesitant. 'But I'll have to pass on lunch, I'm afraid. One of the midwives on the delivery suite today has gone home sick, so I'm heading upstairs after clinic to cover.'

A small frown of disappointment tugged at his mouth. 'Okay, but make sure you grab something to eat. We've had a busy morning down here, and it sounds like you're headed into a busy afternoon.' He looked at her in *that* way. As if, in that moment, she was all he saw.

'I will.' Zara nodded, touched that despite being busy, despite their one night being nothing serious, he cared about *her*. It had been a long time since anyone had put her first. She even put herself last, although she couldn't blame anyone else for that. 'And about Friday…' She glanced at the door, still balanced on a knife edge of indecision. She could almost hear Sharon yell, *Go for it, woman!* And it wasn't as if it could go anywhere. He was leaving in a few weeks and neither of them wanted a serious relationship.

'No pressure,' he said. 'You don't have to answer now. Just think about it.'

Just then Sharon bustled into the room, complaining to no one in particular about the shortage of midwives on duty. Zara stepped away from Conrad, taking a guilty gulp of her scalding coffee and desperately trying to act normal in front of her friend.

'Hi, Sharon,' Conrad said, picking up his own drink. He

shot Zara one last glance she prayed Sharon hadn't seen and then left the break room.

'What were you two whispering about?' Sharon asked, flicking on the kettle. The woman never missed a trick.

'Nothing. Just discussing a patient.' It wasn't a lie, exactly, more of an omission. 'Jane Phillips has been transferred off HDU.'

'That's good. How was your weekend?' her friend asked, pouring hot water onto a teabag in a mug. 'Did you do anything for New Year's in the end?' Sharon had invited her to a party at her house, but she'd declined, knowing there would most likely be some single man there that Sharon would tactlessly thrust upon Zara.

She flushed, kicking herself that she hadn't anticipated questions and planned answers that didn't come with revealing blushes. 'Not much. I was working New Year's Day.'

'You should have come over to ours,' Sharon said, stirring her tea. 'Rod invited some people from work. One of them is a lovely guy your age. Smart. Good job. Works in the IT department.' She took a sip of tea and watched Zara over the rim of her mug. 'Want his number?'

'Sharon…' Zara sighed, busying herself with adding another splash of milk to her coffee to cool it down. Perhaps she should take the guy's number just to shut her friend up.

'Don't give me that,' Sharon said. 'It's not healthy always being alone.'

Zara tried not to think about New Year's Eve and Conrad. 'I'm not alone. I have Zach.'

'You know what I mean.' Sharon huffed impatiently. 'You're twenty-six, Zara. You should stop putting your needs last and take better care of yourself. Most people your age are at it like rabbits.'

Zara snorted and flushed again. She'd waited five years to let a man close enough for intimacy, but now that she had, all she could think about was Conrad and his mad bedroom skills. And he wanted to see her again...

'It's not the sex that puts me off,' she admitted. 'It's just—'

'I know. You've been hurt, so you struggle to trust men.'

Zara looked up sharply. Her friend wasn't wrong. What would she say if she knew Zara was denying herself more casual sex with the department hottie, just because, since Lorenzo, ignoring men had become a bad habit?

Sharon's expression brimmed with sympathy. 'Not all men are selfish and irresponsible, you know.'

'I know that,' Zara said, wondering how, despite all her tough talk and fierce independence, she'd allowed Conrad to charm his way under her defences.

'I know that you're focussed on raising Zach. I know you want the best for him, as if you're making up for his lack of a father, but it's important that you're happy too.'

'You're right.' Zara nodded, unable for once to argue. She had been putting her own needs last. And if Conrad was willing to wait for her, to snatch chances to be with her when Zach was at her mother's, she'd be a fool to pass that up, wouldn't she? 'Would it make you feel any better to know I've made a new year's resolution to take better care of myself going forward?'

A brief fling with Conrad was a perfect temporary situation, as if the universe had dropped a sexy, single toy into her lap. She should take what was on offer—a good time, nothing serious—and simply enjoy a long-overdue sexual adventure.

'Yes,' Sharon said, scooping up her mug and following Zara from the break room. They needed to get back to work.

'Then stop worrying,' Zara said, pausing outside her clinic room to shoot her friend a reassuring smile. She was going to do it, to see Conrad again. And now that she'd made up her mind, Friday seemed a long way off.

CHAPTER SEVEN

Conrad had just finished seeing his final patient of the morning, when there was another knock at the door. 'Come in,' he called, looking up to see Zara poke her head through the opening.

'Zara!' Their eyes locked. 'Come in.' She had her bag over her shoulder so she was obviously headed up to the ward.

'I just wanted to catch you,' she said breathlessly, her eyes bright with excitement. 'I've thought about it and my answer is *yes*.'

Conrad stood and came around to her side of the desk, unable to dampen his smile. 'That's fantastic. So we can do something Friday?'

She nodded and stepped close, her pupils dilating. Realisation dawned, his heart rate spiking. She had *that* look in her eyes. He reached for her at the same moment she hurled herself into his arms. Their lips clashed. He scooped one arm around her back while the other tilted her face up to his deepening kiss.

'Thank goodness you caved,' he said breathlessly after tearing his mouth from hers. 'I've wanted to do this for the past two days.' His lips found hers once more and he pushed her back against the closed door.

'Me too.' Zara gripped his waist and dragged him close.

'But no one can know about this, okay? The gossip would be unbearable.'

'Okay…' Conrad frowned, his mind blanking when she pulled his lips back to hers. 'Although I'm not a fan of secrets.' But his desire for her outweighed everything. And besides, he was only in England for another couple of weeks so did it really matter?

'I know, but if Sharon finds out about us, she'll want to play cupid. The woman is relentless. She's even tried to fix me up this morning with some guy who works with her husband.'

A sudden flare of possessiveness heated his blood.

'And it's not like this can go anywhere,' she continued. 'Neither of us are looking to date and we live in different countries.'

'I can't argue with any of that,' he said. And he couldn't. He cupped her face and brushed her lips with his. 'So you'll meet me Friday, when Zach is at your mum's? Give me something to look forward to.' He kissed the side of her neck, his hand cupping her breast so she sighed, her body sagging against his.

'I'll meet you Friday,' she said, shuddering. 'But it's just sex, agreed?'

Conrad didn't play games. He wasn't making her any promises, but Zara knew what she wanted and, more importantly, what she didn't want. And so did he.

'No arguments from me.' He smiled, reeling when she gripped the lapels of his white coat, pressed a kiss to his lips and then shoved him away.

'I have to go. Until Friday.' She straightened her uniform and reached for the door handle.

'Zara,' he said as she swung the door open. 'I can't wait.' He adjusted the knot of his tie, his heart thumping wildly.

She grinned. Suddenly, it was as if they were transported back to that moment in the garden when they'd laughed together over the escaped rabbit and then kissed, their passion for each other burning quickly out of control.

With a final flirty look, she left. He dragged in a deep breath. It was going to be a very long week.

By nine p.m. Friday, Conrad had just about given up hope that Zara would keep her word, when there was a rap of knuckles on the door. He leapt off the sofa with the eagerness of a kid on Christmas morning and swung open the door, his pulse frantic.

'Hi. You look lovely.'

'Hi.' Zara smiled and hurried inside out of the cold.

No sooner had he closed the door behind her than she hurled herself into his arms, her lips meeting his in a desperate kiss. After days of restless anticipation, of secret looks on the ward and pretending she was just another midwife, her desperation resonated deeply with him.

'That was the longest week of my life,' he said when Zara let him up for air. 'How's Zach, by the way?'

'He's fine. He loves his Friday sleepovers at Grandma's,' she said, shrugging off her coat and immediately tugging at his shirt buttons. 'I want you.' She trailed her lips seductively down the side of his neck, making him groan.

He nodded in agreement, his desire for her as acute as their first time thanks to the build-up. 'What about Derby... dancing?' he asked, half-heartedly putting up a feeble fight.

'Who needs dancing?' she said, her demanding hands everywhere at once: inside his shirt, in his hair, tugging at his neck to bring their lips back together. 'I'm making up for lost time.'

Absorbing every kiss, Conrad stumbled into the nearby lounge where they collapsed onto the sofa together. Truth was, he didn't care one jot about Derby. What could the city really have to offer to rival Zara, naked and playful in his bed? He'd never wanted anyone as much as he wanted her right then.

'Your famous dry spell?' he said with a smile as she sat astride his lap and removed her sweater. Conrad's brain short-circuited at the sight of her amazing breasts clad in the sexy black lace of her bra. He sat up, capturing her lovely lips once more so she shuddered in his arms.

'I can't believe I ignored this side of myself for so long,' she said on a sigh as he popped her bra clasp and leaned forward to capture one of her nipples in his mouth. 'Seeing you at the hospital and not being able to kiss you has been hell.'

'I know,' he said when she tugged his shirt overhead and reached for the button on his jeans. 'I spent the entire week walking around the hospital, looking for secret places I could lure you. I found a large cleaning cupboard outside the postnatal ward that looked very promising.'

Zara laughed, smiled down at him indulgently. 'Hold that thought. You never know when it might come in handy.'

His laughter died as she shoved him down on the sofa and traced her lips down his chest and his abs, moaning as she unzipped his jeans. Conrad froze, recognising that wicked look in her eyes. When she freed him from his underwear and took him into her mouth he almost passed out, so sharp was the ache of pleasure in his gut. She drove him crazy, the yearning and waiting a sick kind of sensual torture, so that now he was on edge, his stamina shot to pieces as he watched her pleasure him with her mouth.

Then he sprang into action. 'Let's go,' he said, standing and pulling her to her feet. In the bedroom, they stripped off the rest of their clothes with unhurried determination, their stares locked. When they were naked together on the bed, he kissed his way from her lips to her breasts, from her stomach to between her legs. He couldn't seem to get enough of her, or stop touching her, kissing her, relishing her every moan and sigh.

'Conrad.' Zara gasped, her fingers twining restlessly in his hair as she looked down at him, the way he'd watched her. His name on her lips did something to him, something primal and possessive. He wanted to hear it over and over.

'Do you want me as much as I want you?' he asked in the pause for the condom.

'Yes,' she said. 'I tried to fight it, but I don't know what you've done to me. It's as if you've flicked a switch to my libido. I'm suddenly addicted to sex.'

Satisfied, he smiled and lay on top of her, kissing up her cries and moans as his fingers moved between her legs. They were obviously intoxicated by each other. When he finally pushed inside her, the hunger he'd tried to ignore since New Year's Eve consumed him so he had to close his eyes for a second against the rush of desire.

'This is the best sex I've ever had,' she said, pulling his lips down to her kiss, her hips moving against his.

'Me too,' he said, entwining their fingers and pressing her hand into the mattress as he moved over her. She stared up at him with arousal and wonder and joy. He could get used to putting that look on her face, just as he couldn't imagine tiring of the way she made him feel, almost as if he'd been waiting his whole life for a woman like her. But that was crazy and just lust talking. Sex that good could mess with your mind.

He kissed her more thoroughly, moving slowly inside her, drawing out the pleasure until their skin was slicked with perspiration and they were both so desperate for release they finally came together, their mingled cries filling the darkened room. As their hearts banged together, Conrad pressed his lips to hers, struggling to withdraw from the heat of her body and struggling to abandon the dizzying high they generated together. It had been years since he'd felt this connected to a woman, but maybe it was simply because they had so much in common beyond sexual chemistry: their grief, their work, her son and his nephew.

Finally, he rolled onto his back and pulled her under his arm, pressing his lips to her forehead. 'You are the hottest midwife I've ever met. I'm so glad you wanted more than just one night.'

She laughed. 'You, Dr Reed, were simply too much temptation.'

'I've created a monster,' he said, smiling, drawing her lips up to his.

When she laughed, he couldn't help but kiss her again.

Afterwards, Conrad switched on some chilled music and padded through to the kitchen naked, returning to bed with two large glasses of red wine.

'Do you mind that we didn't go to Derby?' Zara asked, taking one and placing it on the bedside table.

'Of course not.' He joined her in bed, tilted up her chin and brushed her lips with his. 'I seriously doubt there's anything in the city that's anywhere close to as great as what we just did.'

'You're not wrong.' Zara chuckled, her laughter turning to fear when he reached for her hand under the duvet. Holding his hand felt way too natural and somehow more intimate than all the other things they'd done. But relying on each other at work, supporting each other emotionally through the tricky cases, made this connection between them understandably intense. It didn't mean anything. It couldn't.

'Can I ask you something?' she said, to distract herself from those confusing thoughts.

'Of course,' he said, slinging his arm around her shoulders.

'You said you don't date any more. You said you'd tell me why,' she said, snuggling into his side. 'Did someone break your heart?'

He stilled and sighed, giving her a glimpse into his feelings on the subject. 'I was in love once, a long time ago. But I moved too fast and she didn't feel the same way, so she broke up with me. Since then, I've kept things casual.'

Zara pressed a kiss to his chest over the rapid thump of his heart. 'I'm sorry you were hurt, Conrad.'

'Don't worry.' His arm tightened around her. 'I'm over it. What about you?' he asked, switching the focus. 'You're twenty-six and a complete bombshell. Did Zach's father break *your* heart?'

Zara laughed and looked up, her ego preening. 'Bombshell, eh? I'll have to remember that compliment next time I'm cleaning out Billy Boy's hutch in my wellies.'

Conrad smiled softly, clearly waiting for a real answer.

'I wouldn't say he broke my heart as such. His name was

Lorenzo,' she said, her stomach twisting with embarrassment. 'I was so young when I met him, and very naive. It wasn't a great love story, just a holiday fling—exciting, intense, exotic.'

Her heart raced, her discomfort soothed by the rhythmic slide of Conrad's fingers up and down her arm. 'He said he loved me, but I didn't really believe him,' she went on. 'He worked as a waiter at the Spanish resort where me and my friends were staying. I knew there'd been other foreign girls before me, and there would be more after me.'

'So you weren't that naive, then,' he pointed out. 'Just young and enjoying yourself. There's no harm in that.'

Zara shrugged, dragging in a deep breath, the next part of the story sure to resurface the humiliation she'd felt after her final phone call to Lorenzo. 'When I came home, I'd accepted that we probably wouldn't see each other again, even though we'd swapped phone numbers. Then a couple of weeks later I found out I was pregnant.'

Conrad nodded, urging her to continue.

'I was still in shock myself when I called Lorenzo,' she said, her breathing shallow as she relived the difficult emotions. 'I didn't really know what I expected from him, but it was more than the nothing I received. I figured he might want to come to the UK to meet his child, or ask me to bring the baby to Spain, even if he and I weren't going to be together. But he did none of those things. He got angry when I refused to consider a termination. Said I was a stupid, immature girl and hung up on me.'

Conrad's harsh frown distorted his mouth. '*He* sounds like the immature one, if you ask me. So he let you both down? You and Zach?'

Zara shrugged, feeling a little sick as her protective urges for her son flared up. 'I was upset in the beginning, obviously. I didn't understand how someone could know they had a child in the world and not want to meet them.'

'I couldn't do it,' he said and Zara pressed her lips to his, instinct telling her his assertion was genuine. Where Lorenzo had been a boy, Conrad was a real man.

'Me neither,' she added, wishing she'd made a baby with someone more like Conrad. 'As my pregnancy progressed, I thought he might change his mind once he'd had time to come to terms with it, call one day out of the blue. But he didn't. After a while, I stopped waiting for the phone to ring.'

'I'm so sorry that you had to go it alone. That must have been hard, especially in the beginning.'

She shook her head, brushing aside his empathy. 'I had both my parents for support initially. And once Zach was born, I focussed on being his mother, on making sure he didn't pay for my recklessness, for a mistake in choosing the wrong father for him.'

Conrad glanced at her sharply. 'Maybe the mistake was Lorenzo's, not yours. After all, you're the one who's been there for your son, every day from before he was born. You carried him, delivered him and raised him, doing the work of two parents.'

Zara shrugged, dismissing his praise, but her heart swelling with maternal pride. 'I'm so lucky. He's a great young man.'

'Maybe it's because he has a great mother,' he said, refusing to allow her to brush him off. 'You know, just because you consider you made a mistake, doesn't mean you need to pay the price for ever. We're allowed to be naive and daring when we're young. To get carried away by our feelings and have intense romances.'

She frowned. Had she decided that raising Zach alone was some sort of penance for making a mistake with Lorenzo? Was that why she'd ignored her own needs for so long?

'You sound like Sharon,' she said, a fresh flutter of anticipation in her stomach. This fling with Conrad had certainly whet her appetite for sex.

'I guess I'm saying that you definitely don't *need* a man,' Conrad continued, turning serious, 'but one day, you might want a relationship. Don't close yourself off to that possibility or put yourself last. You're young. You still have so much living to do, and your happiness is as important as Zach's.'

Zara held her breath, torn. She liked that he cared about her well-being. But she'd spent so long going it alone, she didn't really know how to let someone, a man, that close. Maybe when this fling was over she'd be ready to start dating, for real. But could she find someone who not only wanted her, but also wanted to help her raise Zach? The way her stomach pinched with worry, that seemed like a pretty tall order.

Rather than admit those deep fears, Zara wrapped her arms around Conrad's neck, drawing his mouth down to hers. 'You are such a romantic, Dr Reed.'

'Am I?' he asked, seeming genuinely puzzled.

Zara nodded, wondering anew at the mystery woman who'd broken Conrad's heart. 'Let's hope, one day, we can both move on. Meeting you has certainly shown me that what I really need right now is a wild sexual adventure, the kind I missed out on by becoming a mum relatively young.'

'A wild sexual adventure?' He perked up. 'And that's where I come in, is it?' His expression turned to playful delight as he wrapped his arm around her waist, dragging her under him for a passionate kiss.

'It is.' She nodded and giggled. 'Feel up to the challenge?'

'Oh, I think so.' He grinned, brushed his lips over hers. 'Any time you want secret, late-night sex, you know exactly where to find me.' His hand skimmed her hip and her waist, cupping her breast where his thumb teased her nipple.

As Conrad set about proving that he was indeed the man for the job, Zara lost herself in their playful passion, forgetting all about their exes and past heartaches. As he'd said, life was short and so was this fling. Best to enjoy it while it lasted, because the last thing it could be was for ever.

CHAPTER EIGHT

IT WAS THE start of the following week before Zara saw Conrad again. Her weekend had been filled with the usual mum duties and domestic chores. She'd arrived at work that morning with an extra spring in her step, excited that their paths might cross once more. But there was no time now for goofy grins or sexy daydreams.

Zara had paged Conrad to urgently review an inpatient he'd admitted the day before. The woman, who was at thirty-five weeks' gestation, was being monitored following premature rupture of the membranes, or PROM.

As he marched onto the maternity ward with his SHO, Max, in tow, Zara sighed with relief and quickly intercepted him.

'Dr Reed,' she said. 'I need you to review Mrs Hutchins, the patient you admitted yesterday with pre-term PROM.'

The barely perceptible flicker of heat and recognition in his stare was, of course, gratifying, but it became quickly shrouded in concern and professionalism. They might be very pleased to see each other after days apart, but their patients always came first.

'What's going on?' he asked, pausing outside the patient's room to hurriedly wash and dry his hands.

'Her observations have been stable,' Zara said, bringing him up to speed. 'No sign of labour or infection and she's had her steroids. But this morning, after showering, the patient reported she felt something prolapsing internally. I think it's the umbilical cord. We've confined her to bed and placed her in the head down position to relieve any pressure on the cord.'

Conrad pulled on a face mask, his stare etched with the same concern for the patient that Zara felt. 'How's the foetal heart rate? Any signs of distress?'

Zara shook her head. 'It's stable, too. No bradycardias to report.' But they both knew the risks with premature rupture of the membranes. Infection, premature labour and foetal distress were serious enough compilations. But umbilical cord prolapse or compression could be life-threatening, especially for the baby.

'Okay,' Conrad said with a decisive nod. 'You did the right thing in calling me.' He met her stare, his conveying reassurance and faith. 'Let's take a look.'

They entered the room, where Sharon was with the patient. After greeting Mrs Hutchins, Conrad pulled on sterile gloves. 'I need to examine you, Mrs Hutchins.'

Zara waited nervously, trying to keep her concerns for the patient and her unborn baby from her expression. When he'd finished his examination, Conrad glanced at Zara and gave her a worrying nod of confirmation. 'You're right. It *is* the cord.'

Zara swallowed her fear. She'd never personally come across a case of umbilical cord prolapse before. She'd never been more relived that he was there.

Conrad turned to the patient. 'Mrs Hutchins, that feeling you have of something prolapsing inside is the baby's umbilical cord. It's slipped down outside the uterus. There's a risk that if we leave it, the blood supply to the baby could be compromised. I'm afraid we're going to need to deliver the baby with an emergency Caesarean section today.'

The patient nodded tearfully, her stare full of understandable alarm, but Zara was so grateful for the calm authority in Conrad's voice. She'd found it reassuring, so hopefully the patient had also.

Zara took Mrs Hutchins' hand. 'Try not to worry. The baby is fine at the moment. We just need to deliver him or her quickly and safely, okay?'

'Have you called Mr Hutchins?' Conrad asked Sharon, tossing his gloves in the bin and pulling out his phone while Max took some blood from the patient's arm in preparation for surgery.

'Yes,' Sharon said. 'He's working in Manchester today, so he might be a while. But he's on his way.'

From the corner of the room, Conrad made a quick but hushed call to the obstetrics theatre and the anaesthetist, glancing Zara's way with a concerned stare. She knew what he was thinking: there was no time to wait for the husband. Any shift of the baby's position could compress the cord and interfere with the baby's blood supply.

Having hung up the phone, Conrad addressed the patient once more. 'I'd be happier if we deliver this baby right now, Mrs Hutchins. I don't think we can wait for dad. Better for him to meet the little one safely delivered. Do you agree?'

The woman nodded, and Conrad unlocked the wheels of the bed. Seeing the grip the patient still had on Zara's hand, he met her stare. 'Zara, are you up for a trip to Theatre?'

She shot him a grateful nod and turned to the patient. 'I'll stay with you until your husband arrives.'

'Then let's go have this baby,' Conrad said, his own expression impressively calm as, together, they wheeled the patient towards the lifts and headed for Theatre.

With relief pounding through his veins following the emergency C-section, Conrad placed the healthy newborn baby girl onto her mother's chest for some immediate skin-to-skin contact.

'Congratulations. You have a daughter.'

As the neonatal nurses hovered nearby, ready to whisk the pre-term baby away for some initial checks and to be weighed, Zara and Mrs Hutchins stared at the newborn in wonder. Conrad's stare met Zara's over the tops of their theatre masks. Tears shone in her eyes, a raft of emotions shifting there—relief, gratitude, respect. Conrad lapped it up, his heart beating wildly that he and Zara could share this special, professional moment.

In a short time, things had gone from terrifyingly urgent to the happiest outcome, the kind their work was renowned for: a safely delivered and healthy baby. But today, maybe because Zara was there with him in Theatre, the rush he normally felt was amplified tenfold.

Yes, this was his job and he and Zara were just having casual sex. But ever since his brother's violent and untimely death, Conrad had become increasingly aware of how quickly life could change. You could lose what you cared about in a heartbeat.

Focussed on the fundal massage of the uterus and the delivery of the placenta, Conrad quietly guided Max through the surgical closure of the uterine incision while Zara and neonatal team cared for the mother and baby. With the surgery complete, he removed his gloves and gown and spoke to the patient, who was now cradling her sleeping baby adoringly.

'We got there a little earlier than planned, but it looks like she's doing really well.' He smiled, loving this part of his job—the end result. 'I hope Mr Hutchins isn't too upset that we started without him.'

'Thank you for delivering her safely, Doctor,' the patient said, her eyes shining with tears as she rested a hand on his arm. 'She's perfect and I'm so grateful to you and the whole team.'

Conrad swallowed, her gratitude catching him off guard for a second, maybe because Zara was present and listening, watching on with shining eyes.

'I'll come and check on you back on the ward,' he said. Before he moved away, he glanced at Zara, who was looking at him every bit as adoringly as Mrs Hutchins. A moment of silent communication and emotional support passed between them.

You did a good job. I couldn't have done it without you. Thank you.

Did she trust him the way he trusted her? It seemed crazy given they'd only known each other a couple of weeks. But maybe the feast or famine nature of their fling, the stolen moments of intimacy they snatched when they could, made every moment, together or apart, more intense. Maybe that explained their building connection.

Reluctantly, he left Theatre, tossing his face mask and disposable hat into the bin before washing up. He was just about to head for the coffee room, where he hoped some much-needed caffeine would settle his thoughts, when he spied Sharon.

'How did it go?' she asked, her frown easing as he nodded his head.

'All good. A textbook C-section. The baby is a bit small, but otherwise seems healthy. Zara is still with them.' He glanced back towards Theatre, as if reluctant to leave without Zara.

Sharon chuckled. 'There was no way Zara was letting go of that woman's hand. She hates not being able to see a delivery through to the end. I swear if she didn't have Zach to care for, some days she probably wouldn't go home at all.'

He nodded. 'She's a great midwife.' And an amazing woman and mother. He hadn't come to England looking for a romantic relationship. He'd come to forget about the twisted love triangle he'd been dragged into by Marcus and Tessa. To grieve for Marcus without the constant reminders of the betrayals of the past. To give Tessa the space she'd requested when he'd tried to be there for James. But there was something about Zara he couldn't help but allow close. Closer than he'd allowed anyone since he'd learned the truth about his brother and his ex.

'She is. I keep telling her what a catch she is,' Sharon said. 'But Zach's father really let them down.'

He smiled, non-committal. He'd been surprised by how much Zara had shared with him last Friday night about her feelings of betrayal, rejection and humiliation. Maybe she was starting to trust him. And like Sharon, it really bothered Conrad that Zara blamed herself for a youthful mistake, when Zach's father had simply walked away without taking any responsibility for his son.

'Are you enjoying working here?' Sharon asked, switching subjects.

'It's great,' he said, with genuine feeling. 'I'm getting lots of experience and more surgical time than in Brisbane.'

'Maybe you should keep your eye open for a consultant post here. There are a couple of older obstetricians who are close to retirement age.'

'Maybe I will,' he said. 'But I'm not in any rush. No point applying for a consultant post until I know where I want to settle.' For now, he couldn't really think beyond going back to fix things with his brother's wife. They were both grieving, but now that Conrad had seen Zara's devotion to Zach, he could understand why Tessa had told him to back off. Perhaps he *had* been overprotective of James at a time when he was still processing his own grief for Marcus.

'See you later,' Sharon said, turning and exiting the department, leaving Conrad wondering how he was going to walk away from Zara when the time came.

Conrad was about to head for a nearby stairwell, when he heard his name being called. Zara caught up with him, wordlessly widening her eyes and tilting her head in the direction of the stairs. With his heart bounding, he followed. The door swung closed at his back, and Zara hurled herself into his arms, her lips clashing with his in a breathy kiss that almost knocked him off his feet.

'That was amazing,' she said, after pulling back to look up at him, her hands gripping his face. 'You are amazing. Thank you for letting me be a part of that delivery.'

Euphoria rushed Conrad's blood. He didn't need her praise, but it felt good to know their professional regard, their trust, was mutual. 'It was a team effort. I couldn't have done it without you, and, as it happens, I think you're amazing, too.' Now his feelings of closeness made sense. Their relationship *was* intense. How could it not be? They were sleeping together, essentially living together and working together.

She smiled, kissed him again, and, despite them being at work, despite the fact that they might be discovered, Conrad couldn't help but kiss her back. He slid his tongue against hers and pressed her up against the closed door as desire hijacked his system.

'How can I want you all the time?' she said, when they came up for air, her body shifting restlessly against his, a reminder of how she felt naked in his arms, her passionate cries ringing out.

Dopamine flooded his brain, swiftly followed by a sense of panic, a desperation to be alone with her once more. Not Friday night, but now.

'Can I see you tonight?' he whispered against her lips in between her desperate kisses. Suddenly, Friday seemed like a long way off. Too long. Clearly his physical need for her had reached uncontrollable levels, otherwise he wouldn't be risking discovery by kissing her at work. But in a couple of weeks, he'd be flying home to sort out his personal life. In the meantime, he wanted as much of Zara as he could get.

'I can't,' she said, with a sigh. 'It's a school night. I... I don't want to confuse Zach.'

Conrad's stomach sank, even though he understood. 'Of course not. I totally understand. I don't want that either.' He'd always known that Zach was her number one priority and he respected her for putting her son first. 'You're a great mother, Zara. I hope you know that.'

He was desperately trying not to judge Tessa's parenting, but a part of him couldn't help but worry that her withdrawal from the Reed family wasn't in James's best interests. Surely the boy needed his father's family, now more than ever. But maybe Tessa needed time to build new routines for her and James, in the same way Zara protected Zach.

'I just can't seem to get enough of you,' he admitted, pushing the hair back from her face and brushing her lips with his, one last time. Then he reined himself back under control as he stepped back, put some distance between their bodies.

'Me neither,' she said, her teeth snagging her bottom lip in a very distracting way. 'Unless...' She hooked her index finger into the V-neck of his scrub top so he couldn't step too far away. 'I could text you once Zach is asleep.' She blinked up at him playfully. 'Perhaps you could tiptoe up for a sneaky glass of wine.'

His pulse went crazy, his need for her outweighing his dislike of *sneaking around*. But he understood her reasons and it wasn't as though *their* clandestine activities were hurting anyone.

'I'd love to, but only if you're sure,' he said. 'Honestly, no pressure. I respect your boundaries. The last thing I want to do is make you feel uncomfortable or confuse Zach.' Not that Zara was ready to introduce the boy to some strange man.

'I'm sure,' she said. 'I'll text you tonight. I'd better get back to Mrs Hutchins.' She smiled, her stare sweeping over him in a way that was full of promise. Then she pulled open the door, blew him a cheeky kiss and disappeared.

Conrad dragged a ragged breath, stunned by the force of his addiction to Zara Wood. But he needed to be careful, to keep his emotions in check the way he'd done since rushing things with Tessa. He couldn't get carried away by their harmonious working relationship and great sex. He didn't want to hurt Zara or get hurt himself, and, as he'd said to Sharon, his life was back in Australia. His one comfort was that Zara seemed to know what she wanted, and it wasn't a real relationship.

CHAPTER NINE

THE NEXT MORNING, as soon as Conrad opened his eyes, a grin stretched his mouth, his first thought of Zara. She *had* texted him last night, once Zach had fallen asleep. They'd shared a bottle of wine by the fire, whispering like a couple of teenagers up late without parental knowledge. Wine had led to kissing, kissing to nakedness after Zara had sneaked him into her bedroom and covered his mouth with her hand to dampen any noise as they'd climaxed together. The clandestine nature of their desperate coupling had made it somehow hotter. Although Zara was almost too hot to handle, just as she was.

Conrad stretched out his body after a great night's sleep and headed for the shower. Given that he was covering the on call that coming weekend, he had today off, but he couldn't just lie around thinking about his favourite midwife. Perhaps he'd go for a walk. Head into the hills around Morholme, get some fresh air and think about what he would say to Tessa when he returned to Australia. Just as he respected Zara's boundaries, he would respect Tessa's, but he still wanted to be a part of James's life.

When he emerged from the bathroom ten minutes later, he heard squeals of laughter from outside. He quickly dressed and opened the curtains. The unexpected sight that greeted him forced out a bark of delighted laughter.

The garden, the fields beyond, the surrounding rooftops were all blanketed in a thick layer of snow.

Conrad's pulse picked up with excitement. Aside from a few skiing holidays in New Zealand when he was a teenager, he had little experience of snow. He'd certainly never lived anywhere with cold enough winter temperatures for snowfall.

Just then, a little boy he assumed was Zach ran past his window, his cheeks ruddy from the cold and a pair of multi-coloured gloves dangling from the sleeves of his coat by string. Conrad smiled at the boy's infectious joy, imagining how James too would love to play in the snow. A flood of sadness swamped him for all the moments in his son's life that Marcus would miss. It made Conrad all the more determined to patch things up with Tessa when he returned home so he could be there for James, not as a substitute father, but as an uncle who would be there if needed.

Zara appeared and, just like that, Conrad's sadness lessened. She chased after Zach, her hair caked with powdery snow and her breath misting the air in front of her as she laughed. She hurled a snowball, striking Zach in the back.

Conrad smiled wider. They were obviously having a snowball fight and, with a direct hit to head versus one to the torso, Zach was clearly winning.

In that second, Zara looked up and spied Conrad at the window. He raised his hand in a wave, his pulse galloping as usual as their eyes met. He prepared to move away from the window, reluctant to interrupt their fun. But before he could step back, Zara scooped two handfuls of snow from the ground, formed a tight ball between her palms and threw the snowball in his direction. It struck the window with a thump, right at Conrad's eye level. But for the pane of glass, it would have been a direct hit to the face.

Triumph gleamed in Zara's stare as she laughed, delighted with herself. 'Afraid of a little snow?' she called, beckoning him to join them at the door to the flat.

Conrad headed through to the kitchen and pulled open the door to a rush of frigid air and the crisp scent of fresh snow.

'Conrad,' Zara said, from his doorstep, 'this is Zach.' She looked down at her son. 'Conrad is from Australia.'

Conrad shook the boy's hand. 'Good to meet you, Zach. Looks like you're having a fun time and it seems you're better at snowball fights than your mother.'

'We're building a snowman,' Zach said proudly, stooping to grab another two handfuls of the irresistible powder.

'That sounds awesome. I've never done that.'

'Really?' Zach asked, looking up at him with astonishment.

'I don't think they have snow in Conrad's country,' Zara explained, her eyes full of pitying laughter.

Conrad smiled, pleased to see her, given she was supposed to be at the hospital right now. 'You didn't go into work?' he asked.

She shook her head. 'It's a snow day. School's closed, and the roads out here are impassable. But don't worry, they'll be out with the gritters soon. They'll have the roads cleared by tomorrow. Best to enjoy it while it lasts.'

'Do you want to help us build a snowman?' Zach asked Conrad. 'It's going to be so cool.'

'Good idea.' Zara nodded and ruffled Zach's hair.

Conrad hesitated, reluctant to gatecrash their precious family time. 'Are you sure?' he asked, respectful of her boundaries.

'Definitely,' she said, with a smile. 'Come and play.'

'Okay, thanks, Zach.' Conrad reached for his trainers, which were near the door. 'I'd love to help build a snowman.'

'You'll have soggy feet in seconds wearing those,' Zara said, glancing at the trainers.

'I only have these and my work shoes with me. I didn't pack for snow.' He looked at her feet. She and Zach were wearing gumboots.

'I still have my dad's wellies in the shed.' Zara smiled. 'They might fit you. Let me go grab them.'

While Conrad quickly donned his coat, Zach wandered off to retrieve his yellow plastic spade, the kind you'd take to the beach for building sandcastles. Within seconds Zara returned with boots. Conrad shoved his feet into them and stepped outside. The snow was inches thick, blanketing the entire garden, even the path. He stepped gingerly to avoid slipping, the rubber soles of the boots squeaking against the compacted snow.

'Come on,' she said, urging him to her and Zach's half of the garden where they'd already made a good start on the body of the snowman, a mound taller than Zach.

'Now we can make him even taller, Mum,' Zach said, excitedly patting handfuls of snow onto the mound. He looked up at Conrad. 'How tall are you?'

'I'm six foot two,' Conrad said, reaching for two handfuls of snow. 'Let's see if we can make him taller than me.'

'Yeah,' Zach cheered, enthusiastically piling snow higher and higher as Zara cast Conrad a look full of gratitude.

They threw themselves into the challenge, laughing as the mound grew taller and taller. Within seconds Conrad's fingers were frozen and the cuffs of his coat were damp, but he was having too much fun to care.

'Let's make a giant snowball for the head,' said Zach to Conrad, running to the far end of the garden where the snow was thick and undisturbed.

'Careful, mate, it's slippery on the path,' Conrad called out before he could stop himself.

Zara cast him an amused and curious stare. 'He's fine. Don't worry—he's English. He's made of tough stuff.'

Conrad winced. 'Sorry. I just wouldn't want him to fall and whack his head.'

'Thank you for looking out for him,' she said, her expression softening.

Conrad shrugged, adjusting his thinking as he joined Zach, who was rolling a snowball through the snow to help it grow. Of course, Zach wasn't *his* responsibility, but he couldn't help but be protective of the little guy, who reminded Conrad so much of James he experienced another pang of missing his nephew. Fresh guilt rushed him, because his overprotectiveness had upset Tessa, had contributed to pushing her and James away. He knew that. It was something he would need to fix.

By the time he and Zach returned from their trip around the garden, the snowball head was five times the size of the one they'd started with.

'Ready to put the head on top?' he asked Zach, who nodded and looked up at his mother expectantly.

'Is it okay if I put him on my shoulders?' Conrad asked Zara. 'You can pass him the head and he can crown the snowman.'

'Of course,' she said, smiling when Conrad lifted Zach, and the boy squealed with delighted laughter.

'It's the tallest snowman ever,' the boy said, his impressed stare wide. 'Thanks, Conrad.'

When Zach rushed off to grab some fallen branches for arms, Conrad glanced over at Zara. 'Thanks for inviting me,' he said, knowing that she wouldn't have taken the decision to introduce him to Zach lightly.

'Thanks for helping,' she said, tilting her head towards the snowman. 'We couldn't have made it that tall without you. My son clearly thinks you're the coolest thing since sliced bread.'

Conrad smiled, a lump in his chest. For an unguarded second, he could so easily imagine himself a part of this little family. He hoped he and Zara would keep in touch when he returned to Australia. Perhaps she'd even visit him there, given it was on her list. But whether they stayed friends or not, the day he'd built his first snowman with her and Zach would be one he'd always remember.

CHAPTER TEN

LATER THAT EVENING, Zara sipped her wine, a shudder of contentment passing through her like an electric current, bringing her to life. The surprise day off had been magical. After the snowman, she'd invited Conrad to join her and Zach for lunch—cheese on toast and soup—then an afternoon movie, followed by board games and pasta for dinner.

In the armchair by the fire, Conrad read Zach his favourite bedtime story. Her son was totally smitten by the lodger, who'd shown him some of Australia's native animals and taught him how to say, *G'day, mate*. When Conrad had once more lifted Zach onto his shoulders to crown the head of the snowman with an old bobble hat belonging to Zara's dad, she'd wanted to cry at the look of uninhibited joy on her son's face.

Now that all the excitement of the day had died down, icy fingers of doubt once more crept down her spine. She was taking a big risk with Conrad, blurring the boundaries she'd previously never needed to enforce because she'd always kept men at arm's length and away from Zach. Today, the snow had somehow helped her to justify her out-of-character behaviour. She kept telling herself that Conrad was different. Temporary. Risk-free. But the day had left her both happy and unsettled.

Maybe because, for a blinding second, as they'd played

together in the snow, she'd imagined the three of them were a family. Conrad would clearly be an amazing male role model.

'Right, time for bed, young man,' she said after Conrad finished the story and closed the book. Her boy looked exhausted from the day's excitement, and it would be business as usual tomorrow for them both—Zach back to school and Zara to work.

Zach dutifully hopped off the chair. 'G'day, mate,' he said to Conrad, offering him a final fist bump—another wonderfully exotic thing Conrad had taught him—before he dashed off to clean his teeth.

With her stomach churning with both fear and longing, Zara tucked Zach in, kissed him goodnight, and rejoined Conrad, who was picking up plastic blocks and jigsaw pieces from the floor.

'Thanks,' she said, taking a seat on the sofa. 'You don't have to do that.'

He tossed the blocks into the box. 'Thanks for including me in your day.' He grabbed her hand and raised it to his lips, placing a brief kiss there, his stare intense. 'I know how wonderfully protective you are of Zach. I'll always remember building my first snowman with you two.'

Because Zara wanted to hurl herself into his arms and couldn't, she reached for her wine and took a massive gulp.

'I should go,' he said, hesitantly.

Zara shook her head. She should let him go, but that other side of her, the woman, not the mum, craved a little more of his company. 'Stay for a while,' she urged, patting the sofa beside her and topping up both their glasses. 'Finish your wine.'

'Okay.' Conrad folded himself onto the sofa and stretched his arm along the back.

'Zach's completely exhausted,' Zara said, desire and gratitude making her sigh. 'We don't usually pack that much excitement into one day—snow and an exotic new friend, teaching him Australian words and cool fist bumps. Thank you.' Her throat ached anew with fear that Zach was missing out on a positive male influence. Suddenly, she felt jealous of James on Zach's behalf. The poor boy had lost his father, but he still had an amazing uncle, whereas Zara was an only child.

Conrad smiled indulgently, his stare shifting from her mouth to her eyes and turning intense in that way he had of making her feel seen. 'He's a great kid. I don't know if anyone has told you lately, but you're an incredible mum.'

'Thanks for saying that.' Zara swallowed the lump in her throat and looked away. 'It's a good job you'll be leaving soon,' she added with a teasing smile. 'A normally frazzled working mother could get used to those kinds of compliments.' And after the lovely day they'd spent together, after seeing how good Conrad was with Zach, she desperately needed the reminder that this sexy Australian with a big heart wasn't going to be around for ever.

In the beginning the temporary nature of their fling had been a huge part of his appeal. But after today, she couldn't help but wonder what might have been if he lived in the UK. A dangerous thought.

'You shouldn't doubt yourself,' he said with a frown, his fingers slowly stroking the nape of her neck in a way that turned her on.

'Sometimes, it's hard not to,' Zara admitted with a shrug that was part shudder from his touch. 'I think all parents worry that they're doing a good enough job. Parenting is the hardest thing I've ever done. Sometimes, I worry that I've ruined Zach's life by choosing the wrong man to have a baby with. I'm dreading the day he blames me because he doesn't have a father like the other kids.'

Would her boy one day resent her for her mistake? She'd always told him that his father lived in a different country, insisting she could take care of Zach as much as a mum *and* a dad combined. But those vague explanations wouldn't cut it for ever. Zach was a smart kid.

'That day may never come.' Conrad took her hand in his. 'It's like you said—you see to it that he has everything he needs. I hope my brother's wife does half as good a job with James. Man, I wish he'd been here today. He would have loved the snow and loved Zach.'

She met his stare, her pulse flying from his words and the way he looked at her, as if she was something special. Or maybe she was just seeing things because Conrad was addictive, their fling the most fun she'd had in years. But just because it had started out as nothing serious, didn't mean it wasn't…intense.

'You really love James, don't you?' she said, recalling the way he'd been protective of Zach earlier, understandable after what had happened to his brother.

'I do, of course.' He stilled, growing pensive. 'Kids have that way of making you love them.'

She understood the highs and lows of how it felt to love a child. The moments of sheer joy interspersed with the concerns that your parenting might not be up to scratch.

'You're right, they do.' She nodded, choked, because Conrad would be a wonderful father, the kind that Zach deserved. Whoa…that was an unrealistic leap.

'I was thinking about all the days, all the milestones and celebrations that my brother will miss.' His expression darkened with pain and Zara squeezed his fingers to silently let him know she was there for support.

'When Marcus made me promise that I would always look out for James after he was born, neither of us imagined that Marcus wouldn't be around to fill that role himself.' He glanced at their clasped hands, his fingers restless against hers so she guessed there was more he wanted to say, more he was feeling.

'Of course not.' Zara understood grief, and how it could come from nowhere when you least expected it. 'Are you worried about fulfilling your promise?' Since his brother died, Conrad had clearly become a more prominent male role model in his nephew's life.

'I guess.' Conrad looked up as if she'd hit the nail on the head. 'My relationship with Tessa is...complex.'

'Why?' she asked, her pulse buzzing in her fingertips with anticipation.

He watched her for a second then seemed to come to some sort of internal decision. He held her stare, doubt shifting across his expression. 'Because we used to date.'

Zara frowned, his words jarring. 'You and your sister-in-law?' That was the last thing she'd expected him to say.

'Yes.' He nodded, winced, glanced away.

Stunned, Zara fought the jealous twisting of her stomach. 'Tessa is the woman you loved? The one who broke your heart?' The one who'd left him because he'd come on too strong, too soon? Only she'd left him and turned to his brother, of all people. How confusing for Conrad.

'We'd split up long before she got together with Marcus,' he said, sounding defensive, as if he was trying to minimise how he felt about the situation. 'But as you can imagine, there's always been this kind of tension between the three of us. And it's only worsened since Marcus was killed.'

'Of course, it would be...awkward,' she said, still reeling and struggling to find the right words. Instinct told her that, for Conrad, *tension* was an over-simplification, but she could understand why he'd focussed on casual relationships since. There must be a part of him that had felt betrayed.

'Were you over her when they got together?' she asked, a hot ball of envy lodging in her chest. Was he still in love with this woman? After all, this Tessa was the reason he didn't date.

'I was. I hadn't seen her in months. Then one day, Marcus invited me out for a beer and told me that he and Tessa had hooked up one night after running into one another at a bar. They'd been seeing each other in secret, behind my back, and Tessa was pregnant.'

Zara hid her shocked gasp. No wonder he hated secrets. No wonder he'd needed space and distance in order to properly grieve for his brother.

'How did it make you feel?' she asked, her throat aching for Conrad, who must have felt humiliated and confused and horribly torn.

He laughed, the sound mirthless, not quite meeting her gaze. 'How I felt about it didn't really matter. By the time he'd confessed it was a *fait accompli*. Tessa was having Marcus's baby, and he was going to marry her. I had the sense he'd only told me then because he knew he'd have to come clean soon, before she started showing.'

'I'm sorry,' she whispered. 'That must have been so hard on you.' Watching Marcus date Tessa, knowing that they'd gone behind his back, feeling as if he *had* to be okay with the arrangement.

His head snapped up as if she was the first to acknowledge his feelings in this complex triangle. 'I was shocked, obviously. Marcus and I were close until then. I trusted my brother more than anyone else.'

'Of course you did.' And that brotherly bond would have made the betrayal worse for Conrad. Zara waited, stroking his hand. He was downplaying it, maybe because he'd been forced to accept it.

'I didn't want to make a big deal of it,' he went on, 'or make them feel bad because they'd fallen in love. I had no lingering feelings for Tessa, so why shouldn't the two of them be happy together, especially as they were going to be parents?'

'Feelings aren't as straightforward as that,' she said. 'Your trust had been damaged. And there's an unwritten rule about exes. There must have been a part of you that felt let down. Confused. Maybe even trapped in a situation out of your control.'

No wonder he'd stopped dating seriously.

Conrad kept his gaze downcast so she knew she was close to the mark. 'I didn't want to cause a family rift or put my parents in the awkward position of having to choose a side, choose a son. They were understandably excited about the birth of their first grandchild, as they had every right to be. And then there was a wedding to plan. Everyone else just accepted it and moved on.'

'So you felt you had to do the same. As if *your* feelings, *your* hurt and betrayal didn't matter.' Zara's heart clenched painfully. He'd swallowed down his feelings for the sake of family harmony and because he loved his brother, but he obviously hadn't fully reconciled those feelings.

He shrugged, evasive. 'With time to get used to the idea, I moved on.' His mouth twitched into an approximation of a smile but it didn't reach his eyes. 'I was genuinely happy for them when they got married and James was born. They were obviously in love, and James, like Zach, is a great kid.'

Zara nodded, choked by longing. He was so kind and honourable and dependable. And he'd been forced into unhealthy coping mechanisms—setting his feelings aside, keeping his relationships casual—by circumstances brought about by the actions of others.

'Did you ever talk about it with Marcus? Tell him how you'd felt betrayed that they'd sneaked around behind your back?' she asked, hoping that, for Conrad's sake, they'd resolved it before Marcus died.

He lifted one shoulder. 'We skirted the issue a few times. I think he knew how I felt on some level. He always seemed a little guilty whenever he looked at me after that. But then life moved on. He became a husband and a father. It seemed pointless to drag up the past.'

Only now, she saw how Conrad seemed stuck in that same past.

'I'm in no way minimising your feelings, or excusing what Marcus did,' she said, 'but he must have felt guilty for hurting you and torn between his feelings for you, the brother he loved, and those for Tessa. People say we can't help who we fall in love with.'

Or was that a myth? Marcus and Tessa hadn't been forced to act on their attraction.

'I agree,' he said, meeting her stare so she saw the pain and vulnerability he hid with his 'out for a good time' persona. 'Although there must have been a moment, early on, when they both consciously crossed that line. They both chose to ignore my feelings, to sneak around. But it was Marcus that I trusted.'

And Marcus had let him down and then died.

'So it never really got resolved?' she asked, her heart breaking for the wasted opportunity. For Conrad's damaged trust and bottled-up emotions and how they held him back, even now, years later.

He shook his head, his shoulders slumped with regret. 'No. We patched over it, but it was always there like a festering wound between Marcus and me or whenever the three of us were together. I guess a part of me figured that, one day, we'd resolve it, but now it's too late. Marcus is gone. I had to bury all the things I hadn't said to him the day we buried my brother.'

'I'm so sorry.' Zara wrapped her arm around his shoulders and held him close, their hearts banging together. 'But he would want you to be happy, just like he wanted you to be a part of his son's life, because he loved you. You can still say the things you wished you had. You can talk to him and let go of the past. It's never too late to forgive him.'

'I have forgiven him.' He pulled back and peered at her, his stare full of sadness. 'No point holding a grudge with a dead man.'

Zara nodded, uncertain if that was really true. She hoped so, for Conrad's sake. She didn't want to push him, but she was wired to care. She couldn't help but wonder if, on some level, he was stuck in the past, trying to untangle the threads of his mistrust and betrayal from his grief. He'd run away from the mess, after all.

As if he wanted to draw a line under his confession,

he leaned in and pressed his lips to hers. He cupped her face, and she shuddered, relaxed her body against his and kissed him back.

'Thanks for listening to me vent,' he said when they paused for breath. But the vulnerability was gone from his stare, replaced by the desire she'd grown used to seeing whenever they kissed. 'You are a very special woman, Zara Wood.'

'Thanks for confiding in me,' she said, touched that he'd trusted her enough to open up.

But no matter how close she felt to him, no matter how much she trusted him, otherwise she'd never have introduced him to Zach, she had no right to try and fix him. This wasn't a relationship, just sex. And she had her own problems to work through. It was one thing to embark on a temporary fling with a sexy colleague who was passing through town, a whole other scenario when it came to dating someone seriously. Finding a man she could, not only trust with *her* feelings, but also risk making a permanent fixture in her son's life, would be no easy task. That was why she'd put it off for so long.

'I think Zach must be asleep by now,' she whispered. 'Do you want to stay a bit longer?' She needed to remember they were just having a good time. No matter how wonderful Conrad was with Zach, no matter how much she craved both his company and his touch, no matter how much she might wish he were sticking around, this was still nothing serious. It couldn't be.

'I'd love to.' He cupped her cheek and smiled, the flare of heat in his eyes telling her that, for now, they seemed to be addicted to each other. Time was running out. They'd be foolish not to snatch every opportunity to satiate that hunger.

Trembling inside after such an emotional day, she stood and drew him to his feet, leading him silently to her bedroom. With every footstep, she reiterated how this was temporary. Conrad would soon be heading home to the other side of the world, to his loved ones and a consultant job. She couldn't become sidetracked by his confusion and fears and trust issues. She should simply focus on this sexual journey that had begun just for fun.

She didn't want to have regrets, but nor did she want to be hurt. And if she wasn't careful, she'd confuse the professional respect and sexual connection they shared with feelings. This fling had never been about feelings, because they both had trust issues. She understood that clearly, now more than ever before.

CHAPTER ELEVEN

AS HE MOVED inside Zara, Conrad's heart thudded so hard he was certain she'd feel it and understand he was caught at the centre of an emotional storm. The minute he'd opened up to her about Marcus and let her close, he'd wanted to bury himself inside her and chase away his demons and doubts with pleasure. And after such a fantastic and unexpected day spent together, part of him wanted the night to last for ever. But their chat, the way she'd effortlessly seen things he'd been reluctant to admit, perhaps even to himself, had left him feeling raw and exposed. How had she understood that being betrayed by the one person he'd trusted most in the world, his brother, had left him questioning exactly who he could ever possibly trust?

'Why is this so good?' she whispered, wrapping her legs around his hips, crossing her ankles in the small of his back, staring up at him with desire and faith as if they'd forged a new stronger bond because of their shared trust issues.

The minute they'd touched, slowly and silently stripping each other in the dim light of the bedside lamp, Conrad's urgency had turned into fierce longing he couldn't explain. He felt so close to her, he knew he would never forget his time in England. But he couldn't pretend that the relationship that had begun for fun was still under his control.

Now, with his stare locked with hers and their fingers entwined, he couldn't seem to get close enough to Zara. He couldn't breathe. Couldn't bring himself to think about the ticking clock or the time, in the not too distant future, when this would end.

'Because you're so sexy,' he said as he unhurriedly rocked his hips, refusing to think beyond the here and now. It was good because it was casual and temporary. But if he was honest, the full picture was far more nuanced. And terrifying.

Their connection was rare. She maybe didn't know it because she'd avoided casual sex since her Spanish fling, but *he* knew. It had been many years since he'd felt so in sync with a woman. Around her, his problems seemed smaller. Losing himself in their passion chased his doubts and regrets from his mind. Spending time with her, both in and out of work, put other areas of his life into sharper perspective and made him feel as if anything were possible.

'Or maybe it's because you make everything fun, even sex.' She smiled up at him and then moaned when he captured the other nipple in his mouth. 'Part of me wasn't living before you, before this.'

He groaned, moved by her admission. He'd always known that this was temporary. He would soon be heading home. He couldn't get used to the way one glimpse of Zara, one smile, brightened his day, because he'd have to leave her behind. But right then, in that moment, maybe because he'd opened up to her about Marcus's confusing disloyalty, he couldn't imagine walking away without feeling…regret. As if some part of him had been merely surviving before Zara.

'Conrad,' she moaned, wrapping her arms around his shoulders, bringing his lips back to hers, sliding her tongue into his mouth so he forgot everything but how she made him feel physically. He drove them higher and higher, moving faster and faster, nearing the point of no return, a place where he could ignore how she seemed to have changed him, the way she saw straight through him.

Her orgasm crested with a cry. He reared back, watching her fall apart, her pleasure snapping his restraint so he followed her with a groan, holding onto her tightly until the body-racking spasms died away, leaving them both spent. Panting hard, Conrad buried his face against the side of her neck and breathed in the scent of her hair, still yet to come back down from the incredible high, more aware than ever of how different this seemed. No longer just sex.

What was she doing to him? How could every time they slept together be better than the last and somehow more meaningful than any experience he'd had in years? Because he trusted *her*. That was why he'd shown her the broken version of himself tonight. He hadn't let anyone that close in a long time. But for Zara, maybe because they'd learned to trust each other at work or because she'd introduced him to her son today, or because he was leaving anyway, he'd felt safe to finally open up.

'Are you okay?' she whispered, skimming her fingers up and down his back.

'Hmm,' he mumbled, trying not to freak out as he withdrew from her body. He was far from just *okay*. He was both rejuvenated and confused. Euphoric and scared. As if, in letting her so close, some crucial part of him would never be the same. 'I've just never told anyone else what I told you earlier...' Conrad rolled onto his back.

Zara propped herself up on one elbow and watched him

with a concerned frown. 'If you ever need to talk, I'm here. And I want you to know that your feelings *do* matter.'

'Thank you,' he said, too conflicted and choked to say more or even to look at her. She was too wonderful, a great listener who really cared about people. She saw him far too clearly, and part of him was desperate to keep this light and fun, nothing serious, the way it had begun.

'I know he hurt you,' she said, touching his arm. 'But I don't think your brother would want you to be emotionally stranded.'

'You never met him,' he said, even though he knew she was right. Sometimes, alone with his endlessly looping thoughts, he felt stymied. Marcus was gone. It was too late to tell him how he'd felt disregarded six years ago, but nor could Conrad seem to move on from the fact that he'd been deceived by the one person in the world he'd thought he could trust. But he wasn't ready to hear what Marcus might think or say.

'I know.' Her frown deepened with hurt. 'But he obviously loved you. I don't need to have met him to know that he wouldn't want you to be alone for ever because he'd damaged your trust in people.'

'I'll get over it,' he said, scrubbing a hand over his face and then sitting up.

'What would you say to him now, if you could?' Zara pushed, her hand on his back.

Conrad closed his eyes, part of him regretting that Zara understood him so well because he'd lowered his guard. 'I don't know.' But he'd imagined versions of the conversation a hundred times.

'I think if he hadn't been killed, you two would have worked through your issues in time. I think your relationship would have healed, because you're brothers who loved each other. I think when he asked you to be there for James, he was showing you how sorry he was and how much he respected you.'

'Maybe you're right,' he said, his throat choked and his skin crawling, because she was forcing him to examine the mess more closely. 'I'd like to be able to remember all the good times we shared and not just the one time he let me down.'

Maybe he did have unresolved feelings of betrayal that were stopping him from grieving properly. Maybe that was why he'd acted so overprotective of James. He'd never had the chance to make things right with Marcus. He didn't want to risk that he might have regrets when it came to his nephew. Maybe Zara was right: it was time to talk to his brother as if he were in the room and say all the things he'd wanted to say.

'I should go, let you get some sleep,' he said, standing. Padding to the bathroom, he tried to pull himself together in private. What was this woman doing to him, peeling away his layers like that? Yes, he felt as if he could tell Zara anything, and *he'd* been the one who'd chosen to open up, but they weren't in a proper relationship. Neither of them wanted that and even if they changed their minds, it was a dead end. She lived here and he came from the other side of the world. It would clearly take a lot for Zara to overcome her own trust issues and allow a man into Zach's life. This *had* to be temporary. He *had* to go home and sort out the mess he'd left behind. He couldn't make Zara any promises or rely on her emotional support while he tried to grieve for his brother.

He returned a little more composed, pulling on his jeans

and sweater, the act of dressing like donning a much-needed suit of armour.

'I'm on the early shift tomorrow,' she said, her expression still hurt as she climbed from the bed, covering her nakedness with a fluffy dressing gown. 'I might see you on the ward.'

Guilt lashed him. She'd opened her home and her family to him today and he'd repaid her by spilling his guts and then shutting down. But she'd made him see that he'd never actually processed that damaged trust he'd felt, and now it was all tangled up with his grief over Marcus, the issue resurfacing. How was he supposed to work through all of that with Marcus gone?

'I have a ward round tomorrow,' he said, scared that by confiding in Zara, something that had come so naturally at the time, he'd failed to keep her at arm's length. But if he'd let her in, that was *his* problem, not hers. He gripped her shoulders and brushed a kiss over her lips. 'Thanks for today. I'm so honoured that you introduced me to Zach. He's a wonderful boy. You should be very proud.'

She nodded, her eyes shining with emotion as she blinked. 'You're welcome. Thanks for helping out with the snowman.'

Because he sensed she wanted to say more and he needed to collect his thoughts after such an emotional day, he moved towards the bedroom door.

'Conrad,' she said, stalling him, her breathing fast and her stare searching. 'Will you be okay?'

Conrad pressed his lips together, the urge to rush back to her and hold her in his arms until he felt his usual self almost overwhelming. Instead, he gritted his teeth, offered her his best approximation of a smile and nodded. 'See you tomorrow.'

Whatever the hell was going on inside him, whatever it was that explained his restlessness, he needed to pull it together away from Zara. Because the way she looked at him, as if she understood him and cared about his feelings, was seriously messing with his head.

CHAPTER TWELVE

THE FOLLOWING DAY, while trying to put his feelings from the night before behind him, Conrad was halfway through his ward round on the postnatal ward when he became aware of a raised male voice. He looked up in alarm, spying Zara at the other end of the ward. Some man, obviously someone's relative, was yelling at her, his face puce with anger.

With a surge of adrenaline, all of Conrad's protective instincts fired at once. He abandoned his ward round and marched in their direction.

'I don't care if it's normal,' the belligerent relative said to Zara as Conrad approached. 'It's your job to do something.' He pointed a meaty finger, aggressively. 'My wife is very upset.'

'I understand that, sir,' Zara said, casting Conrad a quick glance before standing her ground against the hulk of a man. 'But baby blues are very common, especially after a difficult delivery like the one your wife has been through.'

The man gritted his teeth in frustration and Conrad fought the urge to put his body between Zara and this angry guy. 'What's the problem here?' he asked, coming to Zara's defence whether she needed him or not because, just as she cared about him, he cared about *her*.

'No problem, Dr Reed,' Zara said, flicking him an impatient stare. 'I was just explaining to Mr Hancock that post-partum distress and sadness is a perfectly normal hormonal reaction to giving birth.' She kept her voice impressively calm as she addressed the man, whereas Conrad was in full-on fight-or-flight mode, and Mr Hancock was one infraction away from being marched off the ward.

'The best way to help your wife,' Zara explained soothingly, as if Conrad weren't there, 'is with plenty of reassurance and affection. The crying will pass.'

How could she be so calm, when he was genuinely scared for her safety? He couldn't stop himself from butting in. 'We don't need raised voices,' Conrad said pointedly to Mr Hancock. 'This is a maternity ward. Your wife isn't the only woman here who's just had a baby. Your outburst might be upsetting other patients. If you can't moderate your tone, you might want to go outside for some fresh air.'

'Thank you, Dr Reed,' Zara said impatiently. 'I've got this.' She had that same pitying look on her face that she'd given him as he'd left her place the night before.

Conrad baulked, feeling as if he were unravelling. He wished he could bite his tongue and not interfere. It was obvious Zara didn't need or want his help. She was an experienced midwife who valued her independence. But he couldn't help but feel protective. She was half this guy's size. If things turned physical, she could be seriously hurt.

'If you or your wife have specific concerns about the care she's receiving,' Zara went on calmly when the man stubbornly stood his ground, 'we can talk those through. Dr Reed is doing his ward round at the moment, so he'll soon be in to review your wife, but, as I said, the best medicine is love and reassurance.'

Finally, to Conrad's relief, the man ducked his head,

looking sheepish. 'I'm sorry,' he said to Zara, his colour high. 'I've just never seen my wife that upset. I...don't know how to help.'

Unlike Conrad, who was slow to forgive such an unwarranted attack, Zara softened, her head tilted in sympathy. 'Why don't you make her a cup of tea?' she suggested, indicating the ward kitchen a few doors away.

Mr Hancock nodded, his body deflating. 'A cup of tea... good idea,' he said and shuffled off towards the kitchen.

Conrad stared after him, his fear still a metallic taste in his mouth. He was half tempted to drag Mr Hancock back and make him apologise to Zara again. In fact, the way he was feeling nothing short of a formal written apology would do.

'Can we have a quick word?' Zara said, her mouth tight with annoyance. She headed for the office, knowing he'd follow.

'I know I shouldn't have interrupted that second time,' he said, closing the door behind them and wishing he could drag her into his arms until he was able to breathe easy once more. 'But I just didn't care for the way he was talking to you.'

Zara watched him for a few seconds, a small frown tugging down her mouth. 'Maybe you should have allowed me to handle it from the start,' she replied, her voice clipped with frustration. 'I had the situation under control. In fact, I think your presence made him worse. I think you overreacted, Conrad.'

'Overreacted?' He gaped, his heart rate still thundering away. 'Did you see the size of that guy? He seemed angry enough to get physical.'

'He wouldn't have laid a finger on me,' Zara said, with

a dismissive shake of her head and a lengthy sigh. 'He was just upset because his wife has been crying non-stop since her emergency C-section, that's all. Some men, often the big gruff ones actually, hate feeling out of control. They don't know what to do with themselves.'

'I'm not too fond of it myself,' Conrad muttered under his breath, because last night he'd let Zara too close and now it felt too late to claw back control. It was making him second-guess everything. 'But that's no excuse for raising his voice at you.'

Just as it had for Mr Hancock, Zara's expression softened with sympathy. 'I've experienced worse, Conrad. Look, I understand why you're overprotective, why you see risk everywhere, but I had the situation in hand. If I'd needed you, I would have called for you.'

Now it was his turn to frown. Of course she didn't need *him*. She didn't need any man. Not when she preferred to rely on herself. But was he hypersensitive to danger?

'I don't see risk everywhere,' he muttered, dismissing the idea that he cared too much. The last thing he wanted was to feel vulnerable and out of control like Mr Hancock. 'Of course I'm still trying to process such a senseless act of violence against my brother, a man who had just been doing his job, a man who, like you, had been trying to help someone. In some ways, I'll never understand what happened to him.'

She nodded, another of those pitying looks on her face. 'Anyone would struggle to make sense of that,' she said, her voice soft with empathy.

'And just like paramedics, hospital staff get assaulted, both verbally and physically, all the time.' He couldn't help but want to shield her. He cared about her and her son.

How could he not after everything they'd shared these past weeks? But maybe he *did* care too much. He'd let Zara close, opened up to her about Marcus, and now he couldn't seem to stop the tide of emotions. Whereas Zara was still coolly keeping men, including him, at a distance, the way she'd done since Zach was born.

'But I wasn't assaulted,' she said, quietly but firmly. 'I was dealing with the situation, and I know all about the risk-assessment procedures on the ward.'

Faced with her calm logic, he felt his stomach roll. He felt made of glass. Suddenly this fling felt way too serious. How had they arrived there so fast? Had he pitched it wrong again? Been too eager? Allowed her too close and rushed into something that wasn't reciprocated? He tried to breathe slower, dismissing the need to panic.

Zara sighed, looking at him the way she'd looked at Mr Hancock, with patience and empathy. 'I can't help but be concerned about you after last night. Perhaps your over-protective feelings—for James, for Zach, for me—are a symptom of your grief, Conrad. Maybe if you processed some of the betrayal over what Marcus did to you, maybe if you truly forgave him for hurting you, for going behind your back and making you feel that your feelings didn't matter, you could start to properly grieve for him. Otherwise how are you ever going to move on and trust someone enough for another serious relationship?'

Conrad stiffened. She was right about his unresolved feelings, ones he was still trying to untangle so he could return to Australia with a clear head. Did his concern come across as overprotectiveness? Tessa had accused him of the same thing, after all.

He sighed, scrubbing a hand through his hair. 'Maybe

you're right, but I'm not the only one struggling to let go of the past, Zara. It seems it's okay for you to want to help me, but not the other way around.'

Had he blurred the line between them, confused sex with feelings? He'd started to trust Zara after all, not just professionally, but personally too. Why else would he have confided in her last night? Why else would he feel so off balance since?

'That's not true.' She frowned.

'Isn't it? You're so independent. It's one of your great strengths. But it's okay to let people help you. To allow people to care. That doesn't make you weak.'

'I know that,' she snapped, her eyes darting away.

'Do you? You don't always have to go it alone, you know. Or are you so busy punishing yourself for your mistake that you push people away so you don't have to trust them?' Conrad had assumed she'd started to trust *him*. Now he wasn't so sure. 'How are *you* ever going to have a real relationship if you won't let anyone close?'

They faced each other, stares locked, breathing hard, their accusations echoing around the room.

'I need to get back to work,' she said after a moment, her voice flat. 'I guess we're both still scared to trust for our own reasons. Going it alone has become a habit born of necessity for me. Trusting someone means letting them close to my precious boy, so you can understand why I'm protective.'

'Of course I can.' Conrad exhaled, feeling depressed. Where he'd started to imagine they might have a future, she still wasn't ready for a relationship. And even if she were, he was leaving anyway. He wasn't making her any promises. Not when he needed to return home, to work through his grief and patch up his strained relationship with Tessa so he could be there for James and keep his promise to his brother.

'I'm sorry that I interfered with Mr Hancock,' he said. 'I won't do it again.'

She raised her chin. 'I'm sorry that I offered unsolicited advice about Marcus. What do I know about relationships? At least you've had real ones before, even if you're no longer interested.'

Her words jarred, stabbing at his ribs. She wasn't wrong: he wasn't ready either. He and Zara were similar, both scared to be gullible, scared to trust, to open their hearts to something real. But last night as he'd lain awake for ages, trying to sleep, he'd tentatively wondered if, because of Zara, he might be ready to move on and start trusting people again. He'd imagined a scenario where he and Zara lived in the same country, where they might have a chance at a real relationship, be a real family with Zach. But now that she was still intent on going it alone...his doubts roared back to life.

'I'll let you go,' he said, his heart racing. He hated the distance, both physical and emotional, between them. 'I need to finish my ward round.'

'Maybe we can talk again after work?' she suggested, heading for the door. 'Once Zach is asleep.'

He nodded and tried to smile. Then he watched her leave.

As he strode back down the ward, he couldn't shake the feeling of foreboding. Somehow, he and Zara had strayed from the casual good time they'd set out to enjoy. Even if they both wanted something real, they'd each spent years avoiding relationships. Even if they lived in the same country, there would be no guarantee that they could make it work.

He *did* care about her, that much was obvious. He just needed to keep a lid on the depth of his feelings. He'd been out of sync with a woman before when he'd dated Tessa. He'd rushed in and she'd held back, and when he'd confessed he'd fallen in love with her, she'd ended it then moved on to his brother. It wasn't that she hadn't wanted a serious relationship, she just hadn't wanted Conrad.

Resolved to double down and re-erect the barriers he'd let Zara slip past, he restarted his ward round. After all, he *had* to go home. His life was in Australia. He had to resolve things with Tessa and see James. And the panic that came whenever he thought about leaving the UK and leaving Zara behind? Clearly, that feeling wasn't reciprocated, so he'd need to do his best to ignore it.

CHAPTER THIRTEEN

LATER THAT NIGHT, Zara lay naked on top of Conrad, her face resting on the slowing thump of his heart. She'd invited him up after Zach had fallen asleep so they could talk after their earlier fight. But somehow, they'd barely apologised before they'd reached for each other, kissing voraciously as they'd stumbled towards the bedroom, shedding clothes. It was as if they each understood the futility of arguing, given that their time was running out. Instead, they'd communicated by touch, his regret left over every inch of her skin by his kisses and hers conveyed via their locked stares as he'd moved inside her, their passion for each other an all-consuming fire of which neither of them seemed to be in control.

Now, Conrad's fingers trailed up her back. Zara lay still in his arms as her mind raced and shivers of doubt raised goose pimples on her skin. She was in trouble, despite all her tough talk and independence. Addicted to his touch that made her feel alive, his secret smile that showed her his inner vulnerabilities, drawn to the way he cared deeply about people, including Zara.

And she cared too. How could she not when he'd been so horribly betrayed by the one person he'd thought he could always trust, his brother? When he had so much to offer but was scared to move beyond casual, scared or even unable to allow himself to be loved in case he got hurt again? It seemed like a vicious circle. She wanted him, more and more with every passing day. But since they'd been snowed in and he'd truly opened up to her, all the reasons this could never be anything but sex seemed glaringly obvious.

'You were right about me,' she whispered, needing him to know that, despite her earlier accusations and denials, he wasn't the only one struggling to let go of the past. 'I have been keeping people, well, men, away.'

She still carried doubts that she was ready for a real relationship. But since their closeness had deepened by working together, since she'd witnessed him interacting with her son, since he'd opened up to her about his ex and his brother, she'd begun to imagine that, with the right man, maybe she could trust her instincts again and open up her heart. Maybe she could risk letting another man, the right man, close to Zach.

His fingers stilled against her skin. 'I know. It's like you said, we've both had our trust damaged.'

Zara's throat burned with fear. Despite the way they touched each other, as if their sexual adventure was no longer just about having a good time but something more, Conrad was as broken as Zara. Whatever her feelings and imaginings, *he* couldn't be the right man. He didn't want a serious relationship, because he'd been betrayed. And he had another boy, James, to love and protect, far away in Australia.

'Perhaps I have been punishing myself,' she said, needing to be as brave as she'd urged Conrad to be. 'I've hid behind the need to put Zach first, when, really, I was just scared to trust my instincts, because they've steered me wrong before with Lorenzo.'

Scared to believe in feelings she'd had little use for these past six years while she'd put her own needs last to focus on motherhood. Scared to open her and Zach's life up to someone who might hurt them all over again.

His heart raced under her cheek, his body still as if he was holding his breath, waiting.

'But I'm also protecting Zach. I have to be careful who I allow close to him. I don't want him getting attached to someone who isn't going to stick around. For me to let someone close, I'd need to be really serious about them.' By definition, she and Conrad were *nothing serious*, and he wasn't sticking around.

'Of course,' he said, saying no more.

Recalling how he'd shut down her attempts to talk about moving on the night before, recalling their fight earlier, she felt her doubts multiply. In spite of his feelings of protectiveness, attraction, respect for Zara, he was obviously struggling with that unresolved betrayal, hiding his trust issues behind casual relationships, stuck because Marcus had died before Conrad could properly forgive him. How could he ever want a serious relationship again, when he'd been forced to swallow down those feelings? When he couldn't trust people not to let him down and hurt him?

Cupping her chin, Conrad tilted her face up so their eyes met. 'You are such an amazing person.'

She nodded, her vision swimming, because meeting Conrad had given her hope for the future. Not that her future could include him. But could she really find someone willing to love both her and Zach? Could she risk being that vulnerable, knowing the pain of possible rejection, knowing it could hurt her and her beloved little boy? The alternative was to live her future the way she'd lived the past six years, by just surviving.

'Don't let that fear hold you back for ever,' he said. 'You can't swear off relationships at the age of twenty. You deserve to be happy, too.'

He brushed her lips with his and euphoria flooded her body, that happiness he said she deserved. She wanted to step into the picture he painted. But when she lowered her guard enough to think about dating, she always pictured Conrad—them working together, romantic dates followed by intense love-making, her, Zach and Conrad laughing together the way they had the day of the snow.

But that was crazy, naive, the kind of dream younger Zara would have entertained, and look where that had led. To heartache and loneliness. Conrad was still caught up in the past and not even thinking about relationships, and she'd always known this would be temporary and that he'd go home. She'd most likely never see him again. If she wasn't careful with her wild imaginings, if she made another mistake, allowed another man close enough to hurt her, the consequences would be bigger, because Zach was old enough to understand and remember and feel rejected.

When she pulled back from his kiss, Zara deliberately changed the subject so she could dismiss the fear that it might be too late to protect herself where he was concerned. 'What about you? What will you do when you go back to Australia? Do you have a consultant job lined up?'

'No,' he said, stiffening slightly. 'I've applied for more locum work in Brisbane.'

'Why?' she asked, confused. 'Isn't it time you became a consultant?' Conrad was an experienced senior registrar. She understood why he'd wanted to locum in England—

a temporary post that had allowed him to gain some distance from his complicated relationship with Tessa, and to grieve. But more locum work in Brisbane made no sense.

'I'm just not ready,' he said, sounding defensive. 'I don't know where I want to settle.'

Zara's heart sank. If she'd needed more confirmation that he was still struggling with the past, still running away from his feelings of betrayal, this was it. If he wasn't ready to settle in Australia, he was even less likely to be thinking about relationships, whereas naive Zara was getting carried away again.

'But surely you'd stay where your family are,' she said sitting up and drawing the sheet over her body. 'Where James is? Brisbane?'

Ever since he'd told her of his and Tessa's history, she'd tried valiantly to ignore her jealous imaginings of them fixing their relationship and maybe getting back together one day. Who Conrad dated in the future, who he fell in love with, was none of Zara's business. She had no claim to him. But clearly, she was already way too emotionally invested.

'Yes, that's the plan,' he said, cagily. 'But, I don't know... I've really enjoyed my time working in the NHS. It's made me think about the kind of consultant post I want.'

Zara froze, her breath trapped in her lungs. He couldn't mean he'd considered moving to the UK, could he? She was too scared to ask. But her reaction to the idea, the elation that hijacked her pulse, spoke volumes. She was already in deep. If Conrad lived in England, if he wanted a real relationship, she'd want to continue to see him, to build on what they had and see where it could go. She would even, albeit slowly, allow him and Zach to get to know each other, because she trusted him and liked the kind of man he was.

But none of that could be.

'What about James?' she whispered, terrified and torn to shreds by her conflicted feelings. Part of her, that newly awakened part that clearly had feelings for Conrad, wanted him to stay. But she couldn't ask him to, nor could she rely on her instincts, her feelings, not when they'd steered her so wrong before.

'Yes. That's where I always end up, too,' he said, his voice quiet and thoughtful. 'I owe it to my brother to make sure James is okay, to patch up things with Tessa so I can be the uncle he needs. So I'll go back to Brisbane, and just... see how things pan out, I guess.'

Zara's dangerous excitement drained away, leaving chills behind. How stupid was she to get her hopes up like that? Had she learned nothing from Lorenzo's rejection? No amount of waiting patiently or staring at the phone would make it ring, just as no amount of naive wishing would make someone care when they didn't, or *couldn't* because they'd been hurt before too.

'Speaking of James,' he said, 'I wanted to ask you something.'

Her pulse accelerated again, but this time she shut down the foolish hope.

'There's a steam train exhibition at the weekend I thought Zach might like,' he said, his stare full of boyish excitement the way it had been the day they'd built a snowman. 'I'm on call Saturday, but we could go Sunday. You can ride on the train, and they serve high tea on board. We could make a day of it.'

Zara swallowed, her head all over the place, knowing she'd have to decline. It sounded innocent enough, and, like James, Zach loved trains. But exposing her son to any more of Conrad when he was already pretty smitten with 'the Aussie lodger' and when Conrad was leaving soon was too risky. If she spent another day with Conrad, watching him interact wonderfully with Zach again, she'd never be able to keep her volatile feelings in check. She couldn't let him any closer. If she did, she might not survive him leaving.

'Um...can I think about it?' she said, her eyes stinging. 'I usually catch up on housework and laundry at the weekend,' she finished lamely. But there was no point wishing for the impossible. She'd learned that the hard way while waiting for Zach's father to have a change of heart and seek a relationship with his son.

'Of course,' he said, his voice flat, pricking at her guilt.

This time it was Zara who got up from the bed first and locked herself in the bathroom. She faced her reflection, resolved to protect herself better, given their time was running out and Conrad would soon be gone. The only sure-fire way to safeguard her emotions as resolutely as she protected Zach was to end this now. To stop sleeping with him and part as friends.

She glanced at the closed door, her heart banging away painfully under her ribs as she imagined him on the other side—sexy, confused by her caginess, emotionally vulnerable because he was as susceptible to rejection as Zara. She couldn't imagine she possessed the strength to work with him and not want him with the same burning ferocity she'd always felt. Maybe she could hold on for one more week. Lock down her confusing feelings, take as much of him physically as she could get in the time they had left and face the emotional consequences when he stepped on the plane.

CHAPTER FOURTEEN

LATER THAT WEEK, Conrad was on his way to the delivery ward after a morning of surgeries, when he received an urgent call from his SHO, Max. He rushed to the ward, his adrenaline pumping. When he entered the delivery suite, Zara, Sharon and Max were with the patient, an anaesthetist and paediatrician standing by in the corner of the room.

'What's the situation?' Conrad asked, meeting Zara's concerned stare as he quickly pulled on some gloves.

'Shoulder dystocia,' Zara said, valiantly keeping the alarm he saw in her eyes from her voice. 'The baby's head was delivered three minutes ago. Mum's name is Gail.'

Zara appeared understandably panicked as the labouring woman gave a moan to signal another contraction. But there was no time to comfort either of them. Shoulder dystocia, a serious birth complication with consequences for the health of the mother and baby, meant the baby's shoulders were trapped in the mother's pelvis, delaying the birth of the body.

Conrad took the position beside Zara in place of his SHO, too focussed on the emergency to wonder why Zara had called Max and not him. He quickly examined the patient, glancing at the foetal heart rate monitor for signs that the baby was in distress.

'Okay,' he said, taking charge. 'Let's try the McRoberts

manoeuvre. Zara, you take the right leg, Max the left. Gail, the baby is a little stuck. We need to shift your position to help deliver the shoulders.'

As another contraction began and at Conrad's nod, his assistants flexed the patient's hips, bringing her knees up towards her armpits while Conrad placed his hand on her lower abdomen and applied pressure to the front of the pelvis. 'Push now, as hard as you can,' he instructed the patient.

With everyone present seemingly holding their breath, willing the situation to resolve, the baby moved slightly, but then retreated back into the birth canal.

As Gail collapsed back onto the pillow, clearly exhausted, Conrad looked up and made eye contact with a worried-looking Zara. A week ago he'd have seen respect and faith and encouragement in her stare, but now he just saw doubt. He wanted to reassure her that, together, they could safely deliver this baby, to ask her to believe in him, but even if there was time, even if they'd been alone, he was no longer as sure of Zara. Things had changed between them, as if they were both protecting themselves for the inevitable end of their fling, which was, of course, eminently sensible.

'One more push now,' Conrad said as the next contraction started. 'We're nearly there.' They performed the manoeuvre again, and this time, the shoulders were successfully delivered to a collective sigh of relief around the room.

Conrad completed the delivery of the newborn, placing the baby onto Gail's stomach before he quickly clamped and cut the cord and noted the baby's Apgar score.

'Well done, Gail,' he said. 'He seems fine, but the paediatrician will give him a quick check over, okay? Then he's all yours. Congratulations.'

He glanced up at Zara, yearning for that closeness he'd grown accustomed to whenever they worked together, but Zara seemed distracted. He couldn't help but recall how she'd withdrawn from him the other night when he'd suggested an outing with Zach. He understood that she was choosing to protect her son, and maybe herself, too. And he couldn't blame her. After all, he was making her no promises. In fact, ever since their fight, he too was desperately trying to protect himself.

But ever since the snowman, since the night he'd told her about Marcus and Tessa, he'd also started to imagine a different future for them, one where, instead of ending their fling when he left for Australia, he returned to England and they picked up where they'd left off. Dated for real. A serious relationship. But just because he was trying to manage his own confusion and doubts by selfishly blurring the lines, didn't mean Zara owed him anything. She'd admitted to always relying on herself, and he could understand why, given how she'd been hurt.

Despite the crazy ideas spinning in his head, the ways they could continue to see each other, he repeatedly came up against the same brick wall: Zara wasn't ready to take that risk for a relationship. If Conrad allowed her any closer or pushed for some grand gesture where one of them shifted their entire life to the other's country, he might discover that it was *him* she didn't want. Better to keep any promises off the table, to fly to Australia next week as planned and sort out his personal life. Maybe then his head would clear and he could think straight.

With all the excitement over and with his stomach still

twisting with doubt, Conrad washed up and headed for the office to make a note in the patient's file. That complete, he went in search of Zara, finding her in the ward kitchen.

'What happened?' he asked, trying and failing to keep the accusation from his voice. 'Why didn't you call *me*?'

She looked up at him and sighed, her fatigue obvious. 'It all happened so quickly. Everything was progressing normally until it suddenly wasn't. Max was already on the ward.'

She ducked her stare from his and busied herself making toast. Reluctant to cause another argument, Conrad bit his tongue. He wasn't doubting her story, but there was something off with her. She couldn't look at him. A sickening sense of déjà vu took him back to that first week, when they hadn't really known each other at all. When she'd been prickly, keeping him at arm's length, locking down any need for feelings as she'd done since she'd been hurt by that last guy.

Conrad sighed, terrified that the intense feelings he couldn't seem to contain, ones that fuelled those fantasies of uprooting his life and moving to the UK on the off chance that Zara might be interested, were his alone. He'd rushed into things before, with Tessa. From the way Zara seemed to be pulling back, reluctant to expose Zach to Conrad, reducing her professional reliance on him, Zara was obviously still happy to go it alone.

'Are you okay?' he asked, concerned because obstetric emergencies took their toll on everyone concerned and shoulder dystocia, which was fortunately relatively rare, could alarm the most experienced midwife.

'I'm fine,' she said, finally looking his way. 'It's been a long shift, that's all. I'm tired.'

He was just about to reach out and touch her, the urge automatic, when Sharon bustled into the kitchen. The older midwife paused, shooting Conrad a peculiar look before she moved to the sink and filled a water jug.

'How are you, Sharon?' Conrad asked. 'That was a bit of a shock for us all, I think.'

'I'm glad for the outcome,' Sharon said, catching Zara's eye before she looked Conrad's way. 'A great team effort.'

While Zara finished making the toast, Sharon discreetly made her exit, but something in the older woman's manner flushed his body with uncomfortable heat. The hairs on the back of Conrad's neck stood on end. Was he being paranoid? He sensed they'd talked about him behind his back. But surely Zara wouldn't do that after everything he'd confided in her and after she'd insisted on secrecy?

When they were alone again, he lowered his voice. 'Does she know about us?' he asked, his paranoia spilling free.

Zara shook her head, looking insulted. 'I haven't told her, but she suspects I'm seeing someone.' She looked up and met his stare. 'I'm rubbish at hiding my *post-sex glow*, apparently.' She rolled her eyes, her humour returning for a second. But the smile was tinged with sadness, as if she too sensed this disconnect between them and had no energy to fix it.

As he recalled her obvious fatigue, a surge of compassion welled inside him. He knew first-hand how shift work could mess with your sleep patterns and she also had Zach to care for.

'Listen,' he said, lowering his voice. 'I know it's Friday.' He paused, knowing she would understand he was speaking about their standing late-night arrangement when Zach was sleeping over at his grandmother's. 'But why don't you get an early night tonight?'

He would miss her, ache for her, but maybe he was being selfish. Maybe a bit of distance would help them both gain some perspective. After all, by next weekend this would be over and he'd be on a plane back to Australia. Then, touching her, kissing her reaching for her in the night, would be physically impossible.

She placed a steaming mug of tea on the tray and looked up. 'That's not a bad idea, actually. I could do with an early night.'

Conrad nodded, his pulse whooshing through his head. He wanted to kiss her, to ease her burden somehow, to care for her the way she cared for everyone around her, but he wasn't her boyfriend. She didn't need or want one of those and he was leaving anyway.

'About this weekend...' Zara's mouth flattened into a frown, her stare darting away. 'I'm sorry, but I don't think it's a good idea.' She looked up, something in her expression hardening, reminding him of the woman he'd first met, a woman who'd needed no one. 'Ever since the snowman, Zach has been asking about you non-stop. You made quite the impression on him. I'm scared that if he spends any more time with you, when you're gone, he'll be sad. I don't want to make it worse for him, no matter what I want for myself. I *have* to put him first.'

Conrad nodded, his stomach sinking. 'Of course, you do. I understand. I wouldn't want him to be sad either.' Of course she was protecting Zach. Her priorities were what they'd always been. Conrad's hadn't changed either. They'd always been on this trajectory, their fling temporary. He'd just got carried away by his feelings, lured by the idea that if they lived in the same country, it could be more than temporary. And that vulnerable, irrational part of him that had let her closer than he'd let anyone in six years couldn't help but feel a moment's bitterness. He'd been useful for a sexual adventure, but could never be anything serious, not when she was still dead set on holding men away.

She nodded, picking up the tray as if the conversation was closed. 'Thanks for understanding.'

'Just out of curiosity,' he said, before she could leave, his heart leaping in his chest, 'and because I clearly like to torture myself, if I wasn't flying to Australia next week, would your answer have been any different?'

Hypothetically, had they ever stood a chance of something more than just sex?

'I don't know,' she whispered, looking down. 'But I do know that I'm always going to choose to protect Zach. I'm his mother, so it comes with the territory.' She shrugged, sadly.

Conrad nodded, unable to argue with her inevitable and admirable choice, but crushed all the same.

'I'd better take this tea to Gail, before it goes cold.' She moved past him with the tray.

'Zara,' he said, before she'd gone too far. 'I'll miss you tonight.'

'Me too,' she said, walking away anyway.

But then they both needed to get used to doing that, because time was running out.

CHAPTER FIFTEEN

LATER THAT NIGHT, Conrad's door opened and Zara rushed into his arms out of the cold. 'I tried to stay away, but I couldn't do it. I know it's only going to make it worse when you leave, but I can't seem to care. I just want you until I can't have you any more.'

She stood on tiptoes, raised her mouth to his, kissing him deeply, passionately, her heart soaring when he returned her kisses, like for like.

'Thank goodness,' he said, kicking closed the door.

Even before she heard it slam, she was tugging at his clothes. 'Hurry,' she urged, needing him with terrifying desperation. 'I need you.'

She gasped as one of his hands grasped her backside and the other cupped her breast, his lips caressing the ticklish spots on her neck. She'd spent the entire rest of the day trying to justify this rendezvous, telling herself that as long as she kept Conrad away from Zach, only *her* feelings were at risk. Telling herself she could handle the emotional danger if she focussed on the sex. Telling herself she'd deal with any fallout when he was gone, just as she'd always relied on herself.

'I was sitting here, staring at the door, willing you to change your mind.' He kissed her again, stripping off her jumper and jeans before scooping her from the floor and carrying her into the bedroom with her legs wrapped around his waist. 'I'm so glad you did.'

He tumbled them onto the bed, his hips, the hard jut of his erection, between her legs, where she wanted him. But there were still too many layers between them and not enough skin-to-skin contact.

'Conrad,' she moaned, caressing his erection through his jeans as she pushed her tongue into his mouth. When he stood to remove his clothing and reached for the bedside drawer and the stash of condoms he kept there, she shimmied off her underwear.

'Will it stop?' she asked as he joined her on the bed, pressing kisses all over her body. 'This burning need? Tell me it will stop when you go,' she begged, needing to hear that she'd go back to normal, even if it was a lie.

He looked up, confusion and lust slashed across his handsome face. 'I don't know. I hope so. For both our sakes.' Then he buried his face between her legs, kissing her deeply with a tortured groan.

Because his touch, this wild passion, were the only things that could block out the loud ticking of the clock in her head, Zara lost herself to the oblivion of pleasure. While she was focussed on the way he made her body come alive, she didn't have to think about how, but for the fact he wasn't the right man to risk her heart with, she could so easily fall for him. She'd let him close, closer than anyone else, ever, and one day soon, she had to pay the price for that recklessness. But not yet. For a few more days she could hold off the inevitable sadness that would come when he left.

When he reared back, covered himself with the condom and pushed inside her, she clung to him, all but wrecked by the force of their uncontrollable need for each other. But this had always been too good, intense, a thrilling and passionate risk. 'Yes,' she cried as he gripped her hand and moved his hips, slow and deep.

'I can't stop wanting you,' he said, his face a mask of dark desire as he raised her thigh over his hip so he sank deeper, his body scorching her every place they connected. 'I can't stop counting the days.'

'Don't,' she said, shaking her head. 'Let's just enjoy every second, no regrets.' This had started with sex. Only fitting that they should keep it about sex, until the very end.

She'd had a minor wobble there for a few days, allowed her imagination to run wild with impossible what ifs, but her head was back on straight now.

'Zara,' he groaned as their bodies moved in unison, his thrusts pushing her higher and higher towards the release she'd come for. As the rhythm of their bodies built to a crescendo, Zara focussed on the pleasure, her orgasm ripping through her in powerful waves until all she could do was hold him as he crushed her in his arms, burying his face against the side of her neck, groaning.

When his body stilled, Zara closed her eyes and breathed him in, trying to memorise his unique scent, already certain she was falling for Conrad Reed. But that was okay. She'd come to terms with it, compartmentalised it the way she'd done for so many other parts of her life since becoming a mother. When you had a child you needed to put first, your own feelings didn't really matter.

Conrad raised his face from the crook of her neck, his eyes stormy. 'Part of me wishes I could stay,' he whispered, kissing the palm of her hand, and Zara's heart clenched.

She nodded and pushed his hair back from his face. 'Part of me wishes you didn't have to go. But we always knew it was temporary. I'll never forget my wild sexual adventure with you.'

Witnessing the doubt her words caused, she shifted under his weight. Their wishes made sense. Their relationship had always been intense, even when it was just fun. But wishes weren't reality, and when she was finally ready to fully open up her heart to a real adult relationship, she needed to be a hundred per cent certain it was with the right man, preferably one who lived in the same country. She wouldn't risk confusing Zach, nor would she expose her sweet little boy to any more rejection.

He rolled to the side and released her. Zara stood and hunted around for her scattered clothes.

'You don't want to stay?' he asked, his voice uncertain, so she winced with guilt. If only she'd possessed the stamina to resist him tonight, to start weaning herself off instead of selfishly taking every kiss and touch she could get.

'Just because I couldn't fight the temptation to be with you, I'm still tired.' Zara swallowed down the almost overwhelming urge to climb back into his warm bed and hold him all night long. 'I'll sleep better in my own bed.'

She pulled on her clothes, pressed one last kiss to his lips and hurried out into the bitterly cold night, where, finally, she was able to draw a deep breath. Only as hard as she tried to forget it, the look of confusion, doubt and hurt on his face as she'd left kept her awake for half of the night.

CHAPTER SIXTEEN

On Conrad's final day at Abbey Hill Hospital, Zara sat in the break room just outside the delivery suite with Sharon, feeling as if her world were about to implode. Zach had been sick all weekend with a cold, so she'd had to swap shifts with Bella. Since working three night shifts in a row, she hadn't seen Conrad since last Friday, when they'd made love as if preparing for the end of the world and then she'd fled. But with every day that passed where they didn't see each other, she felt a sick kind of triumph, as if she was already winning the battle of missing him, even before he'd left the country.

She picked at her salad, her head all over the place and her appetite non-existent. Now that the day of Conrad's departure was nearly upon them, Zara had a more pressing dilemma than fearing she might not get over the most intense relationship of her life—her late period.

'Two across,' Sharon said, breaking into Zara's reverie. 'A sudden attack. Four letters. Starts with an R.' Sharon was focussed on the crossword puzzle at the back of one of the magazines lying around the break room, as if this were just any other day. Of course, Sharon wasn't aware that Zara had slept with the sexy Australian locum, that she'd embarked on a foolish fling with him and developed deep feelings for him. That she might, if fate were cruel enough to throw not one, but two unplanned pregnancies her way, be having his baby.

'Raid,' Zara said absently, grateful to have something else to think about other than the fear burning a hole in her chest. She and Conrad had always used condoms, but they'd also had a lot of sex.

Sensing something was off with her friend, Sharon looked up from the magazine crossword. 'What's wrong? You've been off all morning.'

'I'm just tired,' Zara tried to bluff. But one look at Sharon's serious expression told her there was no point in trying to hide her concerns from the other woman. They were probably written all over Zara's face.

'I realised this morning that my period is a couple of days late, that's all,' she said with a sigh. Just saying the words sent her mind into a panic. What if she was pregnant? Would she have to raise this baby alone, too? She and Conrad weren't a couple. He was leaving tomorrow. And Australia was even further away than Spain...

But surely history wouldn't repeat itself...? Surely she couldn't have made another mistake? She swallowed, feeling queasy. How could she have been so reckless again? Yes, she'd practised safe sex and taken every possible precaution, but she should have known better than to take risks with a man who came from the other side of the world. A man who was emotionally unavailable because, like her, he was scared to rush into another relationship. A man she'd always known she couldn't have.

Sharon frowned, obviously concerned. 'Have you taken a pregnancy test?'

'I've been busy today, delivering other people's babies,' she said lamely, shaking her head and pushing away her lunch.

Part of her had wanted to stay happily in denial, hoping that if she left it long enough, her period would start and there'd be no need to wait for those pink lines to appear. No need to tell Conrad of the possibility. No need to know that it wouldn't make any difference to their readiness for a relationship. Just the possibility of a pregnancy had reopened feelings from the past—shame at her own stupidity, guilt that she might be about to mess Zach's life up even more, a resurgence of Lorenzo's cruel rejection—feelings she'd thought she'd conquered, but obviously hadn't.

'Busy having sex, by the sounds of it,' Sharon said. At Zara's sharp look, her friend turned sympathetic. 'Is your mystery man our sexy Australian locum by any chance?'

Zara gaped, her jaw slack as she ducked her head away from Sharon's expression of pity. 'How did you figure that out?'

'I have eyes,' Sharon said, closing the magazine. 'Perhaps you're too close to see it, but he looks at you with this kind of feral hunger. He seems devastated when you're not on the ward and smiles more when you're around. It's kind of obvious. We've all noticed.'

Zara blinked away the sting in her eyes, feeling stupid and naive. Could everyone she worked with also see how close she'd come to falling hard for Conrad? And now she might be having his baby...

'Yes, well, so much for "getting back out there" and "having a good time".' She threw two of Sharon's favourite arguments for why Zara should date back at her. 'Now look where I've ended up.'

Sharon tilted her head in sympathy. 'It might be negative. You won't know until you take the test.'

Zara nodded, feeling sick and imagining it was down to morning sickness. Of course, her practical friend was right. 'I'll grab one from the hospital pharmacy on my way home. Take it tonight,' Zara said, glancing at the clock, her stomach twisting as she packed away her uneaten lunch. Their break time was over.

'What if it is positive?' Sharon cautiously asked. 'I'm guessing he's still planning to leave tomorrow?'

'Of course he is. It was nothing serious. Just a sexual fling, the kind you've been telling me to have for the past six years.' Time to put to bed any naive notion that she and Conrad could possibly have a future. She had Zach to think about. Conrad had his own life to lead, grieving to do, his nephew to support.

'Unless it *is* positive,' Sharon pushed, 'which might change things...'

'It won't.' Zara shook her head, cutting Sharon off. She refused to think of that possibility. 'I'm almost certain it will be negative, and even if we wanted a relationship, which neither of us does, because we've both got trust issues, we're from different continents. We both have jobs and lives and commitments. Real life doesn't always work out.'

She swallowed, aware of the sickening similarities between her holiday fling with Lorenzo and her fling with Conrad. She'd known going into both that neither of them would last.

'Then I'll say no more.' Sharon stood, picked up her bag and eyed Zara with compassion that set Zara's teeth on edge. 'But please text me when you know the result of the test or I'll worry, too.'

'I will. And please don't tell anyone else about me and Conrad. I forced him to keep it a secret, because it was nothing serious and always temporary. I didn't want you lot teasing me, and I knew I'd never hear the last of it, having put off dating for so long.' She couldn't bring herself to say the word sex now, not when what she and Conrad had been doing felt bigger than just sex. It felt like a relationship. A *real* relationship. But of course, it wasn't.

'Of course I won't,' Sharon said, looking worried.

'And please don't look at me like that,' Zara pleaded. 'Everything is going to be fine. The test will be negative. Conrad will leave tomorrow. And life will go back to normal around here.'

As they left the break room together and headed back to the delivery ward, Zara wondered how many times she'd have to repeat the last point until she believed it.

Later that afternoon, Conrad had just finished discharging some patients with Max, when an alarm sounded outside the delivery ward. He took off running, aware of footsteps behind him. At the lifts, a flashing light told him some sort of emergency was occurring inside. He skidded to a halt, glancing around, relieved to see that Sharon and Zara were there too.

But there was no time to talk. A second later, the lift doors opened. A couple in their twenties were inside, the man supporting his heavily pregnant partner from behind. The woman clearly in second-stage labour.

'The baby's coming. Now!' she cried in a state of panic.

'I can't walk any further.' With that, a contraction took hold and she bared down, her weight supported by her partner.

'We'll get supplies,' Sharon said, grabbing Max and running back to the delivery ward.

Conrad pulled some gloves from the pocket of his scrubs, passing Zara a pair before pulling on his own. Together, they crouched side by side in front of the woman, blocking the lift doors from closing.

'What's your name?' Zara asked.

'Jessica,' the woman panted, moaning as another contraction began.

'We can't move her.' Zara shot Conrad a look.

'I agree,' he said as Sharon and Max returned with medical supplies and extra pairs of hands. Sharon unfolded a mobile privacy screen across the opening of the lift behind Zara and Conrad, blocking the view of anyone who happened to walk past.

With the screen in place, Conrad raised the woman's dress to her waist and Zara removed her underwear and quickly examined her. 'I can feel the head,' Zara said, meeting Conrad's stare. 'She's fully dilated.'

He nodded, grateful that she was there. Her calm manner was exactly what they needed, because, whether they liked it or not, they'd be delivering this baby in the lift, any second now.

'Jessica, you need to listen to us,' Zara said, fitting the cardiotocography or CTG sensors around Jessica's abdomen to pick up the baby's heart rate. 'When we tell you to stop pushing, we need you to pant, okay?'

The woman nodded, her eyes wild with fear and pain. Conrad laid the towels and a sheet that Sharon passed to him on the floor of the lift. Jessica's moan heralded the start of the next contraction. While she pushed, crouched in front of and supported by her partner, Conrad and Zara held their hands out at the ready to catch the baby if things happened quickly.

'Okay, pant now, Jessica,' Zara instructed the patient as the baby's head emerged.

Conrad quickly loosened the umbilical cord from around the baby's neck, while Sharon passed in more clean towels. Zara had just managed to spread them over her lap, when the rest of the baby was delivered into Zara and Conrad's waiting hands.

'It's a girl, Jessica,' Conrad said with a smile of relief, noting the baby's Apgar score. He and Zara held onto the newborn who'd been so eager to arrive, smiling at each other, laughing now the adrenaline rush was over.

While the parents laughed and cried and peered in wonder at their daughter, Zara cleaned up the baby with a towel and then handed her over. Conrad injected Jessica's thigh with syntocinon to help the uterus contract down to deliver the placenta and then he clamped and cut the umbilical cord.

'We're going to move you to a delivery suite now, Jessica,' Conrad said as Sharon wheeled in a wheelchair. 'So you can deliver the placenta.'

He glanced at Zara, hoping to see the same euphoria he felt in her eyes. That they'd delivered this baby together, practically hand in hand, made him feel closer to her than ever. But to his utter alarm, she looked close to tears. She wouldn't look at him. What was going on?

In a flurry of activity, Jessica was helped into the wheelchair by Zara and her husband, while Sharon and Max collected up the equipment.

'Do you want me to help with third stage?' Conrad asked Zara, reluctant to just walk away after such an emotionally fraught delivery. He wanted to wrap his arms around Zara and kiss away her frown.

'I've got it,' she said, barely looking his way. But perhaps she was simply focussed on the patient, on completion of the third stage of labour and performing the baby's neonatal checks after such an unorthodox delivery.

As Zara whisked Jessica and her newborn to a nearby delivery suite, ward orderlies started the clean-up, wheeling in a laundry bin and removing the screens. A hospital security guard appeared to lock the lift doors open while the cleaning was carried out. Concerned about Zara, Conrad wheeled the portable oxygen cylinder they fortunately hadn't needed and followed Sharon onto the ward and into the utility room.

'Well, that was a first,' Sharon said with a chuckle, disposing of the used syringe in the sharps bin.

Conrad nodded, parking the oxygen cylinder against the wall. 'Is Zara okay? She seemed...upset.' He knew the two women were close. Perhaps Zara had confided in Sharon about him leaving tomorrow.

Sharon ducked her head guiltily as she busied herself with the clear-up, and Conrad immediately knew that she knew about their fling.

'She'll be fine...' Sharon said, busying herself and not looking at him. 'Births can be an emotional experience, as you know, and she's probably just distracted. I told her to get a pregnancy test as soon as possible, that way she'll know for certain, although—' She broke off, finally realising that she'd maybe said too much.

Conrad froze, his blood chilling. Zara was pregnant?

Sharon turned to face him, clearly horrified that she'd let it slip. 'You didn't know, did you?' she said, her hand covering her mouth. 'I'm so sorry. I just assumed… It just slipped out. She's not certain,' she rushed on. 'In fact she's adamant it will be negative. She's going to buy a test on the way home… Perhaps she didn't want to tell you until she knew for sure.'

Conrad's stomach rolled. Not only did Sharon seem to know all about him and Zara and their fling, Zara had also confided in her friend that she might be pregnant. And yet she hadn't confided in *him*? Not even when he was the father. She obviously didn't trust him.

Sharon sagged in defeat, resting her back against the edge of the sink. 'What will you do?'

Conrad scrubbed a hand over his face, his mind racing with possibilities. 'Talk to her, of course. Make sure she's okay. I had no idea.' He'd always wanted a family of his own with the right woman, someone he loved, who loved him back and wanted him in her life…

Sharon nodded. 'I think that's a good plan. The two of you obviously have some stuff to sort out.'

Just then, Max poked his head into the room. 'There's a woman with an ectopic pregnancy in A & E.'

Conrad nodded and moved towards the door on auto-pilot, glancing back at Sharon. 'I have to go. Clearly it's going to be one of those crazy days.'

Sharon tilted her head, concern in her eyes. 'Want me to pass on a message to Zara?'

Conrad shook his head, feeling sick. The waiting emergency meant he had no time to think and no idea what he wanted to say to Zara anyway. 'Thanks, but I'll catch her later.'

Shelving his sense of betrayal that Zara had gone behind his back to her friend before coming to him, he hurried down the stairs to A & E with Max.

CHAPTER SEVENTEEN

THAT NIGHT, AFTER an evening spent operating on the ectopic pregnancy case, Conrad took his usual seat on Zara's sofa, his chest hollowed out with a sad sense of inevitability. So many times this past month he'd sat in this very seat, laughing with this woman, talking to her, kissing. He'd poured his heart out, told her about his brother, his grief, his shameful feelings of betrayal. Now he wasn't sure that he'd really known her at all. Because the pain he'd felt earlier at the hospital when he'd realised she'd kept a secret and gone behind his back to her friend had burned him alive. It was as if he'd never meant anything to her.

'Sharon said she'd let slip that my period was late,' Zara said, taking the seat beside him. 'I told you there was no privacy at work.'

'Is that all you care about? Secrets?' he asked, because, as far as he was concerned, an unplanned pregnancy with this woman wouldn't have been the worst thing in the world. He cared about her and her son. He trusted her. He'd assumed she'd trusted him. That they were moving in the right direction. That, but for his departure to Australia, they'd both want to continue their relationship. Before he'd found out that there might be a baby, he'd even been plotting ways he could return to the UK so he could see her again and take what had started as something casual and fun as the foundation for a real relationship.

But now, he was almost scared to find out how she felt. For some reason, maybe because he was reminded of the last time he'd cared about a woman and she too had gone behind his back, it felt that Zara was about to break up with him. But there was no need. They'd never been an item.

'Of course not,' she said, her frown turning to an encouraging smile. 'But it's okay. I'm *not* pregnant.' Her face lit up. 'I took a test when I got home from work this afternoon and it's negative.'

He met her stare, seeing nothing but relief and that distance she'd worn for the past week, whereas Conrad felt crushed. His heart, which had been pounding, plummeted to his boots. He hadn't properly had time to think about how he felt about Sharon's revelation, but with Zara's confirmation that there was no baby, all he felt was desolate disappointment.

'That's a relief,' he mumbled automatically, picking up on Zara's feelings on the matter. No point missing something that had never been. And now he knew exactly how out of sync his feelings were with Zara's.

'Yes.' She looked down at her hands in her lap. 'So you can leave tomorrow with your mind at rest. There's no reason to feel obligated or to stay in touch.'

She was practically pushing him out of the door. Obviously Zara's feelings for him were nowhere near as strong as his for her. He'd moved too fast again. Judged it wrong. Poured out his heart to a woman who could never need or want him because she still wasn't ready to let him, or any other man, close.

'I'm sorry that you had to find out from Sharon,' she

said, meeting his stare. 'I didn't intend to tell her, but she knows me so well. She knew I was worried about something.'

'You could have told *me*,' he said, hating that, for a few hours, he might have hypothetically fathered a child and been the last to know, just as he'd been the last to know when his brother had fallen for his ex. 'Especially when you knew that the last woman I cared about also went behind my back.'

'You're right,' she admitted, looking shamefaced. 'I'm sorry. But after Zach being sick all weekend and after my night shifts, I only noticed the date this morning. I didn't want to text you and there was no point worrying you if I wasn't pregnant, which as it turned out was the right call, because I'm not.' She smiled brightly then, and he shrank inside a little more.

'And more importantly, you don't need me or my emotional support, right? You never have, not when you can go it alone, same as always.'

She was so terrified of trusting the wrong guy, and she clearly didn't trust *him*. Whereas he'd been looking for more locum work nearby, taking Sharon's advice and wondering if there'd soon be a consultant job available in Derby and wondering how quickly he could return to the UK.

'That's not fair,' she said with a frown. 'I didn't set out to tell Sharon first, but she *is* my friend. And I didn't tell her that we've been having sex. She'd already figured it out by herself.'

Conrad nodded, glancing away, his doubts so acute, he wondered if he was once more overreacting. It wouldn't surprise him. His feelings were out of control, after all.

One minute he was convinced he had to leave as planned, the next he was plotting ways to stay.

'So that's all I am to you still? Just sex?' he asked, the panicked thudding of his heart intensifying. He and Zara could only work if they were on the same wavelength. For over a week, he'd tentatively tried and failed to draw out her feelings.

She blinked, opened her mouth to answer but no words emerged.

'I'm leaving tomorrow,' he pushed, needing to hear her declare herself before he walked away. 'I've been trying to give you space and not put pressure on the situation, because I've done that before and it didn't work out well for me. But I can't leave without at least raising the possibility of a relationship between us.'

She frowned, her eyes darting away and he had his answer. 'I'm not sure what you expect me to say to that, Conrad.' She dragged in a shaky breath. 'That I don't want you to leave tomorrow? That I *have* thought about us trying to have a real relationship?'

'Have you?' he asked, his chest tight. 'You haven't brought it up. Perhaps you were just going to wave goodbye without a backward glance.' Whereas he'd never felt more torn in two, even before the pregnancy scare.

'Of course I've thought about it, and I can't see how it could work,' she whispered, her stare imploring so he wanted to hold her. 'You live in Australia. Your family is there. James. And mine is here. With Zach to consider, I'm not free to just think about myself and my own wants.'

He knew all of that, but, for him, those reasons weren't permanent obstacles. Unless it wasn't that she didn't want a relationship, she just didn't want *him*.

'You're still not over the last serious relationship you had,' she said, 'otherwise you'd have no doubts about what you want. You'd be able to forgive your brother and move on. But you're stuck, Conrad, and the worst part is that I can understand why, and I don't blame you.' She sagged, as if exhausted.

He'd nodded along as she'd spoken, unable to argue with a single word. He *did* have doubts, because he'd felt Zara slipping away. He *was* stuck, but he'd started to feel that he could move on. For Conrad, the many obstacles she'd just articulated perfectly had seemed, for a moment, surmountable. But only if they felt the same way about each other, which obviously wasn't the case.

'When I want something serious,' she went on, 'I need a man who is sure about me *and* about Zach. Even if you lived here, even if you'd worked through your betrayal and grief, that would still be a big commitment. This, us, began as nothing serious. Trying to turn it into something else just feels…too hard.' She looked up, her eyes shining with emotions but her chin raised resolutely. She'd made up her mind.

'I understand,' he said, his insides hollow. 'I've been trying to change the rules, I know that.' Because she'd changed *him*. She'd made him see that he could let go of the past. 'I just hoped you might want more than a good time.'

'I'm not sure what I want in terms of a relationship,' she went on, reaching for him and then thinking better of it, her hand falling to her lap. 'But I know I can't afford to make another mistake like last time. I have to put Zach first.'

'So I would be a mistake?' She put him in the same category as Zach's father. She didn't want him. Couldn't trust him. Wasn't willing to take a risk for him.

She shook her head violently. 'No, of course not. I don't

know. This is the first time I've had to think about relationships since I became a mother. I'm just trying to do the right thing, for me and Zach, because I don't want either of us to be hurt.' She shook her head in defeat.

'It's okay, Zara. Maybe you're right—it *is* too hard. I'm leaving and I'm not making you any promises. I don't have all the answers. I just knew how I felt—that I'd do almost anything to try and make us work. But now there's no baby, I guess we don't have to worry about it.'

He stood, needing to get away. How could he have been so wrong about her? Yes, they both still struggled with trust, but while he'd been thinking of moving his entire life to be with her and Zach, to build a relationship with her, she'd been preparing to walk away, to push him away and keep her feelings safe.

'I'm sorry,' she said, sadly, looking up at him.

'So am I.' Conrad nodded, his stomach in knots. He wanted to throw out a glib comment like, *If you ever make it to Australia, give me a call.* But he'd never felt less like smiling.

'Take care, Zara,' he said instead. 'Of Zach and yourself.' And then he left.

CHAPTER EIGHTEEN

THE NEXT DAY, with her heart torn to shreds, Zara walked past the doctor's office on the postnatal ward and automatically glanced inside. Of course, there was no chance now of a clandestine glimpse of Conrad, just as there was no point hugging her secret close as she'd done every other day of their fling. It was over. He was gone. By the time she arrived home from her early shift, his flat would be empty and he'd be on the train to London for his evening flight to Brisbane. And it was for the best.

Seeing again his relieved expression when she'd confirmed there was no baby, Zara swallowed down the vicious pang of longing in her chest and shuffled towards the nurses' station. What had she expected? That he'd want to make a family with her and Zach? That he would move his entire life to be with them?

Their final conversation spun sickeningly in her mind. How had it gone so wrong at the end? And why, when it was always meant to be temporary, when he'd always planned to return to Australia, did she feel guilty and scared that she'd made a horrible mistake in refusing to talk about a future?

'Where's the new registrar?' Sharon said in an impatient voice as she shuffled items on the desk and then located a pen. 'I need them to prescribe some painkillers for the woman in bed ten.'

Zara shrugged, making some non-committal noise as she wiped two patient names from the whiteboard behind the desk. What did she care for the new registrar? The only thing that mattered was that the new doctor wouldn't be Conrad. She swallowed convulsively, her eyes stinging.

'What are you doing?' Sharon asked, snapping Zara's attention back to the present.

Zara looked up to see that she'd wiped the whiteboard clean of every name. Defeated and close to breaking down, she replaced the whiteboard eraser, her shoulders slumping. 'I'll write the names back up,' she muttered.

'I don't care about the names,' Sharon said, taking Zara's elbow and ushering her inside the vacant nurses' office, clearly sensing something was very wrong. 'What's going on with you today?' Sharon demanded, closing the door. 'Is it Zach?'

Mention of her son made things worse. Because she'd not only let Conrad down, let herself down because she was scared to admit the depth of her feelings, she'd also taken something from Zach. Her son didn't need a mother who moped around, living a half-life. And now that Conrad was gone, she saw so clearly how her fling with him had brought her back to life. But if she tried to explain the entire situation to her friend, she'd definitely break down, the well of emotion rising in her throat almost overwhelming.

'No, Zach is fine.' Zara shook her head, trying to reassure her friend that it was nothing serious. 'I just got distracted,' Zara said feebly.

'I'm not talking about the whiteboard.' Sharon fisted her hands on her hips. 'You look close to tears. I've never seen you cry.' Sharon urged Zara into a seat, taking the one opposite. 'It's Conrad, isn't it? You weren't just having sex—

you've fallen in love with him, haven't you? And now he's going back to Australia.'

Zara spluttered, mortified. 'No! Don't be silly.' Although she'd come pretty close to falling. Why else would she feel so...bereft now that he'd left?

'Are you sure?' Sharon pressed, her expression somehow both stern and sympathetic. 'Because you've been walking around like a zombie all morning and the only change is that he's flying back to Australia later this evening.'

Feeling weak with hypoglycaemia—she had zero appetite—Zara collapsed back into the chair. 'I told you: it was just sex, but obviously it's over now. I'll be fine. I'll get over it. I'm just...adjusting, that's all.'

But now that the 'L' word was out there, she couldn't ignore it. Could Sharon be right? Had she actually fallen deeply in love with Conrad? Could that explain the frantic panic making her desperate to rewind time and handle their final conversation differently? How stupid would she be if it were true? She wasn't having his baby, but Australia was even further away than Spain, and even if she was in love with him, Conrad could never love her back, could he...?

'How did he take the news about the test being negative?' Sharon asked, her voice cautious.

Zara shrugged. 'Fine, obviously. He was relieved.'

'Was he?' Sharon frowned. 'Are you sure?'

Zara looked up sharply. 'Of course he was. We were never in a relationship and he lives in Australia. Why? What do you know...?' Fear snaked down her spine.

'Nothing,' Sharon said, her expression serious. 'It's just that yesterday when I mentioned you were going to take a test, I thought he looked...excited for a second. But maybe I was wrong.'

Zara dropped her face into her hands, her mind reeling. She'd been so caught up in her own emotions—panic that she'd made another mistake, guilt that she'd told Sharon and hurt Conrad, fear that he'd reject her, just like Lorenzo, and she'd be devastated—that she'd taken Conrad's relief at face value. She'd told him a relationship with him would be too hard and as good as shoved him onto the plane.

But what if Sharon was right? What if he'd been trying to say he wanted a relationship and she'd finally and definitively pushed him away out of fear?

Closing her eyes, she saw his face as it had been last night, his expression flat with disappointment, his stare hollow with betrayal, because she'd not only let him down, she'd also clung to the safety of her independence and kept him out emotionally. How could she have been such a coward? He'd wanted to talk about the possibility of a relationship and she'd refused, dismissed him and the idea, let him believe she didn't want him enough, when, in truth, if Conrad wanted a real relationship with her, she'd move her and Zach to the ends of the earth for him.

With a sudden gasp, she looked up. It hit her like a blow. Sharon was right. She'd fallen in love with Conrad and she'd run scared from him and from her feelings. Why, in the cold light of day, with Conrad gone, did it now seem so obvious?

Seeing the moment of realisation on Zara's face, Sharon nodded and placed her hand on Zara's knee. 'What happened after you told him about the negative test?' she asked, her voice tinged with sickening sympathy that turned Zara's veins to ice.

'I told him I was scared to make another mistake. And then to make certain I'd killed it stone dead, when he wanted to talk about the possibility of a relationship between us, I pointed out that it was too hard and pushed him away.' She hung her head in shame.

Sharon said nothing, which was somehow worse than a stern lecture or an *I told you so*.

'Oh, no...' Zara moaned, feeling sick. 'I was so terrified of making a mistake again that I've actually gone and made the biggest one of my life, haven't I?' She looked up and lasered her friend with a stare, as if demanding a denial would fix it.

But just as they had with Lorenzo, her actions had consequences. Only this time, with Conrad, those consequences were more devastating. She was in love with a wonderful man she'd sent away without telling him of her feelings.

His words from the night before returned to haunt her.

I just knew how I felt—that I'd do almost anything to try and make us work.

He'd obviously been trying to tell her he wanted more. What if he *was* ready to have a serious relationship again and wanted one with her but she'd pushed him away because she'd still been scared to risk her heart? He wouldn't likely declare his feelings and move his whole life to England on the off chance that she might one day wake up and want to date him for real. Could he forgive her? Could he possibly love her back one day? Because now that she was thinking about it, she was pretty certain that was what she felt for Conrad. That over the past few weeks, despite every barrier she'd put up against it, she had fallen in love with him.

Sharon pressed her lips together in a stubborn line. 'Could you back up a bit? Call him and tell him you want to try and do long distance, maybe tell him how you feel about him? Maybe you could visit him in Australia and see how it goes?'

Zara shook her head. Would Conrad want to hear it? 'I think it's too late,' she said, tears threatening. She'd hurt Conrad because she was scared to hope for a real relationship. She'd convinced herself she just wanted sex, nothing serious, but Conrad had been right: she'd spent years punishing herself for the mistake of Lorenzo and denying herself romance and sex and love. And she'd found all of those things with Conrad.

'Even if he wasn't leaving tonight,' she went on, 'neither of us has been in a serious relationship for years. What if he won't give me a second chance?' Conrad had so much to work through—forgiving Marcus, reuniting with James and reconciling with Tessa, looking for a consultant job. But now that she'd woken up to the fact that she was in love with him, that serious relationship she'd put off for so long while she punished herself and lived in fear was suddenly the *only* thing she wanted.

'That sounds like the old Zara talking,' Sharon said softly. 'The one who seemed to be going through the motions of her life, not needing anyone else. The one whose smile was rare. If I'm honest, that Zara was a bit uptight.' Sharon smiled apologetically and reached for Zara's hand. 'You've come alive this past month.'

Zara nodded, her smile wobbling and her eyes smarting with tears. 'I know. It's him.'

'It's the two of you together,' Sharon stated. 'You complement each other. That's when the magic happens, when sex and connection turn into love.'

Zara sniffed, trying to pull herself together. They were at work, after all. And just because she loved him, didn't mean he had the same feelings for her. Could he want her and Zach? Because they came as a pair. She needed to apologise for running scared and find out.

Suddenly energised, Zara stood. 'I'll call him when my shift ends. Before he gets on that plane.' She glanced at the watch pinned to her uniform for the time. She could tell him how stupid she'd been. Confess that she had feelings for him and ask if there was any way they could make a real, serious relationship work. No more secrets. Should she also tell him she was in love with him? Or would he think that was too much, too soon?

'There's the Zara I've wanted to see all these years,' Sharon said with a smile of encouragement. 'We're quiet today and overstaffed. Why don't you finish up early? Call him now? I'll cover you.'

'Really?' Zara asked, her eyes filling with tears.

'Of course,' Sharon said. 'I've been rooting for you to find someone for years. Don't keep me hanging. Go.'

'Thanks. I'll let you know how it goes.' Throwing her arms around Sharon, Zara rushed to the doctor's office, where she'd left her bag, coat and phone.

CHAPTER NINETEEN

FROM THE DERBY to London train, Conrad opened his emails in an attempt to forget about the devastating final conversation he'd had with Zara. Last night, after leaving Zara's place, he'd messaged his parents to tell them he'd be leaving as planned and would see them soon. Until that very moment, he'd agonised over the decision of whether to leave or stay. But what was the point in delaying his departure from the UK when Zara had made it clear that she'd had her fun and that their fling was over?

Hollowness built inside him at the memories of their fight. Not that they'd raised their voices. It had been more of a quiet acceptance that they'd finally arrived at the end of their journey. Only for him, it hadn't been over. Before they'd become distracted by the possibility of a pregnancy and by Zara's explanations about Sharon, he'd wanted to force Zara's hand. To confront her with the idea of them seeing each other again, either in England, or Australia.

But he'd soon realised there'd been no sense pushing it; she didn't want *him*. She was scared to risk her heart, scared to make a mistake, scared to expose Zach to a man who might not stick around. And Conrad couldn't blame her. It wasn't as if he even lived in the UK. Not only did Zara have to think about Zach, just as Conrad needed to look out for James, but their situation was also complicated by a whole world of distance.

With a sigh of inevitability, and to distract himself from the pain gnawing a hole in his chest, Conrad opened the email reply from his mother. He scanned the message, reaching the last paragraph.

In other news, Tessa called. It seems she's turned a bit of a corner and is feeling up to being more social. She brought James to visit yesterday, asked about your travels and then asked if Dad and I can help out with school pickups when she goes back to work...

Conrad tried to focus on the words his mother had written, but the news didn't fill him with the relief he'd imagined. He was happy for his parents, for Tessa, for James. Families needed to pull together, especially in times of grief. But as something shifted from Conrad's shoulders, a weight he hadn't known he'd carried easing, he realised with a start that the mess he'd run away from wasn't his responsibility. Maybe because ever since the night he'd told Zara about Marcus's betrayal, he'd also started talking to his brother in his head. He'd taken Zara's advice and begun to properly work through forgiving Marcus. He still had much grieving to do, of course. But that was no reason for him to be alone, to pass by a relationship with an amazing woman who'd brought *him* back to life.

Zara had been right—he *had* been stuck and hiding from his feelings. She'd helped him to see that he was still clinging to that sense of betrayal, because he was scared to let anyone close again or to fall in love. Scared that he'd lose another person he cared about or be betrayed or rejected.

Only he hadn't been able to keep Zara out. She'd found a way under his guard anyway.

But at the first sign of trouble, he'd run again. He'd allowed her to push him away when he'd wanted to fight for them, to tell her his feelings and how he wanted a serious relationship. How he wanted her *and* Zach.

Sending a hurried reply to his mother, Conrad fought his rising sense of panic. Life was too short for regrets. He might have said that a hundred times, but it was only with Zara that he'd truly believed it. He saw now, with crystal clarity, that he'd been going through the motions before he'd met Zara. He'd called her out on hiding behind the mistake she'd made, on punishing herself, when he'd been hiding too. For all his talk of embracing the good times, the best times he'd had in years had been with Zara. Only a complete idiot would walk away from that before making sure there was no way in hell he could make it work.

Zara's reproach resounded in his head, as if she were in the train carriage with him, hurtling towards London.

I'm not sure what you expect me to say to that, Conrad. That I don't want you to leave...? That I have *thought about us trying to have a real relationship?*

Did that mean that if he lived in England, or if she lived in Australia, she'd want a serious relationship with him? Didn't he owe it to himself, to them both, to find out? Now!

Fresh panic seized him by the throat. He couldn't leave England like this, sloping off with his tail between his legs, scared to tell her that he wanted more than a fling. Scared to know if she wanted the same. He wasn't ready to give up on them just because they had commitments and lived in different countries. There must be a way to make something so good work. He'd move heaven and earth to enable them to be together if that was what she wanted. But first, he had to tell her what *he* wanted.

With his mind working properly for the first time in what felt like days, he typed a few extra lines to his mother.

Change of plan this end. Might not make flight today after all. Will keep you posted.

He pressed send, jerked to his feet and grabbed his bag. Then, manhandling his suitcase from the luggage rack, he positioned himself in the exit, so when the train stopped at the next station, he could get off and swap platforms.

His heart galloped with yearning and possibility. It wasn't over, not when he'd neglected to tell her that his feelings for her were no longer casual or *nothing serious*. And he needed to do that in person. Zara was at work. She wouldn't answer her phone if he called. There was only one way to make her understand how he felt about her and that was to head back to Derby.

CHAPTER TWENTY

WITH HER HEART THUNDERING, Zara ducked into the doctor's office on the postnatal ward and fished her phone out of her bag. With trembling fingers, she held her breath as the phone powered on, willing time to stand still or go backwards so she could make this right. What if he couldn't wait to get back to the Sunshine Coast, where he would easily forget about her and their brief fling? What if he got on the plane before she could tell him she was sorry and that she loved him? What if she missed her chance to be happy because she'd made the massive mistake of pushing him away?

With her veins full of icy panic, the screen of her phone lit up. She was just about to unlock it and dial Conrad, when several alert sounds came in, one after another.

Ping, ping, ping.

She opened the most recent text, elated to see it was from Conrad.

Phone low on charge. Can't call again but we need to talk.

Zara sagged with relief. He wanted to talk. That sounded promising. Seeing she also had three voicemails from him, she grabbed her coat and bag and put the phone to her ear so she could listen to the message as she walked to the car.

Hopefully Conrad would have recharged his phone somewhere by the time she called him back.

She'd just stepped from the office, his voicemail playing in her ear—'Zara, we need to talk…'—when she looked up to find Conrad striding down the ward towards her pulling his suitcase.

Dropping the phone to her side, she gaped at the wonderful sight of him in person. 'What are you doing here?' she said, her throat raw with longing, her mind foggy with confusion. 'Did you miss your flight?'

He shook his head, dropped his bags to the floor and cupped her face between both his palms. Then his lips covered hers and he dragged her into his arms.

Zara dropped everything, including her phone, which clattered to the floor with its voicemail from Conrad still playing. She tunnelled her fingers into his hair and parted her lips, kissing him back with everything she had, as if it were her last chance ever. She was too high to care that the other midwives might see, not to mention the patients. He was here. He wanted to talk. He was kissing her. Nothing else mattered.

She clung to him, yelping in protest when he tore his mouth from hers. 'I need to talk to you,' he said, panting hard, his stare flicking wildly between her eyes.

She nodded, dragging him into the doctor's office and closing the door, her hand in his. 'Conrad, I'm so sorry about last night,' she said, launching into her apology. 'Are you okay? What happened?' She swept her gaze over him, still doubting he was real.

Conrad shook his head. 'I'm fine. I got off the train. I came back to tell you I've figured everything out,' he said, gripping her hand as if he'd never let her go. 'I'm in love with you, Zara.'

Zara frowned, her heart clenching with wild longing. His words made no sense. Had she heard him right? He loved her?

'I realised it on the platform in Kettering,' he went on, scrubbing a hand through his hair. 'Wherever the hell that is.'

Despite the confusion and euphoria ransacking her body, Zara laughed and Conrad cupped her face with an indulgent smile.

'I was sitting on the train,' he rushed on, 'and I realised that I'd run away again, without telling you how I feel about you.'

'Me too,' she cried, gripping him tighter. 'I'm so sorry that I pushed you away. That I made you doubt. I want you to know that I *do* trust you. That you could never be a mistake. That I don't care how hard it is, I want to make us work.'

He cut her off with another kiss. 'I know you're scared,' he said when he pulled back, 'and I am too. But I love you, harder than I've ever been in love before.'

She tried to interject but he shook his head and continued. 'You were right about me. I *was* hiding from the past, running away from it, shielding myself with casual relationships so I didn't have to face the risk of anyone else betraying me or finding out that no one could ever love me. But my fear isn't enough of a reason to walk away from you, from the most real relationship I've ever had. I want you, Zara. You *and* Zach.'

'Conrad,' she said, trying to get a word in, to tell him that *she* loved him, too, but he rushed on.

'I'm ready to let go of the past, Zara, and actually build a real, serious relationship with you, if you'll let me.'

'Conrad, I want that, too. But what about your job in Australia? Your family? James?' Tears stung Zara's eyes, his words were so wonderful, but she'd still have to let him go, at least in the short term.

'Yes.' He nodded, his stare softening. 'I still need to address all of that, but that shouldn't stop us being together. I don't know how exactly—I'll move here, or you and Zach can come to Brisbane or we'll alternate. The point is, I want to be with you. I love you, Zara. That's what I want—us. You, me and Zach. But…what do you want?'

Zara laughed, her tears finally spilling free. 'Well, if you'd let me get a word in, I'd have told you that I want to be with you too. That's why I was leaving early just now, to call you and tell you how I feel. I didn't want you to get in the plane without knowing.' She looked down from the joy sparkling in his beautiful eyes, ashamed. 'I'm so sorry about last night. The way I pushed you away.' She looked up and met his stare. 'You're right: I was scared. Terrified, actually. For a moment, I thought history was repeating itself with that pregnancy scare. I thought you could never love me. Never want me and Zach. But this, with you, has been the first real, grown-up relationship I've ever had.'

'I know it's moving crazy fast.' Conrad frowned, his stare so intense, she gasped. 'But we owe it to ourselves to see where this could go. I know you're scared to make another mistake, but I won't let you down, Zara. You or Zach.'

She nodded. 'I know you won't. And it's *not* too fast.

I've waited six years for this, for *you*. We could never be a mistake, because I finally know now what love truly feels like. Real, grown-up love. I love you too, Conrad.'

His brows pinched together as hope bloomed in his eyes. 'You do?'

'Yes.' Zara laughed, cried, threw her arms around his neck and pressed her lips to his stunned mouth. 'I didn't properly realise it until today when Sharon helpfully pointed it out. But somewhere along my wild sexual adventure, I fell in love with you. I think it might have been when I watched you build your first snowman.'

Conrad grinned, kissed her and then pulled back, falling serious. 'About Zach. I know he's your top priority, but I want you to know that I love him too, because he's yours. I want to help you raise him and one day, when you're ready, I want him to be *ours*.'

Zara blinked, her throat aching. 'You are so wonderful.' Joy burst past her lips in a wave of laughter he kissed up as he wiped the tears from her cheeks.

They stared at each other with goofy grins on their faces for so long, Zara felt guilty for hogging the office. 'What shall we do now?' she asked, her hands caressing his face as if committing him to memory, knowing that she couldn't keep him, because he still needed to go back to Australia. 'Can you still make your flight?'

She would miss him. But she was already planning to apply for some annual leave so she could take Zach to visit him in Brisbane.

'There's more snow due, apparently,' Conrad said, drawing her into his arms once more. 'I saw it on the news before my phone died. If you'll have me, I'll come home with you tonight and take another flight to Brisbane in a few days.'

She smiled. 'I think that could be arranged. You can't fly anywhere if you're snowed in, maybe even trapped in my bed.'

His smile widened, his stare loaded with sensual promise. 'How soon before you could visit me in Australia? I need to tie up loose ends back home, to see James and my parents, but then I want to come back here, to be with you. To make this work. This time our relationship will be out in the open and *very* serious, so I hope you're prepared.'

Zara smiled, laughed, pressed her lips to his. 'I'll only come to Australia if you promise me a tour of the Sunshine Coast. It's been a long time since I've worn a bikini.'

'I think that could be arranged,' he replied, throwing her words back at her. Then he dragged her close for another deep and passionate kiss.

Neither of them noticed the office door being pushed open or Sharon stepping aside so anyone within peering distance could see them kiss. It was only when the applause and cheering started that Zara broke away from Conrad, and they turned, blushing to see their audience of teary-eyed midwives and mums cradling their new babies.

'Let's get out of here,' Zara said to Conrad, once her laughter had died down. 'We can pick up Zach from school and make plans for our visit to Australia. He'll be so excited.'

Conrad reached for her hand and they left the ward to more whoops and cheering, the loudest from Sharon, who yelled, 'Go get him, Zara.'

Zara met Conrad's beaming stare, her heart ready to explode. 'I fully intend to,' she said, slinging her arm around his waist.

He pressed a kiss to her lips, smiled that killer smile and winked. 'I'm all yours.'

EPILOGUE

One year later

THAT JANUARY IN BRISBANE, summer temperatures reached record highs. So the only sensible place for a wedding was on the beach. North of Brisbane, on a white sand cove on the island of K'gari, Zara and Conrad stood under a white linen awning, making their vows before a small gathering of friends and family.

Zara curled her bare toes into the sand and gripped Conrad's hands tighter in hers, certain that for the rest of her life, she'd hold him close—her best friend, her lover, her husband. Love and passion and devotion shone from his grey eyes, all but melting the simple strapless wedding dress she wore clean off. She couldn't wait to get him alone, couldn't wait to start this new adventure with him: their marriage. But first, she planned to enjoy every second of their wedding day.

'As Zara and Conrad have exchanged their vows of togetherness and exchanged rings, symbols of for ever,' their wedding celebrant said to their small congregation of guests, which included Pam, Zara's mother, and Sharon and Rod, who'd also made the journey, 'they move forward, their lives entwined as husband and wife and as parents to Zach.'

Their loved ones cheered and clapped as Zara surged up on tiptoes, her lips clashing with Conrad's in their first kiss as husband and wife. As always, she lost herself to their chemistry, holding him tight, kissing him hard, laughing against his smile, because falling in love with Conrad Reed had brought her endless joy.

'I love you,' he said, pulling back to peer down at her with desire and something close to adoration. And the feelings were very much reciprocated.

'I love you too,' she said, laughing through her tears as she reflected on the past year, where they'd bounced around between Australia and England, finally settling in Brisbane where they now worked in the same hospital.

Her lips found his once more and everything slotted perfectly into place. But she could only enjoy kissing her new husband for a few seconds, as two little boys, their two ring-bearers, Zach and James, pulled them apart with embarrassed squeals.

Conrad laughed, his hands resting on Zach's and James's shoulders. Zara's heart burst with love for him. He was such an amazing father and uncle, and the boys had become close friends.

As their guests surged forward to offer congratulations, hugs and kisses, Zara counted herself the luckiest woman alive. She had everything she could possibly want.

'Congratulations,' Sharon said as she hugged Zara close. 'I told you that you needed to live a little, have a little fun, didn't I? And look how it all turned out.'

Zara laughed at her smug friend, her stare meeting Conrad's. 'You're right. It's been the best time of my life.' Not that she regretted a single second of the journey that had brought her to Conrad, the man she loved.

Later, after photos on the beach, her husband snagged her hand and held her back as their guests wandered back to the lodge where their wedding party would take place.

Stepping into his arms, she raised her lips to his kiss. He cupped her face, that secret smile in his eyes as he peered down at her. 'Any regrets?' he asked playfully, secure in her love because she showed him what he meant to her every day.

'Just one,' she said, slipping her hands around his waist. 'Our celebrations are going to be way too long. I have to wait hours before I can get my hands on all this.' She slid her palms up his chest, over his white linen shirt, caressing his defined pecs.

'I know what you mean,' he said, his stare full of sensual promise as he gave her body a heated glance. 'But that's what a honeymoon is for. I love the boys, dearly,' he said about James and Zach, 'but I can't wait to have you all to myself for an entire week. Brace yourself for another wild sexual adventure, Mrs Reed.' He grinned and brushed her lips with his.

Zara melted into his arms, grateful to Conrad's parents, who would watch Zach for the week they'd be away in Fiji.

'So you think you're the man for the job, do you?' she teased, sighing into another kiss. She wasn't going to be able to keep her hands or her lips off him today.

Playfully, he cracked his knuckles. 'I'll certainly give it my best shot.'

They smiled, kissed again, this one turning heated enough to make Zara's breath catch.

'Mum...stop kissing,' Zach called from across the beach.

Zara and Conrad laughed and headed after their friends

and family, arm in arm. 'I'm not sure I can make that promise,' she said, looking up at the love of her life.

'Me neither,' Conrad said, pausing to press his lips to hers. 'But I can promise that I'll always love you.'

'Me too.'

* * * * *

Las Vegas Night With Her Best Friend

Tina Beckett

MILLS & BOON

Three-times Golden Heart® finalist **Tina Beckett** learned to pack her suitcases almost before she learned to read. Born to a military family, she has lived in the United States, Puerto Rico, Portugal and Brazil. In addition to travelling, Tina loves to cuddle with her pug, Alex, spend time with her family, and hit the trails on her horse. Learn more about Tina from her website, or 'friend' her on Facebook.

To my family.

Thank you for being my rock!

PROLOGUE

EVA MILAGRE LOOKED at the first picture in the small stack and blinked. Tried to process what she was seeing. Her last name might mean *miracle* in Portuguese, but right now it didn't look like even a miracle could save her marriage.

"You investigated Brad?"

Her friend on the barstool next to her wrapped an arm around her shoulder. "I'm so sorry, Evie. After you told me his hours had been all wonky and that he'd been evasive about his last overnight trip, it sent up several red flags."

Her gaze didn't waver. The picture showed her husband hugging another woman. A raven-haired beauty that made Evie feel tired and rumpled in her scrubs with strands of hair escaping from her clip and falling wildly around her face. It could be something totally innocent. An embrace after closing a deal at his investment firm. But there was no way Darby would be showing her pictures of her husband hugging another woman if it wasn't something bad. Really bad.

Her thumb hesitated—Evie didn't want to see anything else. "And the rest of these?"

"They're worse. I hoped he'd prove me wrong. He didn't."

Her friend turned toward her, holding out her hand. "I didn't think you'd believe me without those. I know how much you love him."

The thing was, Evie was no longer sure that she did. The pictures just sealed the deal. She handed them back. "And his firm?"

Brad hadn't shown her the financial statements for his business this year, which she found odd as well. He'd always been so proud of what he'd accomplished, going out on his own almost three years ago. When she'd asked about them, he said he was late in filing them this year.

"He filed for bankruptcy a month ago and gave up the lease on his office space."

Bankruptcy? God. He'd been leaving home every single day at the same time, kissing her on the mouth and telling her he'd miss her before walking out the door of their home. She'd heard nothing about any kind of trouble. And she'd put a big chunk of her own money toward him opening that business and had trusted him to...

She'd trusted him. Too much. And it looked like she was going to pay the price for that. Swallowing hard, she bit back tears of anger and frustration. "Thank you. I just can't fathom how he would do something like this."

"I know. I can't believe it, either. We both went to college with the guy, and he was voted the most likely to succeed."

"It looks like he succeeded alright." Her laugh held more than a hint of desperation as her fingers tightened around the stack of photos. "Only not in the area I expected." All she could see in her mind's eye was the woman he was evidently having an affair with. Since they hadn't had sex in the last six months, the reason made far too much sense—he'd used the excuse of work overload and stress, and she hadn't challenged him on it. In fact, she'd been secretly relieved, since she could relate to both of those things. She'd been feeling stressed and tired herself recently, their talks of having a baby going up on a shelf until things settled down. Thank God they weren't still trying. What if she'd been pregnant?

"Do you want to stay with me for a few days?"

A sense of relief washed over her. At least she wouldn't have to face him. Tonight, anyway. "That would be wonderful." She held up her hand for another drink and after the bartender brought it over, she took a gulp of the spiked fruity drink. "I can't promise I'll be in any shape to drive after this." She put her glass back to her lips and drank again.

"Don't worry. I've got this."

"Thanks." She picked up her phone and pushed the button that would connect her with her soon-to-be ex. She wasn't surprised when it went straight to voice mail. She decided to just get it over with. "I won't be home tonight, but when I do come back to the apartment, I expect you to be packed up and gone."

The second she disconnected, her phone rang. It was Brad. She didn't answer. She was pretty sure he would figure out that the jig was up. But she hoped he did as she asked. Because tomorrow morning she was going to head to town, find a lawyer and file for divorce. It was something that probably would have happened, anyway, even without Darby's news. Neither one of them seemed happy with where they were anymore.

Her friend glanced at the phone she'd placed on the polished bar after silencing it. "Do you think he'll leave without a fight?"

Evie took another drink. "I don't know. I'm pretty sure he has someplace to go, unless she's married, too."

"She's not."

Another laugh came out. "You are nothing if not thorough, Darbs."

Her friend gave her a searching look. "I hope you know this is not how I wanted this to play out."

Now, that was the first thing her friend had said that she took issue with. "You and Max always had issues with Brad."

Ugh. Why had she even said Max's name in the same sentence as Brad's? She and Darby and Max had always been close friends. But something had changed between her and Max when she started dating Brad and they got married. He hadn't even come to her wedding, saying that he had a medical conference to go to. His absence had cut deep. And he'd made it pretty clear, even before the wedding, that he was no fan of her fiancé.

"We both cared enough about you to tell you there were some areas of concern."

Except Max really hadn't spelled out anything specific. He'd just seemed peeved whenever Brad was around. Soon, he'd practically dropped out of her life.

"And yet you never investigated him before now."

"I was a cop when you got married, remember? Running an illicit investigation is frowned on in those circles."

Why was Evie blaming her friend for something she'd

gotten herself into? "I'm sorry, Darbs. I had no right to say that."

Her friend's transition from being a police detective to a private investigator had been heartbreaking. A bullet to her leg would have left her friend chained to a desk, so she'd decided to resign and open up her own PI office, where literally chasing down suspects was no longer required. Instead, she chased them via a keyboard or, in Brad's case, through the lens of a camera.

"It's okay." Darby shifted in her seat, barely catching her cane before it fell from its perch. Her limp wasn't as noticeable as it had been years ago, but Evie knew it still hurt when she'd been on her feet too long. "I can investigate now, though. And so don't expect me not to run your next beau through the wringer."

"Next beau? Nope. I think it's one and done as far as that goes."

"Famous last words, Evie."

"Famous or not, they're true." And she meant it. She didn't see herself going down her current path with anyone else. How could she ever trust a man again? First Max backed out of her life, and now her husband. That didn't mean she'd be entering the nearest convent and taking a vow of chastity. It just meant she was no longer going to equate sleeping with someone with being in love with that someone. No matter whom it might be.

CHAPTER ONE

"DAMMIT." TODAY HADN'T started off well for Maximilian Hunt. He'd gotten numbers back on two of his patients and neither one of those reports had been good. He leaned back in his chair and pinched the bridge of his nose, trying to staunch the vague rumblings of a headache. He could appease the migraine gods by telling himself that neither of those patients were without options. Both had been newly diagnosed and were just starting treatment. But he always hoped for a misdiagnosis that went in the patient's favor, rather than the other way around.

He made a note to call both of them in for an appointment to discuss things. One of his least favorite tasks in his job.

A knock at the door made him push aside those thoughts. "Come in."

The door opened, and Evie peered past it. He could barely see her face.

He hadn't seen her in almost a month. And it's how he'd hoped to keep it. Ever since Darby had called him to tell him the news a year ago, that Evie's marriage was over and the reason for it, he'd had a hard time not chasing down Brad and letting him know how little he thought of him. The bastard had hurt someone he cared about very much.

But now, Evie was divorced, and she could move forward with her life. Darby had been on him to join them for dinner, like old times before Brad had come on the scene, but he wasn't sure he wanted to go back to those times or seeing Evie every week.

And he wasn't sure why.

Oh, hell, he knew. And that's precisely why he was so reluctant. Seeing her with another man had churned his gut in a way he hadn't expected. In a way he hadn't wanted to dissect. He still didn't.

His college friend opened the door a little farther and frowned from across the room. "Do you mind if I talk to you for a minute?"

"Not at all." He motioned to the two chairs that sat across from him. He did mind. Kind of. But there was no way he was going to say that. Especially not when she sauntered across the room, her hips encased in her snug skirt swaying ever so slightly with every step.

Dammit!

The word from a few moments earlier swept through his skull again, crashing into one side of his brain with enough force to make him wince.

He gritted his teeth and waited for her to take a seat. This was why he'd been happy to see a wedding band on her ring finger. He was attracted to her. Even when they'd been just friends. But he knew himself well enough to know that he was the last person that should be in a relationship with anyone. Work took up eighty-five to ninety percent of his brain cells, leaving precious little to invest in anything more than the friendship he, Evie and Darby had always had. Mainly because it had always been light and easy.

At least until one specific night had destroyed any semblance of light. Or easy. He and Evie had kissed under the glittering lights of the Las Vegas strip after the trio had gone to see a production of *Wicked*. Darby had caught a taxi and gone home, and left Max with Evie. She'd looked up at him, laughing at something stupid he'd said, and it just happened. That kiss. It had only lasted a second—a light playful peck that he hadn't expected to rock him to his core, but it had. And it was a mistake. Because just like the two main characters in the musical they'd just seen, their paths led them in opposite directions. He'd been married to his job. He still was. And Evie was married to... Well, he wasn't sure what she was married to now, but it wasn't Brad. Not anymore. And that made him feel...

Uneasy. Because that kiss had happened just before she started dating Brad. And he sure as hell didn't want things to go back to that time before her marriage. Because he might want to kiss her again. And he would end up hurting her. Just like her ex had. Well, not in the same way, since Max would never cheat, but he also wasn't good relationship material.

And Evie was not a one-night-stand kind of girl. She never had been, and he'd respected the hell out of that. But Max could never give anyone more than that. And he had no desire to change. Life was easier when it was just him.

When she made no move to say anything, he decided to push a little bit. "You wanted to talk about something?"

"More like ask something. I'm kind of desperate actually, but feel free to say no." Her mouth twisted in a way that might have made him smile under different circumstances.

"Desperate?"

"Yes. I've asked several other doctors, but they all turned me down."

For what? Did he even want to know? Especially since his head was imagining all kinds of scenarios. All of them revisiting that kiss from years ago.

"Turned you down for what?"

"The gala."

Hell. The annual hospital fundraising event? She'd always brought Brad in the past and he'd pointedly avoided crossing paths with the couple any more than necessary, other than the cursory greetings he gave most of his other acquaintances. And he'd made it a point never to go to those galas.

"Are you asking me to be your date?" The words slipped out before he'd had a chance to examine them for stupidity.

Her eyes widened as if horrified. "My...date?"

Okay, so that's obviously not what she meant. And he felt like a fool for even thinking along those lines. But did she have to look so stupefied?

Yes, she did. Because it helped him relax into his seat.

Before he could think of a funny rejoinder, not that there was anything humorous about the situation, she quickly added, "I—I wanted to ask for your help planning it."

Did that mean she already had a date? He pushed that question from his head. He was feeling more and more angry with the way this conversation was going.

"I thought there was a small committee that handled the gala every year."

"There was. But Dr. Parker, who normally headed it, moved to Texas to teach at a university there. And the rest of the committee stepped down, saying it was time to hand the reins over to someone else. I kind of fell into the role. And was assured that it was a piece of cake."

"How big of a piece?"

That made her smile. "Like maybe a whole sheet cake. And so far, no one wants anything to do with it. The venue has been the same for the past ten years, so that is already set up. And I'm hoping the same goes for the caterer and so forth."

He was evidently her last stop, since she'd been turned down by every other person she'd asked. So she actually was desperate, although it stung a bit that she acted like she had nowhere else to turn. But still, he wasn't sure he could stomach disappointing her. Especially after the year she'd had. She'd had to sell her apartment and split the proceeds with her ex despite the fact that she'd sunk a bunch of money into his investment firm. According to Darbs, anyway, who told him way more than he wanted to know. It made Max want to step in and fix everything, and he knew he couldn't. Not this time. But maybe this was one area where he could help.

"So what would you need from me?"

"Just to be a sounding board and maybe make some phone calls to past sponsors to see if they wanted to help with this year's gala. I know Darby doesn't work here, and she won't be involved, but maybe we can all meet for dinner—it'll kind of be like old times. I'm sure she won't mind if we talk shop for part of it."

Was she making sure he knew that they wouldn't be dining alone?

Darby had still been pestering him to join them, and he'd always managed to have something else to do. And he wasn't even sure why. Except that having Evie here in his office was messing with his equilibrium, the way it used to before she'd gotten married. It had to be some weird phenomenon like muscle memory that was coming back to haunt him.

But trying to explain that to her wouldn't be in anyone's best interest. Because she might think his interest in her was more than just friendship and it wasn't. He wouldn't let it be, because it could only end one way: with their friendship imploding in the worst possible way. Max was not interested in relationships. Never had been. But for now, all he could do was nod and repeat her words back.

"Just like old times."

"So you'll help me?"

"Yes. When is the gala again?"

She snorted. "That's right. You don't attend them."

"Nope. And don't expect that to change, just because I'm helping plan it."

Her head tilted. "Is that a challenge?"

"Just a statement of fact."

She gave a smile that had his libido sitting up and taking notice despite all of his inner speeches. "Well, we'll just see about that, shall we?"

What had she thought she was doing? Max had made it pretty clear that he'd been avoiding her for the last year—actually it had been longer than that—and she had to go and flirt with him?

It wasn't exactly flirting. It was the back-and-forth repartee they used to have before something had changed. When their friendship was light and easy, and so uncomplicated. Before her marriage.

She'd thought that had been the problem. He hadn't exactly liked Brad, and he'd made it pretty clear once they started dating. Had said that he didn't trust the guy. She'd laughed off his warnings at the time. But, looking back, it was easy to see who'd been the better judge of character.

But she wasn't about to admit that to him. Or to anyone, except for Darby, even though Max had to know by now what had broken up her marriage.

Maybe some part of her was still looking to get back to those earlier times, because they'd been happy. *She'd* been happy. Their little friendship trio. Her and Max and Darby. Her best friends in the world. In fact, at one time she thought that she and Max might even... But then he'd suddenly pulled away, and she'd been wounded deeply. Brad had come along soon after that with his smooth confidence and obvious interest. It had been a balm to her bruised ego. The rest was history. Only instead of bringing back Max, it had seemed to push him away even further. But then she'd gotten married and with the business of life had been able to push the friendship to a back burner. Until now. There'd been a reason that he was the last person she'd asked to help her with the gala, and she had fully expected him to refuse.

Only he hadn't.

She laid her head on her desk and groaned, letting the cool surface of the wood absorb some of the embarrassment over that coy smile she'd sent him as she'd stood to leave his office. She hadn't meant anything by it. But what if he thought she did? If she'd been hoping to mend fences with him, that was probably off the table now.

Her eyes tracked up to look at the clock on her wall. Time to get back to work. She had a busy day ahead of her. Especially now, since she'd just bitten off more cake than she could possibly chew. And there was a staff meeting at three with the hospital's new CEO about the gala. He wanted all department heads there. Evie wasn't a department head, but because she was now in charge of planning the event, he'd sent a memo specifically asking that she be there. So she would. Maybe the meeting would even land a few more volunteers to help with the planning.

Max's headache hadn't let up and he'd barely made it to the smaller of the two conference rooms before Arthur Robbins, the hospital's new CEO, got up to speak. He slid into his chair and caught sight of Evie sitting a short distance away. She hadn't noticed him yet, since she was talking to someone to her left, and it gave him a chance to properly study her. She was a little thinner than she'd been a year ago, probably due to the stress of the divorce. But it was good to see her smiling again. She hadn't seemed happy in…a while.

And how the hell did he know that? Because while he might not have been chummy with her over the last few years, he still found himself noticing things about her when he did see her. And the last year of her marriage with Brad had found her smiles few and far between. She'd become serious and focused on her work. Kind of like Max. Not that that was a bad thing. But Evie's personality used to be geared more toward being happy and lighthearted. She'd always had a witty rejoinder. But those had practically disappeared.

He'd glimpsed a bit of that lightheartedness just as she was getting ready to leave his office after asking him for help. She'd thrown him a look and a grin that had shifted something in his chest.

Dr. Robbins got up and received a smattering of applause as he took the podium. Max shifted his attention from Evie to the man. Robbins had once been a plastic surgeon and although he was in his mid-fifties, he could easily pass for early thirties. And with his easy smile and confident bearing, he was probably the perfect person to take on the role after Morgan Howard had retired last year.

"Thanks for coming. I've gotten to meet most of you in person over the last several weeks, but for those of you who don't know me, I'm Art Robbins, and I look forward to working alongside you to make this hospital reach its highest potential."

Something about the way he said that made Max shift

in his chair. Was he saying the hospital had lacked something under the last CEO? Morgan Howard had been much loved, his compassionate nature evident in almost everything he did.

Robbins went on to talk about the gala and how he'd looked at the figures the event had brought in over the last several years. "And there's no denying they're solid numbers, but I feel they could be even better with a little work. I'd like to thank Eva Milagre for heading up the committee. A committee that will make this the best event in this hospital's history."

The man had mangled the pronunciation of Evie's last name, making *Milagre* somehow rhyme with *pedigree*. And yet, when Max glanced her way, she hadn't moved in her chair.

"But we can only make it the best if we all plan our schedules so that as many of us are there as possible. After all, it's a party, and who doesn't like to attend a good party?"

Had Evie gone to the man and complained about him not attending the party in the past? Had that been what the smile in his office had been about? Whatever part of him that had been moved by it hardened to stone.

"And it *will* be a party, but I'd also like to think of this as a work event. Where we can go and mingle with prospective donors. Having faces to put with the names people see listed in the hospital's foyer is always a good thing. I really want to see those donations double or even triple this year. So I want each of you to pick up a flyer and a sign-up sheet that I have up here at the front. Please encourage your folks who aren't scheduled to work that night to attend if at all possible. Again, look at it as a work event, just like the meeting this morning."

Although the man smiled as he said the words, had Max sensed a vague threat hidden in there? When he glanced at Evie again, she was staring back at him, giving him a slight shrug. He had no idea what that meant. But he planned on finding out. Just as soon as this meeting was over.

Fifteen minutes later, it was, and he went up and got the flyer and sign-up sheet while the CEO was in conversation with someone else. He waited at the back of the room and watched Evie go up to the man and shake hands with him as if sealing a deal. He tensed further before ducking out of the room and waiting for her to appear. When she did, he struggled to keep his tone civil as he asked her to join him for coffee. She glanced at him, blinking as if surprised at the request, but nodded. Once they were in the cafeteria, seated with their cups, he studied her for a second before saying anything.

"Was Robbins's speech for my benefit?"

"Wh-what?"

"You know, talking about everyone needing to attend the gala. It's never been a requirement before and we both know it. Is that what you meant when you said 'we'll just see about that'?"

There was a long pause and then understanding dawned in her eyes. "No, of course not. My saying that was a joke. I had no idea Robbins was going to talk about any of that today. I'm as shocked as you are. And for your information, I don't agree with making it a required work event. It used to be looked at as part of the perks of being a staff member, that you could get dressed up in your finest clothes and have fun and eat a fantastic meal on the hospital's nickel. I think what he's done will kill the spirit of the event."

So she hadn't put him up to it. Now, Max felt like a jerk for even thinking it. He knew her better than that. At least he used to think he did. Was he just searching for reasons to be mad at her? If so, that wasn't fair to her.

"I'm sorry, Evie. I think I'm just looking for someone to blame and you happened to be a convenient target."

"It's okay."

He reached across and touched her hand, the warmth of her skin immediately waking up something inside of him. Pulling away, he smiled. "Thanks, Evie."

"Not a problem. And I hate to bring it up, but is there a good time when we can meet to talk about some of the specifics? I can ask Darby to come and we can make a night of it, if you want. But if staff is going to be, er, *encouraged* to attend, then our guest list just increased by about a hundred people from what we had last year. Robbins also wants me to try to increase our pool of sponsors by at least fifty. So that brings the guest list even higher."

"Maybe you should have told him you'd do that as soon as he learned how to pronounce your name."

She laughed. "I'm used to it."

Max lifted one eyebrow. "I remember being schooled on how to say it when we first met."

Her nose crinkled in a way he found adorable. "Because people who are my friends and family should be able to pronounce it."

Even after she'd gotten married, she'd kept her last name, just hyphenated it for documents. But at work, she'd always just been Dr. Milagre. He assumed if he and Evie had gotten married she would have done the same.

That pulled him up short. They weren't married and never would be, so it was a moot point. "Speaking of meeting to talk about logistics, most of my evenings are free." He didn't exactly have a big social calendar, and although he dated casually from time to time, there was no one in the picture at the moment. "And I'll see if I can come up with a list of people who might want to attend the gala as sponsors."

"That would be great, Max. I'll text Darbs and see what dates she has available." She stood. "I have an appointment in a few minutes, so I need to go, but I'll touch base later this afternoon on possible meeting times and places."

That was the third time she'd mentioned inviting Darby. Was that her way of saying that she was uncomfortable being alone with him? He was probably reading too much into something that he should be thankful for. Because she might not be worried about them being alone, he sure as hell was, and he wasn't sure why.

"Sounds good."

With that, she disposed of her trash and headed out of the cafeteria, leaving him at the table to mull over his options as far as avoiding going to the gala. From what Robbins had said, there were no options. And since he

had patients of his own to see, he waited for the elevator
Evie had gotten into to close its doors before he headed
out there himself.

CHAPTER TWO

"HELLO, MRS. COLLINS. How are you today?"

"Okay, I guess." Even as Evie walked in the door, though, she could tell that one of her favorite patients was not okay. She was struggling. It was there in the increased rise and fall of her chest and in the breathlessness with which she'd said her words.

"Is your inhaler not working?" Margaret Collins had been Evie's patient for several years. She had controlled asthma, so it was odd to see her breathing so out of whack.

"It's been taking more puffs from it to get things back to where they should be."

Evie frowned. "Have you been sick recently?"

"No, which is why this is so weird. I feel fine otherwise."

"Why don't I give you a quick once-over first."

A list of possibilities scrambled through her head, each trying to make itself heard. Blood clot in the lungs, COVID and pneumonia were among the top choices.

She looked at the vitals her nurse had taken and then listened to the woman's chest sounds. Her left lung sounded clear, but when she listened to the right, she heard decreased breath sounds. And her pulse was hovering on the low end of the nineties. It didn't exactly knock any of her potential ailments off the pile, but it did shift them slightly. "Are you okay if I call for an X-ray?"

"Yes, whatever you need to do. I trust you."

She heard that a lot from patients, and she understood where they were coming from. But she also wanted them to trust their bodies. To know when they weren't working the way they should be.

Evie called down to Radiology to see if they had an opening and it turned out they did. Normally, she had to wait for a slot to become available. Since Margaret was her last patient before her lunch break, she opted to walk her down there and get her signed in. "Once they get the results they'll call and let me know, and then I'll get in touch with you, okay? I don't want to prescribe additional medications until we know what we're dealing with."

"I just want to be able to catch my breath."

"I want you to, too. We'll work on that."

"Sounds good."

Evie walked out of Radiology and headed for the cafeteria. She got her food and sat down, glad to be off her feet. She saw Arthur Robbins on the far side of the room and wished she had opted to go to one of the local coffee shops instead, but she was here now. And maybe he wouldn't even notice her. Right about then, his gaze swung toward her and he gave her a quick wave before rising and heading her way.

Oh, great. She wasn't really in the mood to hear about anything gala-related, but since she was in charge of it, she probably didn't have much of a choice. And it had been almost a week since the staff meeting, so he probably wanted an update. That was too bad because she'd called the venue where they used to hold the gala and while they said they could accommodate the projected hundred and fifty extra attendees, they couldn't add anyone else without them being over the fire marshal's limits. Which would mean they might have to find a new venue and, if so, they would lose their hefty deposit on this one. Maybe she could talk Dr. Robbins out of the new requirements and ask him to institute them next year instead. After all, then people would have more notice, since the gala was in two months. She was pretty sure trying to find a new place in that condensed period of time was going to be nothing short of a headache.

He stood over her table with a fixed smile on his face. "How's the planning coming?"

It was now or never. "I have some concerns that I'd like to talk to you about. Is there any chance of setting up a meeting?"

"My schedule is pretty tight right now. Can you give me a quick rundown?"

She did as best she could after being put on the spot.

"So what I hear you saying is that the current venue can handle our projections of a hundred and fifty extra guests."

"Yes, but—"

"We'll simply limit the number of tickets to that number and leave it at that."

"And if that leaves some of the prospective donors out in the cold?"

His smile widened, but the man didn't look pleased

at being pressed. "From where I'm standing, Nevada isn't looking too chilly these days. Besides, invitations to last year's donors have already gone out and we've asked them to RSVP by next week. That should give you a rough number and you can go from there."

Not *we*, but *she* could go from there. There was one more thing she needed to run by him. "Okay. Also, our previous CEO did the welcomes and so forth, so I wondered if you'd be carrying on with that tradition."

"I wouldn't miss it. I'm working on my speech even as we speak."

Actually, there was something chilly in Nevada. Their new leader. Whereas Morgan Howard had been warm and welcoming, Dr. Robbins seemed cool and aloof. And he wanted this year's fundraiser to double or triple in donations?

She forced a smile and thanked him. He then walked away to another table, that same smile firmly in place. Maybe she was misjudging the man, but something about him made her edgy. She couldn't read him like she could Howard. Somehow, unless he was a very good actor, she didn't think his persona was going to foster a lot of new interest in giving to the hospital. If anything, Evie was fairly certain that donations were going to be down unless the doctors themselves could make those connections. Maybe that's what Robbins was counting on and why he'd instituted the new attendance requirement.

Maybe that's also why no one else wanted to be on the committee. Had the man's reputation preceded him? Evie didn't usually listen to the hospital's gossip chain, but maybe in this instance she should have tried. Because if something didn't change, this gala could wind up being a colossal failure. And she could see that failure being dropped right in her lap. Not that she couldn't take a little criticism. But she loved this hospital and wanted it to get the funds it needed to grow and help more patients.

Her phone pinged, and when she glanced down, she saw it was the hospital's radiology department. Wow, that was fast. She'd just left Margaret down there less than fifteen minutes ago. She answered the phone and waited as the tech gave his findings.

The results made her close her eyes and let out a long shuddering breath. "Okay, thank you for letting me know. Is Mrs. Collins still there?"

"No, sorry. We sent her on her way. Did you want us to keep her?"

"No, it's fine. Thanks again." She disconnected and sat there, her lunch untouched as she tried to process the one possibility she hadn't put on her list.

Margaret Collins had a mass in the lower lobe of her left lung.

Max waited for Evie to arrive at his office, just like she had a week ago. But this time, she'd given him advance notice and said it wasn't about the gala. But her voice had been strained in a way that said she was worried about something. Something involving a patient.

Since Evie was a pulmonologist, her concern was probably related to a finding during a test. And that she suspected a tumor or she wouldn't be running to him with it.

He remembered when his mom had been diagnosed

with cancer. She'd come home and said she needed to talk to his dad alone. Because of the way she'd said it, he'd stood outside the door and listened, horrified at what he was hearing. Brain cancer? That couldn't be right. He'd burst into the room, a thousand questions in his mind and his eyes burning with tears.

His dad had sat motionless at the dining room table, and rather than being there as a support for his wife, he'd lifted a bottle of what Max later knew to be alcohol and drank deeply from it while his mom comforted them both. She had told them it would be alright, that the doctors had a plan and she'd be starting chemo in less than a month.

In the end, his mom hadn't had a month. Her tumor had hemorrhaged and she died on the operating table. And his dad hadn't stopped drinking. Not during her short illness and not afterward. He remembered checking the bedroom before going to school to make sure his dad was still breathing. Max, who was still grieving the loss of his mom, had been suddenly thrust into the role of caregiver, a job he neither wanted nor felt capable of. But it was either that, or end up an orphan. So he coaxed his dad to eat and put him to bed when he was too drunk to get there on his own.

And in that time, Max had decided that he was going to help people like his mom, because in doing so, maybe more people wouldn't wind up like his father, a shadow of the strong person he'd once been.

The knock at his door drove him from his thoughts. "Come in."

Evie entered and this time she didn't wait to be asked,

she just sat in one of the chairs. She had nothing in her hands, but that didn't surprise him, since all of the patients' records were now kept in an automated system. So there was no need to tote around physical X-rays or paper records. "I have a patient who I think has cancer."

"Give me her name."

He looked up the chart and went through the findings. "No MRI yet?"

"No, just the X-ray. I expected it to show pneumonia or something different, but not this."

"I get it. I take it she's gone home."

"Yes. And is waiting on my call."

"I'll need a biopsy to know for sure. But I want to do an MRI first to get a better look at whatever this is. Do you want me to make the call?" He wasn't sure why he asked that. It would be protocol for Evie to contact the patient and let her know that she needed to be seen by an oncologist. But he sensed something in her demeanor that said this was going to be a hard one. Besides, she had come directly to him rather than writing up an order that would land on the desk of one of his office staff, who would then call him to set up an appointment.

She paused for a minute as if thinking about it. "No, she's my patient. At least for now."

"She'll always be your patient, Evie. I'm only treating one part of her."

"So am I. But she's…a special one, even though none of my patients are supposed to be any more special than the others."

He was right. He'd always been good at reading Evie. Even during that quick kiss all those years ago, he'd sensed that she wanted something more from him. Something that he couldn't give her. Not just because he was afraid of ruining their friendship if something went bad. But because of his dad and how he'd become after his mom died. He'd become a shell of himself and had never recovered. Max had seen many partners lose loved ones. Every day a new one walked through the door of his office. But if Max didn't have a partner, he couldn't lose them. Couldn't grieve his way into a pit of despair.

He knew that kind of thinking was skewed, but he'd already lost two parents. And he'd lost his dad long before he'd died of cirrhosis last year, right before Evie and her husband split up. Max's soul felt as dry as the drought that was currently afflicting Las Vegas. It had been months since the last bit of rain had come their way and severe water restrictions were currently in force.

Evie was looking at him strangely, and he realized his thoughts had wandered for longer than he'd realized.

He stood up from his desk. "Do you have time for a walk out in the courtyard before your next patient?" He hadn't been much of a friend since her split from her husband, and if he wasn't careful, he was going to do exactly what he'd told himself he was trying *not* to do: lose her friendship.

"Thanks. I'd like that."

The relief in her voice said he'd done the right thing. "We can talk about the gala for a few minutes and kill two birds with one stone."

Except Max wasn't sure what the first bird was, except maybe the fact that he'd missed her. Had missed seeing her on a regular basis. Had missed laughing with

her and going on their dinner dates and excursions with
Darby. They still hadn't had that dinner she'd mentioned
about planning the gala. Or had she decided she didn't
need his help after all?

"Good. Because the venue the hospital usually uses
can only accommodate a certain number of folks, and
by requiring that staff go, Dr. Robbins is reducing the
number of potential donors that can attend. It's one of
the reasons that in the past, staff was invited but attendance wasn't required. I do get why they want department heads there, though."

He stood, waiting for her to do the same, his eyebrows
going up. "Ah, so you think I've been remiss in my ob-
ligations by not going."

"Not remiss." She smiled. "Just antisocial."

That made him laugh. Because she knew him. In an
even deeper way than Darby did. Darby had actually
gone to medical school for a year or two before realizing
the health-care field wasn't for her and had made the leap
to the police, much to the dismay of her parents. She'd
breezed through training. Had been the maid of honor at
Evie and Brad's wedding, and then been wounded in the
line of duty a year later, opting to resign when it became
clear that her leg would never regain full function. But
she seemed happy with what she was doing and claimed
that there was nothing better than being your own boss.

Max was beginning to see the benefits of that after
the doozy of a staff meeting they'd had. He'd even toyed
with opening his own practice. But he loved hospital
work. Loved working with other specialties—seeing
the *life* that ran through this place. Oncology could be

rewarding, but it was also draining and heartbreaking at times. The atmosphere at the hospital helped mitigate those aspects of his job.

Even the gala was probably not the onerous chore he'd made it out to be.

"So how do you plan to balance the staff-to-donor ratio?"

"I saw Robbins in the cafeteria and when I mentioned my concerns, he basically batted them back at me, saying he wasn't worried." One of her shoulders went up. "I'm hoping the sign-up sheet will give me a better idea of what we're dealing with. It's kind of short notice to say that everyone has to go. There are people who've already planned vacations and so forth. He did say that exceptions could be made for those folks who absolutely couldn't come."

"Hmm...maybe I should plan a vacation for that time."

"No way, chum. You know that you never take actual vacations."

It was true. Both Darby and Evie had gotten on him about that. He did take time off. But he almost always stayed home and didn't do anything special unless it was dinner with her and Darbs. Even when his dad died, he'd only taken off the day of his funeral. And he'd looked stiff and awkward whenever anyone approached him. But, Evie being Evie, she had said she got why he was that way. He'd told her the story about his dad's drinking and when it had started.

She also got why he abstained from alcohol and had always been her and Darby's designated driver. At least until he'd stopped coming to their dinners. Things had never been the same between the three of them since then. But now—with the gala—maybe he had a chance to rectify that. Unless—like the medications he prescribed—he decided that the risk outweighed the benefits. The jury was still out on that one.

They found themselves out in the large courtyard. The space was carved out of the middle of the medical center. It could only be accessed through the hospital. There was no lush greenery out here. Just interesting rock formations dotted with succulent plants and a central sculpture. But the place had a beauty of its own, just like the desert, as triangular sun sails and the tall walls of the hospital provided shade over a multitude of seating areas. And a flagstone path wound through the space, giving patients and staff alike a spot to contemplate their day. It was really lovely, and at night there were countless strings of fairy lights that gave it a beautiful, romantic appearance. Several staff members had even held their nuptials under those lights.

Max glanced around. "Too bad this space isn't being used for the gala. It would give visitors a chance to actually see the hospital and know where their dollars were going."

Evie cocked her head. "Actually, it probably would be big enough. It must be at least as big as the ballroom at the hotel. Tables could be set up throughout the space and a sound system could take care of making sure everyone could hear what was going on. But I don't know if it's possible to cancel the reservations at the hotel."

"If not this year, then maybe next year."

"Yes..."

She seemed to see the space with new eyes. And he loved watching her mind work. It was there in the way she perused her surroundings, in each twitch of those full pink lips. In the way her head tilted ever so slightly to the left.

He couldn't help but stare.

Since Max had never attended the event, he had no idea what the atmosphere was like, but surely the hospital could match or even surpass whatever was done off campus at these events. And with catering and being able to rent almost anything, right down to tablecloths and silverware, surely it was doable. Although no one could guarantee the weather would cooperate. But with rain looking like more and more of a luxury right now...

"I think it would be lovely. An intimate setting, rather than the formality of an elegantly appointed hotel. We could still erect a temporary dance floor from wood planking in the far left corner, where we have benches arranged in that large circle."

That area was often used as a venue for small lectures or for students and their families who were touring the hospital, hoping to be accepted into one of the local universities. They could visit and chat with other students, as well as staff who would talk about the hospital. So it was already set up as a gathering space, just not for the size or scale of a large event such as the gala.

She glanced at him with eyes that were bright and expectant. "Would you be more apt to come to the gala if it were held at the hospital?"

"Since it's now required, isn't that a moot point?"

"But what if it wasn't? What if this were any other year and held on the hospital grounds."

He thought for a minute. "Then, yes. Because I know that I could always go hide in my office if I got too bored."

"Exactly. I think more staff would want to come. Especially if they knew they could escape to either the staff lounge, the café, or any of the other waiting-room areas. They wouldn't be confined to a table or any one space. They could mingle and visit with each other the way they can't when they're at work. I think it would be a win-win. For everyone."

"You might be right." In fact, she probably was right. "The question is, will Robbins go for it?"

"Ugh. He's kind of a wild card. All I can do is come up with a plan and try to sell it to him. Do you think you could draw up a replica of what such an event might look like?"

She remembered that he liked to sketch? It shouldn't be surprising. During that awkward period after their kiss, he'd wanted to make up for his weird reaction, so he'd drawn a scene from *Wicked* from memory and had wrapped it and sent it to her house. She hadn't said much about it, but she had come up to him the day after she got it and had looked in his face, and simply said, "Thank you." But he could tell she was touched by the gesture. It helped them get past that terrible phase that could have turned terminal. He was grateful that it hadn't.

Was thankful he still had her friendship, even if he had been remiss in nurturing that over the last year and more. But like he'd thought earlier, maybe he could make up for that. At least a little. And as a friend, he could do this for her.

"Send me a list of what you want included in the drawing and I'll see what I can do. I can't promise it'll pass muster with Robbins, but maybe it'll give him a hint of what such an event could be like."

"Thanks, Max. I truly mean that."

He smiled. "I'm happy to do it."

"One more thing. If you have time in the next week or two, I'd like to call the hotel and see if they'll let us look at the venue. I was there last year, but don't remember exactly how things were laid out, since I wasn't involved in the planning. Maybe they'll even have pictures of what the room looks like set up. And I can walk out here in the courtyard and do a comparison, to see if we can fit buffet lines and the number of tables we'll need."

He glanced around before a thought came to him. "The courtyard opens to the atrium area of the hospital. Its size makes a big impression, with high ceilings, and it's not cluttered with a lot of furniture. We could spill over into it. Or maybe even set up the catering area in there. And I bet we could get some fans set up in strategic places to help keep things cool, although once the sun goes down that shouldn't be a problem."

"True." She smiled and gripped his hand, giving it a squeeze. "I'm liking this idea more and more. In fact, maybe we can even use it this year. We could have the formal part of the gala at the hotel and then have something set up in the courtyard, where people could come once that's over, if they want to see what the hospital is like. Something informal juxtaposed against the stiff formality of the event itself."

It was all he could do not to press the hand she'd squeezed against his pant leg to erase the feeling of her warm soft skin against his.

"I think Robbins would go for that. He has to have actually liked the hospital to have accepted the position as CEO of it. Surely he'd want to show it off?"

"I agree. And maybe that will make the idea of having the gala in house next year more appealing. That, along with the beautiful rendering you're going to draw."

One side of his mouth went up. "No pressure, though, right?"

"Oh, I'll press as hard as it takes to make you say yes."

And what if she'd pressed the night of that kiss all those years ago? What if she'd pulled him closer and deepened that kiss. Would he have taken her home? Carried her to bed and stayed there with her the entire night?

Not something he wanted to think about right now. Especially not with the way she was looking at him. As if he could do anything.

It's just a drawing, Max.

He needed to remember that, before he started ascribing personal motives to something that was anything but.

She pulled a pad out of her pocket and scribbled some notes on it. "Before I forget anything," she muttered.

Was she talking to him or to herself? A minute later she ripped the small sheet off and handed it to him. "It's just some of the things that I thought could be included in the drawing. If I think of anything else over the next few hours, I'll send you a text, okay?"

He perused the list. She wasn't kidding when she said she didn't want to forget anything. Ambiance, dance floor, seating that included tables and comfortable groupings of nice chairs, DJ station, food tables, bar, open doors to the atrium, additional strings of lights…

He sent her a grin. "I don't think we could fit anything else out here if we tried."

"You don't think it's over-the-top, do you?"

"I think this CEO is expecting exactly that. So, no." He glanced at the list again. "I'll start working on this tonight and hopefully have it to you within the next couple of days."

"That would be perfect. Thanks so much, Max."

"My pleasure." And it would be. He'd felt badly about what Brad had done to her, but hadn't known what to say or do to help her get over that. Instead, for the last year, he'd pretty much walked the other way whenever he caught sight of her. Not because of Brad, but because of himself. And he couldn't think of anything more selfish than that. Maybe he had a little more of his dad in him than he liked to think. The only thing he didn't do was drink.

Maybe it was time to make up for that lapse. And if a simple drawing would help, then he'd do ten of them.

"Oh, and about your patient with the mass, I'll let you know when we set up the appointment, if you're interested."

"Yes, thank you. I'd like to be there for the consult, if it works with my schedule. That is if you're okay with that."

"Yep. Not a problem at all."

"Great." She pocketed her notebook and glanced at her watch. "Speaking of patients, I'd better get back to it."

"Me, too. Talk soon."

They parted ways, and he realized he was looking forward to talking to her, even to collaborating with her on the gala. And he wasn't sure if that was a good thing or something that would come back to bite him. But he'd worry about that if and when it happened.

CHAPTER THREE

"Wow. You weren't kidding when you said you'd get me something in a few days."

He'd placed a large drawing of the courtyard against the wall and was now standing across from her, watching as she perused his work. Her office was slightly smaller than his, and although he had been in her space before, it was different this time somehow. And she wasn't sure how she felt about it. It reminded her so much of the time he'd gifted her that drawing from the play they'd seen, and even though this wasn't the same thing at all, it still brought back all of the emotions and feelings that receiving that gift had elicited. Especially since it had come after that disastrous kiss. And right before he seemed to go AWOL from their friendship.

And maybe it was because he'd been absent for so long that his very presence seemed to overwhelm the space...and her. Not so much with his size, but his sheer magnetism. It was there in his raw masculinity, the scent of his soap or shampoo or whatever he used, and, of course, those green, green eyes that made her want to get lost in them. She'd always felt that way about him no matter where they were. He'd always been a big part of their trio of friends. So his absence, especially over the last year, had been sorely felt. In fact, even when she'd been married to Brad, Max had been hit or miss as far as being there because she knew he hadn't liked her ex.

But at the time, his withdrawal had made processing that kiss a little easier. Made the realization that nothing would ever come of it a little more bearable, despite the tremendous hurt she'd felt. Because back then, she'd nurtured a tiny bit of hope that things might evolve from there. But he'd apologized and said he didn't want what had happened to affect their friendship. Except that it had. It was then that he'd started making excuses about why he couldn't go out with them. Not always, but enough that she deduced that it was because of her and what had happened. Darby had even asked about it, and although Evie was pretty sure she knew the reason for it, she didn't want to admit it. Didn't want her friend's sympathy over something that couldn't be changed.

She'd realized she had to make a life for herself. She couldn't go on mooning after a man who'd never had a steady girlfriend and had made it clear that he wasn't the marrying kind. Evie was. Brad had proved that. Or at least she'd thought he had, until Darby had presented her with those awful photos. The aftermath of her and Brad's breakup had been just as awful. He'd hounded her for two months, trying to get her to change her mind. And once he realized there was no going back, he'd turned nasty and had sued her for half of her earnings, forcing the sale of their apartment.

She'd lived in Darby's spare bedroom until the divorce was final. Three months in all. Only then did she feel like she could get her own place without worrying

Brad would somehow come after that, too. Only now did she feel like she was starting to recover from the trauma of that time.

With everything that had happened, she saw some wisdom in Max's aversion to relationships. And Evie could say she was now firmly on the side of Team Single. And she wasn't about to change that anytime soon.

She forced her mind back to the drawing when she realized she was staring sightlessly at it. Moving closer, she crouched on the floor across from it and took in what he'd done.

How had he gotten so much detail into it?

The courtyard space had been divided into four different zones. A section for hors d'oeuvres and drinks was right off the entrance to the foyer of the hospital. Rather than the buffet tables she'd envisioned in the atrium, he'd put romantic lighting on each table and drawn in waitstaff carrying trays of champagne and canapés.

Off to the left were the benches that were already in the space, but Max had put small side tables where people could talk and place the food and drinks they'd carried from zone one. It looked like he'd had potted plants brought in to give at least a small illusion of green space, and give people hope that there might be rain in the near future, even if none was forecast at the moment. A shortage of water was a very real concern in this part of Nevada. And there was no relief in sight. Just more sunshine and blistering summertime temperatures.

Fortunately, once the sun set, cooler temperatures moved in, which was one reason Sin City had such a booming nightlife. The gala setting looked like any one of those fancy resorts that were packed into the city. Only this had a vibe that was more intimate. A vibe that encouraged confessions…and maybe even huge donations. She glanced at Max for a moment before returning her attention to the canvas. The only colors on the otherwise black-and-white rendition were the faces of those populating the drawing. While featureless, those faces gave the appearance of life and warmth. And she loved it.

The third zone was the dance floor that they'd talked about. Twinkle lights hung overhead and lined the edges of the low wooden platform that appeared to be made out of hardwood flooring. On it, couples floated across the space in all of their finery.

"You're making me nervous." Max's low voice vibrated over her, causing her heart to skip a beat or two. "You're not saying anything."

"Because I'm blown away by it. All of it. This is beyond fantastic. If Dr. Robbins doesn't go for the idea, then I'll be shocked. Oh, and I like that you left the last zone as a strolling path."

There was one couple holding hands as they walked past the huge sculpture and rock formations that were in the area. It opened up a pit in her stomach that made it hard to breathe for a minute. Because she could imagine Max and herself in place of the pair in the picture. But it wasn't true and never would be. Because the fact of the matter was, she would stroll that path alone. Brad had betrayed her and Max hadn't wanted her.

The hurt from the past rose up all over again and threatened to swallow her.

But she wasn't really being fair to Max. He didn't want anyone—it wasn't a rejection of her in particular. And if she was smart, she would get rid of whatever vestiges of romantic notions she might harbor for the man before she lost him again. She'd been enjoying having him back in her life over this last week—she could see how it had been an impetus to start moving forward again after a year of feeling stagnant and unwanted.

And now she felt wanted again? Ugh! She hoped she wasn't pinning her self-worth on how Max acted or didn't act toward her. If she did that, she'd just end up pushing him away again. Besides, those feelings weren't real. They were from not having anyone in her life right now. Maybe she should think about dating again. After all, Brad had been gone for a year and even if he came groveling back, she didn't want him—would never be able to trust him after what he'd done.

"I thought after the meal at the other venue, people might want to move around a little bit to burn some of it off."

She forced a smile, glanced back at him and stood. "And holding hands as they do. That was a romantic touch."

He gave a half shrug, part of his smile fading. "Purely a selling feature. Just like the couples on the dance floor."

"Ah, I see. Because Max Hunt doesn't have a romantic bone in his body."

She wasn't sure why she said it, especially in tones that were a little more waspish than necessary as evidenced by the muscle that was now pulsing in his cheek. Probably feeling guilty over her thoughts from a min-

ute ago, she sighed and added, "Sorry. That was un-
called for."

"No, it's okay. I can wish romance on others, even if
I don't want any for myself."

"You don't think you'll ever be involved with anyone?" And there she went again. She wasn't asking for
herself—at least that's what she told herself. She just
thought Max deserved the happiness that came with
companionship. Despite the way that she and Brad had
ended, she had been happy with him for most of their
marriage—even if it was more a comfortable feeling of
familiarity rather than a rush of chaotic emotions that she
had trouble sorting out. At least with Brad she'd known
what to expect. Well, except at the end.

He gave her a quick glance before looking away, but
not before she caught something almost poignant in his
expression. "I don't think so. My mom's death was hard
on my dad. He became someone I no longer recognized
and I'd really rather not go through something like that."

"Not every partner dies so young."

"No. But in my family's case that's how it happened.
And the process leading from her cancer diagnosis to
her passing is something I'd rather not put any kids I
might have through."

Her head tilted. "And yet you became a cancer doctor."

He didn't answer for a second, but finally he nodded.
"It was because of my mom. But that doesn't have anything to do with my not wanting a serious relationship.
The fact of the matter is that I like my life the way it is
now and I don't want to risk that over something that

might not—that probably *won't*—last. After all, look at you and Brad."

"Wow, okay. I get it. It's none of my business."

He closed his eyes. "Sorry, Evie. I didn't mean it that way. I'm just trying to show that even when you think something is going to last forever, it doesn't always. I try to live my life honestly. And don't ever want anyone to get the wrong idea and be hurt because of something I've said...or done."

Was he warning her off? If so it wasn't necessary. She'd gotten his message a long time ago. "I get it. I'm really not interested in a relationship, either. Like you said, there's me and Brad."

He was silent for a moment, then she felt warm hands on her shoulders. He gave her a light squeeze before letting her go. "I'm sorry, Evie. That man deserved worse than what he got. And you deserved better."

He evidently knew her ex had tried to take her for everything she had. Probably from Darbs. Thankfully, once the divorce was final, he moved away with the woman he'd been seeing. She had no real idea where he was right now and had no interest in knowing.

She took out her phone and snapped a shot of the picture as a way of changing the subject. "I'll send this to Robbins. Can I keep the drawing in my office, in case he wants to see the original?"

"Of course. I thought maybe you'd want some tweaks."

"Are you kidding? This is a masterpiece. It's perfect the way it is. But don't be surprised if it goes up on the wall of the hospital somewhere, or if our new head guy ropes you into doing some other drawings."

"Nope. I only do them for a few special people."

And Evie was one of those people? All of her self-lectures from moments earlier flew out the window and in their place something warm and tingly stirred in the pit of her stomach. She had to bite her lip for a minute to stop the sensation from spreading. The last thing she wanted was for Max to realize how much those words meant to her. So she again changed the subject. "Any news on Margaret Collins?"

"The patient you referred to me?"

"Yes."

"I actually have an appointment scheduled with her for this afternoon. Do you still want to be there?"

She thought for a moment. It wasn't absolutely necessary that she attended. Margaret would be in good hands, since she trusted Max implicitly. But she would like to be. Would that seem odd to him that she would want to support her patient?

"I don't want it to seem weird or for you to feel like I don't trust your judgment."

"Why would it seem weird? Family members sit in all the time. As her pulmonary specialist, it makes sense that you would want to know what her treatment will be so that you can help carry it out."

When he said it like that, it didn't sound strange at all.

"Thanks, Max. I'll take you up on that then. What time is her appointment?"

"At three thirty. Are you free then?"

"I should be. My appointments tend to be in the morning. And I do a second set of rounds in the afternoon. So I'll just pop over to the appointment and then come back."

He nodded. "Speaking of popping over, I hadn't meant to stay as long as I did, so unless you have any other questions about the drawing, I'll head back over to my office."

"No questions, just a huge thank-you. I'll let you know what Robbins says."

"Great. I'll see you around three thirty, then."

Speaking of which, she needed to write that down before she forgot. Not that she was likely to. Her insides were already doing loops at the prospect of seeing him again so soon. Talk about a downpour in the midst of a drought. It had been a long time since she and Max had spoken so freely to one another, and she was going to turn her face up to the rain and enjoy it while she could. And ignore the fact that, like living in the desert, the rain wasn't likely to last.

As the day went on, Max became less and less sure about having Evie sit in on Mrs. Collins's appointment. There had been something unsettling about being closed in her office while she studied his drawing, especially since she'd asked him about whether or not he might consider being in a relationship.

Had she even realized that she'd used a fingertip to trace the couple he'd drawn who'd been walking together in the picture? He had shuddered, as if she'd been running her fingers along his skin rather than an inanimate object. He still hadn't gotten that image out of his head. When he'd kissed her in front of that theater, her palm had curled over the back of his neck. The warmth of her skin against his had served to jerk him back to awareness just as the mental image of them in bed had slid through his brain.

That same image had risen up as she'd touched that drawing, the intimacy of the act making him picture them together all over again. It made his nerves prickle to life, along with another part of him that needed to be kept on a short leash. Before something bad happened. Not that sex was bad. And with her it was guaranteed to be good. Very, very good. But it couldn't happen if he had any hope of salvaging their friendship—a friendship that was just now being brought back online.

Was the burst of lust something remembered from their past? There'd been that same shivery sensation that he'd thought he'd banished long ago. Or was this something entirely new? If so, he needed to put it in the past and leave it with his other baggage. Because if he couldn't...

Well, then there would be no more meetings in anyone's offices and no more collaborations on anything work-related or not. And the friendship that he'd hoped to salvage would be dead in the water. Again.

His phone pinged and his emotions went on high alert until he glanced at the reading and saw that it was Darby. He immediately relaxed and read the text. She'd actually written the word *squee* followed by an absurd number of exclamation marks. The message went on.

Evie texted me a copy of your drawing and I love it. She said she's headed to the CEO's office to show it to him.

He's going to go berserk. If he doesn't, then he doesn't deserve to run that hospital.

That made him smile. He couldn't picture Dr. Robbins going berserk about anything unless it was something related to dollar signs. He texted back.

Don't get your hopes up too high. He's not the most demonstrative man, from what I've seen of him.

Was he sad that Evie hadn't asked him to accompany her to the CEO's office? He'd be lying if he said no. But he'd also hinted to Evie that he had a busy afternoon ahead of him. Maybe she was afraid Robbins wouldn't like his plans, despite what she'd said. Except that Darby had also seemed to think his rendering was worth presenting to the man.

His phone pinged again.

Well, I think this will float his boat. Besides, he'd be crazy not to go for this. It'll give him a chance to show off his hospital to potential investors. I can't wait to hear what he thinks.

He smiled.

Thanks for the vote of confidence.

Once Darby signed off, he was left with a strange sensation. He had no idea what had caused it or why it was so unsettling, but it was. It could be that it was better for him not to be there. Because he didn't want to witness the sense of disappointment flit across Evie's face. He'd already lived through that once before and didn't want to go through it again. If only she knew that he'd saved her from a relationship failure that was as bad, if not worse, than what she'd gone through with Brad.

Oh, he wouldn't have cheated on her, except with his job. And he certainly wouldn't have gone after her money. But he knew himself well enough to know that he would be withholding some of himself. It was a defense mechanism that he'd brought into play while he was taking care of his dad. Oh, he'd taken care of his physical needs, but he'd felt powerless to help him with anything more than that. Because he'd expected to someday come home and find his dad dead, either by drinking himself to death or worse. Thankfully, it hadn't come down to that. He'd just damaged his liver beyond repair instead. That damage hadn't shown its face until Max was long grown up and out of the house.

The damage done to Max emotionally, back then, hadn't reared its head until later, either. Until he'd started thinking about Evie in ways that had nothing to do with friendship. It had paralyzed him and made him realize something inside of him was missing. Something that had to do with him trying to meet someone's needs in a way that went beyond the physical joining of two bodies. Because he knew that was all that he'd be able to give her. And she'd eventually come to hate him for it.

He shook his head and stood up to stretch his back. He needed to go do something besides just sit here and think about the past. Or about Evie. He glanced at his watch. It was lunchtime, so he might as well go out of the hospital. Maybe he could throw off some of his thoughts. Besides, he was pretty certain he would find out what Dr. Robbins thought of the ideas soon enough. And they weren't even his ideas. They were Evie's. All he'd done was put them to paper. So he'd go and eat and sit somewhere where his thoughts would not be consumed with hospital stuff.

So, he headed down the street, hopefully leaving the clutter in his head far behind.

Margaret Collins looked relieved, which struck Evie as odd. She would have expected her older patient to be defeated by a possible cancer diagnosis, but she didn't seem fazed. "Evie, dear, I'm so happy you were able to come."

She'd said it as if it was a birthday party or some happier occasion. An inkling of worry erupted in the back of her head. She'd never known her patient to think with less than a clear head, but this sounded… Well, it didn't seem like a normal reaction.

When she glanced at Max, she saw a troubled frown. Evidently she wasn't the only one to find Margaret's words odd.

"I thought Dr. Milagre should be here so that she'd know what treatment your tumor needs and would be able to know how to treat the breathing aspects."

"Of course. I never meant anything other than that. She's just always been so sweet to me, even before this, when I had COVID and no one knew if I'd live or die. But Dr. Milagre never seemed to have any doubts." She glanced at Evie. "You were always so encouraging and your sense of hope was contagious. It still is, which is why I'm glad you're here."

Evie's concerns eased. "Your willingness to follow a treatment plan and to never stop fighting played a major role in your recovery. I'm counting on that same determination to get you through this as well."

At seventy-two years of age, some might have not wanted to put the woman through cancer surgery or chemo, but other than her asthma, Margaret had always been remarkably healthy. At least from what her records said and what Evie herself had seen. She was an amazing woman, and she reminded Evie of her own grandmother, who'd come over from Brazil and had made a home in a new place with her family. She'd lived to the ripe old age of ninety-six. And if COVID hadn't come along, her grandma might still be alive. But instead, it had taken her life, even while sparing Margaret's. She sincerely hoped her patient had another decade or two to live.

"We're going to do an MRI today and get a better look at what we're dealing with. We'll inject a little dye into your system to see how much of the tumor is being fed by your blood vessels. Then we'll schedule a biopsy. Do you have family who can come and take you home from that, since you'll need anesthesia to do the procedure."

"My son can. He lives a few miles from my place. The only reason he's not here today is because I didn't tell him. Not yet, anyway. I wanted to have a better idea of what I'm facing before bringing anyone else in my family into it."

Max perched on a stool in front of her and looked

her in the eye. "You're going to want to call him for this one."

"You're that sure?"

"Sure enough. I really want someone here for you. There will be a lot of information thrown at you in a short amount of time. It would be good for someone else to be a second set of ears. No one remembers everything."

He was right. After Darby had shown her those pictures of Brad, her mind had been a mess and she'd barely remembered anything said afterward. It hadn't been a medical emergency, but she'd still been glad Darby had been there for her and had been her support system. She'd even come with Evie when it came time to tell her parents what was happening. Her dad had threatened to come for Brad, and at least give him a piece of his mind. She and Darby had talked him out of it, eventually convincing him that it wouldn't change anything and could only make things worse.

Brad hadn't been worth it. He still wasn't.

"I'll ask him as soon as you know for sure that it's cancer."

Max laid his hand on Margaret's. "We won't know that for sure without the biopsy."

"But you'll have a better idea of what it is with the test today, right?"

"We should have."

Margaret nodded and turned her hand over to squeeze his. "If the test seems to indicate it is, then I'll tell him."

"Good."

"Then let's get this show on the road then, shall we?

The sooner we know, the sooner we can get this thing out of my chest. Or at least I'll hope that we can."

Max turned to look at Evie. "How is the next hour looking for you?"

"I can't think of anywhere I'd rather be." She quickly added, in case Max got the wrong idea, "Than with you, Margaret."

The older woman swiped her fingers under one of her eyes before glaring at them both. "These damned allergies…"

Allergies or not, Evie was glad she could be here for Margaret, no matter what the results turned out to be.

She hadn't had time to even tell Max that Dr. Robbins had loved the sketch and had agreed, even on such short notice, that they should incorporate the ideas into this year's gala. They would still do the speeches and appeals at the hotel ballroom, but they would shorten that portion of it to an hour or two, enough to serve dinner and get through the fundraising portion. But then they would invite everyone over to the hospital to enjoy some desserts and drinks. Robbins had gone so far as to say they would hire a taxi service to drive those home who had imbibed more than they should have. And this way, staff members who were on duty would be able to pop into the courtyard for a few minutes and at least get a few refreshments.

So while Margaret was getting her MRI, she thanked Max again for the drawing. "He's giving us everything we wanted."

His eyebrows went up. "Maybe he's not as hard-nosed as he seemed. And since people can come and go as they please once they get to the hospital, there shouldn't be a problem with overcrowding."

"No. There shouldn't. They're going to rotate some board members and have them take people on tours of the hospital, so it won't be everyone out in the court-yard all at once."

His eyes focused on the images going across the screen as they were taken. He swore softly.

"What is it?"

"It's hypervascular," he said, pointing at the tumor. "And I'm pretty sure it's metastatic, probably from her breast, liver or somewhere else. An angiosarcoma."

"Oh, no." Her whispered words were part prayer. An angiosarcoma was a rare cancer and Max was right—lung involvement almost always originated from some-where else. Which meant it might have also metastasized to the brain or other organs. "Will you still need a bi-opsy?"

"To be one-hundred-percent certain, yes. But if it's what I think it is, it'll be aggressive."

"I know." Evie's heart plummeted and all of a sudden fundraisers and whether or not they got to hold part of the gala on hospital grounds seemed so unimportant.

"I want to stay while you tell her."

He nodded. "I figured as much."

They helped Margaret down from the MRI table. She looked at their faces. "It's bad news, isn't it?"

"It's not the best."

"I see." She stood there for a minute before sitting gingerly down on the wheelchair they'd used to bring her into the room. "Are there treatments?"

"Yes. Chemotherapy and possibly some radiation. But we don't think the lung is the primary site. We think it came there from somewhere else."

She twisted her hands in her lap. "Oh, my. That is bad news, isn't it?"

"Like I said, I still want to do the biopsy. And it's time to bring your family members in on this and let them know what's going on. You mentioned your son lives nearby."

"He does. I have a daughter, too, but she lives in Maine at the moment. That's such a long way to travel…"

"Why don't you let her decide if that's too far or not."

They wheeled her to Max's office and Evie sat beside her and held her hand as Max continued to give her more information.

Margaret interrupted once to ask how soon he'd want her to have the biopsy.

"As soon as possible. We'll want to begin treatment right afterward. Will your son be able to stay with you?"

"He's married with three teenaged daughters. How can I ask him to do that?"

"I understand. But I have to be honest. You'll need support during treatment. I won't lie and say it'll be easy, because it won't."

She gave him a frank look. "Is it even worth it, in your opinion? If this were your mom, would you suggest she go through chemo?"

He paused for several long seconds and Evie's heart contracted. She knew the story of Max's mom and it was a heartbreaking one.

"My mom never got the chance to go through chemo.

Her cancer was found too late and she died before she could start treatment. But to answer your question, yes, I would want her to at least try one course to see if there was any improvement."

"I'm sorry about your mom. She must have been a special lady, because you're a good man."

Max smiled. "Well, some might argue with that assessment."

He glanced at Evie, his mouth twisting sideways. Did he think she was one of the people who might argue with that assessment? Not on her life. And she was going to make sure he knew it. Just as soon as his appointment with Margaret was over.

CHAPTER FOUR

"DO YOU THINK I don't think you're a good person?"

Max frowned. The question had come right on the heels of his patient leaving the room. "What? Where did this come from?"

"When Margaret said you were a good man, you looked right at me when you said there were people who might not agree with that assessment."

"I'm sure that was a coincidence." It hadn't been, though. He had looked at Evie, but he just hadn't realized she'd caught the movement. Until now.

"I'm pretty sure it wasn't." She took a step closer. "You are a good man. Why would you even think otherwise?"

"You're reading too much into all of this." His heart thumped hard a time or two before going back into a normal rhythm. She was standing just a foot away from him, her head tilted up to gaze at him, the brown of her eyes soft and knowing. As if she knew all of his secrets and was hell-bent on prying them from him one by one.

"Am I?" Her hand went up to touch his face. "Is this because of your mom? You were only a kid back then. You couldn't have stopped what happened to her."

"I know that." A coil of emotion unspooled from

somewhere inside of him. "There are days, though—days like today—when I wonder why I went into a specialty that is rife with so much heartbreak. Margaret is probably not going to survive this, you know."

"I know. But if it goes into remission she could have some good years ahead of her. Years when she'll be able to see her grandkids grow up and live her life to the fullest. That has to be worth something, despite the heartache."

Her fingers were still touching him, moving over his jawline in a way that made him shudder. And dammit, he needed this. Needed to feel something other than the desperation of all of the Margaret Collinses of the world, although she seemed remarkably at peace with whatever might happen.

"Evie…" He closed his eyes and balled his hands by his sides to keep from gripping her arms and pulling her closer. Much closer.

"It's okay, Max. You don't always have to be strong."

He felt arms go around him and her cheek pressed against his chest. She was hugging him. Hell, she was only trying to comfort him. So why did the urges going through his body right now have nothing to do with comfort? Or hugging?

But he did have to be strong. Because to be anything other than that would be dangerous. Not just for him, but for Evie, too.

He opened his eyes and looked down at where she was pressed against him. And God help him, his arms went around her and hugged her close, one hand sliding up into the silky strands of her hair and gripping it.

A tiny sound came from her throat, and at first he thought he was holding her too tight and was hurting her. But then he realized it wasn't about that. It was something else entirely.

His hands went to her shoulders and eased her away, and Max looked down into her face as he did. Her eyes, rimmed with impossibly dark lashes, were moist with emotion, and suddenly he knew there wasn't enough strength in the world to stop him from doing what he was about to do.

Except before he could even make a move to do exactly that, Evie went up on her tiptoes and pressed her lips to his in a kiss that was as soft as a butterfly's wings and as deadly as a cobra's strike. Because it ignited a maelstrom inside of him that took over all rational thought. And soon, the kiss was anything but soft. His hand went to the back of her head and held her as his mouth covered hers, his tongue sliding between her lips only to be welcomed home as she opened to allow him any and all access. And he accepted her invitation, his palms going to her back and sliding down until her hips were pressed firmly against his. And this time, the sound she made wasn't imagined. It was real, very real, and if this went much further she was going to be on his couch and rolled under his body until there was nothing separating them, and they could...

Hell, no. She didn't deserve this. Didn't deserve someone that would just take what she was offering and give nothing in return. Because even as his body clamored for it, his mind knew that was all that would be in it for him.

He pulled his mouth free. "Evie. Stop...please."

She tried to move closer again and this time he somehow summoned some superhuman strength and set her away from him. "We can't."

Evie stared at him for a second, the back of one of her hands pressed against her mouth. Then she straightened, her fingers going to her hair and dragging through the mussed locks.

"We can't what, exactly?"

He motioned to his couch, letting the bald implication speak for itself. He didn't want any warm fuzzies entering the conversation and muddying the waters. Hell! She'd tried to argue that he was a good man? Well, he was about to disabuse her of any such thoughts. Because what he'd been thinking had been the opposite of good or noble.

She frowned. "You think I was angling for you to sleep with me?"

"Weren't you? Because that was sure the direction my thoughts were headed. I'd be damned surprised if yours weren't there as well."

They stared at each other, both of them still breathing hard. Then she shrugged. "So what if they were? We're both adults. It's not like I'm asking you for a ring." Except there was a quick flash of pain in her eyes that cut him to the core.

God, he didn't want to hurt her. Had tried so hard over the years to keep from doing exactly what he was doing now. "Evie, I know you aren't. But I just can't give you what you deser—"

She took a step back. "Don't! I know all of the blah blah blahs you're about to recite. You're not the marrying kind. You don't do relationships. You don't want forevers. You'll remind me *again* of how Brad and I wound up. Well, let me let you in on a little secret, Max. I did learn something from my marriage, even if you think I didn't. I'm not after any of those things. Not forevers, not declarations of love, not emotional pleas for more than you can muster." She sucked down an audible breath. "So your overinflated opinion that anyone who sleeps with you must immediately fall head over heels in love with you is way off base. But just in case you're still worried, let me make it as clear as I can. You won't have to turn down a night of pleasure with me ever again. Because this truly was our last dance."

Is that was she thought? He gave a hard laugh. Because if he was worried about anyone immediately falling in love with someone, it was the other way around.

"Something funny?"

Only then did he realize how that had probably sounded to her. But there was no way he could explain that he wasn't laughing because of what she'd said. It was because the reality of those "blah blah blahs" she'd named was still true. Even after all these years.

Rather than respond, he just shook his head.

"Perfect. Well, I guess that about sums it up for both of us." She turned to go, and then said over her shoulder, "Please let me know when Margaret's biopsy is scheduled. I want to be here for it."

As much as he wanted this conversation to be over, he didn't want her to leave like this. "Evie—"

She stopped him with an uplifted hand. "Don't worry. This won't affect our professional relationship. Or our friendship. I know that was another one of your arguments the last time we kissed. But we got through that... kind of. So we can get through this, too."

"Wait."

She turned back and stared at him, eyebrows raised as she waited for him to say something else. But for once his brain was blank. Because what could he say? Everything that she'd just thrown at him was true.

He shook his head. "Nothing. Except, I'm sorry."

"Well, don't be. Because I'm not. See you around the hospital."

With that she was out the door, leaving him to wonder if she would ever speak to him again. Because despite what she'd said, he couldn't think of any way that this wouldn't affect their friendship. Not this time. Because this kiss wasn't the same as the last one. Not in any way, shape or form. It was way worse. Because it had meant something. If not to her, then to him.

Darby nudged her leg under the table. "What is wrong with you?"

"Nothing."

"No. Don't even try that stuff with me. It doesn't work. Since Max conveniently had surgery tonight— *again*—and said he couldn't make our dinner, I take it he's the reason for those slumped shoulders."

Yes, he was. But Evie honestly didn't know how to fix it at this point. When he'd laughed at her for saying that he expected her to fall in love with him if they slept together, a scorching pain had ripped through her. Because it might have been true. If they slept together she probably would fall for him. He'd helped her see what a huge mistake that would have been. But along with the pain, there'd been anger. Furious words had tumbled around her brain, and she'd had to grit her teeth before she lashed out and used them to cut him to the ground. Instead, she'd stormed out of his office like an indignant child.

But now that she'd had time to think, she realized she'd overreacted and hadn't given him a chance to say anything else. Because she'd been scared. Scared he would avoid her like he had the last time this had happened. And it looked like he was. Even Darby could see it for what it was.

She decided to come clean. "I kissed him and he seemed to kiss me back. Until he wasn't and started backpedaling so fast that things became a blur of anger and regret. I'm pretty sure that's why he's not here."

Darby's mouth fell open and her eyebrows shot up, reaching near her hairline. "You kissed *him*?"

"Well, I mean, I think he was about to kiss me, but then I just kind of...beat him to it." She tried to put her thoughts into words. "It just happened. I'm not even sure why or how."

"Wow. Did you guys talk about it?"

She shrugged. "I talked at it. And around it. And through it. And then I stormed out of his office."

"You didn't." Her eyes rounded. "I know it's not funny, but I'm picturing you slamming his door behind you. That is not like you. At all."

"I know." Her chin dropped into her hand and she

probably looked every bit as miserable as she felt. "But I don't know how to repair the damage."

"You go and talk to him again. And again. As many times as it takes for him to screw his head back on straight. I know the guy has a thing against commitment, but from what I'm hearing, you didn't ask for one."

"Correct. I don't want one. I don't know that I'll ever get married again after what happened with Brad. But he even threw that in my face."

"God. I can't blame you for storming out, then. Maybe we'll all just be groovy old singletons when we turn seventy."

Although Darby had nothing against marriage, she just hadn't met the right person yet. And after one failed engagement, it didn't seem like she was in a hurry to change her status on social media.

"Maybe. And you're right. I probably do need to go talk to him. The kiss was just impulsive. It meant nothing. I just need to get him to understand that."

"That's probably a good idea." Darby reached over and squeezed her hand. "Plus, it's hard to do the planning for the gala if you end up being the only one on the committee. And since part of the event will now be held at the hospital, there's a lot of last-minute things to organize, like caterers and DJs and linen services, right?"

"I know. I'll try to talk to him. And if that doesn't work, I'll have to find someone else who'll be willing to help out."

"He'll come around. He probably just feels awkward about everything right now. You could try to reschedule dinner, but until things are resolved between you two, it's probably just going to be lather, rinse, repeat, with him finding excuses not to come."

Although Darbs wasn't trying to make her feel guilty, she just felt more and more miserable as dinner went on and ended with her just picking at her food.

"You need to go home, Evie. Get some rest. Things will probably look better tomorrow."

Her friend was right. Even though Max was avoiding her at the moment, she couldn't really see him not following through with what he'd committed to do. He wasn't anticommitment in general, just when it came to relationships.

They paid their bill and then headed out the door. She turned when she heard her name murmured in a low, familiar tone. Shock made her stand completely still.

Max was standing there in black jeans and a turquoise polo shirt, looking completely at ease. And completely gorgeous.

Oh, Lord, what did he want?

She couldn't think of a single thing to say, just stood there looking at him like an idiot. It was Darby who broke the silence. "Sorry you missed dinner. I hope your emergency worked out okay."

One side of his mouth quirked. "The jury is still out on that. Sorry about tonight, though."

It was then that she realized he wasn't talking about his supposed surgery, but about what had happened between the two of them. She didn't think she could hash it out in public like this, though. It was one thing to tell Darby in confidence, but to then have things laid out like his surgical instruments?

Thankfully, Darby again saved the day as she leaned on her cane and said, "Well, I've got an early morning, and my leg is giving me fits tonight, so I'll say good night."

"See you later. I hope your leg feels better," Evie replied, giving her friend a hug.

Darby whispered, "Good luck" in her ear.

Ah, so it wasn't the leg giving her fits, she was just giving Evie a chance to talk to Max alone. He was here, so he must be ready to talk things through, right? Or maybe he was coming to say "sorry, but I can't help you with the gala after all."

Darby had caught a cab and was on her way home, leaving her and Max standing in front of the restaurant.

"Walk with me?"

"Okay."

They started down the street, heading toward the Vegas strip, where some of the most famous Las Vegas casinos were located. They strolled in silence for about five minutes before he spoke. "I don't like the way we left things the other day."

A sense of relief swept over her. "I don't, either. And I'm sorry for stomping off the way I did. I really do value our friendship and don't want to lose it over something stupid." She hesitated. "I feel like the last time this happened, you avoided me for a long time, and it hurt. And I missed you. Can we just forget that any of this happened?"

She'd spoken the truth. She had missed him. And it had hurt. Hopefully he would take those two things at face value and accept them for the apology that it was meant to be.

"I missed you, too. And I realized when I had to make up a story in order not to come tonight, then I was headed in the wrong direction. Again. I'm sorry, Evie."

"I'm sorry, too. So we're good?"

"We're good."

Her eyes closed and a feeling of gratitude washed over her. She wanted to hug him but was afraid it would ruin things if she did. So she simply smiled and thanked him.

"So do you want to give me a rundown about what still needs to be done for the gala?"

"I actually wasn't sure you were going to continue on the committee, but I'm glad you are." She pulled a list from inside of her purse and showed it to him. "Anything spark your interest?"

He pointed to an item on the list. "I actually know a guy who DJs for a living if that would help. Nothing off the wall and I think it would fit in with the atmosphere Dr. Robbins is going for."

"You mean cold and cranky?"

Max laughed. "I have to admit, that's a fair assessment. I bet his bedside manner was phenomenal."

"I bet. But at least he liked our idea. If it works out, he thinks we might be able to have it completely at the hospital next year. We can use the atrium for dinner and the presentations and then the courtyard for the after party."

"He actually called it an 'after party'?"

Her mouth twisted. "No. He called it a 'greet and mingle.' But, anyway, if you know a DJ, that would be great, if he's available for the time slot we need him for."

"Which is...?"

She thought for a second. "The actual gala starts at seven and Dr. Robbins wants it to go until around eight thirty. Then those who wanted to would all head over to the hospital. We're thinking that most will want to if we advertise that there will be dancing and a bar."

"So from eight forty-five until, say, eleven?"

"That sounds about right."

He made a note in his phone. "I'll call him in the morning and let you know for sure. Now, what else?"

They went through the rest of the items with Max selecting a few more things from the list. "Does that help?"

"Absolutely." She paused for a minute as something struck her. "Is Margaret's biopsy tomorrow? I was afraid that was the surgery you were talking about."

"No, I would have let you know if it was tonight. It's tomorrow at ten thirty. Her son will bring her in at six to do pre-op stuff. And then we'll go from there."

"Did her daughter fly in?"

"Yes, she did, actually. I was proud of Margaret for calling and asking her to."

"Her kids are great. I've met both of them over the years."

They stopped to wait for the light to change, signaling they could cross the street. "Having a great support group will help a lot. She's going to need it, if the biopsy tells me my suspicions are right."

"The hospital also has support groups for those with different types of cancers. I'll encourage her to try some of them out. I'm sure she will find one that she likes.

It'll help if there are some familiar faces in the infusion room."

They crossed the street and found themselves in the middle of a large throng of people waiting to get into one of the shows. They moved to the outside of the cluster, skirting it as best they could. Maybe they should have gone a different way. But she actually loved the crowds and the liveliness of Vegas. Just by walking its streets, no one would ever guess that there was an unprecedented water shortage going on right now. Except for the hotel notices that had been posted saying that for those staying for extended periods, they would only change linens and towels once a week, things were pretty much business as usual.

"I'm sure she will. And she has a great treatment team behind her, too," Evie said. She meant it. Max and his staff were good at their jobs and their reviews showed it. Not that Evie herself put a lot of stock in those things. After all, anyone could have an off day and either be shorter than necessary with a patient, or too cautious when it came to treatment.

"Well, thanks for that. But she has a good doctor in you as well. If you hadn't found that mass on her lung, who knows how long it would have been before it was found. You may very well have saved her life."

"Well, mutual admiration society aside, let's keep on trying to save her life."

"Not a question. We're all going to fight hard for her." He glanced down the street and then back at her. "Do you have room for some ice cream from Delacort? It's just ahead."

She smiled. "Are you kidding. Delacort is my favorite spot. Their raspberry sorbet is to die for."

"I remember. I also remember the one time they ran out of it."

She laughed. "That wasn't one of my finer moments."

"You weren't rude. You just looked like you were going to burst into tears."

He remembered that? "Well then, let's hope they have some tonight, for both of our sakes."

He laughed and the sound sent a shiver over her. Maybe because she hadn't been sure she would ever hear it again. The urge to link her fingers through his made her curl her palm into itself until it was a fist. She wasn't going to risk doing anything that could be misconstrued. Especially not right after they'd kissed and made up.

Ha! No. Kissing could also be misconstrued. Even figurative kissing.

Instead, she took a deep breath of cool dry air and let herself enjoy simply being with him.

Delacort was a few stores ahead and although Vegas wasn't particularly renowned for its ice cream, it should be, she mused. Or at least this one store should be. It was churned fresh every day and if you happened to go in while they still had their machines going, the place was filled with wonderful scents of cream and sugar and the various flavorings.

The line wasn't too long and they were soon back on the street with their selections. Max's was in a little bowl, while her raspberry sorbet—which, thankfully, they had plenty of—was scooped into a chocolate-lined cone. The tip of the cone was also filled with chocolate and was so good when taking the very last bite of the confection.

"Yum." She took a small bite, and the fresh taste of fruit melted on her tongue, leaving it wanting more. "How's yours?" She glanced at him to see him smiling at her obvious enjoyment of her ice cream. "What? I don't get over this way very often. So it's a treat when I do."

"I know. And mine is as good as it always is."

"I can't believe you don't want it in a cone. But you never have, have you?"

"No. I never have. I like the ice cream all by itself."

Heading back the way they came, she happened to glance to the side and gasped before she could stop herself.

"What?"

"Oh, nothing. I just didn't realize that *Walter Grapevine* was showing here in Vegas."

"Walter who?" He looked so puzzled that she had to laugh.

"It's an off-Broadway musical I've been wanting to see. I was hoping it would come here."

"I've never heard of it."

She wasn't surprised. "It's a smaller production, but it's gotten rave reviews."

"I'll have to look it up."

The topic gravitated back toward the gala as they walked back toward the restaurant.

When they got there, he glanced at her. "Did you drive?"

"No. Darby and I both took a cab together—why?"

"I'll take you home."

"You don't have to. Really, Max, I'm out of your way."

He gave a light shrug. "Only by a few minutes. It's not a big deal."

The parking garage was just a block from the restaurant. Max paid the attendant and they waited as the car was brought up to them. "I'm sorry you ended up having to pay for parking when you didn't even get to eat."

"I had Delacort's finest. I can't complain."

She smiled. "Thanks again, Max. For being able to get past what happened."

"I could say the same for you."

The rest of the trip was made with the kind of small talk that Evie had missed. They talked about work and the gala, and just life. She gave him the address of the apartment she'd bought just after selling her and Brad's previous one. It was just a mile away from where she'd lived before and, despite the anger she'd felt at the time, she was thankfully free of memories that might have plagued her if Brad hadn't needed the funds from a quick sale. It had worked out for the best. And she was happy with the new place.

He pulled into one of the guest parking spots and turned to face her. "I'll let you know tomorrow about the DJ either before or after the biopsy."

"Sounds good. I have an appointment tomorrow after work to go look at the venue, just so I can see the space and find out when it'll be open to us to get the setup done. From what I can see we have a linen service, caterer, someone to set up the sound and a florist coming in. I'm pretty sure I understood that those companies were already contracted last year during the previous gala, but I want to make sure none of those changed. And since last year's coordinator moved to a new hospital, I'm not sure how much he can help us."

"Do you want me to come with you?"

"Do you have time?"

"I do. When does your shift end?"

She had to stop and think a minute. "Five o'clock or whenever I finish my rounds."

"How about if we meet in the lobby at five thirty? You can let me know if you get hung up."

"That works. You'll let me know, too, if it doesn't work?"

"I will."

With that, she said goodbye and stepped out of the car. He made no move to back out of the spot, so she started to walk toward the lobby of the apartment building, feeling his eyes on her with each step. He was just being polite, but it made her self-conscious, something it shouldn't have. Evidently, things hadn't gone completely back to the way they were before, but all she could do was give it time and hope that each day would bring a new sense of normalcy and friendship.

CHAPTER FIVE

SHE WAS UP THERE. Max could sense it. He didn't even need to look. He'd caught a hint of movement in the observation room around five minutes ago. She'd been held up with a patient right as the procedure was starting, but by the time he'd placed the camera for the video-assisted thoracoscopy he would use to perform the biopsy, he knew she'd made it.

He made the other two incisions he would use for his instruments and got back to work. They'd know pretty quickly what they were dealing with and if the mass was benign, he might even be able to get it out during this session. If it was malignant, they would need a PET scan to see where else it was and to help them figure out a treatment protocol.

Watching the screen to his right, he made his way to the tumor and used the grasping tool to hold a section of the lung while cutting off a small piece, then quickly moved in to cauterize the area. The danger with vascular tumors was they could hemorrhage, filling the surgical field with blood. Fortunately, it looked like he'd gotten all of the vessels. After pulling the sample free, he dropped it into the collection cup one of the nurses brought over.

"Can you get that over to the lab?" he asked, although he really didn't need to. She would know what to do.

"On my way."

Now, it was a waiting game to see if he closed her up or removed the tumor. This time he did glance up and saw he was right. Evie was up there. She nodded to him and he returned the gesture before turning back to his patient.

He had a piano concerto playing on the speakers, which was usually his music of choice during surgical procedures. It was soothing, with no distracting words to get tangled inside his head. Every surgeon had their own playlists, or none at all. He had one or two colleagues who wanted it completely quiet.

Ten minutes later, the nurse returned with a name. "Metastatic breast angiosarcoma."

Damn. There were times he just didn't want to be right. This was one of those times. He wasn't going to take the tumor out. And depending on the results of the PET scan…

Well, he would cross that bridge when he came to it. She would need to be in the hospital until the chest tube came out, probably a couple of days. And he would need to go out and talk with the family members who had come to the hospital. He knew her two adult children were here, but had no idea if Margaret had living siblings or not.

He glanced up at Evie and shook his head. Her eyes closed for a minute before she opened them and acknowledged his gesture. It was a damn shame that it couldn't have worked out in their favor. But you had to play the cards you were dealt. He'd learned that the hard way when his mom was taken from him. And then again when his dad drank himself into oblivion.

Both he and Evie were aware that with every patient who came across their paths, there was the possibility that a life would end and that there'd be nothing they could do to stop that death. And Max hated this part of the job. He hated even more that this patient was special to Evie, and that there was nothing he could do to change her odds of survival.

He checked to make sure there was no bleeding before he inserted the chest tube and withdrew the instruments he'd used to take the biopsy, then closed up two of the holes with a stitch or two and tightened the opening where the tubing was to keep it secure.

Then he made sure she woke up from the anesthesia without any problems before he started to head out the door. Margaret reached up with a shaky hand and squeezed his, making him swallow hard. He squeezed back. "I'll come check on you once they get you in your room, okay?"

She nodded, but didn't say anything. Not that he expected her to. He wouldn't tell her the results of the biopsy until she was truly awake and could understand what was going on around her.

Evie met him at the door. "You were right, weren't you?"

"Yes, but it doesn't make it any easier."

She leaned her shoulder against his for a second. "You're doing what you were trained to do, Max. You're not responsible for whether or not it's a good outcome."

Evie's voice was low and soothing, and he realized she was trying to comfort him. Shades of what his mom had done with his dad filtered through and he stood up straighter. "You don't need to tell me what I already know."

As soon as he said the words, he clenched his teeth. "Ah, God, I'm sorry, Evie. It just bites that things like this happen to people who don't deserve them."

"I know. And you don't have to apologize. I was trying to talk to myself as much as I was you. I wished for so much better for Margaret."

"We might not be able to take away the diagnosis, but we can do our damnedest to make sure her treatment gives her the best quality of life possible. I've never believed in extending life just to extend it, though, if those months are going to be lived in misery. I wouldn't want it for myself and I don't want it for my patients."

"I'm in complete agreement, Max."

"Do you want to come with me while I talk to the family?"

"Yes. Her kids will recognize me, and I went to Thanksgiving dinner at their house after Brad and I... Well, my parents were in Brazil visiting extended family at the time, and I didn't want to be alone so I accepted their invitation."

And Max had been too busy trying to avoid her—to avoid the complicated feelings that came along with her divorce—to recognize that she might have been lonely during those first holidays without her ex. She'd been staying with Darby, so he'd just assumed... He sighed.

"I haven't been a very good friend, Evie. I don't know why you put up with me."

Her head jerked to look at him. "I didn't say that to make you feel bad. It was more to let you know that I have a history with this family."

"I know. And somehow, that makes it worse. I'll try to do better."

She smiled. "You are. Just don't disappear from mine and Darby's lives again, okay?"

"I won't." It was a promise he hoped to hell he'd be able to keep. Especially as he'd made an impulsive purchase yesterday evening. He wasn't sure what he'd been thinking, or if she'd even go with him. He could always offer the other ticket to Darby and let them go together. But he truly wanted to make it up to Evie and he couldn't think of a better way to do that than to offer her something she loved. And while Darby had liked *Wicked*, she'd confessed that musicals really weren't her thing.

They got to the waiting area and presented a united front when talking to Margaret's family, telling them what they knew so far—that this tumor was aggressive and they needed to find out where else it might be hiding before coming up with a treatment plan.

When her son asked if this was terminal, Max nodded. "I'm afraid so, but I can't give you any more information until we've done some other testing."

As soon as those words were out in the open, brother and sister embraced, with Margaret's daughter breaking into tears. Evie went over and hugged each of them, then promised they would do all they could to keep Margaret comfortable.

After they left the room. Max stood in the hallway for a minute, his own eyes burning before he said, "I do have some more patients to see and I want to check on Margaret. What time is our tour of the venue?"

"At six, so we can meet in the parking lot at five thirty, like we planned. I can drive, or we can catch a taxi, whichever you prefer."

"You drive?" He gave a half snort. "The last time I was in a car with you, you nearly killed us both."

Her eyes widened. "Because some jerk came through a red light and nearly T-boned us. It was my quick thinking that saved you from being squashed like a bug."

"A bug, eh? Quite the opinion you have of me, Dr. Milagre."

"Just stating the facts."

It should seem strange that they could joke after that meeting with Margaret's family, but sometimes inviting some lighter moments in was the only thing that kept him going in the midst of difficult diagnoses. And he was thankful Evie had played along rather than chase the sadness that was Margaret Collins's case.

"Wow." It was the only thing Evie could think of to say as she stood in the cavernous room that would house the initial part of the gala. "It's hard to comprehend how big this room is when it's full of tables and chairs and decorations."

"It is pretty big." Max stood there, his hands shoved in his pockets, and glanced around. "I can see why they chose this place."

"Yeah, me, too."

Right now, the room was devoid of anything except for scaffolding, which was set up in the middle of the room. Some workmen were hanging what looked to be paper lanterns from the ceiling.

With walls that were off white with just a hint of green, the space was bright and airy, a large chandelier giving it an opulence that the hospital's courtyard couldn't match. But maybe it didn't have to. The two places had a completely different feel, but the hospital space would perhaps come across as somewhere that everyone could let their hair down and shrug off the cares of the day. Heaven knew that's what Evie used it for on an almost daily basis. In fact, as her divorce was dragging out, she'd spent many hours out there on one of the secluded benches, needing time to find herself again.

But getting away from the hospital grounds was proving to be nice, too. Margaret Collins's diagnosis had been heartbreaking, something that would haunt her for a while if the PET scans came back with the cancer in multiple places. At least here she could think about something else for a little while.

Really? Then why was it still running through her mind? She did her best to shake it off.

"I think I remember the buffet tables over on the right by the door. Probably because that allowed things to be refilled without staff having to drag food and drink carts through the seating areas."

"That makes sense," he said.

Movement out of the corner of her eye caught her attention. One of the workmen was straining to reach a lantern that was hanging askew, and was leaning way past the railing on the metal scaffolding. She shuddered. That was definitely not a job for the faint of heart. Evie was not a fan of superhigh places. Darbs had talked her into going on one of those drop towers and had said it wasn't as high as it looked from the ground. But it was. It was every bit as high. Once she'd gotten to the top, she'd been pretty sure she wasn't going to survive the plunge to the ground. She expected her heart to give out half-way down. It hadn't given out. But she had given Darby a piece of her mind. One look at her face must have told her something, because her friend had stopped laughing and hugged her instead. "I'm sorry, Evie," she'd said. "I didn't think you would be that scared."

But she had been. Almost as scared as she'd been when Darby had shown her those pictures of Brad and she'd realized that her life was about to radically change. The last year had been harder than she ever could have imagined, and while the betrayal had eroded her confidence in her ability to judge character, it had also caused her to grow stronger and more independent. And it looked like she and Max were on their way to mending their friendship. A silver lining, for sure. Only time would tell if it would last.

One of the hotel's staff came into the room and headed their way. "Do you have any questions? Or any special requests?"

Evie shook her head. "I can't think of anything at the moment." She glanced at Max, who shook his head.

"Well, if you do, please feel free to get in touch with me." The woman handed her a card.

"I will, thank you."

She left and Evie sighed. "Can you think of anything else we need to see?"

"Not off the top of my head, but then again, I haven't been to one of these events."

She grinned up at him. "Well, that's all about to change."

"I guess so." There was a pause and then he added, "Speaking of events, would you be interested in—"

Just then, she heard a shout from above her and glanced up just in time to see the scaffolding tilting to the side. The man who'd been leaning quickly moved back to the middle, but it did nothing to right the structure. Instead, like something out of a movie, it continued to tilt farther and farther, gaining speed as the legs on that side collapsed inward. Two of the men were clinging to the side boards, but one of them slid down the side and hit the ground with a loud thunk and lay there unmoving. Max hurried over to him, and as the same employee who'd talked to them a few minutes ago appeared in the doorway, Evie yelled, "Call 911!"

A cell phone appeared in the person's hand and she assumed she was calling for help.

Max was near the collapsed side of the structure, taking vitals, but when Evie glanced at the scaffolding, she realized if it fell farther, or boards started to rain down, they were going to land right on Max and the victim. And if those men holding on for their lives couldn't maintain their grip, they were going to have two more injuries, or worse.

"Hold on!" she yelled up to them. "Help is on the way."

At least she hoped it was. She made her way to Max.

"We need to move him. That thing could collapse completely and come down on both of you."

"His leg's broken at the very least, and I'm thinking he has head trauma. One of his pupils is blown."

She knew the dangers of moving someone with unknown injuries, but if the scaffolding continued to fail...

The sound of something mechanical caught her attention and she saw a small skid loader being driven into the room. The driver moved the vehicle to the collapsed side of the scaffolding and raised the mechanism so that it bolstered the structure. Smart. Maybe that would help hold it in place until help could arrive.

As if summoned out of thin air, two firefighters appeared in the doorway and immediately entered the room and assessed the situation. One of them nodded at the forklift operator. "Thanks."

Max continued to monitor the downed man as they waited for the EMTs to arrive.

The other firefighter moved to the far side of the scaffolding and called up, "Are you injured?"

Both of the men stated that they were okay.

"Is it safe to try to climb down?" one asked. "We don't want it to completely collapse."

"If you feel you can. If not, we have some harnesses being unloaded even as we speak."

One of the men swung his legs over the side and picked his way down diagonally. The second soon followed his lead, taking the very same path.

Evie held her breath as they continued down, but they both seemed sure about the placement of their hands and feet. When the first one got to the firefighter who'd spoken to them, he allowed himself to be helped onto the ground, where he sat down in a rush. The second firefighter had him put his head between his knees. Evie hurried over to them.

"How is he?" she asked the firefighter.

"Honestly? He's extremely lucky."

Squatting next to him, she took his pulse as the other man was helped off the structure.

Then the place was suddenly teeming with police and EMTs, who rushed in with their bags and each went to a different victim. But the men who climbed down were found to be in perfect condition, except for having the living daylights scared out of them. And this was nothing like the drop tower, because while Evie had been scared out of her mind, the rational side of her knew that she was in no real danger. These men, however? They'd known very well that they could die at any given moment. It gave her a hard dose of reality. In all her years of practicing medicine, that whole scenario of "is there a doctor in the house?" had never happened to her. Until now.

She asked one of the emergency services guys, "Which hospital are you taking them to?"

"Vegas Memorial."

Their hospital. "That's great. We're both doctors there."

"I thought I recognized you, although we normally deal more with the ER crew. Looks like it was lucky you were here when it happened."

She glanced at where Max had handed off his patient to another paramedic. She was glad she didn't have to do what these guys did on a regular basis. She was sure if she'd had to climb that scaffolding, she would have. But she was so, so thankful that it hadn't come to that.

She nodded at the forklift driver, who looked like he couldn't have been older than nineteen or twenty. "We were lucky that hotel staff member thought quickly and brought in the skid loader. He may have saved those two men from having the whole structure collapse."

"Agreed."

The EMT guy went over to speak to the man who was leaning against the wall, looking a little pale himself. He shook his hand and patted him on the back. It made Evie smile. She was glad he'd received a little recognition for his act. She doubted he would forget this moment. At least not for a very long time.

She knew she wouldn't, either.

She went back to stand by Max, and nudged him with her shoulder. "You okay?"

"Yes. I'm happy as hell we didn't have to make the decision to move him." The EMTs had stabilized the man's neck and slid a backboard under him.

"They're taking him to our hospital, so we should be able to check in and see how he's doing."

Max's phone pinged and he got it out to look at it. A second later, his lips twisted. "It's Margaret Collins. She's asking to go home."

Her heart cramped. She understood where the woman was coming from. If Evie thought she was going to die, she wouldn't want to be in a hospital, either. She'd want to go home to her own bed. "She can't. Not yet."

"No. That chest tube has to stay in for the next day or so. I need to go."

"I'll come with you. I think we've done everything we can here." Besides, she wanted to ask him what he'd been about to say to her before the scaffolding collapsed. Something about an event she might be interested in?

A police officer came over and asked if he could take a statement from one of them. She guessed she'd have to ask him later. Looking at Max, she said, "You go on. I'll stay here and talk to him."

"You sure?"

"Yes. Tell Margaret that I'll be there to see her in a little while."

"Will do. See you back at the hospital."

As she watched Max's strong back retreat through a doorway, she closed her eyes for a second. That had been so scary. And the thought of that heavy support structure collapsing on top of Max and the victim had rippled through her head and filled her with fear.

It would have been the same if had been Darby.

No, it wouldn't. She loved her friends dearly and would never choose one's life over the other's. But the thought of Max being severely injured or dying hit a visceral spot inside of her.

One that she knew existed, but that she tried to keep buried and out of sight. It was the same one that had held a tiny hope when he'd kissed her all those years ago only to have it snuffed out in an instant.

The police officer asked her a question and she shook off her thoughts and tried to concentrate on what he was saying, thankful for the distraction.

But what was going to happen when the distractions were all gone and she had time to think?

She didn't know. But she'd better figure it out before that happened, or she was going to get herself into a situation she didn't want to be in. And she had no doubt that Max wouldn't want her to be there, either. Because it would mean that she cared about him a little too much and in the wrong way, and that would not be good. For either of them.

CHAPTER SIX

EVIE ARRIVED JUST as he was getting ready to leave Margaret's room. He had talked her into staying until the drain tube came out, but just barely. She was in pain, which was understandable given the procedure she'd had. But it was also her breathing. She feared she was having an asthma attack and the nurse had refused to give her an inhaler without Max's permission. The nurse had evidently called when he'd been in the throes of helping their scaffolding victim, and he'd missed it. He couldn't imagine how scary it must have been to have had her meds withheld. But it wasn't the nurse's fault, either—she'd been following what the chart had said, and Max had wanted either he or Evie to check on her if her breathing problems got worse. And neither of them had been there.

But once he'd gotten to the hospital and had okayed a breathing treatment, Margaret felt a little better. But it was as if she knew her days were numbered and didn't want to spend the remainder of them in the hospital, despite the fact that both of her children were there with her.

He sat with her and shared that he wanted to get a PET scan and that would give them some more information.

It was a tricky balance of not giving the family false hope, but also not bringing down doom and gloom before they knew what they were facing. He might "think" he knew, but until he had the evidence to prove it, he tried to always err on the side of hope. At least whenever it was possible.

He paused just outside the doorway to share with Evie what had been said. When he finished, she nodded. "I would have done the same. I'll go in and visit with her and if she asks I'll reaffirm what you just said."

"Thanks. I'm going to see if our scaffolding guy has arrived yet. Do you want to be updated?"

She glanced at him as if in surprise. "Of course."

"Alright. I'll give you a call once I hear something."

"Sounds good. Thanks." She stopped him before he could leave with a hand on his arm. "Wait. What were you going to say to me at the hotel? Something about some event?"

Damn. In the chaos, he'd totally forgotten about the two tickets he'd bought for the musical. And the doubts he'd had about them going together had seemed to grow the more time that passed. "It was nothing."

"No, seriously. I want to know."

He shifted from one foot to the other. "I actually have two tickets to the musical you wanted to go to. And was wondering—as an olive branch for some of my less intelligent moments over the last couple of years—if you might like to go to it."

Her eyes widened. "Are you serious? You really want to go?"

"Why wouldn't I?" Actually he could think of a hundred reasons why it might not be such a good idea. But now that the words had been tossed into the universe, there was no way he could retract them.

"I wasn't sure if satire was your thing."

"If you decide to go with me, I guess we'll find out."

She laughed. "Well, in that case, I absolutely want to go. When is it?"

That was something he hadn't even given thought to. What if she had to work that night? He found himself hoping they could somehow make it work. "Next Tuesday night at eight."

"Really? That's perfect because I get off at five that night. It'll give me time to go home and change."

Her eyes were sparkling and he was suddenly glad he'd asked her. It made her happy to go, and that made him happy. And he wasn't sure why, other than what he'd said, which had been the truth. He did see it as a way of making up for being an absentee friend. He just hoped it didn't backfire on him. "Well, then that works out for both of us. Talk to you in a little while."

With that, he left the room and headed down to the emergency room, glancing at the courtyard as he crossed the atrium on the ground floor. The sun was out in full force and the sidewalk outside looked dry and parched, a sign that there still hadn't been a drop of rain in almost two months. It was good that what Evie liked to call the "after party" of the gala wouldn't begin at the hospital until after the sun had gone down and things had cooled off.

There would be no mist machines set up or temporary fountains or anything that involved water, since there was no end in sight to the restrictions that had been set in place. Nothing but a good long rain would remedy any of that. Even an ice sculpture, although not forbidden, would probably be frowned on by some of their bene-factors. Evie hadn't wanted anything that could be seen as wasting that precious resource.

When he glanced at the large television as he passed by, there was a report talking about the rain levels being much lower than normal, even for Nevada. They were hovering near the lowest recorded rainfall in the history of the state. The people in Las Vegas who'd opted to try to maintain lawns had found that even the smallest patches had turned brown. Some had decided to rip them up and turn to xeriscape landscaping instead, which had always been popular in desert climates. The hospital had been one of those places that had recently changed landscaping companies to focus on water conservation.

He sighed and kept moving. He'd been born and raised in Las Vegas and had never thought of moving, but some-times the reality of living here could be frustrating with the constant traffic and how busy the strip could be, but it was also full of life and laughter, and people who ex-ited the shows and casinos smiling. Those chapels of love were also a big draw for the area, probably pro-ducing some of the shortest-lived marriages in the his-tory of the US, but even those were fun and light. His parents had been married in one of those chapels, but theirs was one that had endured, at least until his mom's death had cut it short.

And why was he thinking of any of that? Their mar-riage wasn't one of the happy-ever-after stories from the pages of a storybook. And yet, they had been happy. At least until his mom's diagnosis.

Thankfully, the emergency room was bustling with activity and pulled him from his thoughts. He went over to the nurse's desk. "Any idea where the man injured in a scaffolding accident is?"

The nurse glanced at a computer screen. "He's actually in room one. Dr. Wilson is with him."

"Thanks." That was a good call. Todd Wilson was the head of neurology and a great doctor.

He headed over to the room and gave a quick knock before entering. Todd was leaning over the patient, whose eyes were actually open. The neurologist glanced his way. "Ah, Max. I hear you played hero today."

"No, Evie Milagre and I just happened to be in the right place at the right time."

He smiled. "That's not how I hear it. Grady here was just telling me that the rest of that scaffolding could have come down at any time."

Max moved closer. How had the patient even known that? He'd been unconscious at the time. He looked down at the man. "Glad to see you're awake. How are you feeling?"

"I have a massive headache." Grady's voice was rough-edged, probably from pain.

"I'm not surprised. That was quite some fall." Max glanced at his colleague with an unspoken question in his eyes.

"He's pretty lucky. He's got a big knot on the back of his head, and we're going to send him for a CT scan to make sure I'm not missing anything, but I think he's going to be okay."

"Thanks to you, Doc." Grady forced a smile. "Where's your lady friend? I'd like to thank her as well."

Oh, hell. Thank heavens Evie wasn't here to hear that. "She's actually a doctor here at the hospital as well."

"Oh, I thought you were at the hotel looking to see if it would work for your wedding reception. Sorry."

Todd's eyes twinkled. "Wedding reception, eh? Is there something I should know about?"

The neurologist no doubt knew exactly why he and Evie had been at the hotel. "You know my philosophy on marriage."

"Actually, I don't. Care to enlighten us?" He winked at the patient, who smiled.

"Not really. Suffice it to say I won't be visiting any of the area's wedding chapels anytime in the foreseeable future."

Just at that moment, Evie poked her head in the door. Great. This was all he needed. To have this little joke expanded on and dissected.

"I thought I'd come and check on him myself," Evie said. She came into the room. "I'm glad to see you're awake."

He nodded. "I'm glad to wake up and find I'm not sitting on a cloud playing a harp."

He was right. That scaffolding was heavy. If one of the pipes had broken free and landed on him, things might have turned out very differently. But it looked like this was one story that might have a happy ending. He was sure Todd saw his share of tragic outcomes himself, given the line of work he was in.

Evie came closer. "I'm glad you're not, either."

"So you're a doctor, too?"

"Yep. Evie Milagre, nice to meet you. I was there at the hotel as well. Dr. Hunt and I were looking at the venue for the hospital's gala."

Although it was normal to use titles in front of patients, it always seemed weird when Evie referred to him as anything other than Max. Or Maximilian, if she was feeling playful.

The man nodded before wincing. "I thought you were there for a different reason, but Dr. Hunt set us straight pretty quickly."

Her head tilted sideways, and Todd said, "He thought you and Dr. Hunt were getting hitched. Max jumped right on that and assured us that wasn't the case, nor would it ever be the case."

A strange look went through her eyes before she masked it with a smile. He frowned. It had to be a figment of his imagination. After all, she'd married Brad, and other than that kiss in front of the venue where *Wicked* had been playing, there'd never been any indication that she had any interest in him as anything other than a friend.

Except, then there'd been that second kiss, too. That one had thrown him for an even bigger loop. Because he'd been about to let things go a whole lot further than they had. And Evie certainly hadn't seemed opposed to that happening, either. At least not from the way she kissed him. There'd been a slow thoroughness to the way her mouth had molded itself to his. To the way her fingers had tightened their grip on him—as if she never wanted to let him go. It had set him on fire and made it almost impossible to pull away. But he'd had to. For both of their sakes. Because what he'd wanted out of that encounter had been purely physical. And Evie? He had a feeling she wanted more. More than he could give.

Her smile held steady. "Dr. Hunt and I have been friends for a very long time. But we wouldn't last two seconds as a couple." She gave a quick laugh.

What was that supposed to mean, that they wouldn't last for two seconds?

"That's right. Evie is far too picky and controlling for me."

After a second of no response, she finally made a face at him. "And you are far too overbearing and ridiculous for me."

"Oh, really?"

Evie thought he was overbearing? That was kind of a punch to the gut. But was it any worse than him calling her picky and controlling?

No. So maybe she felt like it was just as mean-spirited. But he'd been joking, choosing words that didn't describe her at all. Because the ones that he would have chosen in real life were the ones that made her hard to resist. Even for an old friend.

But he did want to explain that he didn't see her as either of those things, he'd just been trying to be funny in a not-so-funny situation.

He moved closer to her, so that he could shake Grady's

hand. "It's good to see you awake and in good spirits. Let's not have any more scaffolding accidents."

"Yeah, I think I'm going to keep both feet on the ground for the next couple of weeks."

"Good plan. Take care."

Grady nodded. "You, too, Doc. And thanks again."

"You're very welcome."

He went outside to wait for Evie, although he wasn't sure that was the best idea. Maybe he should just leave well enough alone. But he never wanted to hurt someone even unintentionally. And that look she'd given him…

A minute later, she came sailing through the door, throwing a comment behind her as it closed. Her eyes widened when she saw him there.

"Is something wrong? Margaret?"

There was something wrong, but this time it wasn't with Margaret.

"No, I just wanted to make sure you knew I was joking in there, earlier."

"Joking? About which part? About us never being a couple?" She crinkled her nose as if to show him that she was not serious.

"No, about you being picky and controlling. I don't think you're either of those things. It was meant to be funny, but as soon as the words left my lips, I realized they could be construed as something that I really think. I don't."

She nodded, eyebrows going up. "I assume you want me to say that I don't think you're overbearing or ridiculous?"

"It would be nice."

And just like that, their relationship had shifted back over to the fun friendship they'd always had. Except for the last couple of years, when things had gotten so weird. He was suddenly glad he'd gotten those tickets and that he'd asked her to go with him.

"Sorry, Charley. No can do."

He laughed. "Why did I know you were going to say that?"

"Because, like I said to Grady, we've known each other a very long time. And I need to prep you for that musical we're going to see."

"Yes, you do." He paused. "I'm glad you can go."

This time there was no mirth in her smile, but there was a sincerity that came through in her eyes. She touched his arm. "So am I, Max. So am I."

He glanced at his watch, almost sorry that he was due to see a patient in a half hour. "Sorry to seem overbearing and ridiculous, but I need to go."

"Sorry to seem picky and controlling, but so do I. See you around, Max."

With that, she walked away, and damn if it wasn't hard to look away from the curve of her butt as she retreated. But he forced his eyes up and turned, then strode down the corridor at a pace he hoped would leave the mental image of his hands sliding over that shapely derrière behind.

She and Max had a dinner meeting scheduled with Arthur Robbins in a half hour to discuss where they were with the plans for the gala, which was coming up in just over a month. It was hard to believe that much time had passed since they'd agreed to work on it together. She had to admit, it had brought them closer and had seemed to iron out the creases of neglect that had plagued their friendship over the last couple of years. Three weeks ago, she'd never have imagined they'd be going to the theater together.

She'd even purchased two new dresses. A blue cocktail dress for the theater and a long black sequined affair for the gala that was off the shoulder, but had a detachable chiffon mini train in back that just scraped the floor. She would definitely be removing that for the courtyard portion of the gala, so that it didn't get snagged on the concrete walkway. It had been years since she'd bought anything for the galas. She normally just recycled some of her old formals for the events. But she found she just wanted something new this time. And she wasn't sure why.

She was nervous about the meeting. Maybe because the other two times she'd gone to see Dr. Robbins, he'd always seemed underwhelmed by the hard work they'd done on the gala, even when she'd gone to him with Max's sketch. Oh, he'd said he liked it and wanted it to happen, but there'd been no warmth in his voice to back up his words. Was he really that cold?

She also found his choice of restaurants a bit odd. A pancake house. For dinner. Somehow, she couldn't see the formal CEO eating a stack of strawberry pancakes, so this should be interesting. She and Max were going to meet outside the hospital and walk the two blocks to the restaurant. As soon as she got outside the building, though, she started having second thoughts. It was blistering hot, and most of that heat seemed to be emanating from the blacktop. She was pretty sure her rubber-soled shoes were in danger of melting into the pavement.

She glanced around hoping to see Max so they could be on their way, when a car pulled up next to her. When the window rolled down, she realized it was the man in question. "Care for some air-conditioning?"

She closed her eyes in bliss as a hint of cool air drifted toward her from the open window. "Oh, God, yes, yes, yes!"

As soon as she opened the door and stepped into the chilly space, she realized her words could have come across as orgasmic. She let out a laugh. It wouldn't be too far off the mark.

"What?" he asked.

She cast about for an explanation for her ridiculous laugh and came up with a quick response. "I was mentally moaning that it was too hot to walk, and here you came with your already cooled car. It was as if you could read my mind." Actually, she was pretty glad he couldn't because she would be mortified. Just like she was about choosing the word *moaning*. What if those were both Freudian slips? Then she'd just have to make sure there were no more of those.

"I went out to the courtyard to kind of refresh my memory about the layout before the meeting and thought the same thing. That this heat is unbearable. It's why I don't jog during the day."

That's right. The man ran marathons. He'd dragged her to one of them years ago and she thought she was going to die. She'd been short of breath and had sweat buckets, even in the cool of the evening. "It's why I don't jog at any time. Day or night."

"You haven't given running a chance."

"Yeah? Well, it didn't give me much of a chance when I tried it that one time."

His mouth twisted, as if he was amused, then he pulled away from the curb. "I should have insisted we train together, then you would have been fine."

Train together? She was pretty sure that wouldn't have gone any better. Because she would have just stared at his legs and physique, and probably ended up tripping over something and winding up on the ground in an ungraceful heap of sweatiness, which Max would never be able to unsee.

"I'm pretty sure I'm not cut out to run, training or not."

Maybe it was like Max, who'd once told her he wasn't cut out to be married. It was after he'd kissed her after the showing of *Wicked*. And it could have been construed from his reaction that she'd been looking for a proposal. She definitely had not. But she certainly hadn't expected him to overreact to the point that he made it seem that being with her in that way was the most hideous thing he could imagine. She'd been glad when he'd stayed away from her for a while. But then she'd missed him. And ended up regretting what had happened as much, or almost as much, as he'd seemed to.

But at least there was none of that today. In fact, over the last month they'd seemed to have drifted back into their old pattern of friendship. Margaret had gone home and at their appointment a few days ago, she'd seemed to be feeling better. She even acted like she was looking forward to starting treatments next week.

The PET scan had not revealed any lesions in her brain or liver, but had found one in her right breast and a mass in her lung. Chemo, while it wouldn't be curative, could help extend her life while maintaining the quality of it, hopefully for a few more years, depending on how the tumors reacted. But the hope was that they'd shrink enough that they could both be removed through surgery. The chance of recurrence was high, since the cells had already traveled once and were likely to again, but maybe they could keep that from happening for a long while.

He glanced her way. "Well, I certainly wouldn't recommend starting in the middle of the summer."

"Starting what?" Surely, he hadn't read her mind about Margaret.

"Running."

Oh! She'd forgotten that's what they'd been talking about. "I wouldn't recommend my starting it any time of the year. I'll stick to hiking. But you're right. Nothing seems very appealing when it's this hot. I wasn't looking forward to walking to the restaurant."

"Me, either. Speaking of which, we're here." He turned into the lot and they got out of the car and walked into the entrance of the restaurant.

"I wonder if he's here yet."

At that moment, Dr. Robbins came around the corner from the dining area. "I wasn't sure you saw me in there, so thought I'd come over and show you where our table was."

There were only three of them, but the CEO had evidently chosen a large corner booth at the very back of the restaurant. The table could have held double their number, but maybe it was just so they could have some privacy.

They sat down. Evie ended up sandwiched between Max and Dr. Robbins, which was kind of awkward. But at least the CEO was sitting on the other side of where the table formed an *L* so they weren't side by side. The former plastic surgeon intimidated her, for some reason. Then again, she'd heard rumblings from others that she wasn't alone in that feeling.

Just in case, she'd brought her spiral-bound notebook with all of the vendors' names and numbers and had hunted down pictures from last year's gala, since the decor was being done by the same company, who said they would make it almost identical to the previous gala. She figured it was better to play it safe, since having part of it at the hospital was already changing things up quite a bit.

He motioned for a member of the waitstaff. "I've already ordered."

Evie glanced down at her watch as surreptitiously as possible. They were still fifteen minutes early. How long ago had the man arrived? A tickle of dislike made the back of her throat itch. She cleared her throat to banish the sensation, trying to tell herself he wasn't trying to make them feel small and unimportant. But, trying or not, he was. And she didn't like it.

He waited until they'd ordered their meals before saying anything else. "Thanks for coming. I just wanted to see where we were and ask if there's anything you need me to do before the event. I collected the sign-up sheets and see a lot of our folks are planning on being at least here for the hospital portion of the gala."

Evie had wondered where those sheets had gone. One minute they'd been up, and yet when she went to gather them this morning, she'd found they were already gone. So he had her at a disadvantage, since she hadn't actually seen them yet. "I'm glad of that. Max and I went to see the venue last week and it looks like it'll be plenty big to handle the guest list. If I could look at those sign-up sheets, I would appreciate it, just so that I can get the final numbers to the caterer." The sheets had a place to check whether or not the staff members would attend both events—the hotel venue and the hospital—or just one, or neither. She was surprised Robbins wouldn't have realized that she would need them.

"Of course." He pulled out his briefcase and handed her a sheaf of papers. "If I could get those back afterward, I would appreciate it."

That made her frown even as she promised that she would return them. What did he actually need them for? Was he going to keep track of attendance or something? If so, that rankled and the tickle grew stronger. Really, it was none of her business how he ran the hospital. But if he was going to treat the staff like preschoolers that would not go over well with the nurses' union or any other job representatives.

Their drinks came out and so did Dr. Robbins's meal. "Sorry, I have another meeting in an hour, do you mind if I start?"

When she hesitated, Max's leg pressed against hers,

reminding her that she was the head of the committee. "Of course not, go ahead."

As he ate, she and Max shared what they'd gotten done from their prospective lists. And she was proud of both of them. They'd worked hard and had completed everything that could be done at this time. All that was really left to do was to finalize the numbers with the caterers and get a copy of Dr. Robbins's speech for the sound people in case he needed a teleprompter. But when she asked, he set down his fork and fixed her with a look. "I actually try not to give those out in advance, or at least not until the legal department takes a look at it. Just in case something gets leaked that shouldn't be."

Although he wasn't accusing her directly, it still bothered her that he would say something like that. They'd each done their jobs well and had given him reports without anyone fearing that something untoward would be done with those reports. But again, maybe something had happened in the past that made him leery of trusting anyone. But he would eventually have to trust his staff, or else he was going to find working at Vegas Memorial very uncomfortable.

"Will we be able to get a copy at all? The reason I'm asking is that we can have a teleprompter set up if you would like one."

Their last CEO had treated the staff more like family, and most of those people were still here. If the atmosphere changed too drastically, she could picture a mass exodus, making the hospital a shell of what it had been under Morgan Howard's term. She wondered if Morgan was keeping up with the goings-on at the hospital or if he was just content to go about his retirement with nary a thought about any potential problems crossing his mind. She kind of hoped it was the latter. She didn't think he'd like the direction things were now taking. In fact, she didn't, either. But she wasn't the one in charge.

Dr. Robbins finished his bite and then leveled another look at her. "No teleprompter needed. Do you need a copy other than for that?"

Max again pressed his knee to hers as if sensing her blood pressure was shooting through the roof. And it was. But he wasn't the only one who could keep a level head. She could be as civil as the next person.

"No. No need."

When he set down his napkin, she wondered if he had heard the undertones of her response without her being aware they were even there. But if so, he didn't mention it. "Well, I'm off to my next meeting. Thanks for all your work on the gala. The hospital thanks you and will pick up the tab for your meals."

Oh, you mean the meals in the place that you chose for this meeting?

But, of course, she didn't say that, just smiled and thanked him back, as did Max, who seemed a lot more sincere than her words had been.

Then he was gone, leaving his empty plate and a bad taste in Evie's mouth.

"What a dick." Her half-muttered words made Max laugh.

"Tell me what you really think."

She rolled her eyes at him. "I think Darby has the right

idea about being her own boss. That's looking pretty attractive right now."

Their food came out and was placed in front of them, while the waitress whisked away Robbins's empty plates.

She glanced at Max. "Any thoughts?"

"None that I'd better voice aloud."

She relaxed, scooting away from him a bit so he had more room to eat, since the CEO was gone. His eyebrows went up, but he didn't say anything.

She thought he'd be glad to have a little more elbow room, so why did he look just the tiniest bit perturbed? But she wasn't going to ask. She was glad Darby wasn't here. That woman was an expert at cataloguing facial expressions and would have been sure to let her know what they meant.

She rolled her eyes even at the thought of having that conversation. But for all of Darby's quirks, they got along great—she was fun and loved to go out for a night on the town. Whereas Evie liked staying at home and relaxing, for the most part. But they balanced each other out and they were all for compromising.

It was one of the problems she and Brad had had, because he wasn't happy spending a lot of time just chilling with a glass of chardonnay and whatever show she happened to be binge-watching. And he didn't like compromising, so Evie had often forced herself to go out for a night on the town or to a casino with him, even when she was tired and grumpy after a long day at work. Instead of each giving and taking, she often found herself on the giving side, growing more and more resentful each time she gave in.

Maybe she'd contributed to him looking elsewhere, but if he'd been that unhappy with their relationship, he should have come to her and talked to her about it. But he hadn't. Instead he'd put in longer and longer hours "at the office." One she'd come to discover he no longer had. And those long hours? Well, they hadn't really been about his job at all.

She shook off the thoughts. "So do you think we'll even get a copy of that speech?"

"I'm actually wondering if he's even written it yet. There's just something about the way he avoided the subject that struck me as more than being worried about leaks or the legal department."

"Well, that's just great. But why? This is his chance to show what a good leader he is and that he can be trusted with their donations. You'd think he'd be anxious to prepare for that. Instead he acts like he's more worried about how we're going to make *him* look."

Max shrugged. "We did our part. And since he couldn't think of anything to criticize or recommend, I'm going to assume he's happy with how things are set up. Now, it's up to him to be a voice the hospital can be proud of."

He'd said it well. And frankly, Evie *was* worried about what he was going to say. The reason past donors had given so freely was due to the warm and caring manner in which Howard conducted himself. If Dr. Robbins hoped to compete with that, he was going to need to step up his game and adopt some of that warmth. He might be an excellent administrator, but the jury was still out on whether or not he would be a good boss. She was surprised the hospital board hadn't pinned him down about what he was going to say. Or maybe he'd given them a copy and she and Max were the only ones he didn't trust with it.

Whatever it was, she could only hope things would go smoothly with the gala. All of it.

She pushed away her plate. "Well, I think that does it for me. Can you think of anything else that needs to be done?"

"Nope. Are you headed home or back to the hospital?"

"Home. I got off work a few minutes early to go to the meeting."

"Great. Do you have time to make a quick pit stop on the way back to the hospital, since your car is still there?"

"Sure? I'm assuming it's not a bathroom break since there's one here in the restaurant."

"Nope, not the bathroom. I'll tell you about it on the way."

CHAPTER SEVEN

MAX WANTED HER opinion on the playlist the DJ had sent him. But rather than just show her the list, he wanted to take her to hear some selections from it so she could get the flavor of the music. The songs would be piped throughout the courtyard, but the booth would be set up behind the temporary dance floor, so that people would feel free to dance or to sit around and watch as others danced the night away.

In the fifteen minutes that it took to get to his friend's little out-of-the-way studio, she didn't say much. Until they arrived and the sign out front proclaimed that this was where DJ Electric Nights was located.

"Oh! I've heard of him. *He's* the friend you were talking about? Why didn't you say so at the meeting?"

"Dr. Robbins isn't the only one who doesn't tell everything he knows. Besides, the guy is from New Jersey, so I doubt he even knows who Dale Night is, or would recognize his stage name."

"His name is Dale? I didn't know that. He always seems so mysterious with that mellow voice and those playlists he comes up with on his show. I can't believe you got him on such short notice."

DJ Electric Nights also had his own radio show, which

made him one of the most sought-after DJs in Vegas. The right side of Max's mouth quirked up. "Fortunately, he had his vacation scheduled for that week, so he's just pushing it back one day for us."

"Oh, I feel bad that he's going to miss vacation time."

"Believe me, I'll owe him. Probably my football season tickets. He hasn't decided yet."

That made her laugh. "That hits you where it hurts."

"But it'll be worth it, won't it? Dale's worth it."

"Of that, I have no doubt." She leaned over and gave him a hug. "Thank you, Max. This means a lot to me. And to the hospital."

She pulled away just before his arms came up to go around her. An instinctive move, but one that he probably shouldn't act on. It was bad enough that he'd wanted to at all. And yet he did. Seeing the happiness on her face when she heard who his DJ friend was made things warm up inside of him.

"You're welcome. Shall we?" He motioned toward the studio.

"Oh, absolutely. Just kick me if I start salivating."

That made his jaw tense. He knew that Dale had this effect on a lot of the women who crossed his path, but somehow the thought of Evie being one of those women made him uneasy and he wasn't sure why. Maybe because she said she'd sworn off marriage and Dale was newly divorced, like she was.

That didn't mean anything. Lots of people got divorced. They didn't marry the next person that crossed their paths, though. Not that either of them were. Dale was also of the no-more-marriage camp. So even if Evie were taken with him, it wasn't likely to be reciprocated. At least he hoped not. Again, why it would even matter was beyond him.

Wasn't that the way he'd been about Brad? Except that Dale was a good guy, and Max had never had a good feeling about Evie's ex. Something that had turned out to be true.

And if she really did like Dale?

Then it was none of his business.

They got out of the car, and headed toward the door. Before they could get there, it flew open and a man bearing a slight resemblance to Jason Momoa stepped out. He wasn't as broad as Momoa, but his stage presence was every bit as striking as that of the actor. And Dale knew it and used that to good effect.

"Max! So good to see you." The man peered past his friend. "But who is this? Don't tell me you have a *girlfriend*?" His friend's eyes were trained on Evie with an interest that made Max tense further. He knew that look. It was on the tip of his tongue to lie and say that yes, he and Evie were involved. But then, he'd have a lot of explaining to do afterward. And that was one conversation he could do without.

"No. No girlfriend. But she is a friend. A *good* one." He tried to inject a subtle note of warning in there, but Dale had never been good at subtle. It was one of the things people found so endearing about him. "Dale Night, meet Eva Milagre."

Dale gave her a slow smile. "Oh, *miracle*. Very nice name. I think I'll call you my miracle girl."

Evie laughed, and it set Max's teeth on edge.

His friend went on. "You came at just the right time. I need *you*, Eva, to listen to a song from the playlist and tell me if I should include it. Or lose it."

"Oh, but I'm sure I don't know anything about playlists or how they're chosen."

"That makes you the perfect person to give me an opinion. I'll show you the ones I already have on the list. The one I'm on the fence about is very different as far as genre goes, but I think the message is perfect for the night." He pointed both of his thumbs at himself. "And *this* Night."

Evie actually giggled again, the sound light and magical. What wasn't magical was Dale calling her his miracle girl. He'd become somewhat of a serial dater since his divorce, but there wasn't much of a chance of him dating Evie. At least, Max hoped not. As far as he knew, she hadn't gone out with anyone since her divorce.

And if she chose Dale to be the first? Hell, what did he do if that happened?

Nothing. You sit back and let it happen.

Like he'd done with Brad?

Every time he'd seen Evie and her ex together, it had made a screw tighten in his gut. The sensation had grown so unbearable that he'd eventually stopped accepting invitations to things where he knew the pair would be. Which meant that his and Evie's friendship had suffered. And in the end, she'd been hurt terribly by someone who was supposed to love her.

That same screw was beginning to turn inside of him. Why now? Just when they were starting to get back on track.

All he knew what that bringing her here might have been a huge miscalculation on his part. He'd hoped she'd be impressed, but this went way beyond that. But he couldn't very well rip her away and say they were leaving. Because she and Dale would both want an explanation for why he was acting that way, and he had none. Not even for himself, since he had no idea where this feeling was coming from. Or what it even was.

They went into the studio and neon lights surrounded them. They were one of DJ Electric Nights's gimmicks. He took a neon light to each gig he had, and whichever one he chose, it was the theme for the music of the evening. Whether it was Lovers in Peril or Love Overcomes or Lovers Inc. Every show he did had a calling card that was a play on words, just like the playlist he selected.

He pointed to one of the lights on the far wall and Max's fingers clenched at the words on it. It said Friends to Lovers with an artistic heart added after the words. Yeah, that was not going to be the theme of the gala, if Max could help it. But Dale was doing him a favor. And if he suddenly overruled the man on his lighting choice, he was going to ask why, and that wasn't something Max was going to admit to under threat of death. Although it was better than Strangers in the Night, right? Maybe, but not by much.

Max had fantasized once or twice about what it might be like to make love to Evie—okay, make that fifty or sixty times—but he wasn't willing to risk what they had on something that couldn't be permanent. It would be the same thing if he was fixated on Darby and acted on that fixation. Things between them would change. They would have to.

And if Dale and Evie spent the night together?

Not something he wanted to think about right now. Or pretty much ever. The last thing he wanted was for her to be hurt again.

Was that all it was?

He chanced a glance at her. She was gazing at his friend expectantly. *Ah, hell.* Why had he even mentioned having a friend who was a DJ?

"Isn't anyone wondering why I might have chosen that as the theme?"

"Theme?" Evie blinked as if coming back to awareness.

Dale laughed. "Okay, well, I'll tell you even if you aren't wondering. This is a fundraiser, right? Where you're hoping that people will be coaxed into donating for the good of the cause. *Right?*"

The emphasis on that last word told Max that his friend was waiting for a response.

He forced himself to answer. "Yes. That's the hope."

"Well, then all of those who aren't already involved with the hospital financially are friends who are basically coming to play dress-up and eat some great food. But the hope is that they'll go from being *friends* to being *lovers*. Let's call it a subliminal message."

Evie laughed. "Aren't those illegal?"

"All music at its heart, Miracle Girl, carries subliminal messages. Even orchestral music with no lyrics. Even the scores to movies. They're all meant to elicit an emotional response—in other words, they hope to move a listener to react in a certain way."

"True," she admitted.

"And *we* hope that listeners at this gala react by opening their pocketbooks and donate to something that gives back to the community in ways that go far beyond its exceptional health care."

Despite his uneasiness, that explanation made sense in a way that Max couldn't argue with. It had gone from a knee-jerk response about Max thinking about how it would be if he and Evie spent the night together, to seeing how carefully his friend had crafted a message for the event. He didn't realize how much work Dale put into these gigs.

As long as he didn't let his job venture into more personal territory.

As if waiting for something more, he turned to Max. "What do you think? Do you think it'll work?"

"I think it will. And we honestly need any help we can get this year."

Evie came over to stand beside him. "That we do."

They glanced at each other, and at her nod, Max saw that she'd had the same thought he had. That the new CEO was going to make it tough to get new sponsors. It actually made him relax a little bit. Maybe all of her attention hadn't been on Dale after all.

And if Dale could inject the warmth that Dr. Robbins lacked, maybe it wasn't going to be as much of a disaster as he'd feared.

"Well..." Dale spread his arms wide. "I'll give you any help I can muster. Now, let's look at the playlist and then I'll tell you about the outlier that's begging me to include it."

He put the list on the table and Max saw that it was a good mix of pop, rock and some lighter ballad-type songs. Most all of them dealt with love of some type. But then a lot of songs had love at the heart of their message. There were a couple of things that Max didn't recognize and Dale played those for them. One was a tearjerker ballad of regret and Max nodded, trying to see the choice through the eyes of the DJ. "The regret of not giving?"

"You got me, man. That's definitely the message for anyone who's hesitating."

Max put a hand on the man's shoulder, relaxing even more. "I've got to hand it to you. There's a reason you're the best in Vegas."

The man's head went back as if shocked by the words. "Just Vegas?"

That made Max laugh. "A little humility might do you some good."

"How about you, Miracle Girl, do you think I'm lacking in that department?"

Max noticed she hadn't said very much, but had instead listened to Dale give his spiel. That Miracle Girl thing bothered him, though. And he wasn't sure why.

"Do you want my honest opinion?"

"I do."

Max would have expected Dale to look a little less confident, but if anything, he had a half-expectant smile on his face. One that he kind of wished he could wipe off. All he could hope for was that Evie was going to knock him down a peg or two.

"I think you're kind of a genius."

Max could feel his eyebrows crunch together, even while the DJ's arms spread wide again.

Far from knocking him down to size, she'd just added to the man's overinflated ego.

"And there it is. Humility, huh?" Dale said. "She can see where I'm going, even if you, my friend, can't. But you will. When you see those dollars pouring in."

What if she really did start dating the man? How would he feel then?

He groaned internally. He felt just like he had when she'd started dating Brad. All he could hope was that it didn't happen. And so he wanted her to be alone? No. But he also knew that Dale wasn't going to give her what she needed. Especially not after what Brad did to her.

"Well, I hope you're right about those dollars." He glanced at Evie. "Are you about ready?"

He hadn't meant to add that last part, it had somehow just slipped out. But now, Evie and Dale were both looking at him like he had two heads. Maybe he did. And one of them was taking exception to what was happening in this room.

He finally put a name to the feeling that was jabbing him in the gut. Jealousy.

Oh, hell to the no.

That's not what it was. It couldn't be, because that would mean...

It would mean nothing. And it would *change* nothing. Max didn't want a relationship. Not even with Evie. No... *especially* not with Evie. He wanted their friendship to go on exactly like it had over the last few weeks and in the years before her marriage. It had been fun and easy, at least for the most part. He was just being protective of her, that was all.

By admiring her body when she moved, or hoping she'd throw a little extra attention his way?

Like she was at Dale?

No. He wasn't hoping for that. Because—again—he didn't want a relationship.

"I still haven't played the outlier," Dale said.

Right now, the only outlier Max saw was himself. And he really didn't want to be played. Not by Dale. And not by Evie.

"What is it?" Evie asked.

He handed her a piece of paper. "You two read it. And tell me if the lyrics fit the situation or not. Then I'll explain my dilemma."

Max started reading and every muscle in stomach that wasn't already knotted went tight. The song talked about being let down so many times before. About being tired of getting hurt. About being tired of searching for answers.

The words could have been lifted straight out of his childhood. About his mom's death and his dad's descent into alcoholism. And his own pain and the hopeless anger he'd felt. And at the heart of it, the inability to change any of what had happened.

And then the chorus kicked in about someone special walking into the singer's life and how it had made a change for the good and how the person had transformed his life. It ended with saying she was his best friend.

He swallowed hard, and the jealousy he'd been feeling

toward Dale seemed to fade away. Because right now, he had bigger concerns. Namely, not seeing himself and Evie in those lyrics. They were just words written by some writer and sung by a random artist. He couldn't even put a tune to the words as he didn't know if he'd ever heard the song before.

Evie glanced up. "Wow. I know this song. And it *has* to be included."

"Ah…okay, Miracle Girl. Tell me why."

"I just think a lot of people will be able to relate to the message. I mean how many of us have been let down by people we care about? I know I have."

He swallowed. She had been. And not just by Brad. Max had let her down as well.

Her soft voice went on. "But then along comes someone who makes us believe that not everyone is like that." She shrugged. "Can't it be said of corporations as well? That we've all been let down by a business or other entity. But then along comes one that goes above and beyond and makes us believe that there's goodness in the world after all. That not every person and business is out for themselves."

Max nodded. He could see her point, and it sounded exactly like what Dale had talked about. How he wanted to make people believe that they were doing the right thing by giving to the hospital. And they would be. They could help more folks who, for some reason or other, couldn't afford medical care.

Dale smiled, a very broad smile that said Evie had given him exactly what he'd wanted to hear. "And that is why I wanted your opinion and exactly what my dilemma is. You say you know this song. What genre is it?"

Evie didn't hesitate. "Country and western."

"Yes! So will it sound off for it to be mixed in with all the others?"

She seemed to think for a minute. "I think the singer is well enough known that a lot of people will recognize it. I'm sure the song has been played at countless weddings at these little chapels around here. It's not an outlier."

Dale steepled his fingers and regarded her, and then he went over to his computer and tapped some keys, before stepping away. The sound of a printer starting up made Max turn to look at a long shelf where several machines were set up. A piece of paper came spitting out of one of those machines, then a second sheet, then a third. Dale went over and collected the pages.

"One for my friend Max. One for me. And one for my Miracle Girl, who gets me."

Evie smiled. "Glad I could help."

Yeah, Max was glad she'd been able to help, too, but if he heard the term Miracle Girl one more time he was going to tell the DJ exactly what he thought of him.

No, he wouldn't. Because for one, he liked Dale. The man had a good heart. Plus, if he said anything, Evie would want to know what was going on with him. And he did agree with them both about including the song. At least the business side of him did. The personal side of him said it was a very tricky business, which could get him into a lot of trouble. Because he knew himself well enough to know he was going to go home and play that song. And then it was going to wander around in his head until after this damn gala. And then, all he could hope was that he never heard it again.

But until then, he was stuck with it. And he had a feeling even if he objected to the tune being on the list, it was going to do no good. It was two against one, which made Max almost want to laugh. Because he didn't have to wonder long to realize that he really was the outlier in this mix. And he didn't like the way that made him feel. At all.

Max stopped in front of her apartment building and turned to smile at her. It was weird, because technically, the curving of his lips could be considered a smile, but it looked more like a pained grimace. In fact, he'd been strangely silent ever since they left his friend's house and she wasn't sure why.

She'd been wildly happy about what the DJ hoped to accomplish by letting his playlist get his message out. And she was pretty sure that every DJ gave an intro here and there to a specific song, or talked about the occasion, whether it was a wedding or birthday party or whatever. He would try to hammer home his message. And from everything she had witnessed, he was going to be successful at it. Who could resist that low sexy voice?

Her lips twisted. Actually, it looked like she could. He'd gotten her alone, while Max was looking at some equipment behind his desk, and asked her to go out with him. She'd had to tell him no, as gently as she could, and she wasn't sure why. Darby had been after her to get back into the dating scene, and Evie had been trying her best to start thinking in that direction. But when it actually came down to acting on her words, she'd chickened out.

DJ Electric Nights would have been the perfect person, because she had no doubt that he was a casual dater who went out with a lot of different women, sleeping with some of them and not sleeping with others. But there was no doubt that when a woman was out with him, he would make them feel like the most special girl in the world.

And God, she needed to feel that way. But she was scared to. And despite her words to Max a couple of weeks ago about not wanting to be in a relationship, the thought of going out with someone who would simply move on to the next person after their time together was done didn't sit as well with her as she'd hoped it would.

In fact, it didn't sit well at all. Maybe because that's exactly what Brad had done. Moved on to the next person. And she was pretty sure nothing was going to change her mind, which was why she should thank her lucky stars that the kiss she'd initiated with Max had been summarily rejected. What if it hadn't been? What if they'd slept together and he'd simply gone on, as if it had meant nothing to him?

She would be devastated.

Which is why she was not going to bed with him.

No, but she would be going to a musical with him in a few short days. What had made him get those tickets? Did he feel sorry for her?

She blinked back to awareness, realizing they were still sitting in front of her place and she'd made no move to get out. Did he think she was expecting a kiss?

Oh, God. She snapped open the mechanism that would allow her to get out of the car and practically fell to the ground in her haste to escape.

"Are you okay?"

"Of course. You?" She couldn't help throwing the question back at him, because he'd seemed to find too much pleasure in watching her try to roll gracefully from the passenger seat. She'd stuck the landing at least.

He turned to look at her. "Can I say something?"

"Sure." Although she wasn't sure she wanted to know what it was that he wanted her to do.

"Be careful around Dale. He dates a lot of women."

She blinked, trying to digest his words before the meaning hit her. "You don't think I can figure that out? I've seen articles about him. I know he's been divorced and that he dates a lot. But I'm not sure what business it is of yours."

"So you're going."

"What?" She stared at him. "What are you talking about?"

"I know he asked you out. When he mentioned the vinyl he had under his desk, I was pretty sure that was just a ruse."

She crossed her arms over her chest and bent down to peer inside the car, wanting to see his expression. "You're right. He did. What of it?"

"I just don't want to see you hurt." His low, gritty voice diffused some of the anger she felt over him acting like he could tell her what she should or shouldn't do.

"I'm not some fragile mouse who can't stick up for herself, Max. And for your information, I'm not going. I knew who he was the minute I met him. But that doesn't mean that I didn't enjoy him flirting with me."

"Flirting? Really?" The faux shock in his voice made a trickle of amusement go through her. "Flirting with Miracle Girl?"

She laughed, suddenly not offended anymore. Max wasn't just being nosey and giving her unwanted advice. He was concerned, and she appreciated that concern, even if it wasn't necessary. "I thought that was rather clever, didn't you?"

When Max didn't say anything, she climbed back into the car so she could face him on his level. "He didn't mean anything by it, Max. It's all part of his persona. I'm sure every person who steps into his studio is presented with the same one-dimensional caricature of his stage name."

"But you bought it. Told him you thought he was a genius."

"I wasn't lying about that. I do think he's a genius, when it comes to what he does—how meticulous he is about preparing for each job. But that doesn't mean I want to go out with him. Yes, it would be fun and exciting, but it could only be taken at face value. I think Dale has problems separating his stage presence from who he is outside of his job. And that's okay. It makes him happy. But when and if I ever decide to date again, I don't want it to be an act. Even though I'm not interested in marriage at this point in my life, I still want things to feel real and important to whoever I'm out with. I don't like games. I never have. So it's a lot, and not even I am sure of what I hope to get out of dating someone. After Brad it's…well, everything is jumbled in my head."

He linked his pinkie with hers for a second and squeezed before letting go. "You don't owe me any explanations. And I'm sorry for intruding. I just…" He shrugged, his voice dropping off in a way that touched her.

"It's okay. I know I don't owe you an explanation. I just didn't want you to think I'd been taken in by anything Dale said or did. Because I wasn't." She reached across and touched his face. "But thank you for being the good friend that you are. It means the world to me that you care enough to not want to see me hurt."

She wasn't prepared for the rough stubble that met her fingertips. It was earthy and real and made her shiver. Made her want to know what it would feel like in the morning after a long night of…

She pulled away, suddenly feeling shaky and uncertain. What had that been? That sudden awareness of him as a man, and not simply as a friend. She'd felt it before, but this was… She was not going to analyze it. She was just going to get out of the car and walk up to her apartment. While she still could. "Well, anyway, thank you."

She started to leave only to have him grab her hand and stop her, his eyes holding hers for a long minute before letting her go. "You're welcome, Evie. Have a good night."

"Y-you, too." With that, she got out and closed the door. With one more look through the window, she gave him a little wave and then walked away as fast as her shaky legs could carry her.

* * *

"That was so good, Max. Thank you for getting the tickets."

"You're welcome. It was fun."

They'd decided to go to Delacort's after the musical, and strolling down the street was reminiscent of the last time they'd gotten ice cream from the place. Only this time, both of them were dressed up. And when he'd seen Evie come to the door in that teal dress, his mouth had gone dry.

Dressing for the theater in Las Vegas meant just about anything went. Ranging from jeans to formal-wear, people basically wore whatever they felt like. And her dress…

The dress was cut so that her shoulders were bare, and it clung to her curves in a way that turned heads—he found that he'd had trouble looking at where he was going. And yet, Evie seemed relaxed and happy and totally unaware of all of that. Maybe because of the show. The musical satire had been both witty and subtle, and the actors had truly been good at what they did.

Max had expected things between them to be a lot more stilted than they'd ended up being. When she'd touched him in the car a few days ago, he hadn't wanted her to get out. He'd wanted to pull her close and hold her in his arms in a way that had nothing to do with friendship. And hell, he'd listened to that song that Dale had chosen for the gala and then had to play it again before turning it off with an irritated sigh.

"It's a shame that Darby isn't a big fan of live entertainment. I think she would have liked this."

Probably, he thought, but right now, Max was glad to have Evie to himself. Seeing her at Dale's had been a wake-up call. Someday she might find that special someone and they would lose their connection again. To hope that it might not happen was not only improbable, but also downright selfish. It would be the same if Darby started dating someone seriously. Most of her time and energy would go to whomever she was in love with. It was the way of the world. Except no matter how many times he told himself that was the case, he knew deep down it wasn't. It had been different when Evie had gotten together with Brad. She hadn't been the one to leave the friendship. Max had. Maybe if he hadn't, he could have spotted the danger signs before it was too late.

And that wasn't quite true, either. It was more than that. But he couldn't quite decide how it was.

He was not in love with Evie. He could not let himself be in love with Evie. To go down that path would just bring so much heartache on both of them. He knew he had a problem with being intimately involved with anyone, but that trait had been seared into his conscience many years ago. He didn't know how to change, nor did he want to. He'd given his all to his dad. Had tried to protect him and be the emotional support he needed after his mom had died. And it hadn't worked. No matter how much he tried, it just hadn't been enough. Max had just ended up burned out and used up emotionally.

Evie's bare shoulder bumped his arm and he swallowed, realizing his ice cream was melting in his cup.

"What are you thinking about?" she asked.

He cast around for an answer, then said, "I wonder if

Walter Grapevine was ever happy." Okay, it was stupid, but at least sticking to the topic of the musical was safe.

"I don't know. I think he just got so used to wallowing in the bad that he never opened himself up to opportunities that could have changed his life. Like when he had the chance to leave his job and go away with Tammy. He didn't. He chose to stay where he was."

This topic was safer? The musical hadn't had a happy ending, even though it couldn't be considered a tragedy, either. At least not from his perspective.

"Is that what you would have done? Give something up for love?"

"I think I tried to. With Brad. But I've learned there are no guarantees in life."

She took the last bite of her raspberry sorbet and dropped her napkin in a nearby trash receptacle. He did the same with his unfinished dessert.

"I've learned that, too."

She glanced at him. "Your mom."

"And my dad. He was completely lost without her."

"I remember you telling me that." She reached for his hand. "I think your dad was kind of a Walter Grapevine figure. He chose to stay in his unhappiness, never looking for anything beyond that."

"I know. But he was so sure there *was* nothing beyond that."

"Like I said, there are no guarantees in life. But it was his choice not to try, wasn't it?" They got to the parking garage and Evie let go of his hand. He immediately missed the connection. As they waited for the valet to bring Max's car, the topic changed yet again, and for that, he was grateful. Because Evie was right. His dad had made his choice and there'd been nothing anyone could do about it.

But hearing her say what he'd known in his heart to be true was somehow freeing. It took the burden off a kid who'd tried so hard to change things, but who couldn't. A ball of emotion rose up, threatening to overwhelm him. He glanced at Evie, and it was as if he was seeing her for the first time.

And yet, he wasn't. These temporary bursts of feeling for her had erupted from time to time over the course of their friendship. Usually when she'd had some sort of insight or tried to make him see hope in situations that seemed bereft of it. In a few days' time it would run its course. It always did. He just had to wait it out.

And if he couldn't? If he did something stupid and ruined everything? Then he was in for the biggest pity party in the history of man.

She might be Dale's Miracle Girl, but Max had to remember she wasn't his. Because there'd never been a big enough miracle to save him from what his past had made of him: a man who, like Walter Grapevine—like his dad—was too afraid of pain and loss to let himself take a chance on love and everything it meant.

CHAPTER EIGHT

EVIE TOUCHED A finger to the picture Max had drawn for her years ago. It was in the entryway of her apartment, exactly where it had been when she'd been married to Brad. Her ex had never asked about it, maybe assuming she'd bought it at some out-of-the-way market. And he'd never seemed bothered by her friendship with Max, although Max had made it fairly clear that he and Brad would never be friends. And he'd pretty much stayed out of the picture during her marriage.

It was funny how Max had much the same reaction to his friend Dale's interest in her that he'd had when she'd been in the initial phases of her relationship with Brad.

Was that a coincidence or something more?

The musical had been so, so wonderful and sitting there next to Max had been…heady. It was the only word she could find to describe it. And it was totally different than when their little trio had gone and watched *Wicked*. Maybe because so much had happened since then. Evie had learned to treasure their friendship again. Was learning to be grateful for this new season in her life in a way that she hadn't been since her divorce from Brad.

She didn't want to be Walter Grapevine. She wanted to live. To enjoy life and friendship and lo— She stopped herself before she could go any further and ruin how lovely last night had been. Max hadn't kissed her when they stood there on the sidewalk in front of her apartment. But he had hugged her and thanked her for a wonderful evening. It had taken her a long time to get to sleep, despite the late hour, and she was still on kind of a high this morning.

She glanced at her watch. Ugh, she needed to get busy or she'd be late for work. After taking one last look at the picture, she headed to the bathroom to get ready.

When she arrived at the hospital, she was shocked to see workers out in the courtyard. She hadn't scheduled anything to be done until two weeks out from the gala, and they were still four weeks out at the point. Maybe Dr. Robbins had requested some repairs or something.

She met Max in the atrium to find he, too, was looking out at the courtyard space, hands shoved into his pockets. "What's going on?" she asked.

"I have no idea. I thought maybe you knew."

"No clue." She blew a breath out. "I think maybe it's time I went to see our new CEO and see if he's behind this."

He glanced at her face. "Are you sure you want to do that?"

"You bet I am. It's one thing to refuse to let us have a copy of his speech. It's another thing to start interfering with our plans without even notifying us. I have workers scheduled to come in two weeks. I have no idea if these are the same ones, or if Robbins has gone out and gotten his own."

"I'll go with you."

"No, I can handle this on my own. Besides, if he fires me, he'll still need you to carry out his plans."

"No way," he said. "If he fires you, I'm gone, too."

That stopped her in her tracks, and she stared at him for a few seconds. "Don't do that, Max. People like Margaret Collins need you."

"They need you, too. If you haven't noticed, you're the first person she calls because you're the one she trusts the most. And I wouldn't have that any other way."

"I promise to *try* not to get myself fired. Does that help?"

"Yes. Let me know how it goes, okay?"

She bumped his shoulder, like she'd done last night. "I will." Looking up into his face, she stopped for a minute. The sun came through the window and cast a light on him that made him glow. He was gorgeous. Why had she never noticed that before? Well, she had, lots of times, but more in the sense of how one friend knew another one was good-looking. But this was a take-your-breath-away kind of response that only came with attraction. Maybe it was because of last night's outing. He'd looked incredible in his suit.

So what? She'd always been attracted to Max. Otherwise, those two kisses—one years ago, and one more recently—never would have happened. But she'd never let herself actually think about what they meant. Until last night and this morning. There'd been an intimacy between them during their trip to the musical that had stopped her cold, even without a single kiss.

Could she really afford to dwell on that, though? It had already gotten her hurt. Twice. That picture in her foyer, as much as she loved it, only served as a reminder of one of those hurts. And yet, she could never bring herself to part with it. He'd made it. For her. And she loved it.

Just like she lov—

No! Do not even think it!

That half-formed thought from this morning threatened to break through yet again. And this time, there was no doubt about what it meant. She needed to get away from here.

"Okay—well, I'm off. I'll let you know how it goes."

He repeated her shoulder-bump move from a moment earlier and it sent another shiver of awareness through her.

"Good luck," he murmured.

"Thanks. I'm going to need it." In more ways than one.

Forcing her thoughts to something else, she went to Robbins's office and checked in with his assistant. Yes, he was in. And no, she wasn't sure if he was busy or not. But she would check.

Evie dropped into one of the chairs in his waiting room and wondered if he was even going to see her or not. If not, then what did she do from here? Just sit around and wonder if her workers were going to have anything to do when they arrived in two weeks?

Hell, she had no idea. But one thing she did know— she was not going to head up any more committees that Robbins had anything to do with. That included next year's gala. As much fun as she'd had with Max planning this one, she didn't think she was ready to sit in front of the CEO and watch him smugly inform her that she wasn't getting a copy of his speech. She hoped the board saw through the man before he did something that would hurt the hospital. He was either really, really smart, and would surprise the heck out of her, or he was a clueless narcissist who only wanted his own way in everything no matter what it did to anyone else.

Robbins came out of his office, and she stood to go shake his hand.

"What can I do for you, Evie?" Was it her imagination or was there a slight edge of irritation to his voice?

"There are some workers out in the courtyard, and I'm not really sure what they're doing. I don't have the preparations for the gala scheduled until two weeks from now. Does this have something to do with that work?"

"Ah, I see. No, this isn't for the gala. Not specifically, anyway. I just thought that maybe there needed to be another sculpture out there to go with the first one. It'll make more of a statement that way, don't you think?"

Except she'd only taken one sculpture into account when it came to the walkways. And if, as he'd said, it was going to be a statement piece, then it might change her plans for out there. "Is it going to be a big? Because that might mean we won't be able to fit as many people out there."

"Hmm, you yourself talked about having people in other areas of the hospital, did you not? So not everyone will be out there at one time."

That was technically true. But when she'd said that she hadn't meant that they could cram the courtyard with a bunch of new stuff, either. But to stand here and argue with him would accomplish nothing. And since he hadn't offered to show her a picture of the new addition, she was stuck. "Okay. I'll wait and see what goes in and then reconfigure the walkways to accommodate it."

"Good. That will work just fine then. Is there anything else?" He brushed his hands together as if he was already done with this conversation.

"I think that does it. Thank you."

With that, she turned to walk away, her jaw set into stiff angry lines to avoid telling the man exactly what he could do with his new sculpture. And God help him if the man erected a statue to himself. She might take a sledgehammer to the thing herself. Of course, she wouldn't, but it didn't hurt to at least pretend that she could.

Blowing out a breath, she suddenly felt a lot lighter. People weren't stupid. She had to believe the board of directors weren't blind, either. And since it wasn't just her who felt this way, others would catch on as well. Max felt the same way as she did.

She wasn't alone. And that was all that mattered. She had a feeling that things would work themselves out. One way or another.

The breathing treatment had an immediate effect on the young athlete, as the ragged coughing stopped, and she was finally able to take deeper breaths. The fourteen-year-old track star had wound up in the emergency room complaining of coughing and shortness of breath during training. There was no history of asthma, but Evie had seen this before.

"Did that help?"

"Yes. I feel so much better. I'm not sure what happened." The girl took another deep breath and let it out with a sigh.

"Have you had this happen before?" She glanced at the girl's mom, who was seated beside her daughter.

"Sometimes at the end of a run, I feel extra tired. But today, I couldn't even finish the race."

Evie held up the spirometer for Delilah to try again now that she'd had a treatment. The girl took it and blew hard. Looking at the result, Evie smiled. "Much, much better than when you came to the hospital."

"So why is this happening?"

She took the instrument and put it on a tray to be sanitized, then came back and sat on a stool in front of the girl. "I think you're experiencing something called exercise-induced bronchoconstriction. It causes the airways to constrict, making it hard to breathe. It's similar to asthma. We actually see it in a lot of asthma patients."

Her mom spoke up. "Does this mean that Delilah has asthma?"

"It's kind of something in between. They used to call it cold-induced asthma, but obviously, we're in the middle of summer here in Nevada and it's not cold. But the thought now is that dry air is the real culprit, and since cold air holds less moisture..." She let her voice trail off before restarting. "We're in the middle of a drought, and although we live in a desert climate where it's almost always dry, there's even less moisture in the air right now. It dries the lining of the lungs and causes them to spasm when she's breathing hard."

"But why does it happen to me and not everyone?"

"We don't really know why it affects some people more than others."

"Does the mean I have to give up track?" Delilah's tone was one of devastation. "I love it so much."

"No, you absolutely don't have to. We're going to start you on an inhaler that you'll use before you start running. It'll help keep the airways open. A longer warm-up period before you start your practice may also help. If those two things don't do the trick, we have some other options we can try." She patted the girl on the shoulder. "The fact that you responded so quickly to the albuterol is a good sign."

Delilah broke into tears and hugged her mom before returning her attention to Evie. "I was so afraid you were going to tell me to quit running."

Evie smiled. "I'm not a runner, so I can't quite relate to the lure of it, but I know someone who is. And he would be pretty devastated if he had to stop, too. I know you guys are a dedicated crew. So keep on running. And I'll keep on doing my best to keep those airways open. Deal?"

"It's a deal."

She gave the girl's mom her card. "I'd like you to call and schedule an appointment so we can follow up on how things are going. Until then, I'll give you a prescription for the inhaler. If there are any questions, give me a call. My cell-phone number is on there."

"She has another meet the day after tomorrow, is it okay for her to go?"

"I'm going to say yes, but do the inhaler before you

start and if you start feeling short of breath at all, stop. We may have to tweak things a bit, but I'm very hopeful."

The mom looked at the card. "Are you sure you don't mind if we call?"

"I'm sure." She didn't give her actual card out to all her patients, but this one was special, and she could tell that running was Delilah's passion. She'd told her the truth—she was going to do everything in her power to help keep that dream alive.

"Any other questions?"

Mom and daughter looked at each other. Then Delilah's mom said, "I don't think so. You'll give us a prescription for the inhaler?"

Evie nodded. "I will. Your breathing seems to be back to normal and the test we just did shows a vast improvement to how you were when you arrived at Vegas Memorial, so I think you're good to go. I'll get your discharge papers and prescription ready, and the nurse will be in to give you everything. And call and let me know how the track meet goes."

"We will."

Delilah jumped off the table, came over and hugged Evie tightly. She hugged the girl back, feeling a kindred spirit. Evie had had people in her corner helping her achieve her dream of becoming a doctor, and she'd vowed to do everything in her power to help other people fulfill their dreams.

She smiled down at the girl. "Take care and I look forward to hearing from you."

After Evie left the room and gave instructions to the front-desk attendant about the girl being discharged, and handed them a prescription, she headed to the elevator. It opened and she was surprised to see Max standing there. "Well, hi there. Fancy seeing you in a place like this." She was in a good mood that no one was going to ruin. Seeing Max just made that mood even better. "Not as fancy as Tuesday night. But then again, neither are you."

He grinned. "I'm crushed."

"Do you have a patient in the ER?"

"No. I was looking for you, actually."

Her heart sailed in her chest. "You were?"

It had been two days since she'd last seen him and the new sculpture in the courtyard had been installed yesterday. She wasn't quite sure what it was. It was oval-shaped and almost looked like some kind of tall obelisk. It stood side by side with the sculpture that was already out there, but the two pieces had nothing in common. But she'd taken measurements so that she could somehow maneuver the pathway between the two structures. It would be a tight squeeze, but there was nothing she could do about it at the moment, since it was obviously there to stay.

"Do you have any more patients?" Max asked.

"No, the one I just saw was actually my last for the day." He was acting a little odd. "Did you want to talk to me about something?"

"Yes, and it could affect the gala."

Her mood suddenly plummeted. "Oh, God, what now? Is there a third sculpture going out in the courtyard?"

"No, but... Can we go somewhere outside of the hospital? I don't know if what I have to say is common knowledge yet."

Okay, those words were as obscure as the new sculpture. "We can. But I'm actually starving, so can we go someplace we can eat? I skipped lunch today."

It had been a crazy day with three emergency cases sprinkled in among her normally scheduled appointments. It had put her behind, so she'd worked right through her lunch break.

"Yep, how about that little Italian place we used to all go to?"

That "little Italian place" was actually a hole in the wall that the three of them ended up falling in love with. It held a lot of great memories of friendship and laughter. And, of course, since Max didn't drink, they had a built-in designated driver, which they always teased him about. But they both respected his reasons for abstaining and were careful not to overimbibe and bring back bad memories for him.

"I love that place. I actually haven't eaten there in ages. And right now, anything's better than the place we went to with Robbins."

"I don't think you're going have to worry about that anymore."

Her head cocked. "I don't understand. Did that restaurant get shut down?"

"Even better. I'll explain over dinner."

As soon as they got settled in the restaurant and she had a glass of wine in front of her, she prodded him. "So what's all this cloak-and-dagger stuff?"

"Cloak-and-dagger pretty much describes it."

She blinked. "Are you being serious right now? Did Darbs investigate someone other than my ex?"

"Huh?"

"Never mind. Tell me what it is."

Max settled back in his seat. "It seems all of us department heads were brought in for a meeting this afternoon with the board of directors and told that Dr. Robbins is no longer with the hospital, effective immediately. They don't want to make a public announcement at this point until they figure out how to proceed."

She stared at him, looking for any sign of humor in his face. Because if he was kidding right now, he was going to be in big trouble. "Tell me you're serious."

"I am. They looked for you when they called us in, since you're in charge of the gala, but you were with your ER case and so they asked me to notify you."

She took a sip of her wine, trying to wrap her head around the fact that the man she'd tangled with about the new structure going up was no longer there. "How did this even happen?"

"His personal assistant went to the board with some concerns she had."

"And they fired the man based on that? And what about the gala? Will it be canceled?"

"No. It's going on as planned, including all of your ideas for using the courtyard for a type of after-party."

"Did Robbins even notify them of our plans?"

"He did, but he didn't tell them about a lot of other things, like his going to a couple of our donors and asking for a personal loan."

Shock held her speechless for a second. "What?"

"They evidently did a background check before hiring him, but missed the fact that the man has a gambling problem and there were some hefty private debts that don't show up on any credit reports. We weren't the only ones who noticed that he was behaving kind of oddly. Some sketchy characters came to his office not long ago when he wasn't there and freaked out Amanda, his personal assistant. That's when she started looking at what he did a little closer. The meeting he was in a hurry to get to when we were with him at the restaurant? Well, it ended up being with a loan shark who was calling in an overdue note, hence the phone call to the donors."

"God. I can't even believe this is happening. Who's going to be the keynote speaker at the gala?"

He leaned even closer, forearms braced on the table. "You're not going to believe this."

This time she laughed. "I pretty much don't believe anything you just told me."

He leaned back, putting his hand on his heart. "It's all true, I swear it. Anyway, the new speaker is going to be Morgan Howard. They're trying to coax him to come back at least until they can vet some other candidates. And do a more thorough job of it this time."

"I love Morgan. I don't begrudge him his retirement, but it'll be hard to fill his shoes. I just think they tried to rush things and didn't dig deep enough into Robbins's finances. I bet they don't make that mistake again."

"Let's hope not."

Their food came. She'd ordered the eggplant parmigiana and Max had chosen the rigatoni. She couldn't help but smile. "Some things never change."

"What do you mean?"

"Isn't the rigatoni what you always got?"

"It is. And you liked the eggplant." He took a bite of his food. "And this is just the same as it always was. I'm glad the owners have always kept things simple, even though they're a lot more popular than they were seven or eight years ago, when we started coming."

"Me, too. And Darbs always liked the Caesar salad."

"With anchovies, of course."

She laughed, feeling inexplicably happy all of a sudden. "Those tiny fish always looked so sad lying on top of a bed of lettuce. I'll have to tell Darby the news. She's had to listen to me moan and grumble about gala stuff for the last few weeks."

She cut into her food and took a bite, as a thought hit her. Once she'd swallowed, she had to ask. "What are they going to do about that ugly thing in the courtyard that Robbins had commissioned?"

"The board didn't say, but I can't imagine them keeping it."

She blew out a breath. "This day has suddenly become perfect. I didn't have to kill a young girl's dreams and now the CEO from hell just got booted out of the hospital."

"Back it up a step. You didn't have to kill a young girl's dreams? Care to elaborate?"

"Just a patient I had today." She rubbed the back of her neck. "Some stories really do end well. And, as doctors, we need those, you know."

"Yes, we do. And then there was the man who fell from the scaffold. His story ended well, too, don't forget."

She sighed. "Yes, and in light of what could have happened, I'm grateful. It could have been so much worse. You could have ended up on the bottom of a pile of heavy metal along with our patient. And those other two men could have—"

"But none of that happened. It was a good day."

"Yes, it was." She thought for a second. "And so was today. First with the news from the board. And then eating at this restaurant again. It brings back so many good memories, doesn't it?"

"Yes, it does. Very good memories." His eyes locked with hers for a minute.

She couldn't stop herself from reaching over and catching his hand and giving it a soft squeeze. "Thanks for being there for me during the gala planning. And for the musical. You don't know how much either of those meant to me. It was like light at the end of what's been a long dark tunnel."

"I know I haven't been there for you during that, and I'm sorry. I know I went MIA during that whole thing with Brad. I kept feeling like I needed to somehow fix things, and yet, I knew I couldn't. And so I stayed away and let Darbs do the heavy lifting."

"I have no doubt if I'd have called, you'd have come."

He hesitated for a minute as if examining some deep part of his psyche. "Yes. If you'd have called, I would have come."

She let go of his hand and took the last sip of her wine. And that was enough sad talk for the night. "Hey, why don't you come over for some coffee. We can watch a movie or something. It's too early to go to sleep, but I don't really want to go out and do anything, either."

Again, he hesitated, and for a minute she thought he might refuse, saying he had something else he had to do. But then he smiled. "Sure, coffee and a movie sound good. And I'm not really in the mood to try to go out, either. How about if I run you back to the hospital and we can pick up your car."

"That sounds perfect." And just in case he was looking for an out, she added, "Don't feel obligated to come, though, if you'd rather just go home and decompress from the day."

The waitress came and handed them their bill. "Just pay at the front desk as you go out."

They waited for her to leave, and then Max said, "I do want to come. Sitting with someone who understands what a 'day in the life' is like is probably just what I need. I'm actually looking forward to the gala now."

"Even though it probably won't be a requirement for staff anymore now that Robbins is gone?"

He nodded. "In retrospect, I knew I should be attending it, but after so many years of sitting it out, it just became a habit. Kind of like Walter Grapevine. Maybe the nudge was a good thing."

"I think Robbins's method was more of a shove."

"Shove or nudge, I'm still going to go. Especially after seeing how much work goes into it."

She smiled. "And since DJ Electric Nights is our disc jockey for the evening?"

"It'll be good to see him do his thing. Just don't let him get too chummy."

"Define chummy." Before he could say anything, she laughed. "I'm kidding. You got your point across last time we talked about him. He's nice, though. I can see why women fall for his charm."

"But not you."

"Not me. Not after what happened with Brad."

"Good call." They paid their bill and headed out to the lot to get Max's car.

Once inside, it only took a couple of minutes until they were at the hospital and he was parked beside her car. "I'll lead the way."

"Sounds good."

With that, she got out of his car and jumped inside hers, then started it and backed it out of the spot. And then she turned it and headed toward home.

CHAPTER NINE

EVIE'S APARTMENT WASN'T far from the old one. Maybe just a block away. She'd said that moving her things from the old place had been a lot easier than she'd thought, since she'd left all the furniture behind for Brad to take with him. All she'd had to do was pack her clothing and her most precious possessions, and she was out of there.

He pulled into a guest spot and turned off the car, then joined her on the sidewalk. "I've only seen your place from the outside. It's nice, though. And I'm sure starting fresh was the better option than staying where you were."

"It was really the only option, since Brad had been out of work for a while and needed the other place to be sold. But it worked out for the best. This apartment doesn't have any memories attached to it other than the ones I put in it. And I tend to be pretty careful about which ones I let in."

He could understand that. When his dad had died, his childhood home had automatically become his. It was paid off, and so he could have moved into it and saved himself some money, but the thought of doing so just made him queasy, so he'd sold the place. He'd donated the money to a well-known cancer-research place in honor of his mom.

Her apartment complex was a tall structure that curved partway around a pool, so that all of the units had at least one window that overlooked it, a great selling feature. They took the elevator up to the third floor.

"Very nice."

"It is nice. But it feels odd to have a big body of water sitting in the middle of the lot when the drought has caused so many changes in our personal usage. I mean, car washes are only allowed on a weekly basis and they've had to cut back on the amount of water per wash."

"Looks like they've saved water in other ways. Didn't there used to be lawn here?"

"There was. And they took it out. But I kind of like it. It's a nod to the reality of where we live, although it would probably be hard if the city were devoid of green spaces."

They stepped into her apartment, which was blissfully cool after the heat that had enveloped them outside. The marble floors probably felt wonderful on her bare feet when she padded around in the mornings.

And just like that, the image of Evie in a silky robe that was loosely belted around her waist came to mind, her nipples standing out in sharp relief against the thin fabric.

Hell, coming here had probably been a huge miscalculation on his part. Because he'd envisioned this as each of them watching a movie enveloped in their own little bubble of space. But when he glanced through the door into her living room, he saw that she had one couch and a chair—which he was certainly going to use. She didn't need to be sharing anything besides room space with her.

Just then, something hanging above the glass table in the foyer caught his eye. He stared at it for a second, realizing what it was. It was the picture he'd drawn her from *Wicked*. She'd taken the canvas and had it framed in black wood that looked ragged and bubbled along the edges, as if it had been in a fire. It was the perfect contrast for the pristine white of the canvas and the black inked images that seemed to jump off the page. He'd almost forgotten what it looked like after all these years.

"Wow. You kept it."

She glanced at where he was looking and gave a half shrug. "I really like it. And the fact that you drew it makes it that much more special."

"And the frame?"

"My dad actually made it, using a flamethrower to blacken the surface and make it look older."

"It makes the black of Elphaba's robe stand out. I never would have thought to do that."

She smiled, touching the frame with light fingertips. "My dad can't draw, but he does have a great eye for putting the right frame with the right print. He did all of the frames in the apartment for me."

As he glanced back into the living room, he saw several other pictures each with a different type of framing material. Most were informal, made out of wood that was either painted or stained. As far as he could see, this was the only one made with a charred appearance. "I'll have to remember that. Does he do them for friends?"

"For you, I'm sure he would."

She tossed her keys in a wooden bowl on the hall table and motioned for him to come into the living room. He took one last look at the picture and followed her.

He wasn't sure how he felt about his work being given such a prominent place in her home. It created a warmth in his chest that could transform into a more dangerous heat given a little encouragement. Encouragement he didn't intend to give it.

So he turned his attention to the living room. Just like he'd seen from where he'd been standing, she only had a few pieces of furniture, including a TV stand with some drawers and another wooden bowl that held a couple of remote controls. She took one of them and turned on a ceiling fan that was suspended from a vaulted ceiling. He was glad because he was still a little warm—both from picturing her in a thin robe and from seeing how much care she'd taken in displaying his artwork.

She motioned him to the sofa, and so he gingerly sat on the long piece of furniture, hoping that she was going to sit in the chair adjacent to it. "Do you want some coffee or tea?"

"Coffee if you have it."

Maybe the coffee would help center him and keep him from falling asleep on her couch, something he did at home quite regularly. He'd kick his shoes off, stretch out on his long leather sofa and sleep an hour or two. But that was not something he was going to do here.

"I do. Black, right?"

"Yes, thanks." He tried to remember how she liked her coffee but came up blank.

When she came out with a tray that held a thick mug

and a more dainty cup with the string from a tea bag dangling over the rim, he knew why. She liked tea rather than coffee. With her Brazilian heritage, he just assumed that coffee was a cultural norm. And yet, she had it in her house. For company?

"You don't drink coffee?"

She bit the corner of her lip. "Not a lot, but buying it is still a habit. Plus when I have company I serve it."

The way she said it was still a habit to buy it made him pause before he realized Brad had probably preferred coffee. Which explained why she always had it in the house.

He wished he could go back and change what had happened to her, but he couldn't any more than he could change what had happened to his mom. Or to his dad. Sometimes, it just had to be accepted that bad things happened and that there was no rhyme or reason for them. There wasn't necessarily a grand scheme that demanded they happen.

He tried to think of something to say about coffee or tea, but came up blank, so instead he asked, "Do you use your pool a lot?"

"Almost never. When I'm home, I'm normally in for the night, and to change into a suit and go down there just seems like work. But most complexes have pools as part of the amenities, so I just go out on the balcony and sit and enjoy looking at it."

"May I?"

"Of course. There's a ceiling fan out there, too, and it's nice and private."

She followed him out to the balcony and unlocked

the sliding glass door. Outside, she had a few potted plants, including rather healthy-looking tomato and pepper plants. There were small red tomatoes on the one bush, but nothing on the other. "Does your pepper not produce?"

"Oh, it does. They just never last because I eat them almost as soon as they're big enough."

There was a double glider swing on the side of the balcony and they settled on it together, thighs lightly touching. Maybe coming out here hadn't been such a good idea after all. He'd been worried about being too close in the living room. This was ten times more intimate. He set his mug on the table beside him and looked through the glass barricade that was the only thing standing between them and falling over the side of the building.

It was warm and dry, and there was no sign of grit on the tiled flooring from the dust storms that periodically rolled through the area, obstructing visibility and creating a mess. Part of the "blessing" of living in the desert.

"It's nice. My house doesn't have one of these. I'd probably be out here every evening." With the fan above them twirling and sending air over his skin, he stretched his legs out and glanced out over the empty pool area.

As if sensing his unspoken question, she said, "The pool normally gets busy after dinner, when the kids are out of school. An hour or so from now. It can get pretty loud."

"I can imagine."

"Are you okay if I go put some shorts on? It tends to be pretty warm out here."

"We can go back in, if you want."

She shook her head. "I like it out here. I just need something a little cooler. I'll be back in a minute."

As soon as she went in, he got up and looked over the balcony at the hardscape below. The sun glinted off the pool with enough force to make him squint. And yet he loved the desert, even during times like then when the heat became unbearable. Because once the sun went down, it almost always cooled down enough to open the windows and let some fresh air in.

Other than the *Walter Grapevine* production, he couldn't remember the last time he and Evie had gotten together and done something that didn't involve work or, more recently, the gala. Or that hadn't included Darby. To be here with her alone was…nice. It had a comfortable feeling, like wearing a favorite pair of jeans. Which made sense, since Evie was one of his favorite people.

She came back out a minute or two later and he turned from his spot to look at her. She had on black Lycra shorts that hugged her frame and made every curve of her hips and backside stand out. And she was wearing a white racerback tank top that showed off thin pink straps that were probably to her bra. The sight made him swallow.

A pink bra? The urge to trace his finger down the path of that strap on her back came with a strength that surprised him. When she leaned over the glass railing, making even more of that tanned skin visible, it became even harder to resist. Because he could just follow the path down, continuing its trajectory even past its boundaries, going over the small of her back until he reached the curve of her buttocks.

He swallowed and when her head suddenly turned and caught him staring, she blinked. "What?"

Hell, what could he say?

"I thought you weren't a runner?"

"Why do you say that?" She glanced down. "Ah, the outfit. Is there some kind of special runner's law that says no one else can wear spandex?"

"No. And it looks good on you."

Why he'd said that last bit was anyone's guess.

"Thanks. I'm normally out here alone. But once I get home from work, I'm ready for the clothes to come off."

"I guess you are." The image of that bathrobe came back to his mind and he wondered if she would lean over the railing just as easily when she was wearing just that. Wondered what it might be like to come up behind her and slide the hem of that robe up the backs of her thighs and...

She turned around and grinned. "That didn't come out quite right."

In a voice that sounded strangled, he said, "I was pretty sure you didn't mean you come out here and dance in the nude."

"You know, when it's dark and the lights are completely off, it probably wouldn't matter if I did. No one could see." Her throaty chuckle did nothing to erase the image of her doing just that.

"Evie..." Did she even know what she was saying? How every picture she painted was being burned into his brain?

"What?" Her eyes widened as her gaze took a quick trip down his body, where he was pretty sure every one of his thoughts was there on full display. "Oh! I didn't realize that you... That what I..."

She bit her lip, then propped her hip on the glass barrier as she stared at him. "Would it really be that awful, Max?" Her words were so soft he'd barely heard them. But she'd said them all the same.

He could pretty much guarantee that whatever might happen between them wouldn't be awful at all. At least not on his end. But was it the smart thing to do?

Hell, did it really matter? She'd made choices she probably regretted and so had he. That didn't mean that this would necessarily be one of those choices, right? They'd kissed and their friendship hadn't gone up in flames.

But he knew something else that might go up in flames. Him. The moment that he touched her.

He should stop with those thoughts. Right now. But the note of uncertainty that he'd heard in her voice as she'd whispered those words had cut him to the core. So, reaching out, his hand encircled her wrist and tugged her closer. "No. It wouldn't be awful. And the way you're making me feel right now says it would be the opposite."

She took another step closer, until their bodies were touching. "Would it?"

Doing what he'd wanted to do just moments earlier, his free hand went to her shoulder and followed the hellish path of that bra strap until it disappeared under her stretchy shirt. He came back up and dipped his hand under the strap, loving the feel of the elastic across her skin as his thumb brushed against her soft skin. The sensation sent prickles across every nerve ending he possessed.

"Hell... I want to go back inside."

He could only hope she could guess why that was and that she was in full agreement with it.

"So do I. But I don't want to watch a movie. Not anymore."

"I was hoping you were going to say that."

With his fingers still around her wrist, he towed her behind him as he reentered the apartment and closed the glass door behind them. Then he turned her to face him. "Are you sure you're okay with this?"

"Yes. More than okay."

As if to emphasize that point, she stood up on tiptoe and kissed him, her lips soft and pliable against his. It only took a second for him to wrap an arm around her waist and fasten her to his body. Then his hand pushed deep into her hair and he kissed her in earnest, his tongue sliding along the seam of her lips until she opened to him. If she thought what she'd seen on the balcony had been obvious, then feeling the effect she had on him must be all the more apparent as he pushed his hips against her belly, loving the pressure along his length.

Except he wanted more than this. So much more. And this time he wasn't going to pull away with some glib speech about saving their friendship. Because if it could survive two kisses, surely it could survive sex. And it would be very good sex. It was in the way she whimpered against his mouth. In the way her mouth closed around his tongue and drove him wild with need.

He needed to find a horizontal surface. And soon. Or this was going to be over before it had even begun.

After pulling away long enough to mutter the word

bed, he moved back in without waiting for a reply, his hand leaving her hair and traveling down the front of her body until he reached her left breast. It was perfection in his palm as he squeezed, finding her nipple in a millisecond.

"Bed." This time it was her voice repeating his earlier thought.

Oh, yeah, he'd wanted to find a bed. He'd almost forgotten. Scooping her up in his arms, he let her direct him to the first open door down a short hallway. Not bothering to shut it behind him, he entered the room and found the bed in the middle of the room. Instead of tossing her onto it and following her down, he turned his back to the mattress and lowered himself onto it. Lying back on the mattress, he took her with him. She quickly scrambled so that she was on top of him, the breast that he'd cupped now pressed tightly against his chest.

It was heaven on earth having her like this. Something he'd never in his wildest dreams ever pictured happening. But it was real. Evie was here with him, kissing him like there was no tomorrow. And maybe there wasn't. But right now he didn't care.

He cupped her bottom, pulling her tight against him and wishing she'd already shucked her clothing. But because she hadn't, he found the waistband of her shorts and pushed his hands beneath it and encountered smooth rounded flesh that sent his body into a frenzy of want and need.

"Evie." He pushed the clothing over her hips, and as if sensing what he was trying to do, she stood up and stripped them off her body, kicking free of them. His mouth watered. But when her hands went to the hem of her shirt, he sat up and stopped her. "Let me."

Pulling her onto his lap so that she straddled his thighs, he gently slid her shirt up her flat belly and over her breasts. When she held her arms high over her head so he could get it off her, he paused for a minute after he'd discarded the garment, one palm sliding up her arm and trapping her wrists in place so he could enjoy the decadent sight of her lacy bra against her skin, her breasts pushing tightly against it as if wanting to be free.

Soon. Very soon. But not before he did this. Letting go of her wrists, he eased her forward until his mouth was against her breast. With it still encased in fabric, he found her nipple and used his teeth to grip it, wetting the lace and scrubbing his tongue across the sensitive part of her.

Evie moaned and pressed closer before she reached down and freed her breast from the cup and drew him back to it.

The sensation was incredible as he pulled hard against the nipple, her hands cupping his head and holding him in place. He finally couldn't take it anymore, so he undid her bra and tossed it across the room. Then he lay back as she remained where she was, her thighs on either side of his.

All that stood between them were his jeans and briefs. But first... He bucked up under her enough to slide his hand into his back pocket, then withdrew his wallet. He hoped to hell he had something in there. It had been a while.

Flipping it open, he found not one, but two condoms.

Plans for how to use that second one were already form-ing inside of his head, but he put them aside for now, along with the second condom, barely able to reach her nightstand with his fingertips. The he used his teeth to rip open the packet he still held in his hand.

Before he could try to maneuver himself to where he could reach, she took the condom from his hand and went up on her knees. Setting it beside his hip, she made short work of undoing his button and fly and freeing him, her hand warm against his oversensitive skin. Her eyes came up and met his with a secretive smile as she pumped up and down with the perfect amount of pres-sure.

It was too much.

"God, Evie. Stop for a minute."

She did, halting her movements and reaching for the condom. She slowly unrolled it down his length while he muttered under his breath and tried to hang on to what little control he had left.

Her fingers drew circles across his abs, making his nerve endings crazy with the mixture of pleasure and ticklishness. He was so attuned to that that he completely missed her hips moving over him until she pressed down hard, taking him deep within her with a single move-ment. He swore out loud, gritting his teeth at the intense rush of pleasure that swept over him.

His fingers gripped her hips in an effort to slow down the wave that was starting to grow and gain strength. But she was relentless, as if needing something only he could give her.

The feeling was mutual. Because what he needed, only she could give.

And there was still that second condom…

Giving himself permission to just go with what was happening, he slid his fingers in between their bodies and found moist curls and that tiny sensitive nub that lay at the very heart of her.

She moaned as he stroked her with both his fingers and his body, using them both to bring her as much pleasure as she was bringing him.

"Max. Yes." Her movements quickened, taking him deeper with each strong pump of her hips. And the wave, which was traveling toward shore, grew to monstrous proportions, and he knew it would soon overtake him.

Just as it hit, she cried out, her hands gripping his shoulders and wildly driving herself onto him. Her body spasmed, once, twice, and then it contracted rhythmically around his flesh, finally forcing him over the edge. He saw white for several long seconds before he became aware of anything other than their frenzied movements and the ragged sound of their breathing.

She slowed the friction just before it became too much, her gripping hands easing their hold and smoothing over his chest.

That had been… More, much more than anything he'd experienced before.

When she finally came to a stop and sat atop him, her eyes landed on him as if seeing him for the first time. And it did something to him. Touched a part of him he wasn't sure he wanted exposed, so he put a hand in the middle of her back and eased her down until she was lying against him. But at least she could no longer see his eyes. Because what he'd seen in hers threatened to rock his world and topple everything he believed to be true.

But those thoughts could wait until tomorrow. When he would be seeing the world with more rational eyes. Until then, he could just lie here and enjoy the slight aftershocks that were still coursing through his body and making him jerk against her a few more times.

He was spent. Didn't want to move. Didn't want to think.

But he didn't really have to, did he? Not yet. He could just relax, revel in the release his body had just had and enjoy the feel of her body against his. Although the fact that he still had clothes on was starting to rob him of some of the joy of lying here with her. He could fix that later, too. But right now...

She wasn't moving and it took him a few minutes to realize she was breathing in deep steady movements that made him smile. She was asleep.

And part of him was glad. Glad she hadn't tried to rationalize what had happened or try to talk through things. He didn't want any of that. He just wanted to be here with her.

If she'd been anyone else, he probably would have already been up and out of here. Or at least up and in the shower. He rarely took the time to wallow in the afterglow of sex. But this time was different, and it stole the part of him that sought to escape.

He didn't want to escape, because this was Evie and she was his...

Max didn't finish that thought because the word *friend* didn't seem to fit in this context.

Don't try. Just lie here and be with her.

So until she woke up, or morning arrived, whichever came first, he was going to do just that. Enjoy being with her.

CHAPTER TEN

THE SOUND OF something buzzing somewhere near his head woke him up. At first, he brushed his hand across his head as if chasing away a pesky insect. Then his eyes opened, and he wasn't sure where he was. Someone's leg was draped over his.

Evie. The events of the previous night rolled over him like a freight train.

They'd had sex.

He swallowed, all of the implications that he'd swatted away yesterday came rushing back. And this time he couldn't just ignore them.

He'd told himself that sex wouldn't affect their friendship, but now that it was staring at him in the cold light of day…

What was he going to do? He'd broken all of the promises he'd made to himself. Not about sex, because that had never been off the table. But his rule was that he not be with someone that he was emotionally involved with.

Had he really broken that rule, though?

Hell yes. Because he was emotionally involved with Evie, he'd just refused to acknowledge it. So again, how was he going to fix this?

The buzzing started again and this time he realized

it wasn't an insect. It was his phone. What time was it, anyway?

He reached for the item on the nightstand and felt the second condom, instead. It, too, filled him with foreboding. He'd had every intention of using it last night. Except he'd fallen asleep. Strike two for his promises.

Grabbing the phone, he sat up to answer it, and felt something on his shoulder. Lips. Very warm lips that trailed up his neck and sent a shudder through him. His eyes lighted on the condom again, and this time it didn't look quite so evil. Quite so nefarious.

He pressed answer on his phone in case it was something urgent and muttered, "'lo?"

"Max, is that you?"

He was awake in a flash when he recognized the voice of his personal assistant. "It is. What's going on?"

Evie stopped kissing him and came around the side to look at him. He held up a finger to signal he would be just a minute. And then what? Was he going to actually move on to round two with her?

The question swirled in his head as Sheila's voice came back to him. "Max, I have some news. Margaret Collins was scheduled for her first treatment today."

That's right. She was. He glanced at his watch. It was only eight in the morning. He wasn't due at the hospital for another hour. "She is, but that's later this afternoon, isn't it?"

"It *was*..."

Those two words came down like a hammer, shattering whatever had happened last night.

"What happened?"

"We're not sure. But her son went to wake her up this morning and found her unresponsive. She died in her sleep."

She died in her sleep.

The guilt that he'd not felt last night came pouring over him in a flood that wouldn't be stopped. His eyes burned and his throat went bone-dry. While he'd been rolling around in this bed with Evie, Margaret Collins had been taking her last breath. A sense of déjà vu went over him that wouldn't stop. She hadn't even made it to her first treatment.

Shades of his mom. Shades of people leaving those they loved. Loved ones being left behind to somehow carry on.

It's not the same thing.

He knew that, but it still didn't stop his heart from trying to jackhammer its way out of his chest.

"Thanks for calling." It was all he could manage to get out before he hit the end button.

He was somehow able to get his feet under him and lever his way out of bed as a fog of regret settled over him, every bit as dark and heavy as the dust storms that ravaged this part of Nevada.

Then Evie was in front of him, wrapped in the bed-sheet. "Max, what happened?"

"Margaret…died last night." He took her by the shoulders, even as he wanted to jerk away from her, the urge to escape beating through his skull. "I'm so sorry, Evie."

Her eyes closed and two tears escaped. "Did she suffer?"

"I don't think so. She passed in her sleep."

Brown eyes stared at him and a hurt almost as deep as when he'd learned his mom had died held him in a paralyzing grip.

He couldn't do this. Couldn't bear to see the devastation in her eyes over what had happened.

Margaret had been Evie's patient for years and so he understood those emotions. But what about the other ones? Like the fact that Margaret Collins had never gotten the chance to prepare? Had never been able to say goodbye to her family?

What if it had been him? Or Evie?

He didn't know. And things right now were so jumbled he couldn't make sense of anything. All he knew was that he couldn't stay here and think about any of that. It was why he'd been so adamant about not getting close to anyone.

And now, he'd gone and done the very thing he knew he shouldn't have. Gotten close in a way that had nothing to do with what they'd done last night.

He let go of her and closed his eyes, hoping he could do what he needed to do. "Evie, I'm sorry. Really, really sorry about Margaret. But I just can't be here right now."

Grabbing his clothes from the floor and pulling them on with a frenzy that came out of nowhere, he tried to put his thoughts on hold. Only they wouldn't go away, and kept swirling inside of him.

"Max, stop a minute."

"I need to get to the office."

"No, you don't." She moved in front of him and threaded her fingers through his. "Please. Talk to me."

"Not now. Maybe later. I just need time to process this."

"Process what? Margaret's passing? Maybe it's better that it happened this way. There was no pain. No suffering."

Maybe not for Margaret. But for her family?

"Not just her passing. I just need time to think. About everything."

"Okay. I get that."

But she didn't. He could tell.

"Call me if you need anything, okay?"

Her hand fell back to her side. "I will." She paused for a second. "Does some of what you need to think about revolve around what happened last night?"

"We can talk about it later."

"So it does."

He swallowed. He didn't want to hurt her, but wasn't that inevitable at this point? The thought of being involved with someone caused a queasiness to churn inside of him that no amount of talking would abolish. It was a knee-jerk reaction that made no sense, and yet, try as he might, he'd never been able to rid himself of it. He was like Walter Grapevine, forever stuck on a dead-end path, but not able—no...not *willing*—to change.

He moved forward and took her hand. "Evie, last night was a mistake."

"A mistake. Why?"

"I can't explain it. But I don't have what it takes to truly give myself over to someone else. Maybe it's from my childhood. Maybe it's engraved into my DNA. I don't know. But I only know I'm not what you need."

She jerked her hand free, her eyebrows going up. "I think *I* should be the one to decide that. But since every single time we start to move toward something deeper, you stop and call it a mistake… Well, this time, I'll believe you. So let's just say it's over and move on."

Hearing her cast the very words he'd been thinking into the universe was a shock. And for a second, he wondered if he'd done the right thing. But right or not, it was too late now.

As if emphasizing her point, she went over to the table, snatched up the condom and walked back over to him. She put it in his hand and curled his fingers around it. "Take it. You'll need it for the next woman you decide to have sex with. Only let me give you a piece of advice. Don't tell her it was a mistake."

Before he could say anything else, she walked past him to the bathroom and went inside, softly closing the door behind her.

He should be glad. Evie had let him off easy. But something about the way she'd said that he'd need that condom for the next woman sent a knife deep into his chest. Is that what she thought he did?

Don't you? Didn't you just think about how you don't have sex with women you care about?

He stared at the object in his hand, horrified at the truth that was staring him right in the face. And then he went over and dropped it into the garbage can by the bed. He finished dressing and left Evie's apartment, getting into his car and driving with no destination in mind. The only thing he wanted to do was escape. Escape the news of Margaret's death. Escape the fact that what had happened with Evie was done for good. And that there was no going back.

* * *

"In short, it was a mistake. According to Max."

She'd met Darby at her office shortly after he'd left her apartment. She couldn't believe how easy it had seemed for him to throw words at her that hurt her to the core.

"Maybe give him some time. I always felt like there was something he wanted to tell you, but just never could."

"I think he pretty much said everything he wanted to say. And when I told him it was over and we should move on, he didn't say a word."

"Do you love him, Evie?"

Those words shocked her into silence for several minutes. Then, in complete misery, she nodded. "I do. I think I have for a very long time. I was just too afraid to admit it to myself." She let out a hard laugh. "And it looks like I was right in being afraid. Thank God, I didn't say it this morning or last night. Because I'm pretty sure he would have thrown it back in my face."

"You don't know that."

"I do. You didn't see the look he gave me when I asked him to stop and talk to me. He acted like I was made of poison."

"I'm so sorry, Evie. Do you want me to talk to him?"

The thought of that filled her with horror. "No. Please don't say anything to him. I don't even want him to know that you know."

"There's no way he won't. He knows how close we are."

She thought for a minute. "You're right. Because here I am less than two hours after he left my apartment. And

I don't really need advice. I just needed to tell someone. Losing Margaret and Max in one day…"

Darby put her cane against her desk and caught her up in a tight hug. "I'm sorry, honey. So, so sorry. I thought… Well, never mind what I thought, because that doesn't matter. And I know you don't want advice, so all I'm going to say is that you need to give yourselves space and time to heal. Maybe you'll both either realize that what happened isn't the end of the world. Or you'll realize it is and that you can't live without each other."

"I don't see that second option ever happening, but I do think you're right about the first one. And since Margaret was the only patient we had in common right now, there shouldn't be a lot of reasons to see each other."

"What about the gala?"

"That planning is all done. No need for any more meetings, and as for the event itself, there should be enough people there that we can avoid crossing paths during it." She shrugged. "I've never thought about leaving Nevada, but maybe I need to go visit some of my relatives in Brazil for a couple of weeks. I have a lot of vacation time saved up. I can be back in time to make sure all of the gala stuff is ready to go."

"I think that's a good idea. I'll miss you. And please don't leave Nevada. Not permanently. Not without giving yourself a lot of time to think and grieve. And this is worth grieving over, Evie. You love him. Let yourself cry and scream and shake your fist at the sky. But don't make a permanent decision while you're feeling like this."

"I won't. I have a few patients I need to wrap up over

the next week and then I'll spend a week or two in Brazil. Once the gala is over, I think I'll be able to screw my head back on straight and figure out my next step."

She wanted to make sure that Delilah, especially, was doing okay before she left. She had a track meet today, so Evie would call this afternoon and find out how it went. And then she had another two patients who were in the middle of adjusting meds and she wanted to see those through as well. And then she'd be free to go to Brazil and try to clear her mind of anything that had to do with Max or what had happened between them. And he was right. This could never happen again, because it would destroy her. So even if she had to walk away from him, from his friendship, she was going to do what she needed to keep from being hurt by him ever again.

Max twirled a pencil between his fingers, then tossed it to the top of the desk and groaned out loud. He'd gone to Margaret's memorial service two days ago and had seen Evie from afar. He'd toyed with going over to her afterward to see how she was doing, but she must have slipped out as soon as it ended. When he looked for her, there was no sign of her.

He hadn't seen her in the hospital, either, but that wasn't all that unusual. Unless their paths happened to cross because one of their patients needed services that the other specialized in, they pretty much kept to their own departments. But he hadn't even caught sight of her since the service. And he couldn't stop thinking about her. About how they'd left things.

No. Not *they*. Him. Max was the one who'd had the

meltdown and had said a lot of things he didn't mean. A lot of things he regretted. And a week after Margaret's death he could see that he'd mentally blamed Evie for getting through to his heart, when all along it had been Max who'd opened the door and let her in.

Blaming her was probably just an excuse to run for the door. What he really hadn't been able to face wasn't Margaret's death—it was what had happened in Evie's bedroom.

But why had he made it into such a tragedy? Why had he felt like the world was ending, when it really was still spinning on its axis just like it always had?

Everything inside of him went silent for several seconds. All thought ceased. His muscles froze, breathing stopped, then it all started back up again when the truth he'd been avoiding exploded onto the scene, scorching everything he thought he knew.

He loved her.

And that was why he'd been so horrified. And so adamant that it had meant nothing, and tried to convince not just himself, but her.

All because of the baggage he carried from his mom and his dad. And it wasn't even their fault. It was his for taking on their problems and acting like they were going to be repeated in his life. They weren't. Max hadn't gone out and drunk himself into a stupor when Evie had let him walk out of her life. Evie wasn't the one who'd died, it was one of their patients. And while that fact made him sad and he had grieved the things that she would never get to do, he was going to be able to move past it and keep on living.

What he wasn't sure of was whether he was going to be able to move past Evie. And he suddenly knew he didn't want to. He wanted to hold her in his arms and say he was sorry for every stupid thing he'd ever said to her. Sleeping with her hadn't been a mistake. It had been the smartest thing he'd ever done. Because it had made him stop and take a good look at what was staring him in the face. What had been staring him in the face since before she'd met Brad. That he loved her. It was why Brad and Dale's interest in her had bothered him so much. Why he hadn't been able to stand the sight of her with another man.

So what was he going to do? He was going to find her and do what he'd just thought about. He was going to take her in his arms and tell her how much he loved her. And beg for her forgiveness for wasting so many years of their lives.

He took a deep breath and picked up the pencil, then tossed it in the air and caught it by its point. But he couldn't do any of that sitting here at his desk. He wasn't sure she could forgive him, or if she even should, but what he was sure of was that he needed to try. Right now. After telling his assistant where she could find him, he headed down the elevator to her department and went to the desk. "Is Dr. Milagre here?"

"No. She actually left for vacation this morning."

A cold wind washed over him. Was that a euphemism for leaving? For good?

"Do you know when she'll be back?"

The woman glanced at a calendar in front of her. "She

said if things went well she'd be back…let's see. Yes, here it is. A week before the gala. July twenty-fifth."

If things went well. And if they didn't? "Okay, thanks."

He left and did the only thing he could think of. He called Darby.

"Nao sei."

God, how many times was Evie going to have to explain to her well-meaning relatives that she didn't know if she was ever going to get married again. Or if she was going to have children before she was forty years old.

She thought coming here had been a good idea, but a week in, it looked like it might have been the worst idea of her life. She missed her job, missed her apartment, but most of all she missed Max. Despite what they'd said to each other, she regretted leaving without getting some kind of closure, even if it meant the end of their friendship. She regretted not having her say and not telling him the truth once she'd realized it: that she loved him. Confessing it didn't demand that he feel the same way, it was simply telling him the truth. How much worse could it be than leaving things the way they had?

Her aunt was saying something and she'd missed it.

"Como?"

"I asked if you'd mind riding with me to the airport to meet a friend. I hate driving in that traffic alone."

"Why don't you take the bus?" The bus that went from São Paulo to the international airport was a lot easier than driving. And it only took about forty minutes.

"It's a special friend, and I want him to be comfortable."

Evie's eyebrows shot up. "Aunt Maria, do you have a *namorado*?" Her aunt had never been married and she was pushing seventy.

"Of course not, *moça*. Grab your purse, we need to go."

Okay, so it had gone from asking Evie if she wanted to go to assuming that she would. But what else did she have to do? She still had two more days before her own flight for the States, and the way she felt right now, it could not arrive fast enough. "Okay, I'll be right back."

Then they were in the car and driving through the snarls of rush-hour traffic, but her aunt, to her credit, was very good at weaving in and out of traffic at just the right moment to keep inching forward. If you made eye contact with the next driver, it was an unspoken rule that they had to let you in. And Aunt Maria was a force of nature when it came to getting people to look at her.

Once they were at the airport, Maria checked the flights while Evie moped in silence. "I found it, let's go."

Her aunt pulled her behind her until they were at the arrivals area. Evie hoped whoever it was got here quickly. All she wanted to do was get back to the house so she could start packing for her return flight. Darby had kept her apprised of how the gala preparations were going—since she and Max were still on speaking terms. The workmen had almost completed the courtyard and the obelisk structure had been carted away to parts unknown.

"There. He is here."

She glanced up, only half interested in whoever it was.

She'd been gone from Brazil for so many years that it was doubtful that she even knew the person. "Where?"

"Just look. You will see him."

Oh, brother. She looked at the throng of people, not seeing a single familiar face. Then her attention snagged on something. An easy move of masculine hips that looked familiar. She frowned and looked closer at the people coming toward them. Then she blinked, every emotion in her suddenly rushing up and getting stuck in her throat.

It couldn't be.

She lost sight of him for a second, then as she frantically swept her gaze across the group, he reappeared behind someone. Oh, God, it was.

Max!

She jerked around to look at her aunt, who only nodded. "Yes, *querida*, it is him."

"But how?"

"Your friend Darby called your mother, who called us and told us he was flying into Brazil. It is why I insisted you come."

Was he here for a conference and her mom had somehow found out? The shot of happiness she'd felt vanished. What if he wasn't here for *her* at all?

Then their eyes met and he stopped, right in the middle of the moving line of people, forcing the crowd to part and go around him like water flowing around a rock.

Then he was moving again, his lanky frame eating up the distance before she had a chance to catch her breath.

Then she was in his arms and he held her so tightly that she really *couldn't* breathe.

Was this happening? Maybe this was all some dream or wishful thinking. Maybe her longing was so strong that she'd summoned a hallucination. And yet, his arms felt real. And he was murmuring something in her ear over and over.

It was her name.

And for some reason it broke her, and she started sobbing, clinging to him like he was the only thing that could save her world. And maybe he wasn't, but he was the closest thing she was going to find.

He pulled back, looking into her face. A thumb came up and captured a drop of moisture. "Happy tears or sad?"

She sucked down a shuddering breath. "That depends on why you're here."

"I'm here for you."

Her eyes closed and she pulled his face down to her, pressing her cheek against his. "Happy. They're happy tears. I love you, Max."

He kissed her, the softest touch, almost making her cry again. She thought she knew what it meant, but she wanted to hear the words. Needed to hear them. He looked at her and nodded. "I love you, too. I was just too afraid to admit it. Or to believe I deserved it. And so I ran. And worse, I called something beautiful a mistake, hoping it would make you pull away. And it did. But it was the stupidest thing I've ever said and it wasn't true. It wasn't a mistake. You'll always be my best friend, Evie. But I'd like the chance for it to be more than that."

"Yes."

He laughed, pulling back and putting an arm around her waist. "Yes, what?"

"Yes to whatever you suggest, as long as it includes having you in my life."

"That's a nonnegotiable." He glanced to the side and saw an older lady who looked far too pleased to not be a part of how he'd gotten to Brazil. "Is this your aunt?"

"Oh, yes." She turned red. "I'm sorry. Aunt Maria, this is Max, my..."

"Teu namorado. Ja sei." The woman stepped forward and kissed him on either cheek. *"Bem vindo ao Brasil."*

Max's head tilted, and Evie laughed. "I'll explain what she said later. But right now, all I want to do is this." She went up on tiptoe and kissed him again. "I just want to hold your hand all the way to my aunt's house. And then I still want to be holding it in two days, as we head home."

"Home," he said. "I like the sound of that." With that, he gripped her hand and followed her aunt to the airport's exit, where they stepped out into brilliant sunshine and the promise of a thousand more days just like this one.

Just then her phone pinged, and she glanced at the readout. "Oh, my God," she whispered.

"What is it?" Max sounded worried.

"It's Darby. She said it's raining in Las Vegas and more is predicted over the next couple of days. The drought is over."

"It certainly is." Only Max wasn't looking at her phone. He was looking at her. And in his expression was more love than she ever dreamed possible.

She squeezed his hand in silent agreement. The drought was over. And she thanked God for the rain.

EPILOGUE

Two years later

MAX CAUGHT SIGHT of Evie coming toward him across the courtyard. It was their second gala as husband and wife and he would never get tired of the sight of her in an evening gown. Even eight months pregnant, she was the most beautiful woman in the room. And she was all his.

At thirty-eight, she was considered a high-risk pregnancy and Max had to fight the urge to coddle her and make her slow down. But Evie swore she would not do anything that would put their baby at risk. Her mom and dad and whole extended family were ecstatic with the fact that their family was about to grow. And Max had been welcomed in as if he'd always belonged, and he loved it. Loved them all. He was even trying to learn Portuguese, although Evie always translated for him.

He tucked her arm through his and dropped a kiss on her head. "Have I told you I loved you lately?"

"Hmm." She hummed the sound in that low throaty way of hers that drove him crazy. "Only about forty times."

"Then I'm behind schedule." He nodded toward the left. "Come dance with me."

"Now? I'm not sure I'll make the best partner." She cupped her belly.

He tipped up her chin and looked into her eyes. "You make the best partner all the time. Please. For me."

"Okay." They walked over to the area where the dance floor had been set up. The same dance floor that had been used for the last two years, since the hospital portion of the gala had been everyone's favorite part. And Evie was still head of that committee. Morgan Howard's successor had finally been chosen and it was actually his son, who was also a doctor. And Morgan Howard the second was every bit as compassionate and savvy as his father was. Everyone loved him.

DJ Electric Nights saw them coming and winked at him. "All set?"

"Yes, we're all set."

Evie looked up at him in question and the music started softly, then slowly got louder. She bit her lip. "Max, you know this song always makes me cry."

"That's why I wanted him to play it." He took her in his arms and slowly moved in time with the music, the country singer's voice coming through with a sure sincerity that said he knew what he was singing about.

Evie laid her head against his chest and closed her eyes as they swayed together. No one else in the world mattered, except the woman in his arms. The first verse moved into the chorus and then flowed to the second stanza. Through each word and phrase, Max took them in and made them into a vow he would never go back on. She was the best thing that had ever happened to him.

The chorus came for the last time and the singer

seemed to hang on to those final words for a long time. Long enough for Max to sing them softly in her ear. "You're my best friend...my best friend."

* * * * *

MEDICAL

Life and love in the world of modern medicine.

Available Next Month

Falling For The Single Mum Next Door Fiona McArthur
A Kiss Under The Northern Lights Susan Carlisle

....

Paramedic's Reunion In Paradise Alison Roberts
Healing The Baby Surgeon's Heart Tessa Scott

....

Hot Nights With The Arctic Doc Luana DaRosa
Nurse's Keralan Temptation Becky Wicks

Keep reading for an excerpt of a new title
from the Romantic Suspense series,
COLTON'S LAST RESORT by Amber Leigh Williams

Prologue

Allison Brewer didn't belong in a morgue. She was a twenty-five-year-old yoga instructor with zero underlying conditions. She never smoked, rarely drank, and was the picture of health and vitality.

Detective Noah Steele sucked in a breath as the coroner, Rod Steinbeck, pulled back the sheet. How many times had he stood over a body at the Yavapai County Coroner's Office? How many times had he stared unflinchingly at death—at what nature did to humans and what human nature did to others?

She looks like she could still be alive, he thought. No cuts or bruises marred her face. There were no ligature marks. She could have been asleep. She looked perfectly at peace. If Noah squinted, he could fool himself into thinking there was a slight smile at the corners of her mouth. Just as there had been when she'd feigned sleep as a girl.

However, an inescapable blue stain spread across her lips. He could deny it all he wanted, but his sister was gone.

"I'm sorry, Noah," Rod said and lifted the sheet over her face again.

"No." The word wasn't soft or hard, loud or quiet. Noah surprised himself by speaking mildly. As if this were any other body…any other case. His mind was somewhere near the ceiling. His gut turned, and his chest ached. But he let that piece of himself float away, detached. He made himself think like he was trained to think. "What're your impressions?"

"Fulton's already been here. It's his case. And for good reason. You're going to need some time to process—"

"Rod." He sounded cold. He was. He was so bitterly cold. And he didn't know how to live with it. He didn't know how to live in a world without Allison. "Next of kin would be informed of any progress made in the investigation. I'm her next of kin. Inform me."

Rod shuffled his feet. Placing his hands at each corner of the head of the steel table, he studied Allison. "I'm not sure I'm comfortable with this."

"She's dead." Noah made himself say it. He needed to hear it, the finality of it. "If Sedona Police wants me to process that, I need to know how and why."

Rod adjusted his glasses. "Look, maybe you should talk to Fulton."

"She was found at the resort," Noah prompted, undeterred, "where she works."

"Mariposa."

"You were on scene there," Noah surmised. "What time did you arrive?"

Rod gave in. "Nine fifteen."

"Where was she?"

"One of the pool cabanas," the coroner explained.

"Tell me what you saw."

"Come on, Noah…"

"Tell me," Noah said. He knew not to raise his voice. If he were hysterical, it would get back to his CO. He'd be put on leave.

He needed to work through this. If he stopped working, stopped thinking objectively, he would lose his mind.

Rod lifted his hands. "She was found face down, but one of the staff performed CPR, so she was on her back when I arrived. Her shoes were missing."

That could've been something, Noah thought, if Allison hadn't had a habit of going around barefoot where she was comfortable, particularly when entering someone's home.

The temperature had dipped into the thirties the night before. *A little cold for no shoes, even for her*, he considered. "What was she wearing?"

"Sport jacket and leggings," Rod explained. "Underneath, she wore a long-sleeved ballet-like top cropped above the navel with crisscrossed bands underneath. It was a matching set, all green."

"What do you figure for time of death?"

"Right now, I'd say she died somewhere between one and two this morning."

She hadn't gone home to bed, Noah mused. "Any cuts, lacerations? Signs of foul play?"

"Some abrasions on the backs of her legs."

"Show me."

Again, Rod paused before he walked to the bottom of the table. Lifting the drape, he revealed one long, pale leg with toes still painted pink. Noah tried not to see the unearthly blue tone of the skin around the nails. He craned his neck when Rod showed him the marks on her calves.

"She was dragged," Noah said as he realized what had happened. Why did the air feel like ice? The cold filled his lungs. They felt wind-burned, and the pain of it made his hands knot into fists.

"That would be my understanding," Rod agreed. He replaced the sheet gingerly.

"Before or after TOD?" Noah asked.

"After."

Noah's brow furrowed. "She was killed somewhere other than the cabana and staged there." His voice had gone rough, but he kept going, searching. "Were there any items with her at the scene?"

"Fulton noted there was no purse, wallet or cell phone. She was identified by members of Mariposa's staff."

"Were her lips blue when you got there?"

"Yes." Rod nodded. "Her fingernails and toes were discolored as well."

Noah scraped his knuckles over the thick growth of beard that covered his jawline. "Who found her?"

"From what I understand," Rod said slowly, "it was a staff member. You'll have to get the name of the person from Fulton."

"Who was there when you arrived on scene?" Noah asked curiously.

"There was a small crowd that had been blocked by officers," Rod told him. "Several members of security, one pool maintenance person and all three of the Coltons."

"Coltons." Noah recognized the name, but he let it hang in the air, waiting for Rod to elaborate.

"The siblings," Rod said. "They own and manage Mariposa. Adam, Laura and Joshua, I believe, are their names."

"What was your impression of them?" Noah asked, homing in.

Rod considered. "The younger one, Joshua, was quiet. Laura didn't say much either. She seemed stricken by the whole thing. The oldest one, Adam…"

When Rod paused, Noah narrowed his eyes. "What about him?"

"He did all the talking," Rod said. "He ordered everyone back and let the uniforms, Fulton, crime scene technicians and myself work. There was no attempt to tamper with the scene. Although I did hear him speaking to Fulton as we readied the body for transport."

"What did he say?" Noah asked, feeling like a dog with a bone.

"He wanted Fulton's word that the investigation would remain discreet," Rod said. "They get some high-profile guests at Mariposa. He didn't want their privacy or, I expect, their experience hindered."

The muscles around Noah's mouth tensed. "A member of their staff is found dead, and the Coltons' first thought is how it's going to affect their clientele? Does that seem right to you?"

"I'm not the detective," Steinbeck noted.

No, Noah considered. *I am.* "You'll do a tox screen?"

"It's routine," Rod replied. "As it stands, I don't have a cause of death for you."

"You'll keep me informed?" Noah asked.

"I'll stay in touch."

Noah forced himself to back away from Allison's body. Deep in some unbottled canyon, he felt himself scream.

"Have your parents been notified?"

The question nearly made him flinch. Rod didn't know. No one did. Not really.

It didn't matter, he told himself. He'd loved her, hadn't he? He'd loved her as his own. "She doesn't have parents," he said. "Neither of us do."

"I'm sorry." Rod placed his hand on Noah's shoulder. "I'll take care of her."

"I know." Noah turned for the door.

"Don't get yourself in trouble over this," Rod warned. "Let Fulton handle it. He'll find out what happened to her."

Noah didn't answer. In seconds, he was out of the autopsy room, down the hall, crossing the lobby. Planting both hands on the glass door, he shoved it open.

Cold air hit him in the face and did nothing for the lethal ice now channeling through his blood.

He thought about stopping, doubling over, bracing his hands on his knees.

He could hear her. Still.

Breathe, Noah. Deep breath in. And let it out.

Noah shook his head firmly, blocking out her voice. He thought of what Rod had said—about the scene and his impressions of the people there.

He took out his keys, walking to the unmarked vehicle that was his. Opening the driver's door, he got behind the wheel and cranked the engine. The sun was sinking swiftly toward the red rock mountains in the distance, but he picked up his phone. Using voice commands, he said, "Hey, Google, set a course for Mariposa Resort & Spa."

He studied the GPS route that popped up on-screen before mounting the phone on the dash. Shifting into Reverse, he cupped the back of the passenger headrest. Turning his head over his shoulder, he backed out of the parking space.

To hell with staying out of Fulton's way. Someone was responsible for Allison's death. He would find out who.

And he was going to nail the Coltons' asses to the floor.

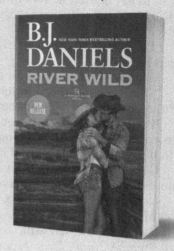

Subscribe and fall in love with a Mills & Boon series today!

You'll be among the first to read stories delivered to your door monthly and enjoy great savings.

WE SIMPLY LOVE ROMANCE

MILLS & BOON

—— JOIN US ——

Sign up to our newsletter to stay up to date with...

- Exclusive member discount codes
- Competitions
- New release book information
- All the latest news on your favourite authors

Plus...
get $10 off your first order.
What's not to love?

Sign up at **millsandboon.com.au/newsletter**